"This page-turner opens a window on what it's like to raise a special-needs child."
— *Parenting*

"This is a book rich in its offerings without being complicated. Cammie McGovern has created a page-turner that will keep you up at night."
— *Myrtle Beach Sun News*

"An airtight thriller that illuminates the exhausting, isolating realities of parenting special-needs children. . . . It's easy to picture [Julia Roberts, who optioned the movie rights] as the tireless Cara; she's sure to savor the emotional intensity that McGovern has bestowed on her remarkable heroine."
— *People*

"A gripping *and* moving read."
— *Redbook*

"Most deeply moving, actually gripping, when Cammie McGovern, herself the mother of an autistic child, brings to the page an empathetic understanding of the lock that autism places on a mother's child."
— *New York Daily News*

"Will set you to wondering about mothering, friendship, loneliness, whom we label 'different' and why. This is a book rich in its offerings without being complicated. It's really about relationships, but author Cammie McGovern has created a page-turner that will keep you up at night trying to solve a murder, worried about, half in love with the children involved. . . . You'll close *Eye Contact* knowing more about loving children as they are, rather than as we expect them to be. . . . You won't feel lectured or hectored; you'll feel entertained by a good read and, in the process, enlightened."
— *The State*

"Amazing . . . Realistic, gripping, deeply moving and heart-warming. Only someone who has a family member who has autism could have portrayed Adam as well as McGovern does."
— *Daily American*

"An unusual literary mystery that combines the elements of a women's novel with the gripping aspects of a good suspense story. Taut writing and alternating viewpoints work effectively to lead the reader down several dead ends en route to an unpredictable and satisfying conclusion. This page-turner is a rewarding look into the life of a mother who must discover the truth."
— *Library Journal*

"Dynamite . . . Meticulously researched and emotionally absorbing, this provocative page-turner also addresses an important issue—how to educate and care for children with special needs." —*Publishers Weekly*

"*Eye Contact* is a page-turner, and I tore through it in twenty-four hours. But it's more than that—it's also a nuanced, poignant exploration of how all of us, with or without autism, struggle to find our place in the world. Cammie McGovern writes with grace and compassion."
—Curtis Sittenfeld, author of *Prep*

"Cammie McGovern makes a satisfying marriage between an exploration of one of modern parenthood's greatest frustrations—autism—and murder mystery. Moreover, she displays considerable insight into the complex, often cruel hierarchies of childhood."
—Lionel Shriver, author of *We Need to Talk About Kevin*

"Once in a blue moon comes a literary thriller so full of our everyday lives that it rocks you back on your heels. This is it! This book. These sweet, funny, heartbreaking characters—these mothers and sons, broken friends and lovers—including one unforgettable little boy whose last gesture in those deadly, mysterious woods recalls our lost innocence. *Eye Contact* is a thrilling mystery tautly told, and beautifully realized. In it, Cammie McGovern leads us through the shadowlands of our own hometowns where words break down and paranoias proliferate, even as we yearn for one lost moment of fluency. This is a book of secrets that will change you."
—Michael Paterniti, *New York Times* bestselling author of *Driving Mr. Albert: A Trip Across America with Einstein's Brain*

"Twin mysteries lie at the heart of this riveting and unforgettable novel: the identity and motives of a child-killer, and the inscrutable workings of an autistic boy's mind. Only a writer like McGovern, whose brilliant gift for storytelling keeps pace with her unflinching emotional acuity, could take on both mysteries and succeed with such power and grace."
—Julie Orringer, author of *How to Breathe Underwater*

"In the tradition of *The Curious Incident of the Dog in the Night-Time*, Cammie McGovern delivers a compelling murder mystery that intrigues as much by what it hides as by what it so deftly reveals—the stark, poignant, deeply intimate moments in the lives of people living with autism and those who love them."
—Patricia Stacey, author of *The Boy Who Loved Windows*

PENGUIN BOOKS

EYE CONTACT

Cammie McGovern was awarded a creative writing fellowship at Stanford University and has received numerous prizes for her short fiction. Her stories have appeared in several magazines and journals, and she is the author of another novel, *The Art of Seeing*. She lives in Amherst, Massachusetts, with her husband and three children, the eldest of whom is autistic. She is one of the founders of Whole Children, a resource center that runs after-school classes and programs for children with special needs.

For more information visit www.cammiemcgovern.com

EYE CONTACT

A NOVEL

Cammie McGovern

PENGUIN BOOKS

PENGUIN BOOKS

Published by the Penguin Group

Penguin Group (USA) Inc., 375 Hudson Street, New York, New York 10014, U.S.A.
Penguin Group (Canada), 90 Eglinton Avenue East, Suite 700, Toronto,
Ontario, Canada M4P 2Y3 (a division of Pearson Penguin Canada Inc.)
Penguin Books Ltd, 80 Strand, London WC2R 0RL, England
Penguin Ireland, 25 St Stephen's Green, Dublin 2, Ireland (a division of Penguin Books Ltd)
Penguin Group (Australia), 250 Camberwell Road, Camberwell, Victoria 3124, Australia
(a division of Pearson Australia Group Pty Ltd)
Penguin Books India Pvt Ltd, 11 Community Centre,
Panchsheel Park, New Delhi – 110 017, India
Penguin Group (NZ), 67 Apollo Drive, Mairangi Bay, Auckland 1311, New Zealand
(a division of Pearson New Zealand Ltd)
Penguin Books (South Africa) (Pty) Ltd, 24 Sturdee Avenue,
Rosebank, Johannesburg 2196, South Africa

Penguin Books Ltd, Registered Offices:
80 Strand, London WC2R 0RL, England

First published in the United States of America by Viking Penguin,
a member of Penguin Group (USA) Inc. 2006
Published in Penguin Books 2007

1 3 5 7 9 10 8 6 4 2

Copyright © Cammie McGovern, 2006
All rights reserved

PUBLISHER'S NOTE
This is a work of fiction. Names, characters, places, and incidents either are the product
of the author's imagination or are used fictitiously, and any resemblance to actual persons,
living or dead, business establishments, events, or locales is entirely coincidental.

ISBN 0-670-03765-6 (hc.)
ISBN 978-0-14-303890-0 (pbk.)
CIP data available

Printed in the United States of America
Set in Galliard
Designed by Amy Hill

Except in the United States of America, this book is sold subject to the condition that it shall not,
by way of trade or otherwise, be lent, resold, hired out, or otherwise circulated without the publisher's prior consent in any form of binding or cover other than that in which it is published and
without a similar condition including this condition being imposed on the subsequent purchaser.

The scanning, uploading and distribution of this book via the Internet or via any other means
without the permission of the publisher is illegal and punishable by law. Please purchase only au-
thorized electronic editions, and do not participate in or encourage electronic piracy of copyrighted
materials. Your support of the author's rights is appreciated.

For the boys I love so much:
Mike, Ethan, Charlie, and Henry

EYE CONTACT

"KEVIN IS FINE," Miss Lattimore, their fifth-grade teacher told them. "Just *fine*. He's had a little bit of brain damage, that's all." She held up her hand, thumb and forefinger out, so they all saw: *Just an inch of brain damage*. "If he has trouble doing certain things, like talking, for instance, or getting around, remember: inside he's just the same." She closed her inch-measuring fingers into a fist and thunked her chest. "He has exactly the same feelings you do."

Cara and Suzette eyed each other. Suzette's father's secretary was Kevin's aunt. They already knew Kevin wasn't fine, that he used a walker and could only operate one side of his face. Drool was a problem, as was the bathroom. Kevin used to be a regular boy no one thought much about until last summer when he rode his bike helmetless down the long hill of Brewster Boulevard into the side of a Pepperidge Farm bread truck and for two days lay in a coma with a missing kidney and bleeding on the brain. Now he was more interesting.

When he appeared in the doorway for his first day back at school, Cara was ready, hands clasped in front of her, a frozen smile of welcome on her face. Weeks ago, she had decided that she would befriend Kevin upon his return—help him with his tray at lunch, unzip his backpack, retrieve his pencil case for him if need be. She wasn't afraid of him, the way everyone else so obviously was, watching as he inched his way into the room, silver metal walker first, his mother—wearing bright red lipstick and a scarf tied over pink sponge curlers—behind. His face was exactly as Suzette had described it: half fine, half fallen like a cake, creasing in on itself, his mouth tilted in a crooked smile that didn't move as he took what felt like the whole morning to get to his seat, one row behind Cara. Miss Lattimore's fist returned to her chest: "We're just happy to have you here, Kevin. Very, very happy."

The coughing and paper shuffling around the room spoke volumes of denial. No one was happy to have Kevin here. He was a cautionary tale, the name all parents now used when their children headed off anywhere on a bicycle. As he moved closer, even Cara, with her Florence Nightingale dreams of rescue, was so stunned by the sight of him, and the terrible decimation one moment of bad judgment could wreak, that when he slid his squeaky walker past her, she did what she promised herself she wouldn't: lowered her eyes to the hem of her minidress, took in her good legs and working hands, tested her face by raising both eyebrows. When he finally took his seat, leaving his walker to block the aisle, Miss Lattimore returned to the lesson and a room full of children so eager to attend to anything besides Kevin that it was possible no one, except Cara, heard a kind of throat clearing that became words, garbled, full of saliva, uttered through half a mouth: "I can see your panties."

Later, Suzette told her there was something wrong with her, to love a boy who would say something like that. "I can't help it," Cara said. "There's something about him."

She and Suzette had been having these conversations since the second grade, when they first met and became friends. If Cara was the romantic, Suzette was the practical soul, the seer of truths, the one who eschewed popularity and all that it required. Currently, the popular-girl trend at lunchtime was weaving lanyards out of long, narrow plastic ribbons of red and black. "Whore colors," one girl explained, and Cara made the mistake of rushing out to buy her own materials. She didn't understand the basic tenet of popularity: that you had to be *asked,* invited into it. You didn't just sit down, your brown bag of materials on the table in front of you. For years, she didn't understand the rules of social discourse; then, in a single exchange, she did: "We sort of sit here," Patty Sweet told her. "Like with our friends."

"Oh," Cara said, pulling her bag into her lap, scooting down the bench.

Afterward, Suzette rolled her eyes. "Like those girls are so great. Please. They have nothing going for them, except they're all skinny and have good hair." Suzette had no use for the popular girls at their school, or anyone else for that matter. She wanted to work with animals someday. "Like in Africa," she said. "Animals are honest. They want food, they eat you."

Though Suzette wouldn't have understood this distinction, Cara didn't long for popularity so much as an ease with people, a way to move more smoothly through the world and be like her fourth-grade teacher, Ms. Simon, who once taught a whole morning with her fly down and laughed afterward when she realized. "So who heard a word I said?" she joked. For Cara, a mistake like that would have clung to her for days, become an explanation for the conversations that piled up in her head, the words she never spoke to the people she spent all day watching.

In Kevin's first week back, Cara watched him as much as she could. Every time she turned around on some fabricated excuse in her mind—

she needed to remember where the pencil sharpener was, needed to glance at the clouds out the windows—he was staring at her, his broken face wearing the same half smile. Privately, she began to doubt the business about brain damage. When she looked into his eyes, she saw depth there, intelligence, a perfectly fine brain trapped in a half-collapsed body.

At the start of the second week, Miss Lattimore began class by whispering, "I need to ask one of you to be Kevin's helper this week." Though Kevin wasn't there (he still arrived at school an hour late every day), she leaned toward the class as if this were a collective secret, something they shouldn't speak of outside their room. Cara's hand shot up, a lone pillar in a sea of uncertainty. To date, Cara had made no mark in this class, had distinguished herself as nothing beyond being the one person with clean fingernails the day Miss Lattimore discussed hand-to-mouth transmission of cold germs. ("I'm not afraid to shake hands with Cara," she'd said. "The rest of you, I'm less sure of.") Now that would change. Miss Lattimore called her up for a private conference at the teacher's desk. "Try to think about things he might need, and help him before he has to ask. I think that's the nicest way." Cara nodded and planned to be the best Kevin-helper ever, so good that no one else would need to apply for the job, it would be hers for the rest of the year.

As it turned out, though, Kevin didn't need much help and hardly ever asked for anything; in fact, he hardly seemed to talk at all. Twice Miss Lattimore called on him in class, and both times everyone watched the concentrated effort that talking required. Both times he failed to get any words out, and Miss Lattimore said, "It's okay, Kevin. Thanks for trying. Maybe next time." They ate lunch together as Miss Lattimore had told them to do, and Cara kept up a steady stream of chatter she'd planned ahead of time to fill what would otherwise be a silent meal. She told him everything she'd been thinking about recently: That she wasn't interested in having tons of friends, that she'd rather be *nice* than *popular,* and sometimes, she'd learned, you can't be both. To her surprise, in Kevin's silent presence, words came easily, opinions, thoughts; suddenly, she had lots of them. She sounded like Suzette, who everyone knew was the smarter of the two of them. She told Kevin she was thinking about being a nurse when she grew up, or a marine biologist, based on visiting tide pools last summer and surprising everyone with the fearless way she reached in to touch the textures that couldn't be predicted ahead of time. "Some anemones look squishy, and then you touch them and they're hard as a bone. Like touching a skull, which would be weird. Who'd want to do that?"

His wandering eyes flicked to hers.

Oh my God, she thought. *His skull has been touched, by many hands probably.* Her heart sped up and she feared some kind of internal combustion, death from embarrassment, a heart attack of stupidity.

Later Miss Lattimore told Cara she did a fine job but she was going to assign a boy from now on. "In case Kevin needs any help in the restroom. It'll be easier this way, less embarrassing to him if he has to ask." Cara stood beside Miss Lattimore's desk, in the second and last private audience she would have with this teacher for the rest of the year, and saw, in a flash of the terrifying insight children sometimes have and then shake off, confused by their own capacity for truth, that she was not alone in loving Kevin for inexplicable reasons: his needs, his silence, the bad hand he had to place with the other on top of his desk. Miss Lattimore loved him, too, and thought about him at night, far more than she should. They each believed their version of the truth about Kevin: to Cara, he was fine, or even better than fine—a brush with death had aged him prematurely and placed an adult in their midst, trapped inside a broken child's body; to Miss Lattimore, he would forever stay the child who climbed on a bicycle and rode for three minutes, his arms outstretched. Perhaps they both hoped for similar things: to erase injury with ministrations, to find a hole, a vacuum to pour their liquid love into, or maybe it was slightly darker, what Suzette had implied in her annoyance at Cara's refusal to eat lunch with her all week. "You just want everyone to notice *you*."

Suzette had been her best friend for three years now. They'd suffered through seven months of Girl Scouts, had jointly quit when denied their artistic creativity badges because the Shrinky Dinks stained-glass project Suzette dreamed up, incorporating bird feathers and aluminum foil pieces, fit no definition of art the leader had read. They had learned to ride bikes together, to swim, to make God's eye yarn stars they hung above their beds. Suzette knew everything about Cara, and had spoken a certain degree of the truth: Cara *did* want to be noticed. Against the hard, plain truth of all Kevin's needs, she saw herself for the first time during those lunches, heard her own voice, felt herself become the person she might one day turn into.

Years down the line, Cara would come to realize she wasn't wrong about Miss Lattimore, either. She would learn firsthand that there are many responses to a child who has "special needs" (as they weren't commonly called then but would be soon), that people seem to feel, in equal measure, compassion, disdain, terror, and pity, yet also this—an equation of possibility: *Here you have this need. Come, sit beside me. Let me fill it.*

Now, at age thirty, Cara sits in the office of her old elementary school, waiting for Margot Tesler, the principal, to return and tell her what's going on with her son, who has been missing long enough for her to be called down here. Most of the time Cara forgets she went to this school some twenty years ago, that if walls could talk, these corridors could speak to a long history of her failures and successes. It only occurs to her in odd moments: kneeling beside a coat cubby as Adam negotiates his way out of snow pants, she'll see a heating vent and remember her and Suzette, bored, decorating the slats in tiny ballpoint-pen *Hellos*, and she'll lean over to see if coats of beige paint might not have erased evidence of her old, now dead friendship.

Though Cara never came to the principal's office as a child, she knows this office well now, with its wall-to-wall bookshelves and conference table big enough to accommodate Adam's yearly education plan review, which sometimes involves eight people hammering out goals, benchmarks, the accommodations necessary as the curriculum grows more demanding with each year. Strangely, Cara has happy associations with being in this room. She isn't friends with any of these people, but she also isn't adversarial, as she suspects some parents of special-needs kids are, with a bottomless list of requests and demands. Cara takes the opposite approach, baking cookies for all her meetings, distributing fudge every Christmas, writing elaborate yearly thank-you notes to everyone on staff, because she's always believed what her mother taught her—that kindness breeds kindness—and if she thanks people, and thanks them again, Adam's world will be cushioned by a bit of remembered gratitude. So far, Cara would argue, her approach has worked. Even when she walked in here, Shirley, the principal's secretary, caught her eye and said, "We love Adam, sweetheart, and we're all going out of our minds. He'll turn up in a minute." Cara nodded and mouthed, *Thank you.*

Adam *is* loved, by the adults of the school anyway, who always talk about his big smile, the dancing joy on his face when he comes in from recess. Though he's still, at age nine, capable of the occasional inexplicable tantrum that embarrasses everyone, he can also be magically uncomplicated: offered the promise of a gumdrop or a chance to listen in on afternoon band practice, he nearly explodes with delight. "No, *really*?"

he'll say, a new favorite expression. "No really? A gumdrop?" In the middle of an elementary school full of children aging too rapidly, dressing like pop stars, carrying cell phones, Adam is, for some of these grandmotherly types, the perfect eternal child—happy with the mundane, a pile of wood chips, a tuft of dryer lint, nothing really. One year, even the principal, sensible Margot, with her boxy orthopedic shoes and terrible crocheted vests, ended an IEP meeting by saying, "Adam is a jewel, Cara, and we all love him. I just wanted to say that."

Cara has always taken such comments as hopeful beacons for the future. Adults love him, and one day he'll be an adult, too! The implication, in her hopeful heart's logic: loved then, too! Appreciated by people who are his age, not thirty years older!

It's a stretch, though, and it requires more work every year to stay optimistic about Adam's future in the face of the growing gap between him and his peers. He's in third grade now, and the list of things he can't do grows longer every year, more exacting, and in her mind more ominous. He can't tell time, can't grasp abstract time concepts: yesterday, tomorrow, next week. He can't play card games, still adds two dice by counting dots. "Shouldn't he be good at this math stuff?" a teacher once asked, thinking obviously: *Rain Man, Dustin Hoffman.* "He's *not,*" Cara said in a rare curt moment. "Autistic kids are all very different, and math is Adam's weakest subject. He's fine with reading. *Fine.* Grade level." She said this emphatically, though there was actually some question about this, too, a lower score on comprehension than he'd gotten six months earlier, which she has to investigate but hasn't gotten around to because there are so many gaps, so many deficits now, countless questions that run through her mind every night: *Why worry about reading when the math is so low? Why worry about math when he is still, three days out of seven, not dressing himself? Why worry about any of these things when it has been nearly a year since he's had a playdate?* Recently she has been falling asleep every night stewing about playdates, thinking: *I've got to try another one soon.* Kids like Adam well enough, or at least they don't mind coming over and playing with his things. Sometimes she'll get the type who will spend the whole time talking to her and she'll watch sweet Adam in the corner, hands clasped in joy at the ease of this get-together, how smoothly it is going, as if he wants to say, *I love my mother and look! So do you!* Afterward, she will have to go over it all, remind him that one has to *talk* to people to be their friend, has to answer questions, has to, for instance, *say hello.* And Adam's face will fall slowly, take in what she is saying in pieces—that it hasn't really been a success, that friendship requires something more complicated than standing in the same room, among the same toys, though Cara, with her own history of failed friendships, can hardly say with any certainty what this should be.

The whole enterprise makes her sad, unable to think about the great gray morass of Adam's future. Math isn't his weakest subject, really. His weakest subject is life, and everything about moving through it. Last week, lost in his own thoughts, Adam very nearly followed the wrong woman off the bus. Cara had to reach out, snap his coat hood, and bark, "Adam, look *up.*" "Oh, oh, oh," he said, his face awash in gratitude and relief: *Almost lost and then saved!* He pressed his forehead against her chest, gasped and giggled and almost cried as he said, over and over, "You're okay, you're okay." Nine years old and in a panic, he still reverses his pronouns, still echoes words of comfort exactly as they've been given to him. "You *are* okay," she said, ruffling his hair as he stood rocking beside her, her baby boy, her preteen, his cheek pressed oddly to the side of her breast.

Now Margot Tesler huffs into the room and sits down across from Cara to explain what happened: Phil, Adam's regular aide, was out sick today, and Teresa, Adam's usual sub, already had an assignment, so he had someone new today, a Mrs. Warshowski, who misunderstood what she was told and believed recess was her break time.

Cara stares at her. Until this moment she hasn't been terribly worried. She assumed he'd be found in one of his strange places, behind a vending machine, under the piano in the music room, that soon there would be some forced laughter and general embarrassment about the commotion this caused. Now she's less sure. "He went out to recess *alone?*"

"The playground supervisors were told. They were perfectly aware."

"But he was outside when he disappeared?"

Margot meets her gaze and nods. "Yes."

Cara stands up. She hasn't considered the idea that he might have been outside, might have really disappeared. She needs to get out there and start looking in all the spots Adam is most likely to have gone. "He must have heard something—a lawn mower maybe. Or some music. Did you check the maintenance room? Sometimes they leave their radio on."

"We checked. He's not there."

Cara gathers her things. "How about the music room? Is the band practicing?"

"We looked. They're not."

"Adam can hear things other people can't. If one kid is playing violin somewhere in the building, he'll probably hear it and try to get closer."

Margot comes around the desk. "We've got people looking inside and outside."

"Let me go find him, Margot. I'm sorry this has caused such a disruption, but I'll find him. He can't have gone far." In the old days, when Adam was younger and more driven by his compulsions to investigate machines, heating vents, water faucets not completely turned off, Cara lost him more often than she liked to admit. She knew the panic, the speed with which he could disappear, but she also knew, intuitively, how to find him: Stop. Listen hard for his humming, his tiny throaty bird noises, or for what he must have heard—music maybe, or the low compelling purr of a machine come to life.

"They may ask for that in a minute or two, but for right now, you need to stay here."

"They? Who is they?"

"The police."

The *police?* "How long has he been gone?"

"A little over an hour. There's a girl missing, too. The police say they think that's a good sign, that it diminishes the possibility of stranger abduction. It's virtually unheard of for someone to take two children at once."

Cara tries to swallow but finds it hard, her mouth filling up with something she can't bear the taste of. She nods but doesn't sit down. "What happened, Margot? Why wasn't anyone watching him?"

"There was actually *more* supervision than usual. Six adults were outside when it happened. There was no stranger on the playground, no unknown cars in the parking lot, no unusual interactions that anyone saw. We're talking to the three classrooms of kids who were outside at the time, trying to find out if any kids talked to them, dared them to hide maybe, as a practical joke, or to walk over to the woods."

The woods, she thinks. Beyond the soccer fields on the far side of the playground, there is a lovely wood glade of pine trees that gives the school its name, Woodside Elementary. "Let me go outside, Margot."

"Not yet. They're doing a systematic search, and for now they ask that you stay here."

Cara looks out the window. "What do they think happened?"

"They think it was a prank. Someone picked two vulnerable kids and told them to do something stupid." Margot shakes her head in disgust.

"That's why I called the police so fast. I want whoever's responsible for this to understand they're in big trouble."

In the past, Cara hasn't worried excessively about bullying. Riding the bus with Adam the first week of school as she does every year, she got a glimpse of how little he registers to other children. They walk past him, look through him, hardly see him, beyond the obvious oddity of a third-grader riding the school bus with his mother. It is sad, of course, and also a relief. If bullies have an intuitive sense for who will burst into tears most easily, most spectacularly, it isn't Adam. He might hum or walk away, but in all likelihood he will hear very little another child says to him. She has to be honest about this, has to remind herself, often, to remain clear on who Adam is and what he is capable of. "If another child told him to do something, I don't think he would. That's not like Adam."

"You never know, Cara. He's changing. Adam's changed a lot this year."

In any other context, she would take this as a cause for celebration. *He's changing! Even the principal noticed!* Now it only seems worrisome. "Who is the girl?"

"Amelia Best?" she says as a question, as if hoping this name might ring a bell, which it doesn't. "She's new this year. Fourth grade. She's been at this school . . . what? Six weeks. Unusually pretty little girl. Very . . ." She tries to find the right word. "Blond."

Adam has disappeared with a notably pretty little girl? For the first time in years, she thinks of her fifth-grade fixation on Kevin Barrows and panics. "Are you sure they're together?"

"We don't know. We know Adam better than we know her. We noticed Adam was missing first, because it's so unlike him. He's so compliant these days that when he didn't line up at the first whistle, Sue knew something was wrong and called the office right away."

"Is it possible an older kid came over from the high school? Or middle school?"

Margot presses her fingertips together. "Theoretically, they're not allowed, but it's possible." The middle school sits within viewing distance of the elementary school—up a hill, with some soccer fields in between. "So I'm afraid I have to ask—where is Adam's father?"

Cara looks up. She hasn't expected this. "He's not . . . in the picture." This is her standard answer, the one nobody ever presses her past.

"Right, I know that, but where is he? I'm only asking because the police have asked several times. Apparently, an absent father is the first place they look."

Cara feels her mouth go dry. "I don't know who his father is . . . exactly."

Margot raises her eyes in surprise. "Oh. So he's *never* been in the picture?"

"No. He wouldn't know."

"At all? Anything about Adam? There's no chance he's involved in this?"

Cara shakes her head. "None."

Margot holds up her hand. "That's all I need to know." She looks out the window of her office, as if she's contemplating going out there right now, telling someone this. Then she turns back, with a new thought: "Do you think if Adam was out on the playground, he could have heard a radio, maybe, playing in the woods?"

Cara's stomach begins to pound, like a second heart. *Let him not be in the woods,* she prays. "Yes," she says softly. "He could have heard something no one else did."

"Would he have gone if, say, he heard voices?"

"No," she whispers because she can't bear the fact that she isn't sure. Adam is her life, her constant companion, the boy she gave up any other life for, but there is a truth to what Margot says: in the last few years, he has been changing. There is a new bravery to him at times, old fears mysteriously dropped. Even in this brief school year, there have been occasions when she warned the teacher needlessly—Adam can't handle fire drills, Adam won't do well in regular PE—both times she's been wrong, has underestimated her son.

Suddenly there is a flurry out in the hallway; two secretaries stand up at once. Through the glass window of the principal's office, Cara can see one of them look directly at her and then away. When the door handle turns and the woman leans in, Cara doesn't look up. "They've found him, Cara. Adam is all right. They're bringing him out now."

Cara exhales, her relief so huge she cannot speak.

"Where was he?"

"In the woods, so he may have some scratches."

"And the girl? Did they find her, too?"

"Yes."

"Is she okay?"

"No."

"What happened?"

"They found her body."

"This Is My Confession," Morgan writes carefully across the top of the page. He wants to make it neat, get this right. "I didn't mean to hurt anyone, except maybe myself, which I understand was stupid, and wrong, and NOT THE ANSWER, but I'm trying to be honest, and that's the truth. Confessions are meant to be a factual re-telling of events in which the writer says, basically, It Was Me. For me to do this right, though, I have to make a few things clear. Number one: I am not, nor have I ever been, the type to get in trouble. In fourth grade, I got very upset about a misunderstanding over some graffiti written on the wall near my seat. When the teacher asked if I understood what school property means, I told her I didn't do it, I wasn't even the *type*. Here's what I've learned, though: People can do certain things even when they are not the type of person to do them."

He is being neat, careful with his writing, staying in the lines, even though he doesn't intend to show this to anyone. He is in study hall, which is a pointless period because no one studies and the proctor, Mr. White, is so old he doesn't care what anyone does, which is mostly talk. Since no one cares, Morgan keeps writing. "Number two: While I'm not going to turn myself in because that would mean having no future for the rest of my life, and maybe going to jail, I am going to work in my own way, every single day to make up for what I've done, which was a terrible mistake."

Morgan looks up at the clock, sees he's out of time, and folds his notebook closed. Twice a week, Tuesdays and Thursdays, he eats lunch with a group that has no name but meets in Room 257. In his mind, Morgan thinks of it as the Group for People Who Need a Group Like This. To him, this means people who have no other friends, though he doesn't know this for a fact. No one has ever said, "I have no friends"; that just seems to be a given in most of their discussions, which so far have been on topics like Having a Conversation, Controlling Your Anger, and Dealing With Anxieties. Morgan doesn't have all of these problems, only some of them. Controlling his anger, for instance, has never been his problem, though people might be less likely to believe that now.

There are five other boys, plus himself, plus Marianne Foster, who runs the group. Some of them have very obvious problems: Derek, for instance, stutters so badly that he hardly speaks. Everything makes Sean anxious: lines in the cafeteria, spoiled fruit, school bells, gym class, the idea of growing up. Chris probably has the widest variety of problems: asthma, eczema, glasses that don't stay on his nose. He is also afraid of water, even in a cup. "I never touch it," he says. "I don't swim, I don't go in boats, I don't drink it or bathe. I wash with a powder my mother sends away for." Someday Morgan wants to ask if Chris *never* showers, or just not very often. Maybe the others want to ask the same question and are afraid to—he can't be sure.

At first, today is like any other day. Marianne starts by asking how people have done on their goals. They each have goals they are working on, though Morgan doesn't know what anyone else's are, except for Howard, who told his the first meeting, not realizing he didn't have to: "I'm working on asking other people questions about themselves and not playing with my penis through my pocket," he said. After that, everyone else chose not to tell his goals.

"All right, then, if nobody wants to share today, we'll press on to what I promised last time I would talk about: your semester project." Marianne turns around and writes on the blackboard: *Volunteering in Our Community*. She explains that for the assignment they'll choose a placement and meet once a week with a person who needs their help. "For instance, it might be an elderly person. What might you do for an elderly person?"

Sean raises his hand. "Excuse me, Marianne, but I've tried something like this once and it made me extremely anxious."

"For right now, Sean, let's just listen to what I'm saying with open ears and an open mind and try not to get too worried before I tell you what you're doing."

"I'm just saying—"

"I understand, okay, Sean? I hear what you're saying."

Morgan likes Marianne, likes that they get to call her Marianne, which he hasn't done with a teacher since preschool. He understands she isn't technically pretty, that her body is fine but her face has more chins than it technically should have, which she explained once was because she has lupus and takes certain medicines that make her face swell. Morgan likes that she tells them things like this, just says them out loud.

She checks her watch. "You're going to be able to pick from four choices: a retirement community, a preschool, a soup kitchen, and bilingual conversation practice for non-native English speakers. Think about what you'd be most interested in doing."

As she speaks, the door opens and a woman from the main office walks in. For an instant, they all look around. Even Marianne looks shocked. "Barbara! You shouldn't—"

This group is a private place, Marianne told them in the beginning. *No one needs to know who's here; no one should ever repeat what's said.* Barbara holds up a hand, a small folded piece of paper in it. "I'm sorry, Marianne, but there's been an emergency."

Marianne takes the note and reads it. "Oh my God, I have to go," she says, standing. "I'm sorry about this, guys. We'll talk more next time."

A minute later, she is gone.

Now she knows, Morgan thinks. *The note must have been about me.*

For all of fifth period, Morgan feels edgy and nervous.

In sixth-period science, an announcement comes over the loudspeaker from the principal, canceling all after-school activities. "Parents are being notified," he tells them. "Everyone is to proceed directly onto school buses following dismissal." Morgan raises his hand, gets a bathroom pass from Mr. Marchetti, then walks to the hallway outside Marianne's office door. He wants to go in there, show her his confession, explain everything, but instead he stands beside the open door to the main office and hears an overlap of raised voices, something about an ambulance: "The police are already there. These kids are going to see it."

"We have to make sure they don't. Get all of them onto a bus or into a parent's car."

"Jesus, Paul."

"That's what we've been told so far. That's all we know. We have no choice."

Morgan hears footsteps coming up behind him, and he moves away, too late.

"Morgan," he hears, and turns around to find Marianne, her face splotched with bright red patches. "I don't know what you just heard, but something very sad has happened." She reaches out a hand and—he can't believe it, he thinks for a minute his heart will stop—takes his. For the first time it occurs to him: *Maybe this isn't about me.* "A girl has died. Over at the elementary school. Everyone will probably know soon enough, so it's better to just say it, I think." She squeezes his hand. "Hopefully, I'm right. What's important now is to follow directions and listen very carefully and do exactly what you are told, okay?"

Morgan nods and holds on to Marianne's hand. He imagines, for an instant, being married to her, living at her house, helping her pick out which turtleneck she'll wear. She bends down, catches his eye. "This is serious, Morgan."

"Oh I know," he says.

For Adam, language has always been a struggle. His first words didn't come until he was three, and then they arrived as only a scatter of nouns, the words most important to him: musical instruments, composers, machines he was fascinated by. By the time he was four, he could identify a clarinet, an oboe, and a bassoon, but couldn't, even when pressed, point to a pair of pants. This is the peculiarity of the autistic brain, the way some pathways work and others do not. Why can one autistic child learn to read before he can organize his mouth into speaking words? Why can another memorize a menu in the time it takes most people to read it? Over the years Cara has learned that the brain can move in lurching dissonance, travel at high speed and no speed simultaneously. Once, in the same four-minute conversation, Adam identified a piece of elevator music as Bach but was unable to give the impressed stranger in the elevator his own name or age. Cara knew he wouldn't be able to because she knew his brain and the walls it contained. "What's your name?" was still a question he couldn't, at age four, answer without prompts, without her touching his chin and starting the answer, "Aaaa . . ." The hard part was the pronoun. To Adam, *your* meant the other person, and how would he know that person's name? There is logic to the countless things he can't do, a way his thinking makes sense.

For years, he never strung his words together, never adopted those baby phrases that get you through a meal: *All gone! More please!* Then, in the course of a single morning four years ago, it changed. Cara remembers all of it, exactly: the lunch she was arranging on his plate, the ham slice, the pickle beside it. Sitting sideways on the chair, one hand mysteriously raised, he began to speak in a heart-stopping monologue: "You can't just step off curbs like that. This is a street, with cars. They go fast and don't *look*. They could run you over, squash you. Flat."

It was a speech she'd delivered the day before on an afternoon walk to the park. For a long time, she couldn't move, didn't dare carry the plate over to the table. Before this he had never put more than three words together, and then he only did it with prompts and rewards, marshmallows and gummy worms, when he found his words and got them out. This was twenty-five, maybe thirty words in a row, handed over for free, sent into the air, just like that, though she knew she couldn't make too much of it. The whole trick to breakthroughs was not going overboard with praise after them. "Wow," she said softly, laying his plate in front of him. "I remember that. When you were standing on the curb. What made you think of it, I wonder?"

Instantly, he was lost again, focused on the food, which took all his concentration, so she kept talking as she was used to doing. "Maybe it scared you when I said that?" He looked at the place over her shoulder where she believed he put his eyes when he was listening to what she said. "That must be it. That must have scared you a lot, I think. It's good to be scared of cars, but remember nothing bad can ever happen when I am with you."

She thinks about those words now, and how patient she has had to be courting him out of his self-imposed absences, to join her in this world with all of its imagined and legitimate dangers. As the main office around her fills up with strangers, Cara prays that he hasn't taken in whatever he's just witnessed. That when she gets to him, she will find him confused by the attention, by the policemen at school, by everything so out of the ordinary when all he did was walk out to the woods at recess. She also knows that Margot is right—he has been changing recently. He has registered and gotten upset about unexpected things— another child on the playground getting a splinter, two children on the bus fighting over gum. Still, there's a chance. Four years ago, when both of Cara's parents died in a car accident, he came to the funeral, came to the wake, came everywhere with her because she couldn't bear to part with him in the days that followed, but in that whole time, surrounded by tears and somber faces, he seemed unaffected. He loved his grandparents but, even so, never once asked where they were or what had happened. For a whole week she let him do whatever he wanted: dribble stones outside, push little pieces of paper through the opening of a soda can. She didn't pull him to a table, didn't line up the flash cards she'd made to build his vocabulary, magazine photographs pasted to colored index cards. She didn't say once, to his body, rocking at her side, "Point to lettuce. Point to plate." She wanted to wait, see what he would do, if the fact of his grandparents' deaths had gotten through to him, and by all evidence it hadn't. The night after the funeral, they ate their hot dogs in the silence that would always reign if she let it. They listened to a tape of *Sesame Street* songs. He had a bath. In bed, she read him the story of Christopher Robin leaving the wood. Did he understand this was about loss and saying good-bye, about love that continued even when you didn't see the people again? No, she finally decided, hoping then it was a blessing, praying now it would still be true: he didn't take in the terrible pain of the world, didn't understand the finality of death.

For some immeasurable time, she isn't allowed to see Adam. He's fine, she is told, he's all right, there's an EMT on the scene checking him out. Finally, a tall, surreally thin policeman leans into her chair: "Are you the mother?" he whispers, and she nods, though of course there must be another mother somewhere, the girl's. "Follow me. And bring your things. We'll need you to go to the station afterward."

She follows the officer outside, stands beside him as he points to an ambulance parked in the middle of the field where, two years ago, she brought Adam for a season of Saturday soccer, fifteen games in which he never touched the ball once. If she asked about soccer now, he would probably remember the oranges at halftime and the shin guards he always wore on his arms for the car ride home. *Please,* she prays, starting toward the ambulance. *Let him be untouched by this. Let him remember this field, look around, and wonder where the oranges are.*

When she gets there, though, she knows before she climbs inside that it is too late.

She has never seen him in this posture before, bent over like this, with his arms gripped to his sides. She races to him, bends down to get his face on her shoulder. "Adam. It's okay. Mom's here." Is he even breathing? She kneels at his feet, her arms around his shoulders. "Just breathe, baby. Keep breathing."

Outside the ambulance door, there is a crowd growing, more police cars, a television news van. She hears someone say, "The mom's with him now," and she finds his face with her hand, cups his cheek. He doesn't move, doesn't respond to her voice. She's never felt anything like this knot he's wrapped himself up into.

For three hours, June Daly, Greenwood's special ed teacher, grades four through six, tells the police officer what she remembers of Amelia: that she usually wore dresses to school (or had for the month and a half she was there); she was cooperative and quiet, but also learning disabled, and perhaps—if the testing had been done that was suggested—even mildly retarded. This wasn't in Amelia's records (which were sketchy and in transit, being sent by her old school), but there were tasks June noticed she couldn't complete in her early assessment: simple addition worksheets, first-grade readers. The officer writes all this down, then comes back to a subject he's already asked about—the boys in her class. "Any of them seem particularly interested in her?"

June looks down at her hands, sees the pinky on her left one is trembling. "No," she says, in answer to the officer's question, though this isn't true, exactly. Amelia was beautiful and the only girl in her class of five students—all the boys were interested in her. They called her nicknames, offered her Tic Tacs, wooed her with jokes, even though she mostly ignored them, sitting in class with the hand-clasped primness of a little librarian. She was an odd mix, though. She could be reticent like that, go days hardly speaking to anyone in class, and then, unpredictably, she could spend a whole morning out of her seat, hovering a nervous two inches from June, leaning onto her arm, resting a chin on June's shoulder. In the early days of school this year, when the summer heat hung on longer than usual and Amelia's nervous hovering became skin-sticking and uncomfortable, June thought of talking to Amelia about personal space; then she never did, fearing it might seem too unfriendly, like an overworked teacher on the brink of burnout though it was only September. And some days it never happened. Some days, Amelia sat self-contained and fine, in her seat all day.

It's not one of her boys, though, she knows that.

"Any unusual behavior after recess?"

"No. My kids aren't particularly adept at duplicity—it takes me about forty-five seconds to know if something's happened at recess, if there's been a fight, and there was nothing today. She simply didn't come back from recess."

She knows what the world thinks of her kids. Years ago, June got into special education because these were the students who intrigued and also terrified her most. It also seemed to be the population with whom the right teacher at the right time could make the greatest difference. And she has made a difference. She thinks of Jimmy, who came to her class as a ten-year-old, reading at a first-grade level, and who now reads aloud proudly from the library of *Captain Underpants* books she has bought with her own money. (One of her reading strategies is providing the books kids are genuinely interested in, which might produce more diaper and fart jokes than she would otherwise care for, but it's worth it to get a book report from Jimmy—as she had two weeks ago—with *booger* and *bowel movement* spelled correctly. "I loved this book," he wrote, "because it's a subject I care about.") She has these success stories, but she also has students she hasn't reached yet, who have sat in her class in wary silence, uncharmed by any of her tricks or jokes. This year, Amelia had been one of those.

"Why was she in the special ed room?"

"Her mother requested it."

"So she had an IEP?"

"Yes. A child can't be placed in my classroom without one."

"What do you remember about her mother from the meeting?"

June remembers a thin woman dressed in a grape-colored suit whose primary goal seemed to be getting Amelia placed out of a regular fourth-grade classroom and into the special ed room. These days, most parents want the opposite: aides, interpreters, whatever it takes to keep their child in the regular classroom. Usually June's room is the last resort, the final straw after months of disruptive, explosive behavior. Because the mother wanted Amelia in special ed, the meeting was a relatively brief one. June must have asked what Amelia liked to do and what she was good at, because she made a point always to ask those questions—to give parents a chance to talk about their child's strengths. She vaguely remembers the mother saying that Amelia loved to draw, but she didn't elaborate, which was odd. Most of those conversations go on and on and have to be stopped by someone coughing and pointing to the wall clock.

"Did you have any contact with the mother after the initial IEP meeting?"

"Yes. Once a week or so, she brought Amelia into school, which isn't uncommon. Sometimes parents do that to check in regularly."

"Hmm . . . Any particular conversations or exchanges that you re-member?"

"I remember one time she asked if I knew anyone Amelia could be friends with. It was hard for her, because she was the only girl in the class."

"Did you have any suggestions?"

"I told her I would ask some fourth-grade teachers. Sometimes we try to pair kids in my room with their regular ed peers who may need a break from their classroom for whatever reason. We give them a project to do. Measuring all the doors in the school, something like that. We've found that's a good way to get math in with active boys."

"But she wasn't an active boy."

"Right."

"So what did she do with her partner?"

June hesitates. What else can she do but admit the truth? She meant to follow up on the mother's request, partner Amelia with another girl. She was going to—she'd even approached one teacher—and in the end, she hadn't done it. She'd never found a friend for the student.

Later, after the police have left with as many of Amelia's belongings as June could find—her writing journal, her notebook, her backpack, even her pink cardigan sweater, still hanging neatly on the back of her chair until the senior officer picked it up, pinched between fingers wearing latex gloves, and placed it in a Ziploc bag—it occurs to June there is one story she didn't tell, one she'd almost forgotten about completely.

It happened late in the morning, the second week of school, or the third, when the room was enjoying a brief quiet spell. Liam, her usual troublemaker, was in with the guidance counselor and Jimmy was home sick, so it was three of them, actually working, bent over a reading assignment, pencils in hand. It was such a rare moment of peace that when the smell first wafted in her direction, she feared the morning would be lost to fart jokes and accusations. But nobody spoke. The stench remained, so heavy in the air that she quietly stood up and opened the door (they were windowless, of course, a center room, low priority), and when it lingered for five, then ten minutes, she quietly asked if anyone needed to use the bathroom. No one did.

She didn't move through the room, didn't try to pinpoint the source of the stench, though she must have suspected. She let it go, released them to the cafeteria for lunch, and staggered to the teachers' lounge. Later, when the afternoon passed uneventfully, smell gone, she went into the girls' bathroom and looked halfheartedly for evidence of a cleanup. She felt guilty by then. *Don't make a janitor face what I can't, don't let another child find soiled panties and make a story of it,* she told herself. She walked from one stall to the next, checking everywhere, around the toilets, the trash. Nothing. When everyone was gone, she checked the boys' room, and found nothing. By then she knew, without a shred of doubt, it was the girl, this fair-haired, quiet Amelia.

Huh, she thought afterward, meaning to make a note of it, to write it down so they could begin to put the pieces together on this puzzling child. And then, one thing and another—how would she explain? she wasn't absolutely sure, didn't see the panties, didn't try to help—she never made the note.

On the day Amelia Best died, her file had all of four pieces of paper in it.

Morgan's mother hates TV, which she says is because she was addicted to it when she was young. "I wasted my childhood watching nothing but trash," she used to say, and Morgan thought she meant literally, watching a garbage can. These are the kinds of mistakes Morgan sometimes makes, until she explains, "No, Morgan, my God. Bad TV, I'm talking about, *The Price Is Right*, *The Love Boat*. That kind of trash."

Usually, Morgan is allowed one hour of TV after she's checked his plan book and all his homework assignments. Now it's clear that after a murder is committed in your neighborhood, TV must be okay because it's still afternoon and they've been watching it steadily for almost two hours, with no mention of his plan book, no talk of homework. Morgan wishes he had his notebook to write down what he's learned, the facts as the reporter lays them out: "Pending autopsy, the girl appears to have died from a single knife wound to the chest."

"Oh my God," his mother says, clapping a hand over her mouth, making him wonder if she is going to throw up. If she throws up, Morgan knows he will, too, because it's happened before, in school, twice to be exact.

But his mother lowers her hand, swallows, and they keep watching.

It's strange to be spending all this time sitting on a sofa beside his mother. Usually for dinner, she makes him some food and stands while he eats, reading a thick pile of stapled pages in her hand. His mother works as a lawyer for an environmental action group, which means if she isn't reading, she's making telephone calls. "I have a compulsive polluter to call tonight," she'll say and he'll shrug, ask no questions. She has her problems and he has his. Now they sit together, blinking at the screen.

A picture of Amelia flashes up—blond hair curled into ringlets, pulled into two ponytails below her ears. The reporter tells them: "We don't know what she was doing in the woods, or how she got out there unnoticed by any playground supervisor." Margot Tesler, the principal, has something to say on this: "Parents need to know this playground is very well supervised. Student safety is the number one priority of this school."

Morgan's mother shakes her head. "Well sure. It is *now*."

The reporter tells them what they know about Amelia: "She liked animals and drawing. She had a bird named Yo Yo." Morgan hears these things and files them away to write down later in his notebook. Then there is this: "Amelia was enrolled in the special education program at the school. Her specific diagnosis, or whether that was a factor in her abduction, is unknown at this time." To Morgan, it seems strange they would say this now that she is dead. Then her mother comes on camera: "We've only lived here six weeks. We came to this school district because the special ed program was supposed to be so great. We moved here from Fitchburg and now this—" She is holding a baby, looking at someone off-camera.

"Oh my God, can you *imagine*?" Morgan's mother says.

Morgan shakes his head. He can't imagine. He's never been to Fitchburg.

Morgan can imagine this much, though. He knows the SPED room at Woodside because last year, when he was still a Woodside student, he volunteered to go there one recess a week and play games with the younger kids. His teacher, Ms. Heinz, suggested it to him. "You'd be sort of a big brother to them. Someone they can look up to," she'd said. Morgan assumed he'd gotten the assignment because even though he was in the sixth grade, he tested at an eighth-grade reading level, which would someday very soon put his brain in high school. He was paired with a boy named Leon who had Down's syndrome and it was okay, as Morgan remembered—a way to get out of recess, anyway, which had always been empty, pointless time to Morgan. Because Leon didn't say much, they usually played checkers while Morgan talked to the teacher, Ms. Daly. It had all been fine until Emma, a girl in his class, told him she'd heard some teachers say they picked people for the job who needed help, too. "Like socializing and stuff," she said. "It's supposed to help everyone." It was the first time someone pointed out what Morgan had never noticed before: that other people had friends, did something on their birthday besides go to a restaurant with their mother. "It's not really your fault, Morgan," Emma had said, twirling a tiny piece of her hair, touching the ends to her tongue. "It's just that nobody really *gets* what you talk about."

A year ago, Morgan used to talk all the time, too much he knows now. That was back in elementary school, when he was still smart and re-cited books and facts he'd read from memory, when he didn't think up movie stories in his head, but imagined his life was a movie, that a cam-era followed him wherever he went, because everything was interesting, even his sock choice. Now he is in middle school, and everything has changed. He understands that he can't be the person he once was who sat in the cafeteria and recited facts about the Trojan War. He under-stands that people laugh when you speak what you're thinking unedited. Now he weighs everything and second-guesses even yes-and-no answers. After that conversation with Emma, he resigned from his SPED room visits, went stiff when Leon tried to hug him in the hall.

After two and a half hours of watching TV, they learn that another child disappeared with Amelia. "He is in police custody, where it is being determined how much, if anything, he saw," the reporter says. There are parents on TV, gathering at the middle school cafeteria for an emergency response meeting. News cameras aren't allowed inside, so they talk to people wearing puffy jackets outside the building. One mother speaks over her scarf. "I want to find out what the school is doing. I want to know if it's safe for my son to come to school tomorrow."

Morgan hasn't thought of this: people will be scared, might not go to school.

Another mother comes on the screen, wearing a fur-lined hood. "I'm just thinking about those two little children. We're praying for Amelia's family. We're praying for Adam."

The reporter's eyes creep off the woman and toward the camera, and even Morgan can see the problem—she's said the name she wasn't sup-posed to, has put it out there: Adam.

Morgan remembers one Adam who was sometimes in the SPED room. Once, he and his aide, Phil, were there playing Boggle at the same recess time he was playing checkers with Leon. He remembers watching them because Morgan used to watch all kids with aides and fantasize about having one of his own. Of course, technically no one wanted an aide and what it said about your coping abilities, but he would imagine the comfort of having his own assigned adult, someone whose job it was to listen to whatever was on his mind, and sometimes he thought it might be worth it. That time, he remembers watching Adam and thinking, *How weird, that kid can read.* And then it was obvious, he could not only read but he was pretty good at Boggle. His list of words ran down the page, was twice as long as Phil's. Morgan leaned closer, to see what Adam was writing. Some were words and some weren't: *Blip, Ting, Bing.* "Those don't count," Morgan had said because this was before Emma had talked to him, before he knew to shut up most of the time.

Phil looked up from his own list. "We play a little different. We play that sounds count."

The sounds are everywhere, too many for Adam to sort out. The *hummzzzzz* of the lights. The *kitchita, kitchitaa* of a Xerox machine that he would find and stand beside if he could because he loves Xerox machines. Loves paper appearing magically from gray lips to settle onto a hard tongue, all square and neat, a white rectangle nestled onto a gray one.

He'd go look, but he doesn't dare. He can't make his body move because moving isn't safe, he remembers now, and must remember forever. He must sit here and keep a watch on his knees, his pants, keep a hold on his arms. These parts he still has. His face may be gone, he doesn't know yet, doesn't dare feel for it.

There is a phone ringing, a pencil writing, a chair wheel squealing, someone chewing gum. Up the hall, there's the hiss of pipes behind a

metal water fountain which he would go to if he could move, but he
can't.

There are also people talking, he thinks. Right here, all around him.
There is no way to follow what they are saying, so he doesn't bother trying. Their silences are hard, though, and make him nervous. He worries
that he's meant to say something to fill them.

"You have to answer," his mother sometimes says. "You can say 'I
don't know.' "

He could say *I don't know.*

He hears his name. He thinks: *I don't know.* But nothing comes, his
mouth doesn't move, because he's almost sure now, his face must be
gone. He can't feel anything, can't smell, can't open his eyes to see. All
he can do is hear every sound.

For two hours, Cara and Adam have sat side by side in plastic chairs
across from a man who looks too young to be a detective. Adam has not
been questioned yet—has, in fact, not spoken a single word, even when
Cara leaned into his ear and whispered "Are you okay?" and "Do you
want some juice?" (both times, he answered only by rocking and humming louder). So far, this detective—Matt Lincoln is his name—has told
her it's fine if she does the talking and so she has answered all his questions: *No, Adam doesn't willingly break rules. No, he has never mentioned this
girl. No, he won't be able to tell us what he saw; he can't tell a story in that way.*

They are waiting for a team of specialists to come: a child psychologist, apparently, a social worker, and a detective specialist from the juve-
nile division. She has figured out that in Adam's presence, all talk of the
crime must be suspended, anything that might plant suggestions or con-
taminate Adam's testimony in any way. "With kids it's hard," Lincoln

had said earlier. "Their memories are shorter, they're more suggestible. That's why we try to do this as fast as possible. The less he sees, the fewer people he talks to, the better his story will be."

Does she need to tell him that this won't be a problem here, that Adam isn't suggestible in the way other children are? Strangely, though he wears no wedding band and looks too young to be a divorced dad, he's the only person they've talked to so far who knows instinctively what to do with Adam. When they first walked in, he bent down in front of Adam, caught his eyes without touching his body, asked him questions that went unanswered, though Cara could see—the way his body stilled, the humming ceased momentarily—that they were heard. When Adam is finally led out of the room by a female police officer who tells them they are ready, Lincoln explains: "I have a nephew with the same thing. My sister's little boy. He's three years old."

Cara hears this and knows what he's probably thinking: three is still young enough to hope for everything—magical cures, full recovery. For a second, she wishes he hadn't told her. Now he'll be watching Adam the whole time for signs of his nephew's future. When Adam was a newly diagnosed preschooler, she hated seeing older children lost in the grip of autistic behaviors for fear it would jinx the blind faith that sustained her. Every time she saw one, she said to herself, *Adam at age twelve won't be like that. Or that. Or that.* Now she doesn't think along those lines anymore. She thinks: *Adam is Adam.*

It has been decided that Cara won't stay with Adam while he's being interviewed. She offered this with the explanation "If I'm there, he tends to let me do all the talking," so that everyone will understand, he *can* talk even if they've seen no evidence of it yet. Once they get inside the observation room, with its eerie silver-gray light and the one-way mirror into the room where Adam will be interviewed, she wonders if this will be a mistake. There are three buckets of toys on the floor, none of which will be in the least bit interesting to Adam.

Once they're seated, Lincoln is all business again, explaining the rules and how it will go. "I have to watch the doctor, make sure she's asking the right questions, not leading Adam in any way. You need to watch Adam, see if there's anything he's doing or saying that might tell us something. The doctor will also be wearing an earpiece that will let us make suggestions Adam won't hear, but she will. The idea here is that anything we can get from Adam, anything at all—skin color, shirt color, facial hair, tall, short, anything—is going to give us a starting point. Right now, we've got very little to go on."

Cara's heart sinks a bit at this. He's a kind man, sympathetic; she wants Adam to magically produce answers that will help him, but how can he when she's never put skin color on his curriculum, never drilled him on the gradations of difference? *It looks brown, but we call it black. Some people think skin color matters, but really it doesn't; underneath everyone is just the same.* How can she teach Adam this, when he's never noticed?

"I have to say, I don't think Adam's going to be able to tell us any of those things. He can't describe a person who isn't standing right in front of him."

He looks at her. "Really? If someone asked him, 'Does your mother have brown hair or blond?' he couldn't say?"

Instinctively, she touches her hair and shakes her head no, though of course she doesn't know for sure. They've never been in this situation before. She's never asked him those questions. "Why don't we see," he says. "Maybe he'll surprise us."

They turn to the window and she finds herself looking for a moment, not at the interview room, but at the outline of this detective's face. He isn't attractive in any standard sense of the word; his face is too boyish, with eyebrows that creep across the bridge of his nose in a way that reminds Cara of a joke Suzette once made describing a teacher: *His eyebrows look like they're shaking hands.* She can only think: how strange it is that someone who doesn't know him, who has only seen Adam at his worst, looking more autistic than he has in years, should hold out more hope for a breakthrough from him than she does.

As they wait, watching the empty room, Lincoln is apparently free to explain some particulars about what they've found: "Here's the thing," he says softly. "We've got a couple of unusual factors here. The first one is: no one noticed these two kids leaving. I mean *no one.* None of the teachers, not a single student, and we've talked to all three classrooms at this point. Something like this, you'd expect a ripple effect—one person dared them, one person saw them, told another person. Nothing like that. As far as we can tell, there was no one else involved in their leaving."

Cara nods. To her this makes sense. Adam wouldn't leave the playground on a dare because he wouldn't recognize what one was.

Lincoln shifts in his seat. "The other thing is: we've got forty officers at the site right now, gathering evidence. Outdoor crime scene like this, hard to tell how useful any of it's going to be. You collect two hundred cigarette butts, five of them with lipstick, what does that tell you? Someone wearing lipstick has been there, smoking. Nothing, basically. The point is, we've got one thing going for us: the ground is soft. It's been raining, right, so we've been able to pull up some footprints—good ones—but only of the kids. We can find lots of evidence of the two kids there, a lot that shows us what we *should* be able to find, but we can't. Bear in mind, adults are heavier, so usually it's much easier to get their footprints. This is the opposite of what you'd expect."

The door opens, and Adam walks into the interview room, followed by a middle-aged female psychologist Cara has met, another woman, and a man Cara hasn't seen before. The psychologist starts by pulling out crayons, paper, and two cloth dolls, one a boy and one a girl. Cara knows these won't work, that Adam won't draw a picture voluntarily, and dolls are meaningless to him—the table might as well be scattered with clothing. Adam sees what the woman is putting on the table and drifts away to the far wall of the room.

"There are also no tire marks on the dirt-road entry. No one—so far—has reported seeing anyone on the road. Now, it's still early and this may very well change. But so far we can't find evidence of anyone else in the woods."

Jesus, Cara thinks as she watches Adam do something he hasn't done in years—stand in the corner of the room, facing the wall, and rock.

"Now, a guy can be good, okay? He can be very meticulous and orga- nized about covering his tracks and cleaning up afterward, which it looks like this guy was, okay? But he can't run around in a little girl's shoes, you know what I'm saying?"

Wait a second. She turns and looks at him: What *is* he saying? "Does someone think *Adam* did this?"

"We've got to consider the possibility. He was there, no evidence any- one else was."

"Adam couldn't have possibly—"

He holds up a hand. "Here's the thing, though. It doesn't really fit. Where would he have gotten a knife? He has no blood on him. He'd have had to do a lot of covering up, burying the evidence, changing his clothes."

"He wouldn't have done that."

"Right. We've talked to his teachers, talked to people who know him. Bottom line is, anyone sitting with him for three minutes is going to pretty much agree he didn't do this thing. So, no, he's not a suspect at this point." Cara takes a deep breath, feels the knot in her stomach loosen. "But we're trying to get a picture of what the hell happened. How did two kids get away and across a soccer field, without being seen? Was this *planned* somehow?"

She shakes her head. How many different ways can she tell him no, Adam wouldn't do that? "Has somebody said they *saw* them together?"

"Yes. At eleven-fifteen, Carla McQuiston, a second-grade teacher, saw them sitting together on the swings." He shuffles through his notes. "She said it looked like they were talking to each other and she was curious what they might be saying. She knows Adam, right?"

"Yes. She was his teacher last year." She turns back to the room, where Adam has started moving compulsively. He's up on his toes, humming and keening, wiggling his fingers in his beloved peripheral vision, looking like a grown version of the toddler she remembers before intensive therapy, eight hours a day, dragged him out of his shell. Those were the days when everything had to be drilled: *Look up, look at me, hands quiet in your lap, no humming, no toe-walking*. In the past, some of these stims have revisited periodically—Adam will hum for a minute, do this business with his fingers—but in five years she's never seen all of them appear at once and take over, lock him up in this way.

"She got closer and realized they weren't talking, they were *singing*."

Oh my God, Cara thinks. Her mouth goes dry.

"She decided not to interrupt what seemed like a nice moment and turned away. For a few minutes, she got involved with some boys rolling rocks down the slide. When she looked back, five minutes later, they were gone. Nobody remembers seeing either one of them after eleven-twenty. All indications are, they left together."

It doesn't help that these people are all strangers. For five minutes Cara watches them struggle valiantly with Adam, who won't sit, won't stop moving in a circle around the periphery of the room. "Three people might be too much in the room. It's making him nervous," she says, though this is only a guess. She can't be sure what will help right now.

Lincoln speaks into the microphone he holds in his hand. A moment later, two of the adults in the room tell Adam they have to go. Alone with Adam, the woman psychologist starts moving, trying to keep pace with Adam's flight around the room.

"What are we, Adam? Are we airplanes or birds?"

Cara knows this strategy—join the child in play that looks empty, force him to attach some meaning to it, make a connection, interact somehow. And if the child won't answer, give him a choice of answers, let him pick one. "Are we flying, Adam, or running?"

Ordinarily Adam is so trained in this technique, he can make a joke out of it, or his version of a joke: "We're fly-running," he'll say. Or, "We're bird-helicopters." Not funny, exactly, but something. Now there's nothing. Two people in an oval, orbiting chase, with no response.

"She needs to tell him quiet hands and quiet feet. Make him attend to what she's saying."

Lincoln hands Cara the microphone. "Tell her."

She does and then listens, a moment later, as her words come out of the doctor's mouth. Adam pauses in the far corner of the room, and Cara watches his face register the confusion of hearing his mother's words come out of a stranger's mouth. *He knows,* Cara thinks. *He knows I'm somewhere watching this.*

His fingertips come up, to press first his chin, then the side of his face. She knows this old habit. As a three-year-old, he used to wake up at night and cry until she lay down beside him, one arm draped like a scarf around his neck, giving him a way to feel his own chin, to know that his head was still on. This has always been the body part he most needs reminding of. His hands he can see; his legs, his stomach. But how can he be certain his face is still there? Eventually she found a ribbed baby blanket that worked as well, and every night since, he's gone to bed with it tucked gently around his neck and chin. These days, for the most part, he sleeps through. Now his fingertips move across his cheeks, arrive at his nose, and, as suddenly as it came on, the worry vanishes. He returns to his buzzing flight around the room.

"This isn't Adam," Cara whispers, though of course, maybe it *is*. The longer she watches, the more afraid she grows: he doesn't look like a boy who's been traumatized; he looks like a boy happy to be doing things he'd forgotten he'd loved. She lets it continue until she can bear it no more. "This isn't working."

"Maybe we could try something else? Get one of the men in there?"

She shakes her head. She has to get Adam home, surround him with his things: his blanket, his food, his operas, her voice. Start the process of returning him to his body again. "This won't work. I *know* my son," she says emphatically, though it's exactly the point she's no longer sure of. In the details of this day, doubt has opened up and spread its wings. *They were on the swing. They sang together. A minute later, they broke all the rules and disappeared.* None of this aligns with the Adam she knows, the Adam she has spent nine years working with, the Adam who now moves like a broken helicopter powered by some instinct to go back in time, and start everything over.

Afterward, Cara and Lincoln speak briefly in the hall. By pulling Adam out of interview after only half an hour, she has earned a collective glance of disapproval from everyone. Once Adam leaves here, nothing he says will be of much use. He'll have watched TV, seen the newspapers; anything he says will be distorted or colored. She wants Adam home, alone with her so she can ease him back into his skin, into being himself again, but she can't help feeling bad. They are failing at an effort that is obviously important. "I'm sorry," she says softly to Lincoln, the only one who accompanies them down the hall to the front door.

"Hey, he did his best. What's important now is making sure you guys are okay."

She has already turned down his suggestion that they find a friend to stay with tonight. "You might feel safer," he said. She shook her head, and told him Adam needed to be in his own home.

"Sure. I understand."

Outside the front door, they stand under the surprise of a darkening sky. Somehow they have lost a whole day inside. "You know, what you said before is true. Adam may surprise us."

He nods, digs his hands into his pockets. "Sure."

"He may wake up tomorrow and start talking about this." This isn't a wholly unreasonable hope; in recent years, he *has* surprised her, coming home from school to tell a perfect, three-sentence story about a girl who spilled her milk and cried in the cafeteria. It doesn't happen often, but it does happen. "So if he says anything, I should call you, right?" Maybe this sounds ridiculous—too little, too late.

"Absolutely." He claps his hands together and turns to the door. "Absolutely. Call."

She watches him walk back into the building. He doesn't mean it, of course. Even a nice man willing to give an autistic boy the benefit of the doubt has his limits. Earlier in the day, she heard a sergeant on the telephone say, matter-of-factly, "The witness is retarded, so we'll see if we get anything." She'd wanted to stand on her chair, offer a stationwide lecture on autism, but in the end what difference would it have made, when Adam has offered up nothing at all?

When she finally gets him home, Cara calls the first person she can think of, Phil, who's been Adam's aide for over a year.

"Oh shit, Cara. This whole thing. I'm just so sorry—" Phil says.

She cuts him off because she doesn't want his sympathy; she needs to ask questions. "Did you ever see Adam with Amelia before?" She assumes the answer will be no, that if Adam and Amelia had talked to each other, she would have heard about it.

"Yeah. A few times, at recess. More lately. I think she started it, but I'm not sure."

Oh God, Cara thinks. *Let it not be a girl with some mission like I was.* "Who *is* she?"

"She might have had some special needs herself, I'm not sure. I never heard anyone talk about her before today. I just noticed that she and Adam sometimes sat together on the swings. Or she came over to him when he sat inside the tires."

"And they *talked* to each other?" An hour earlier, she had told Lincoln this wasn't possible.

"Yes, I think so. I know I heard them singing a few times."

"Why didn't you *tell* me this?"

"I thought I did. I meant to. It wasn't a big deal. It was just a nice little thing. You know." Technically, Phil is too young for this job, twenty-one and working at night on his college degree. He was hired because she had fought for a man, preferably young, had made the school run a newspaper ad until they found one, because she wanted someone who would talk to Adam the way real boys talk, which Phil does. In the year that he's been Adam's aide, she's loved listening to the patter of Phil's slang, the way he'll tell Adam that math might be a bummer, but then it'll be cool, because they'll go outside, shoot some hoops. Usually, she loves the rhythm of Phil's talk, loves hearing Adam say, earnestly, *cool* instead of *yes,* when she offers him dinner. Now she fears this is a story Adam won't have the vocabulary to tell correctly. "Phil, please. This is *Adam* we're talking about."

"I know, Cara. I know what you're saying, but he was *into* her. He liked her clothes. The last few days he'd come in from recess singing some little song about a color and finally I figured out it was the color of her socks that day."

She can hardly bear this detail because she remembers it, too; she can hear him singing *yellow, yellow, yellow* under his breath in the back of the car. *Her socks?* She reminds herself: He's nine years old. The girl was ten. They weren't seventeen caught in the tidal pull of hormonal impulses. Still, the possibility haunts her: *Adam liked her clothes? Dwelled on her socks? Was she some precocious little girl making promises to remove them?*

All his life, Adam has shown more interest in the inside of machines than in any mystery the human body might hold. The closest they've ever come to a discussion of sex is the time he watched Cara go to the bathroom and asked why she peed out her fanny. She pointed out what he'd apparently never noticed before—that she had no penis—and he shrugged, lost interest, went back to whatever he had been doing. She tells herself no, she hasn't missed something crucial, some leap he's made in privacy, apart from her.

But the truth is, if Adam has changed in recent months, so has she, in ways that no one else might recognize or notice but to her feel monumental. When he was still a baby, she didn't know other babies, didn't realize hers was so much harder than most. It was months before she understood that her baby cried louder and longer than other babies, that he was different in many ways: he threw up all or most of everything he ate, his greatest comfort came not in her arms but in his mechanical swing. When he was eight months old, she watched him fly around in his doorway bouncer one day, twisting and spinning wildly, and for the first time she thought: *Wait, is this normal?* When he was a year, she understood, *No it isn't.* She watched other babies at the park babble in their play, point pudgy fingers at dogs and puddles, wave bye-bye, blow kisses, while her own child sat for an hour at a time, content to watch sand slide through his fingers, and she accepted it in stages. First she told herself: *He'll be a late talker.* Gradually, she began to see: *He'll be different in other ways, too.* When he wasn't walking by sixteen months, there was talk of low muscle tone, referrals to a physical therapist, a phone number passed along for early intervention services. Then, when Adam was two and a half, his bow-tied pediatrician sat down on his rolling stool, clipboard on his lap, and said, "He should see a neurologist, get some tests done."

No, she wanted to scream, but didn't. Instead, she asked calmly, "What can a neurologist say—that Adam's delayed? That he's going to be different? I know that. I accept it."

"It may be worse than that, I'm afraid," the doctor told her.

The pediatrician knew, of course, as did anyone who knew anything about toddlers and watched hers: lost in his own world, no language at all, no communication. Still, she waited six months to make the appointment.

How was it possible to live so long in a state of denial? She can only say this: It is. You tell yourself you're not interested in labels, that the problem these days is too many labels. You can understand that your child is too extreme in many ways, both overly sensitive and impervious, and you can believe you are working on those things, that they are steadily improving, albeit not by much, but how is a doctor's assessment going to help get you in and out of a grocery store without a tantrum? You want to have faith, believe in your child's right to be different. You narrow your eyes and see an older boy you remember from high school: the quiet one who was good at math and never looked up from his shoes, or the band member no one noticed until the final talent show when he played a saxophone solo that broke every girl's heart.

You can know he isn't normal and still think it's possible: *Maybe he's extraordinary.*

Once, when Adam was eighteen months old and her parents were still alive, she set him down beside their aging, oversize stereo speakers with classical music playing softly and, for forty-five minutes, he never touched the toy she put in front of him. He lifted his head up, lost to the music, and Cara watched him the whole time, mesmerized by the adult expressions flickering over his face—a lifting of his eyebrows, as if to say *Ah, flutes,* then a lowering: *That's nice, cellos.* Even her father, who for a year had been silent on the subject of this squalling baby, grew more interested and brought out his old vinyl records of operas he'd loved. They held their breath and watched Adam close his eyes to take in the wonder of this new music: surround-sound vibrato in a foreign language. Adam loved opera from the first time he heard it; when a record ended, he cried until someone could get to the turntable, lift the needle up, and start it again. "Pretty remarkable," her father said, making anything seem possible—that Adam was a genius, that her life was going to be different than she expected but not worse. Not worse.

He was three and a half before he was finally diagnosed: too long, too late, she knows now. After the diagnosis came, she shifted gears swiftly, put all her energy into reading books about autism and the children who'd recovered, all with a tireless mother at the center, demanding play, pushing interaction, language, response. She became obsessive because she understood you had to be—that autism was a war and recovery necessitated a clear battle plan. She got her parents' financial support and lined up therapists three hours a day to drill flash cards, build vocabulary, go over, with a shoe box and a toy car, basic prepositions: "Put the car *inside* the box. Now put the car *outside* the box." Interestingly, Adam could learn nouns with relative ease, but every concept involving relationships was a stumbling block for him. Put two things together and ask which is bigger, or heavier, and he struggled, fought, wept in frustration. Outside of therapy, she didn't let up. She *made* him play with her, forced his hands into puppets, wrapped them around Play-Doh, dragged him through rounds of Go Fish and Candy Land, torture he endured for the promise of an opera he could watch at the end. But even when it worked, as it did in incremental steps—he would learn to pretend a banana was a phone, a sofa was a mountain—she would wait for the miracle that was meant to follow such breakthroughs: the initiated conversation, the glimpse of interest in another child's play, and in all honesty—though it was painful to admit, and heartbreaking—it never came.

What he really learned, she guesses now, was how to please her. That to make her happy, he might hold a banana to his ear and speak into its bottom, or pull a sock on his hand and talk with the toe, but none of these activities held any genuine interest for him, none were as compelling as, say, a lawn mower, or a transistor radio tuned to static. Nothing changed him fundamentally from what he began as, a boy most interested in being alone, in studying machines, in privately pursuing complicated music, delivered to him in languages no one they knew spoke.

It wasn't easy to decide to stop fighting quite so hard. It started during the summer, after a long period of resistance to the one goal she'd made for the school vacation: riding a bike. To Adam, a goal like this had no point. What he loved about riding his bike was tilting on his training wheels, watching the wonder of his front tire turn its slow revolutions. He hadn't lifted his eyes, noticed the neighborhood children growing older on every side of him, didn't see that big boys rode real bikes now, certainly didn't recognize that he looked ridiculous.

"This summer the training wheels come off," she had said to Adam back in May, though he didn't register the news until the Saturday morning in June when he watched her work for an hour with pliers and screwdrivers to remove them and then wept in protest. She stuck to her guns, made him work at it every afternoon until her back ached with the effort of holding him up. Eventually, she had to set a timer and promise a reward. "Five minutes on the bike and we'll turn on the hose."

"No bike, please. Hose, thank you."

"I know, babe. I know you want the hose. Look at me. Here's the timer. Here's the hose. Five minutes up and down the driveway, and you're all done. That's it. All done."

"All done. Good-bye."

"Good-bye yourself. Get on the bike. I'm counting to three."

Then one evening they had a particularly trying session; he wouldn't put his feet on the pedals, wouldn't even hold the handlebars, and she got fed up. She told him if he didn't start trying harder, she'd cut up the hose with her garden shears. Later, when she called him for dinner, he didn't answer. She searched the house, all of the places he would ordinarily be, and couldn't find him anywhere. He knew not to walk outside by himself, had never done such a thing before, but when she stepped outside, she heard a noise and followed it, running, to find Adam alone in the garden shed beside his fallen bike pouring a bottle of glue into its gears. "Back on," he said, tears streaming down his face as he pressed the training wheels into the mess. She thought of the hours Adam used to spend riding his tilted bike up the street, eyes on his wheel, ringing his bell at every driveway. She had been so sure that removing the training wheels was the right thing—that it would expand his life, not take away one of his few reliable pleasures. She felt her heart rise up, take hold of her throat. Never again would she be so sure she knew what was right for him, she decided. Never again.

It wasn't negativity that made her list Adam's deficits so emphatically to Lincoln (when for years she'd been doing the opposite, insisting that people see him as more normal than not, forcing open doors, signing him up for soccer, saying, "He'll be fine," though he usually wasn't). It was an attempt to be clear, to love Adam without denial or delusion. *This is my son; he isn't fine,* she was essentially saying, because she believed this was better, that real love acknowledged a child's perimeters, accepted the givens, shouldn't be conditional.

In September, for the first time, her initial teacher conference wasn't a cheerleading performance on her own part, as it had been the year before when she'd gaily insisted, "Adam loves science! Maybe he could participate in the science fair!" only to realize, too late, what a bad idea this was, the effort and self-motivation that volcano models and homemade batteries required. This year she was clearer: "Adam can't handle fire drills, and he doesn't do well in regular PE. He'll need an assigned seat at lunch and a teacher with him."

This was better, she felt sure. In the six weeks of school so far, she'd seen a happier Adam in general, one who wasn't being pushed in directions that were meaningless to him. She wasn't forcing him to learn Uno (the way she did when he was in first grade and saw the other kids playing), wasn't drilling him on Yu-Gi-Oh cards (so that he might recognize a trend if it passed under his nose). She was letting him follow his own impulses this year. After homework was finished, she put on the operas that she had previously limited in the belief that he needed to watch what other kids did, that knowing SpongeBob was important, too.

After she hangs up with Phil, there is only one other call she can think to make, a number she finds easily in the phone book, the only listing with this last name.

"Mrs. Warshowski?" she says.

"Yes?" The voice on the other end sounds older than she expected. Cara introduces herself, and a silence follows that extends so long she fears the woman might hang up. "Look, I know there was a miscommunication about recess. I don't even want to ask you about that. I wanted to ask you about Adam's morning, about what happened before recess."

"I told the police, it wasn't my fault. Nobody told me he was a runner."

"He's not a runner," Cara says, knowing that this is shorthand for kids who slip away, that aides get paid slightly more for working with a runner. "Besides, you weren't out with him at recess. Nobody told you that you were supposed to be. It's not your fault."

"No, I'm talking about before. When he got away in the morning."

Cara hesitates. "He got away in the morning?"

"Didn't anybody tell you? After he got off the bus, I was right there. I told him to stay, I needed to get another student, then I turned around and he was gone. Just like that."

"And you'd told him very clearly to stay with you?"

"Sure, I even signed it. My son is deaf, I'm in the habit, and I could tell he liked it."

Adam did love sign language, and he knew all the basic commands. *Stay* would have been clear to him. This makes no sense. "I take it he wasn't gone long?"

"Ten minutes maybe. Long enough for me to get pretty worried."

"Where did you find him?"

"I thought you knew all this. With *her*. Amelia. In the boys' bathroom."

It doesn't take long to get Lincoln on the phone. "Why didn't you tell me about this bathroom incident?"

"I'm sorry, I thought you knew." Lincoln sighs. "Yes, they were found together in the main boys' bathroom across from the library that morning. Fully dressed. Standing by the sinks. Neither one of them said what they were doing. Both were sent to their classrooms. Technically, school hadn't begun, there were three minutes until the bell. He hadn't done anything wrong—*she* was the one in the boys' bathroom. It's possible he went to the bathroom and she followed him in."

"But this is what makes you think they had planned something?"

"Seems possible, right? They were alone. Three hours later they disappeared."

That night, Adam eats dinner, undresses, bathes, climbs into bed, all in silence. Cara peppers him with questions unrelated to the day. If a murder has driven him into this shell, she'll remind him of everything else there is to pull him out. "What music should we listen to? What can we eat here? Does it feel cold to you, sweetheart?" Her voice has the nervous warble of a hostess pushing her way through a bad dinner party, as if Adam has suddenly become a stranger, someone she hardly recognizes. Finally, she gives up. *Tomorrow,* she thinks wearily. *I'll make him start talking again tomorrow.* Instead, she watches him carefully, and the way his body has closed around itself, his hooded eyes turned within. He's not moving anymore or running circles, so he must register that he's at home, where it's safe enough to hold perfectly still, to sit for twenty minutes on the sofa, then twenty more at the kitchen table, but his absence is so complete, so impenetrable, it feels as if something worse than regression is taking place. Even in the old days when Adam was at his worst—tantrumming in public, screaming for things he couldn't name or even point to—he was there in his body, putting up a fight. She's never seen anything like this total withdrawal before. This walking, swallowing, compliant catatonia.

Later, after Adam has gone to bed, she turns on the TV with Amelia's picture frozen—beautiful and dead—in the corner of what feels like every channel she turns to. When Cara can stand it no more, she turns off the TV and wanders the empty home of her childhood, the house they have occupied but hardly changed since her parents' death. Her mother's tiny handwriting still labels the spices; the doorway to the pantry still bears the pale pencil markings of her own childhood growth—lines with dates, because there were no siblings, no need to label which child they were charting. Once, she pointed these out to Adam: "Look, sweetheart. This is how tall I was when I was your age." Even as she said it, she knew he wouldn't understand such a complicated concept: *Mama little?* Now, she wonders if living here is a mistake after all. As she paces these floors, the past walks beside her, larger and clearer than it should be. It's here now, ghosts whispering accusations, the feeling that the events of this day must be her fault, because trying to conjure the picture of Adam and this girl together on the playground, swinging side by side, she sees only the memory of her fifth-grade self, fixing her sights, like a set of crosshairs, on a pale, injured boy.

AFTER THEIR LAST lunch together in fifth grade, Cara lost the courage to open her mouth in Kevin's presence, though she continued to watch him as they moved from one classroom to another, from elementary school to the junior high up the hill. In the fall of ninth grade, Kevin stunned everyone by coming back to school with a beard so full it looked as if he had fashioned a costume for himself. Though the beard didn't last long (guidance counselors protested, pointed to grooming rules no one had ever heard of before), that was the year Kevin became a regular notation in Cara's diary, not as a crush or a friend, but as an example of someone carrying on in the face of obstacles larger than she could imagine or claim. In December, he got pneumonia and was out of school for four weeks, only to return in January so thin his clothes looked empty, his face creased with new age lines. In tenth grade, the one kidney he had left after the accident began failing. She knew this from Kevin's aunt, who was still a secretary for Suzette's father. From this same woman, she also learned that Kevin struggled with depression, that winters tended to be hard for him, sometimes requiring medication. This was the first time Cara ever heard the word *antidepressant,* and she thought of it every time she saw him at school, laughing with his friends, standing by his locker, thumbing through a guitar magazine, balanced on his forearm, his bad hand hanging uselessly below. She was fifteen by then, and, in all that time, strangely, they'd never spoken to each other since that last fifth-grade lunch.

Perhaps it wasn't that odd. Each new school they moved into had been double the size of the school they left. Though Kevin talked now, his words came slowly, weighted, like an old person with an immigrant's accent. Because Kevin had learning disabilities, his courses were a scattershot of special ed and regular classes. Surprisingly, he took and dressed for regular gym, then sat beside the teacher recording statistics, a role he must have liked, because in eleventh grade he became the unlikely football statistician.

Cara watched Kevin, thought about him, privately cheered his progress, but never, in all that time, expected what happened the first day of their senior year in high school: to walk into her English class and find him sitting there. They stared at each other for so long it would be impossible not to speak, or pretend they didn't recognize each other. "Oh my God," she finally said. "Hi."

He looked down, and blushed. "Hi," he whispered.

That morning, Cara had made a conscious effort to change her look from the baggy shirts and overalls she'd come to school in all her life, to a tight spaghetti-strap T-shirt and tiny shorts. "Jesus, Cara, I can read your bra label," Suzette told her—and did, to prove it. Over the years, they had stayed friends in spite of their differences. While Cara still pined for nods of approval and party invitations from the popular table, Suzette floated obliviously, above it all, her bank account stuffed with the money she made babysitting every weekend. More and more, Suzette cared little about the classes she so easily aced, and instead spent hours in the school art studio, painting canvases Cara had a hard time thinking what to say in response to. Suzette was obviously a good artist—she won awards, everyone said so—but her primary interest was abstract expressionism, which always left Cara nervously trying to guess what the pictures were of: "Wow," she'd say. "I love this one. Is it flowers?"

Suzette would roll her eyes. "It's Teddy," she'd say, her younger brother and frequent subject of her paintings. Three years ago, Suzette's life had been turned inside out when her father fell in love with another woman, leaving her mother to fall apart in the privacy of her bedroom, spending most days in her nightgown, sleeping and flipping through the magazines she kept scattered across his side of the bed. "I don't even want to talk about my mother," Suzette would say, shaking her head. And she wouldn't. Instead she took over the lion's share of the cooking and other household chores, packing Teddy's lunch every morning, and, even though he was eight years old, waiting with him at the bus stop so he wouldn't be alone with the fifth-graders who scared him.

"Teddy is a sensitive soul," she said to explain constructing their after-school schedule around Teddy and his bus drop-offs. "I don't want his life to be any harder."

That was the year Suzette started making and keeping rules. "We have to go to my house. I don't want Teddy to be home alone," she'd say. And though of course their mother was home, Cara never pushed the matter. She knew the divorce had taken a toll on Suzette, had left her scared of anything that suggested change. Cara knew this about Suzette and also knew her own new clothes weren't a mistake. She'd seen it in several surprised faces, saw it now in the half of Kevin's face that revealed emotions.

"Why don't I sit in front of you and it can be just like we're in fifth grade? I can talk on and on and embarrass myself all over again."

Kevin laughed and Cara slid into the seat in front of him, thrilled with her own daring. When they spoke again after class, his voice, soft and halting, surprised her: he breathed between words, like someone with a stutter. "I wanted to try a regular . . . English class. I don't know, though. Reading can give me . . . very bad headaches. My eyes . . ." He seemed to search the sky for the words he needed. "Aren't strong."

"I can help you," she said, simply. Meaning: real help, what he needed, not the showy help of the past, where she peeled the tops off yogurt containers and dipped his spoon in for him. "I could read the books aloud. Make tapes for you. Would that be good?"

He shut his eyes, smiled in his old crooked way. "Yes. It would."

Was it friendship, exactly, what they moved into? The exchange of tapes was always furtive, as if they were both slightly embarrassed, he by the need, she by the effort she unaccountably put into it. She told him it wasn't a big deal, that she was such a slow reader, doing it aloud took no more time, but this wasn't true. Reading aloud, page after page, was a laboriously slow task. Doing it this way, she learned how little she had actually read of these dense books. Dialogue, scenes, first and last sentences of every paragraph. This effort to help left her trapped, not with him, but with the endless descriptions of Puritan life in *The Scarlet Letter*. Finally, after two weeks, she abridged the text. "There's a whole bunch of stuff in here about dresses and what they wear, but I swear it doesn't matter, Kevin," she said into the tiny microphone.

The next day he passed her a note, smiling. "I want to know about their dresses."

She wrote at the bottom, "The weird part is they all wore bathing suits underneath. Little red bikinis."

Soon they had two secrets: the tapes she never mentioned to anyone, including Suzette, and the notes they wrote steadily, all through English class. They were always funny, and maybe the best part was that she was a little funnier. Not by a vast distance, but a little. "How would you de-scribe the hair today?" he wrote, with an arrow pointing to the teacher, Mrs. Green, whose hair was an ever-changing terrain. Some days it was curled into a dramatic flip that separated over her shoulders like indi-vidual sausage links; that day, it was piled on top of her head, high enough to clear the chalkboard. "Conical," she wrote back.

On paper, she learned why he had friends—he was a good straight man, he set up jokes, let the other person tell them—but after a while, she began to worry this had gone too far. He wrote too much, saved their notes. He labeled her tapes *Cara, Part One*, as if she were the book. It felt like a mistake to let him go on, get the wrong idea.

"So, Kevin," she wrote after a month or so of note exchanges. "I don't think I can read the next book for you. I'm getting kind of swamped these days."

For the whole period, the paper didn't come back. Then as they packed up, he dropped the rectangle in her lap. "No prob," it said.

Cara decided it was better not to discuss it. When partners were needed for a class project, she leaned forward in her seat, to a girl named Yolanda, and said to herself, *It's kinder this way. I'm thinking of him.* And it was, presumably. Scott, the one football player in the class, who, ow-ing to his size and his prematurely deep voice, seemed as out of place in the room as Kevin, leaned across two desks and said in the surprising voice they rarely heard: "Kevin, dude, you and me." Cara exhaled in re-lief. *He's not my responsibility,* she thought.

Suzette was the one who pointed out, weeks later, after Cara thought the whole business behind her, "Have you ever noticed how Kevin Bar-rows *stares* at you?"

Cara flushed, swiveled around in her seat. "No he doesn't," she said, feeling her stomach turn to rock. She'd done this herself, created some-thing terrible.

After that, Cara stopped talking to him completely.

At the semester break, when Mrs. Green suggested changing their seats to break up the monotony, Cara took one across the room and left Kevin to sit in behemoth Scott's hulking shadow. She focused all her attention on her new crush, Peter, who she'd met working props on *Guys and Dolls*, the musical he was the star of. Before this, Cara had only dated one boy, Robbie, who had never been a particularly dutiful or attentive boyfriend. Some weekends went by without any calls, and when they were together, Robbie was often restless, wishing their town had more to offer, which left her scrambling for ideas: "My parents will be gone. You could come over," she'd offer, her voice suggestive of things he never picked up on. Sex wasn't nearly as interesting to him as it was to her.

"That's because he's gay," Suzette declared after Cara and Robbie had been dating for three months. "I'm sorry, but it's true."

Cara blinked, dumbfounded by the possibility. "Robbie's not *gay*," she said, new doubt opening a vortex of worry in her stomach.

Robbie *was* gay, as it turned out, a fact revealed six months after they broke up and he came to school one day in a dress polo shirt and a pink triangle sticker on his backpack. Cara had learned her lesson: she tried to hold back this time, let the boy make the effort, come to her, and from the start this one felt different. Peter flirted with her all through rehearsals, until their last performance, when he whispered backstage, "So what are you going to do after this? Go back to being Cara, pretty girl with one friend?" She blinked up at him, shocked that he'd noticed the one defining truth of her life so far—she only had one friend. That night they kissed in the darkened back row of the auditorium seats, and a week later they became the couple that surprised everybody. She saw it on their faces: *Why's Peter with her? Props girl and star?* A month later, she understood the answer when he broke down and confessed, with teary uncertainty, about a friend he'd met at tennis summer camp. "He's just a friend," Peter said, but she was old enough now to recognize these tears and know she'd heard enough.

The weekend after she broke up with Peter, Kevin went into the hospital. His kidney was failing, they were told; he was flying up the organ donor lists. "I think anyone who knows him ought to visit him in the hospital," Mrs. Green told the class. "In these situations, you want to make sure you've done everything you can."

Cara felt as if the whole class were staring at her.

"Look, I'll go with you," Suzette said later. "I think our insane teacher might be right, actually."

Cara hoped the visit would resolve the terrible guilt she felt, that she would stand alone with Kevin in the room, hold his good hand, and whisper apologies as his eyes opened and closed peacefully. Instead, his mother stood in the doorway when they walked up, her forehead corrugated into creases of worry. "What are you doing here?" she said, a greeting that so stunned Cara, she said nothing, leaving Suzette to fill in the gap.

"We're friends of Kevin's from school. We just wanted to say hi."

His mother shook her head. "I don't remember him ever mentioning any girls."

"We've known him a long time. My father's secretary is his aunt Joanne."

His mother pursed her lips and shook her head. "I don't like Joanne. She talks too much. She tells everyone our business."

"Actually, you're probably right," Suzette said. "She does talk too much."

With this, the older woman seemed to soften. She let them into Kevin's room, but only with the promise that they wouldn't stay longer than five minutes and wouldn't talk about anything that might upset Kevin. "He's exhausted and he needs all his strength right now. The most important thing is, he doesn't need any distractions."

When they walked in, he opened his eyes and smiled with the good side of his face. He looked pale, thinner than he had three weeks ago.

"Hi," Cara whispered, unsure what to say with his mother standing there. "So you're not missing much in English. Right now we're writing different introductory paragraphs. Like for essays you're just pretending to write. Argumentative, personal, analytical, whatever."

After this, a silence fell over them and Kevin closed his eyes again. "My body is finally falling apart," he said, and the three of them stood, paralyzed by the truth of this simple statement.

Cara reached for his hand. "No it's not," she whispered, as if it were possible for her to control such things.

After they walked out, Suzette surprised her. "You're right about Kevin," she said, in response to nothing. "All these years I hadn't realized, but he's interesting, isn't he?" Cara turned and looked at her. She couldn't remember Suzette saying even this much about a boy before.

Two weeks later, on the eve of Kevin's transplant, Cara got a letter in the mail, one sheet of notebook paper folded into a white envelope with only her name and address on the front. Inside she found a note, handwritten in large, unevenly spaced letters: *Here is my introductory paragraph. For seven years, I have loved you.*

Kevin survived the operation, though barely. This time, Cara's information came from Scott, the football player, who visited Kevin in the hospital and told everyone that for three days his fever ran so high he spoke gibberish. "I heard it, too. It was wild," Scott said.

As he spoke, Cara thought about the letter she hadn't answered, though Kevin's hospital address was still written on the chalkboard,

double-boxed with DO NOT ERASE printed above it. Mrs. Green still
pointed to it occasionally: "In these situations . . ." she'd say, and Cara
now understood what she meant by this—in matters of life and death.

She bought two cards, one with flowers on the front, one with a car-
toon drawing of a woman with what looked like an animal on her head
that said inside, "Better hair next time." She drafted different messages:
"We've been friends for a long time. I wish I knew you better. I wish it
was possible to know people better." This one struck her as the most
honest and also, potentially, the cruelest. Perhaps she could say, *I feel the
same way*, which occasionally she did, until she considered the awkwardness a full recovery would precipitate, seeing each other at school again,
faces frozen in expectation.

Eventually, she sent the flower card with a single sentence that tried,
as best she could, to incorporate Suzette's sentiment: "I am thinking
about you and so is everyone else." She hoped that would at least mitigate his mother's distrust of her. She imagined his mother reading it
aloud, balancing it on his bedside table, thinking to herself, *Well, that's
something anyway*.

Now Cara sees everything from the mother's perspective, how a
young girl might have left her feeling terrified, powerless. Maybe she
tore it up in fury.

Eventually, Kevin recovered enough to go back home and, though
there was talk of getting assignments to him, Cara never raised her hand
to volunteer for the job. He never returned to school. At graduation, his
name was read and greeted with a thunderous applause he didn't hear
because he wasn't there.

"YOU WANT TO hear what I think about autism?" Martin says, sitting at a tiny bar table across from June.

No, June thinks. *I don't.* It has been a day full of unimaginable horror, and now she finds herself at the end of it, sitting across from Martin, a school guidance counselor she has never particularly liked, though the kids all do, especially the boys who horseshoe around him in the hallway to talk about sports scores. He works hard at his own popularity, dresses in jeans that bag a bit in the way the older, sixth-grade boys wear them, and his lunch-hour talking groups fill up so quickly that other adults sometimes wonder—is it appropriate for kids to be so eager for counseling? In the last year or so, June has avoided lunches and long hallway chats with him. That they are having a drink now is a testimony to the way this day has unmoored them all. They both live alone, and both—she suspects—are afraid to go home tonight.

"I think about this guy my buddy took care of for a while. He was an

adult, okay? Nonverbal. Incontinent. Pretty out of it. But one time I visited my friend at work and a child started crying outside the window of
his apartment and, I swear to God, the guy did everything he could to
get to that kid. Rocking, moaning. My friend had to hold him in his lap.
Both grown men. You ask yourself, did the guy have a connection to
other people—to that kid, to his caretakers? My God. They loved each
other. No sex, no words, all the stuff that jumbles it all up. I sat there
watching and I thought: This is the purest love I've ever seen."

It's odd that Martin is thinking more about Adam when everyone
else has been thinking about Amelia.

"When I was in college, I worked for a summer at a camp for autis-
tics. You want to know what I used to think?" She doesn't answer. He
leans forward to tell her anyway, his thumb and forefinger pinched together. "I used to think: Here are a bunch of kids so brilliant, so truly
ahead of us all, intellectually, they came out of the womb, took one look
around this screwed-up world and said to themselves, 'Good-bye. I'll go
on living but not here. Not on this planet.' "

Does he think *Adam* did it? She shakes her head; they all know Adam
at least a little bit, and no one thinks this. He's doing something she
hates, actually—overromanticizing their most mysterious students—
though it occurs to June that all day she's been wrestling with something
like the feeling he's trying to express. When she thinks back over the few
memories she has, she wonders if Amelia might have been smarter and
more sophisticated than anyone realized. She came out tonight wanting
to ask Martin what he remembers of Amelia, what his impressions were.
Did she seem to him (to a man) to understand her beauty? They have already gotten the news (a surprise, a relief, if such a feeling is possible)
that preliminary tests showed no sign of sexual molestation. That even
though there was a window of time where it could have happened, the
killer was apparently not interested in having sex with her. But here is

what June can't figure out: Was she interested, if not in sex, in the attention an older man might have paid her? Or was it something else—did she go out to the woods to play doctor games with Adam? Was she precocious in that way?

If so, it wasn't obvious. She still dressed like a little girl, in skirts and jumpers; most days, she wore her hair in pigtails. June needs the opinion of someone who might have seen things she hasn't. While she has playground patrol once a week, Martin is out there every day. "Did you ever see Amelia talking to older boys? Doing anything like—I don't know—flirting?"

"No, no. Nothing like that."

"Did she ever touch you?"

He shakes his head, frowning. "Not that I remember."

Strange that this comes as such a relief, but it does. She reaches for her wine, takes a sip. Maybe the problem lies only with her. She's too uptight, too long at this job, too anxious not to have these children she loves mistake her for a parent.

"Did she ever talk to you?" That would be a measure; Martin seemed to have some level of flirtation with every student he talked to.

"Once, that I remember. She asked if I could help her find a rabbit's foot that she'd dropped in the wood chips."

"Did you find it?"

"Yes, eventually. It took a long time. I got interrupted and then I saw her again, still looking for it, and I came back. Eventually we found it inside the tires."

June remembers the rabbit's foot that traveled in Amelia's backpack, lay on her desk, sat on the floor next to her foot. It was the first thing Amelia talked about, June remembers, and suddenly she can hear Amelia's tiny voice again, so soft she actually misheard it the first time, thought she was saying "You want to see my rabid foot?" She can picture

Amelia reaching into her backpack, pulling out a closed fist and, like a child of five or six, holding it out, opening it up, one finger at a time. June thinks of this and, suddenly, the tears she's avoided all day rise up. Before she knows it, she's weeping so steadily Martin has no choice but to rise out of his chair, come around the table, and embrace her in the most awkward bar hug ever. "I'm all right," she says, waving her hand, willing out of her mind the unbearable bits they've learned throughout the day—one knife wound, one punctured lung, surprisingly little blood. ("When he found her, the officer thought she was asleep.") She pictures Amelia offering her the rabbit's foot—the simplest of treasures, most childlike prize—and wonders, honestly, why her first thought in all this was to question Amelia's innocence.

If anyone asks, Cara says her life is easier than it used to be, which is true. Adam doesn't make scenes with every trip to the grocery store; his oldest, most extreme fears—of covered parking lots, of digital clocks, of the unpredictable moves a skateboarder might make—are tempered now. He doesn't respond to these mysterious triggers by screaming so loud he must cover his ears; it's been years since she's scraped him up off a public sidewalk or a store floor.

For most of his life, her strategy has been the same one—she pushes her tentative son into the world by moving ten steps ahead of him and rearranging what he will find when he looks. She has thrown napkins over clocks, stored her own in a drawer; she has learned the places where skateboarders are most likely to be and parked two blocks away, finding a path that won't cross theirs. She has done everything she can to reassure Adam that the world is not such a threatening place to be. "Look up," she'll say, knowing the peculiar things he will love—a mealybug inching down a branch, a man in a bucket truck fixing a wire. She knows the things that will be interesting enough to merit his attention, and in pointing them out she believes she's helped him begin to see more, to look beyond the bug on the branch and see the tree, the sky, the surprising shapes clouds can make.

Now she wonders if everything she's done wasn't a mistake. She has made him look up, look around, led him to believe the world is mostly a benevolent place, that strangers are people one *should* say hello to, that friends will help him and adults are, by and large, a trustworthy group. Has she done all this at the expense of the most obvious lesson of all, the one most children have down by the time they get to kindergarten? *Don't talk to strangers; don't walk into woods where they might be waiting.*

In the morning she wakes to find Adam standing silently at her bedside, his eyes wide with terror, as if he's been there for some time and isn't sure she's alive. She sits up. "It's okay, baby." She tries to read his thoughts, believes that she sometimes can. "I'm all right. I was just asleep."

His face softens into its loveliest expression: eyes wide, a closed-mouth smile. He has always been a beautiful child, with dark wavy hair and huge, soulful brown eyes that people notice. Once on the subway in New York City, a stranger pointed to Adam seated on the floor of the train—the only place he would ride, the only way he felt safe with everything moving—and asked if he had commercial representation. Adam was maybe four at the time, with thick bangs and his big eyes and—it was true—an unusually photogenic quality. Cara blushed and demurred, waving her hand as if the compliment had been directed to her.

All morning, Cara weighs every expression on Adam's face, every flicker of his eyebrows for some indicator of what is going on. Adam has certainly had phases in the past, ups and downs that usually follow a pattern. The beginning of the school year is always hard, and then at the end, when the exhaustion of nine months of school takes its toll, he'll regress again, talk less when he gets home, go limp on tooth brushing or shirt buttoning, tasks he's theoretically mastered. Already she can see something is different, though. This isn't one skill mastered and lost, this is everything. Since he's gained language, he's never gone this long without using it—twenty hours and counting.

She tries different tactics, anything to get a response out of him.

"What do you want for breakfast?" she asks when they are standing in the kitchen. He looks vacantly around, as if this is a room he hardly recognizes. His eyes pause on the stove, the refrigerator, the pantry full of food, each a new mystery. "Do you want spiders maybe? Or worms?" This is an old joke, something she used years ago to teach him yes and no.

She waits forever. Nothing. "Adam? Do you want a hammer for breakfast?"

This should get a giggle out of him—it always has in the past. Instead, he blinks at her mystified. His beautiful face recognizes nothing, this room, these words, even her.

"Hello, Adam? Can you say something?"

Nothing.

She doesn't bother getting dressed that morning. Panic shoots through her, pumps her blood with adrenaline. If Adam has regressed and lost everything, she will have to start from scratch, go back to the beginning, pull out the boxes of flash cards and drill them the way they did six years ago. If he won't talk, she will make him label flash cards. If he can't do that, she will lay them in a row for some "Point to . . ." drills. *This is right,* she tells herself. *Don't waste time. Don't let his brain resettle around what he's seen. Don't let it fill up with a movie that is only blood, his ears plugged with the sound of a little girl's screams.* She'll bring him back with his favorites, she thinks, shuffling through the deck, looking for lawn mowers and musical instruments. These are the gifts she can offer

to her son who has never, in nine years, asked her to buy something—
these pictures she has cut out and glued onto index cards of objects that
he loves: a tractor, a piano, a fan, some keys. Maybe she doesn't even
want to run flash cards, she only wants to hear his yelp of pleasure when
he sees one of his favorites coming. She won't make it too hard, she decides, laying out pictures of a shirt, a piano, a bright red tractor. He's had
these for years. This will be like a game, like the family up the street
whose children are ten and eleven now, but still occasionally play Go
Fish for old times' sake. This is their Go Fish.

She gets him to the table, makes him sit down.

"Okay, sweetheart. Look at me," she says, and he does. He hasn't lost
this. His first command, the first words she was certain he understood.
"Good boy."

His eyes are altered, though, in some way she can't describe. It used
to be that eye contact scared him enough to make his eyes tremble as she
counted off the "one, two, three" he had to look at her to get his pretzel.
Now the tremble is gone and in its place is an emptiness she hasn't seen
before. For five full seconds, they stare at each other.

"Now, point to tractor," she says, wondering if she has made a mistake, let him look too long into her eyes so that he's lost track of the
task at hand. "Right here, Adam." She taps the table. "I see a tractor
somewhere."

His expression doesn't change. His eyes move incrementally, off hers,
to stare at the blank distance over her shoulder. She leans forward, takes
his face in her hands. "Baby, listen to me—you gotta try. I know you can
do this. Point to tractor."

Her breath goes shallow. She wants to shake him—is afraid she actually will—then he narrows his eyes at a spray of sun filtering through the
trees. He seems to have heard something else, not her pleas, but a noise

in the light, something that makes him register, for the first time, that it is morning. His face shifts. His eyebrows seem to say, *What was that?* And then it's gone.

He doesn't look again at her.

He never notices the cards.

His mother is mad. He can hear it in her voice. "Point to tractor," she says and he can, with his eyes but not with his hands. His hands are the problem.

Moving when someone tells him to move is the problem.

"Move," the boy said, his finger pointed in a Battle Zone gun. "Move or I'll shoot."

If he points, his hand will become a gun. He will shoot his mother and accidentally kill her. People die in Battle Zone, he's seen it before: the grassy hill behind the playground littered with bodies of fallen boys.

He thinks about the girl, how her voice is like the sun and shadows she talks about all the time. It is light, skipping, singsongy, and then dark. "I hate those people. All of them," she said. He didn't know who she was talking about, but he watched her hands squeeze into egg ovals. "I hate every one of them." One finger poked out. "*Rat-a-tat-tat.* There. I killed them all. We're not allowed to talk to those kids now. That's the rule."

Balled into fists, her thumb and fingers look like the whorled side of a snail's shell. Or the pictures people draw of a snail's shell. He's never seen a real snail.

He can follow that rule because it is easy; he never talks to kids, either. There are other rules, though, interesting ones: "I can only walk on shadows. If there's no shadows I walk on my own. I walk backward if I have to, so I make a shadow."

The day they went for their walk was sunny. "Plenty of shadows," she said, turning the sink faucet on and off. "We'll have no problem."

And they didn't. Once they walked so close their shadows touched. "Don't let anyone see," she said, "or they'll shoot us with their stupid guns." He followed her because he wanted to hear more of her singing, wanted to see her throat, where the sounds came from and how she bent the notes and then jiggled them. He imagined rubber bands inside her neck stretching and vibrating.

Once, his mother brought him to a piano lesson where the teacher started by opening the piano to show him the inside. For the first time he saw how the sound was made, a million felt hammers gently striking strings, and after that he couldn't bear to play. He wanted only to watch the mechanics of music, which is how he felt with her. He didn't want to sing himself. He wanted to look in her throat, see if it held pianolike surprises.

In the hallway at school, Marianne looks happy to see Morgan. "I'm so glad you're here," she says. "So many kids have stayed home, which is terrible. It just makes everyone more scared." She is wearing a black turtleneck and gray skirt with stockings that have little white balls of dryer lint stuck to them.

"I'm not scared," Morgan says.

"Good. I think it's important that we show whoever did this he can't control our lives."

"Only three people were in math. The teacher was supposed to give a quiz, but he canceled."

She shakes her head, looks around the hallway. "You see, I think that's wrong. Even teachers are staying away. What are they *thinking* about?"

He doesn't know. He doesn't know what anyone else thinks about.

Last night, after he and his mother had watched as much murder coverage as they possibly could, Morgan went into his room, closed the door, and opened his notebook. He had been thinking a great deal about clues, although until now he'd thought about clues to his own crime, not someone else's. Here was a new place to put his thoughts: "This is How I Will Make Up For What I've Done," he wrote. "I will solve this crime and people will understand I'm a good person, not a criminal. If I get a record someday, maybe this will be part of it: *Committed One Crime; Solved Another*." He studies Marianne. "There's something I wanted to ask you about." He's been thinking about this all night, has made up his mind to ask at their next meeting, but now she's standing right here, so why not? "I had an idea about volunteering."

She narrows her eyes, confused. "Volunteering? Oh yes. I'd forgotten about that."

"I was thinking I could do something with that Adam guy. Play games with him after school maybe."

"What Adam guy?"

"At the elementary school. The one who—"

"Oh yes. Yes, of course. I don't know, Morgan. I don't know about that. Why don't you stop by my office later and we can talk about it."

For the rest of the morning, he feels good. He thinks of things he can say to Marianne in their meeting. He knows she likes to stay on topic, so he will: he'll tell her he's volunteered before, with special ed kids, that he liked it fine, he isn't scared of them. Of course, he won't tell her about the terrible job he did, dumping Leon after five sessions, pretending later not to recognize him in the hall.

At lunch Morgan gets his food and moves toward the table in the corner where he always sits alone and tries to eat as unobtrusively as possible, but then he sees Chris, from the group, sitting in his chair. Usually, the boys in group don't talk to each other outside of group. They might say "Hi" and wave, but that's it. Morgan considers taking a new seat, but what if a crowd shows up and yells at him, as people so easily can about seats in the cafeteria? Morgan slides his tray down across from Chris.

"I'm not supposed to be here," Chris says. "I usually eat in one of the offices because crowds make me extremely uncomfortable. I got kicked out today because everyone's got meetings about the murder. Do you believe that?"

Believe what? he wonders. *That a girl got murdered? That there were meetings as a result?* "Yeah," Morgan says. "I believe it."

Chris takes a sip from a juice box. He is eating food no one else would pack in a lunch: sweet potatoes, pineapple chunks, a box of raisins. "I'm extremely allergic," he says when Morgan watches him spear a sweet potato. "One piece of bread and I'm covered in hives. Once I tried pizza, and you want to know what happened?"

Morgan stares at him. "What?"

"Hospital," Chris says. "For three days. Oxygen tent and everything. It was okay, though. I don't mind being in the hospital. At least then you don't have to go to school. If things get bad enough, I might do it again."

Chris is older than Morgan. He has been through a year of middle school already, which makes Morgan wonder what he might mean. "How bad does it get?"

"Believe me, you don't want to know. Wait until winter, when it gets really ugly. You'll be thinking an oxygen tent is nothing. Murder would be a relief."

Morgan stares at Chris.

"Ha!" Chris says, so nervously Morgan wonders if he should put Chris on his list. "Just kidding."

In group, Chris has told stories about a summer camp he went to where, according to him, he was extremely popular and everyone loved him for who he was. "For two weeks I was voted Bunk Camper Overseer," he told them. "Which means—you know—I oversaw things. Then at the end I won for Most Improved Athlete of the Summer." At first, no one believed him because Chris is so thin he can't wear watches or keep most socks pulled up his legs. When Sean asked, *"You* won best athlete?" Chris closed his eyes and shook his head. "Most *improved.* In the beginning I couldn't kick a ball. By the end I made a soccer goal. At final campfire I got a standing ovation." Anytime Chris mentions the summer camp, Morgan wants to come right out and ask him for the name. He tries to imagine standing up in the dusky light of a campfire, accepting an award to the music of a hundred people clapping for him.

Morgan decides to take a risk, tell Chris what is on his mind. "I keep thinking about that guy. Who saw the whole thing."

"What about him?"

"I just keep thinking—I don't know. I don't know what I'm thinking." Talking to someone his own age is confusing; Morgan's mind jumbles into a blur of words that won't organize themselves. "That he almost died, for one thing."

"Well, sure," Chris says. "But see, I don't like to think about those things. I don't like to think about almost dying."

Down the table, a trio of older boys blow straw wrappers in their direction. They watch as the paper tubes float and dance toward them. "Yeah, all right. Very funny. Ha ha," Chris says. "I'm putting them on my list." He seems to be talking to the wrappers.

"What list?" Morgan asks.

"My list, all right? My list of people who are going to get in trouble for harassment very soon. We're trying to eat lunch here, right? This is what I can't stand."

"It's just straw wrappers."

"Yeah, to you maybe. You don't see half of it. You don't see what's really going on."

Maybe Chris is right, Morgan thinks, but when he looks up the table, the boys have walked away.

That afternoon, class schedules are changed to accommodate an all-school assembly about safety with strangers, led by a woman no one has ever seen before. She starts the meeting by standing onstage, a microphone in her hand, and saying nothing for so long that people grow nervous, turn around in their seats looking for a teacher who might explain. Then with a click of her thumb and a tiny peel of feedback, she begins: "You all know why we're here. You all know Amelia Best, a ten-year-old girl, was murdered in broad daylight during school hours about three hundred yards away from where we're sitting right now. You may be children, but you're not stupid. You know the perpetrator hasn't been caught. That a very real danger to all of you—every single one—is still out there."

Morgan watches a girl in front of him start to cry. Beside her, another girl puts an arm around her shoulder. "He's not going to kill you, Amy," she says. "He's *not*." Morgan twists around in his seat, looks to see if other people are crying. No one is.

After the assembly, Morgan walks to Marianne's office. To his surprise, two kids he's never seen before are already waiting outside her office. Just as he arrives, Marianne pokes her head out. "Jeff, why don't you come in, and then you, Fiona. And Morgan—" She smiles. "Do you mind sticking around?"

"Not at all," he says, nodding.

He sits down across from the girl, who in any other context would terrify him. Dressed all in black with dark makeup around her eyes and silver jewelry everywhere possible: her thumbs, her ears, even her nose. Maybe he is studying her too intently, because after a minute or two she surprises him by speaking: "You want to know what I heard?"

He shakes his head.

"I hear that she did it to herself. She was a cutter."

Morgan has a hard time judging jokes, but he's pretty sure this must be one until she looks up to the light and he sees she is crying. He's had this problem himself before. After his conversation with Emma, crying at school was always a danger, and could happen any minute if he wasn't careful. Once, when Leon caught him in the hallway off guard and pulled him into a hug, he came away with his eyes filled, like this girl's. He had to go to the bathroom, sit down on a toilet until it passed. "I don't think so. I think she was killed, like they said."

She turns from the light and stares at him. "But maybe she *wanted* it. Did you ever think about that? Maybe she was a sad girl who wanted something to happen to her. Maybe she saw the guy in the woods and thought, 'I'm going to go out there and see what happens to me.' "

Morgan stares at her. This is the first time a girl has talked to him in middle school. Ever since Emma, he has been so scared of them. He wants to argue with this girl, but the words escape him, he can't think what to say. A minute later, Jeff walks out and the girl stands up.

By the time he gets inside her office, Marianne looks exhausted. "Do you mind if I eat while we talk, Morgan? This has been such a long day, I haven't even gotten a chance." She pulls out a vinyl lunch bag, lifts half a sandwich out of it. "So here's the question, Morgan. Why are you picking this kid to volunteer with?"

"Well, I know him a little bit. I remember him. And I don't know what's wrong with him, but he's not—you know—retarded."

"He's autistic."

"Oh."

"That shouldn't scare you necessarily. It's what makes this potentially a good idea. But we'd have to be very careful."

"Okay." He smiles. He loves that she said "we."

"He's obviously been through a traumatizing experience. Something more terrible than we can imagine. I don't know very much about him, but I brought up your idea in a meeting we just had. I learned that he has a single mother, and he's considered moderately high functioning. They told me that he is generally very affable and well liked and that over at the elementary school, everyone is very worried about the toll this is going to take on him. As far as anyone knows, he hasn't spoken since the murder and has gone into a kind of regression."

Morgan nods. He can't believe she's telling him all this.

"Here's the thing, though. I called over to the elementary school and spoke to the guidance counselor about your idea. She wants to run it by some people, but she didn't automatically say no. What she said was, it might actually be a decent idea. There's more and more research these days that says as these kids get older, the best thing for them is not necessarily more one-on-one time with adults, but simply being with other kids. Especially kids who are willing to be patient with a conversation that might take extra time." She reaches into her bag, pulls out a granola bar. "There's this fascinating study, actually. We've always thought that the plasticity of children's brains stops at a certain point. That with developmentally delayed children early intervention is everything—you try to cram as much in before they're five or six years old, because after that there's not too much you can do. The gains they might make are much slower, more incremental. Now there's new research saying that the cusp of puberty is another opportunity—that the brain opens up again, grows more malleable, and certain strides can be made later as well.

"The point being that I'm going to argue for this. I think it's something to try, at least. But we'd have to have some strict guidelines. This couldn't be about spending time with the kid who saw the murder. You couldn't go in there and ask him about it. Do you understand? That's for the professionals to do. Okay, Morgan? Are you listening?"

Yes, he nods, realizing as she says it, all the possibilities. At home he has started a list of possible suspects, including the school principal, Ms. Tesler, because she keeps sounding so defensive on the news. Last night, she said on TV, "There are one hundred and fifty elementary schools in this state without fences around them," though the reporter hadn't asked any question about fences. When Morgan tried to look up the fact, he found nothing on the Internet about elementary schools and fences and can only assume she is making up facts, which leads him to believe she might be a suspect.

Also on his list is Mr. Herzog, the music teacher who asks people who can't keep rhythm "to please not clap." Mr. Herzog wears brown suits and brown shoes, and once he told them, "I play in a jazz band, but it doesn't matter really, because nobody cares about jazz anymore," which Morgan realizes now is an angry thing to say. Morgan remembers a time he saw Mr. Herzog in the hallway, pushing a rolling cart loaded with black instrument cases, with his head bent down so his glasses slipped off and got run over by the heavy, unstoppable cart. When he picked them up, they hung like a *W* in his hand. "Excuse me," he said, squinting up the hall to Morgan. "But my worthless life just got worse, I'm afraid, and I need a bit of tape. Could you help me?" Morgan remembers all this, but never knew what to make of it before. Now he does. It means Mr. Herzog is sad and possibly mad about many things: jazz, glasses, students with no interest or talent. Maybe Amelia pushed him over the edge—blew chewing gum into a clarinet, made fun of his glasses, something.

Morgan formulates a plan in his mind: if he can't ask Adam about the murder directly, maybe he can make a list of names and work them, one by one, into their conversation.

Around school, June hears the stories that are springing up and taking on a life of their own—whispered at first and then spoken aloud, outside on the playground: *He's going to try again, maybe at Halloween. He wants the kid who saw him, but if he can't get that one, he'll take somebody else.* Teachers have been told that in discussing Amelia's murder with the kids, it is important to be open, to let the kids talk, but to emphasize facts as often as possible, keeping speculation to a minimum. "Here's what we know," they've been told to say. "Here's what we don't know." The more facts they are given, the more reassured kids will feel, so they are meant to use facts to arrive back at the same point: *The police are here, doing all they need to, everyone is safe, everything is fine.* But anyone can see that children hear this and tell themselves something else: *He could be someone we already know. He probably is. A neighbor, a custodian, someone who doesn't look crazy, but is.*

In June's classroom, they have found someone new to suggest every hour: Mr. Fawler, who runs the computer lab and has, more than once, hunted for glasses that were sitting on top of his head. "He carries a pocketknife," Jimmy tells her group, and they are all silenced for a moment, forced to imagine a man so overweight he can't button his cardigan sweaters, standing in the woods, wielding a switchblade. There's also Perry, on the maintenance crew for thirty years and so quiet most students have never heard him speak. "Check it out, you guys. I heard Perry lives with his mother. Like that guy in *Psycho*," Brendan says, and June is floored: Brendan is in fifth grade and he's *seen* this movie? And he expects everyone else has too?

"Please, people," she says, and stares at Brendan hard, not looking over at Leon, though she doesn't have to. They all understand: *There are children here, don't scare them.* She'll have a moment like that—clear cut, unambiguous, and an hour later she'll find herself wanting to dial Teddy's number, whisper into the receiver, *Has anyone checked out Perry, the custodian? Did anyone realize he still lives with his mother?*

Teddy has come over every night since the murder, though sometimes he doesn't get there until eleven or twelve because now, of course, he works double shifts. The first night she saw him, after her drink with Martin, she fell into his arms and wept all over again. Now he walks in and they sit at her kitchen table, hands curled around mugs of tea.

Theoretically, this relationship with Teddy is meant to be a lark. He is six years younger than June and better-looking than any man she's dated in years. In college and graduate school, June sat at the top of all her classes and usually attracted some variation of the same man: brainy and pale, stomach going to paunch, glasses that slipped down his nose as they debated into the night about education and philosophy. Teddy is the opposite of all that: he is beautiful and young; his eyes, a rusty brown, flecked orange; his curly hair, dark blond; his freckled face, as her mother might have said, a map of Ireland. He is a cop she met when he pulled her over for speeding and the first thing he said to her, bending down to her window was "Gosh, hi." He's someone she's never imagined herself with—a boy in a uniform, who is sweet and, on matters of any weight, inarticulate. For a year, she refused to take him seriously. He was a treat she gave herself late at night when he called from the parking lot of Dunkin' Donuts to ask, shyly, what she was doing, as if he didn't want to presume anything, even the empty spot beside her in bed.

"It's fine, Teddy. You can come over."

"Really?" he'd always say. "Now?"

She used to make jokes, point to a gray hair and tell him time will not smile on a match like theirs. "When you're forty, I'll look a hundred and fifty," she used to say. Now she doesn't make these jokes anymore because something has changed. She wonders if they are both feeling this, moving toward a change, something deeper, and more, but they are both feeling too tongue-tied to say anything. For her, this is no longer a lark, or a brainy woman's revenge for a lifetime of being overlooked by the best-looking boys. He isn't just beautiful anymore—he is also smart in the quietest way she's ever seen a man be, thoughtful and reflective, decent and loyal. Part of this is owing to the last five years he's spent taking care of his sister, Suzette, which in her mind makes him all the more compelling, but it also limits their time and keeps him at a certain distance. They never make plans more than two days ahead, never talk about the future, never mention living together, which is impossible, she understands, with Suzette in the picture. Dating Teddy has worked so far because she's accepted the givens: that he will leave on a moment's notice, that a single phone call from Suzette will end an evening inside of three minutes, the time it usually takes him to put his clothes back on. But there's also this: since the murder that turned their world upside down, he has come every night to be with her.

In the beginning, he told her everything he knew about the investigation. "They say there's an eighty percent chance the perpetrator knew the girl before today. He's a family member, a neighbor, someone she's had some contact with in the last six weeks. Chances are, they talked. Maybe she petted his dog, maybe she bought an ice cream from him, something, and he fixated on her. They think he's probably been watching her from the woods for a while. So we'll canvass the neighborhood, knock on doors, and sooner or later we'll find someone who's seen him." That first night, she let herself believe in his certainty. "In twenty-four hours, this'll be over."

Now that hasn't happened and they are obviously stumped, looking for ideas anywhere they can. "She took swimming lessons at the Y, so we're interviewing every person with a pass to that pool, anyone who might have seen her in a bathing suit."

June stares at him. "But there wasn't any sexual assault."

"Supposedly she wore this little pink polka-dot bikini. A few people have mentioned it."

June nods and thinks of her own first reaction—that Amelia, who had always seemed so oblivious to her own beauty, must not have been, that she must have done something, drawn attention to herself somehow.

"There's something I haven't told you," he says, turning his mug in his hands. "About the little boy who was with her."

"Adam?"

He nods. "I knew his mom once. She was an old friend of Suzette's."

"You're *kidding*." It's hard to imagine Suzette with a friend, but then it's hard to imagine her with anyone or anywhere beside the apartment she hasn't left in a year. "Does she know about this? That it's her friend's son?"

"No. Not yet."

Suzette's self-imposed exile from the world began a year ago, after a summer full of visits to the emergency room complaining of chest pains and rapid heartbeat. Teddy was never with her when these episodes happened, and the calls usually came from pay phones and nurses' stations. "I'm at the hospital! I think I'm dying!" Suzette would say, and Teddy would run, mumbling excuses: "It's this heart thing again," or "She says her fingers are numb." When he was told these were the symptoms of a classic panic attack, June would ask what she was afraid of, but there were never clear triggers; once, it happened in a Laundromat, another time, the library. Now June understands better the fruitlessness of that question. That the mind is a powerful thing and the physical symptoms of its unrest are real.

Now Suzette doesn't go out at all and, for June, the strangest part of this withdrawal from the world is the apparent peace Suzette seems to have found in it. By all evidence, she has solved her problems and has needed no more ambulance rides. She reads a great deal, watches TV, keeps up with one friend that June knows of, though she's never met him, a clerk at a store near her apartment. He is always referred to as "just a friend" and, oddly, never by name. He is only mentioned occasionally. "My friend came by yesterday, drove me crazy for three hours." June used to honestly wonder if this friend was real, but then she would see evidence of his presence around the apartment—an ashtray forested with cigarette butts, an empty can of beer (Suzette certainly didn't smoke or drink beer)—and she would understand that, yes, Suzette had a more complicated life than they understood, a web of her own secrets, tying her to the world by invisible threads.

For a long time Teddy put off introducing them. When June finally met Suzette, the surprise was how much she liked her. For someone so afraid of the world, Suzette still kept up with it, kept a ubiquitous TV tuned to news, read two newspapers daily. She was warmer than June expected her to be, even surprisingly sweet about the age difference. "I'm so happy you're not a twenty-two-year-old waitress, I can't tell you," she said.

June wasn't sure what to say. "I never was a twenty-two-year-old waitress, if that's any consolation."

"Neither was I. When I was twenty-two, I was crazy." Except for a remark like this, Suzette seemed mostly fine, certainly capable of surviving on her own. She worked from home as a graphic designer and kept up with her painting, which, from what June could tell, she was pretty good at. When she told Teddy that Suzette seemed healthier than she expected, he nodded. "Yeah, she can seem that way. Fine, like that."

Sometimes she wonders if Teddy is too close and can't see the ways his help might fuel Suzette's problems. Once, she tried to gently suggest this. "Maybe what she needs is medication, Teddy, not you there, doing everything for her."

His response was curt. "She's tried medication. It didn't work."

Now June thinks about Suzette and this connection to Adam. She has only had a handful of encounters with him this year, but she has noticed that his eyes are up more, looking around, taking in other children. Once she watched a line of kids, all taking a turn at whapping a garbage can as they walked in from recess. There was no point to the game, nothing much happened, but here was the surprise: at the end of the line, on his turn, Adam did it, too. It was a tiny thing, really, but for an autistic child, unusual. He watched twenty-two examples and without being prompted, he did it, too. "You should tell Suzette what's going on. Adam's mother is probably going out of her mind. Maybe Suzette can help."

"I don't think so."

"Why not? Maybe it would be good for her. I know Adam's mother—she's a single parent, she'd probably be grateful to hear from an old friend."

"Cara was Suzette's best friend. All through school they were inseparable. After they graduated, they got an apartment together, but something happened. That was when Suzette fell apart." He stares at June for a long time, as if he needs to make sure she understands. "See, Cara was the whole problem."

· · ·

That afternoon, Cara takes Adam's backpack up to her room, gingerly unzips it, and pulls out the communication book Phil has dutifully written daily notes in. She knows she won't find Amelia's name in here—he's not allowed to mention other students by name—but maybe there's something else she can find. She reads through a few entries: *Hard time after recess today. Wouldn't do his math. Spelling test went great! Only one word wrong!* She has needed these notes to know anything at all about Adam's day, but she can see how they tell only half the story. They are all about schoolwork, with almost nothing written of recess or lunch, the only times Cara remembers of her own elementary school days.

In his regular notebook, she finds Boggle lists, handwriting practice sheets, voluminous pages of remedial work, nothing she hasn't already seen, until she gets to the zippered pencil pouch at the bottom. At the beginning of the year, she loaded it with new school supplies that look as if they haven't been touched, except for this surprise: there in the bottom, beneath the newly sharpened pencils, the unused eraser, and the ruler, she finds a fraying white rabbit's foot.

She takes it out and walks over to the sofa where Adam sits, listening to his music. "Adam, sweetheart, what's this?" She holds it out, into his line of vision. Seeing it, he begins to rock slightly. "Was it a present from someone?" She waits, watches his face, but can't read his expression.

It must have been a present, of course. If Cara didn't put it in here, someone else must have given it to him, but did that person know about his pouch, find it at the bottom of his backpack and zip it inside? Or—and this would be far more mysterious—did *Adam* put it in there? It seems so strange, zipped in his pouch, buried deep in his backpack, the best approximation she's ever seen of him trying to hide something from her.

· · ·

The reason Morgan has gone for thirteen years of his life without making a single friend is simple really: there was never time. His interests made demands on him, filled his days. Trains, for instance, took a lot of time because he had to draw them and then write stories in which trains acted out trainlike dramas: derailments, crashes, tornado encounters. These stories necessitated trips to the library, books to copy from, facts to learn. Eventually he understood that nothing he could write or check out of the library matched the satisfaction of buying things. His Viking ship phase lasted only three weeks because there was nothing to buy, but electricity? Planets? Star charts and telescopes? Every new interest has filled their mailbox with catalogs full of the surprising products it is possible to own: a personal planetarium, a cricket-breeding kit, an aquarium for hatching and raising sea monkeys. He's only gotten a fraction of the things he wanted. Some arrived and were almost immediate disappointments. The sea monkeys for instance, which he should have guessed, his mother certainly did. "I told you they'd either be plastic or dead," she said, staring down at the larval shrimp, which looked both, floating across the water's surface.

In between purchases, Morgan kept busy, filling his notebooks with pages of research, with his coin-collection sleeves, and with the gravestone rubbings he made one summer on a trip to Gettysburg, the vacation he insisted on after months of reading everything he could find on the Civil War. These days, his old fixations feel so distant he can hardly recall the pleasure attached to them. Did he really squeal uncontrollably, driving up the long dirt road to the Gettysburg battle site? Did he really run from the car to a cannon and throw his arms around it? ("I promise you, yes," his mother says. "And when we drove away, you cried like a baby.") He doesn't remember this, can't imagine such excitement and desolation over a field of green grass. He has become a boy who must not recognize the child he was, who must kick at piles of notebooks and wonder what he was thinking; a boy who, short fifty cents to buy lunch, will dip into his old fifty-state quarter collection and feel nothing.

The problem with Amelia's murder is that it has him going to notebooks again, filling them up with theories and facts: *Time between Amelia's disappearance and estimated time of death: forty-five minutes.* In Morgan's experience, forty-five minutes can feel like an eternity, especially if conversation is in any way awkward. He piles up more facts and observations on those facts: *Total days Amelia attended Greenwood Elementary School: thirty-one. Number of days absent: zero.* There is also this: they can't find the weapon. Judging from her wounds, it was small, no more than six inches long, one reporter has said. "It was probably an ordinary kitchen knife," she said and then, on a cue from off-camera, "a serrated kitchen knife."

Later that night, Morgan studies Amelia's school picture in the newspaper. He imagines speaking with her ghost, consulting it on questions he can find no answers for. *Did you take any music lessons, or meet Mr. Herzog in those thirty-one days? Did you ever find Ms. Tesler a little unfriendly?* In lieu of getting answers, his mind wanders onto the possibility of conversations that will never take place. He imagines warning Amelia about middle school, the loneliness of walking crowded halls wearing a backpack that weighs twenty-six pounds. "Appreciate your childhood while you can," he tells the ghost-face of the dead girl who appears in his mind anytime he closes his eyes.

In the morning Marianne calls Morgan to say that Adam's mother likes the idea and wants to get started as soon as possible. Would Saturday be all right? "Sure," Morgan says, and hangs up feeling both excited and nervous, which worries him. Sometimes when he's nervous, he can do certain things without being aware of them, like the time he spent most of the geography bee picking his nose, which he didn't realize until his mother told him afterward, laughing so hard there were tears in her eyes. He understood from this that it wasn't really funny, that part of the problem was they both made mistakes like this. Like his mother with her petitions and the card table she unfolds in front of the supermarket entrance. "Do you love your mother?" she shouts at people, meaning Mother Earth, the environment, the fourteen miles of wetlands she gathers signatures to save, though sitting beside her, he can see people's confusion. They look over their shoulder and back at her as if to say, *My mother? Where?*

Morgan used to love spending a day at his mother's wetland stand, watching her approach unsuspecting strangers to say, "Sir? Excuse me, sir? Can you give thirty seconds for your planet?" But in the last year or so, he began to see the way people backed up their carts and took different doors out to avoid getting enmeshed in one of her harangues. He began to feel self-conscious at the way she yelled at them. "If you're not part of the solution, you're part of the problem!"

Morgan wants this to work with Adam, maybe even become friends with him, but he can already see the ways it might fail. Adam could hate him, or scream when he walks in the room. His mother could open the door, look at him, and say, "I've changed my mind." If she tries this, he is prepared to say, "I have to come back, it's part of my class," even though technically this isn't a class, it's only a Group for People Who Have No Friends, and there is no credit, no grade, so for college transcripts, none of this matters. Except that to him, it does. This is his one chance, he believes. If he does this right, he'll be able to go on—make his confession and not go to jail.

When he rings the doorbell in the morning, Adam's mother opens the door. "Morgan, hi. Come in," she says. He can't look her in the eye, can't even look up. From his quick glance, he guesses she's pretty, younger than most mothers, with longer hair. His mother wears her hair short, cut in a style called wash-and-wear. This woman's shoes—the only thing he can look at for any length of time—are dirty, with broken shoelaces that have been tied back together. He thinks: *For some people, shoes aren't a big deal. They are just things you put on your feet in case of glass.*

"Adam's in the den waiting for you. I've got some cookies I've made. I thought maybe we could try playing a game."

"Sure." He folds his jacket over his arm.

"I can take your jacket if you like."

"That's okay. Look, I can't stay for very long."

"That's all right. Shorter might actually be better for Adam. I'll be honest with you, Morgan, this may not work. I can't get him to play a game with me, I've tried. There's no reason to think someone he doesn't know will have better luck, so I don't have any big, high expectations, okay? I just want to remind him that there are *nice* people in the world who he *should* trust. Do you understand?"

No, he doesn't understand, but he nods because that seems like the right thing to do.

"Even if he says nothing, it'll still be a good thing that you came and tried."

"Okay, yeah," Morgan says, fearing if she talks any more he might run out the door.

Adam remembers something else.

In the bathroom, the girl leaned against the sink, one hand resting on the faucet. "Okay, Adam?" she said. "Say 'Okay, I'll go.' "

He wanted the water to turn on but didn't dare do it himself, didn't dare risk touching her on the way. "Okay, I'll go," he said.

There was a sound out in the hallway, someone calling his name, some voice he didn't know, which meant *Don't answer.* The girl heard it, too, and said nothing because she has her own rules, people it's safe and not safe to talk to. No one with red hair ever, or braids, she said once. He doesn't care about those things, doesn't usually notice hair unless it stands up by itself, which his mother says is electricity though he doesn't understand because electricity can kill people and shouldn't be in hair.

Now he doesn't look up. He can't look at the boy his mother has brought in who might be one of the people the girl says they're not allowed to talk to. "Those guys," she says, pointing, though he's never looked. He's only heard their voices.

"Adam, you need to sit down, please. I've got cookies."

He can't turn around.

"Right here, babe. Come sit. I'll count to three if that will help."

He hears a shuffling, the sound of a stranger sitting down.

"One . . . Two . . . Come on, Adam."

He hears his mother get up, move toward him.

"Let's go, sweetheart. I told you we were going to do this, remember? I said Morgan's coming over to play one game with you, that's all. One game and you're done."

"Look," says a voice. The boy's voice. "I was thinking, maybe we could play that sounds count?"

Adam breathes. This isn't what he expected. It's different from the voices he's afraid of hearing. He remembers this one from somewhere and then it comes back to him in pieces. He remembers the band in the background playing "America the Beautiful." He remembers a saxophone he couldn't see but could hear. This is the boy who was once in the Boggle room. If he lives there, he will know things. Maybe he will know the girl with the pink dress. Maybe he will know where she is. Maybe he will know what happened to her after they walked into the woods and started talking to that man.

All morning Cara has worried that she's overbuilt this visit, hoping a thirteen-year-old boy will somehow pull them out of the frozen place they're in. Now she can hardly believe what she's seeing: Morgan's voice helps. Adam's body shifts slightly, and relaxes away from the window. "Come on, baby, over here," she whispers, tapping the chair loud enough for him to hear. And he comes. For the first time in two days, she doesn't have to move him with a prompting hand on his shoulder. She is so astonished to see compliance again, she pushes their luck: "Can you say, 'Hi, Morgan'?"

Her heart almost stops. His mouth opens.

"Hi, Morgan," he says.

It's his voice, his old beautiful voice she's been waiting two days to hear. "Very good," she whispers, knowing if she overpraises him or makes too much of this, he'll get confused, retreat back to the window where he started. Adam's eyes stay on the floor, but he sits down in the chair she has pulled out for him. She doesn't want to waste any time. For this to be a success, they need to get through it fast, ride on the momentum of Adam willingly coming over. "Let's see, should Morgan go first?" She opens the Boggle box, takes out the plastic cube and—Adam's favorite piece—the sand timer. "Here, Morgan. Will you start?"

Morgan shakes the cube and sets it down. She holds the sand timer poised, suspended in anticipation of a single gesture from Adam: Will he pick up his pencil voluntarily? Will he remember this basic component of the game? "Adam?" she says, not moving. *Give him time,* she thinks. *Don't tell him too fast.* And then: just when she's about to point to his pencil, give him that tiny visual clue, his own hand miraculously appears and reaches for it.

"Good boy," she whispers again. "And, go."

The top comes off, the timer starts. Morgan scribbles with the fierce determination of competitive player, and she worries the sound of his pencil scratching will be too much of a distraction for Adam to write any words of his own. For her, it is. She can't write, can't look at letters, can't concentrate at all until she sees Adam's pencil begin to move. There's no time left, but she lets it go, gives Adam a chance to write three words: *dig, pot, top*. Joy explodes in her chest like a tiny bottle rocket.

They've done it. He's back. He's played a game.

Morgan can't believe how grateful Cara seems at the end of his visit. He's eaten five cookies, played a game of Boggle, and said very little, though she acts like it has gone much better than she expected. "I'm just so happy you came over, Morgan. It's made a huge difference to us. I can't thank you enough."

He planned a speech insisting that he will need to come back, but he hasn't planned any words for her holding up his coat like he's still a child and saying, "When can we have you back? Would that be okay? Would you mind coming back? Maybe tomorrow?"

"Oh sure," he says. "I mean, you know. I don't mind."

He can't look at her. He's afraid that if he does, something bad will happen, that he'll say the wrong things, make his confession, break the spell of her praise.

"I know it doesn't seem like much, but Adam *responded* to you," she whispers, though Adam is in the other room, listening to music, not to them. "He felt safe with you. He wasn't scared, and he's been scared of everything since—" Her voice wavers. "Everyone's telling me, take him to the doctor, get him to therapists, send him back to school, but I can't do that to him. School is going to be terrifying to him, right?"

Is she asking him a question that he's meant to answer? He's never had a conversation like this before. He tries this: "Right."

"Then you called, and I thought let's just try this. Bring the world back to him, one child at a time. Let him see it's okay, he's safe."

For the rest of the day, Adam disappears into his silence. Cara studies his back, outlined by the window, and watches his movements. Why did he emerge for a few minutes with Morgan, only to retreat again? There are clues here, she thinks, if only she could read them, add them all up, understand what they mean. She needs to think like Adam thinks, follow the movement of his body and imagine the reasons, the explanations behind them.

They are there, she knows.

For years she didn't understand the pleasure of sand dribbled through his fingers—then an ophthalmologist told her that Adam can see far better than most people, every grain of sand in motion. "I imagine it's quite a beautiful thing," he said. What looks pointless and empty isn't always. She must remember this, look for reasons, watch everything he does.

This reminds her of the time after her parents' death, when the puzzling details around their accident became her obsession and she couldn't stop going over a handful of questions in her mind: Why, in a freezing rain with black ice on the road, was her father, a compulsively cautious driver, going fifty miles an hour in a thirty-mile zone? Why did the people in the car behind them, who called in the accident and waited with them until help arrived, also report seeing him run a stop sign a quarter mile before he lost control? In the terrible days that followed the accident, as their house filled with neighbors and casseroles they would never eat their way through, Cara tried to put the pieces together. They'd gone to the theater that night to see a three-hour movie about World War II. The accident occurred forty minutes after the movie let out, though the theater was only ten minutes from their house. It wasn't like her parents to stop for a drink, but was it possible they had? Why else would her father have driven recklessly in conditions that, more typically, would have slowed him to a crawl, driving the road shoulder with his hazard lights blinking? A year later, she rented the movie they saw that night, thinking it might contain clues—something that had upset her father enough to come out of it driving erratically. Halfway through, she stopped watching. The tragedy of war and mass carnage of young lives offered no comfort or insight into her own terrible loss.

After Morgan's visit, Cara starts a list of observable changes in Adam since the murder.

1. *He walks differently,* she writes, unsure how to describe his new loping hunch with his hands poised, robotically, midair, as if he is carrying an invisible tray.

2. *Except for echoing "Hi, Morgan," he hasn't talked since the murder.*

3. *This rabbit's foot.* A token? A gift? Something he stole? As small as it may seem, to her recollection this has never happened before. Adam has never taken anything belonging to another child.

4. *Socks.* This is perhaps the oddest change of all. Last night, straightening his covers after he'd fallen asleep, she found him wearing socks—a new pair, not the ones he'd worn all day, but ones he'd apparently gotten out of bed, in the dark, to find and put on. All his life, Adam has hated wearing socks; one wrinkle and they'd have to start all over again, smoothing and straightening, getting it just right inside his shoe. She thinks of what Phil said, wonders if socks are somehow a connection to Amelia. Did she like them, so now he likes them as well?

That night, Matt Lincoln surprises her by stopping by. He tells her he was in the neighborhood following some leads and just wanted to check up on them, see how they were doing. She shows him the list she's made, explains what's on it. "You said you had a hard time finding footprints, right?"

"Yes."

"Is it possible the guy might have been barefoot?" Lincoln doesn't say anything. She had just thought of this when he knocked on the door, but now she's thrilled that he's here to share it with. "Because all of a sudden Adam wants to have socks on, all the time, but he hates socks. He's always hated socks. So I'm wondering if maybe that's what he saw: some guy's *feet*."

"Interesting. It's true—bare footprints would be harder to pick up. We could have missed them." He doesn't seem as intrigued as she might have hoped. He goes to the refrigerator and studies the collage of Adam's schoolwork and pictures taped to it. "But look at the temperature that day—you had a high of fifty-eight degrees. How is a guy going to walk barefoot down the road and not get noticed by somebody? Or what—he took off his shoes, went into the woods, killed the girl, and then put them back on? It's an interesting idea, but it's also a long shot."

She can hear the patient disinterest in his voice. He's seen Adam at his worst and has given up on the idea of his being of much use. Two days ago she'd insisted he wouldn't be. Now she's less sure. Everything about Adam is different, and she believes that in these differences lie clues to what happened, if she can interpret them correctly. Earlier in the night, he had come to her holding an old video copy her father had made of *The Magic Flute*. They hadn't watched it for a long time—so long in fact, that her father's handwriting on the case was a sad shock, like finding the closest thing they have to a letter from him, addressed to

Adam. Why this one, she wondered, with its dark witches of the night, forest fairies, and other creatures? Surely it means something—the first video he's asked for, the first request he's made since the murder—but what? "Okay," she said, starting it up, and then turned around to the second surprise of the night: Adam standing behind her, his back to the TV, waiting as if he couldn't bear to watch, could only bring himself to listen to the music. *Okay,* Cara thought, leaving him alone. *One thing at a time.* When she came back an hour later, he hadn't moved.

"Can I make you some tea?" she offers.

Lincoln smiles gratefully. "Yes, thank you." He looks different away from the station, handsomer than she remembers and more awkward also, as if there is something he wants to ask her and isn't sure how.

She wonders if this visit is standard procedure or something slightly more personal, connected to his nephew. One thing she knows: when your child is autistic, your whole extended family wishes they could do more for you. "So how is your nephew doing?" she asks, meaning: *Exactly how autistic is he? Does he talk about trains a little too much or does he not talk at all?*

"He's okay, I guess. They're starting this thing, ABA, with him." He shakes his head. "Did you ever try that?"

"For a while, yes," she says. Applied behavior analysis, ABA, is a time-consuming, often money-draining commitment that involves many hours a week, ideally forty, of the child with a one-on-one therapist breaking down and drilling all components of language acquisition and learning. For Adam, Cara did a modified form of ABA, with trained therapists ten hours a week and herself theoretically filling in the other thirty, drilling compliance and vocabulary flash cards. Though Adam got better, improving incrementally at pointing and repeating, he never got used to the demands the sessions made on him, never started one without protesting, never got through the two hours without crying at some

point. After a while, it drained her resources and her reservoir of determination. When Adam was five, halfway through kindergarten, she decided to let it go: stop the after-school therapy, shelve the notebooks of
carefully recorded data—goals outlined, drills mastered.

"We did it for a while," she repeats, and thinks about Adam at the station, rocking back and forth with his fingers in his ears, looking more
autistic than he had in years. "I thought it was good. It's worked for a lot
of kids." What else can she say? She can hardly point to Adam and say,
Look, see how well?

"David's got some words. Mostly what he does is line up cars, along
his bed, and desk."

She nods. Though Adam never did this, she's heard of it, of course:
the beautiful patterns, Matchbox-car art.

"See, I'm telling my sister, I don't know about ABA. Shouldn't kids
this age be learning how to play, not sitting at a table doing work?"

"But if there's no other way a child is going to learn how to communicate, you do whatever you have to. Adam was never very good at
playing."

He nods. "Yeah."

It's a sad subject, all of this—choosing therapies, trying to imagine
the future that lies ahead. When Adam was three, she couldn't talk about
it with anyone except her parents. "Are you close with your sister?"

"Yes, actually. We're twins."

Cara remembers one set of twins, a boy and a girl she went to high
school with who were two or three years younger. She doesn't remember
their names, only that in their freshman year they ate lunch together
every day in one corner of the cafeteria. "Wait a minute." She looks at his
face again. "Did you go to Whitmore High?"

Apparently this isn't a shock to him, because he nods, smiling again.
"Yes, indeed. Played saxophone for *Guys and Dolls*."

He *did*? Maybe this shouldn't be such a surprise, but it is. High school seems like a different world to her now, though come to think of it, she remembers his sister, that she was pretty, and shy. "How is your sister doing now?"

"She's okay. It's hard. David's their first baby, and he's the first grandchild. Our parents, everyone, is kind of—" He cups his hand around his head, makes a crazy motion. "We're all trying to help. What else can we do, right?"

Listening to him, she feels a pang for the loss of her parents, for the way having people to share it with mitigated the pain after Adam's diagnosis. "If your sister ever wants someone to talk to, she's welcome to call." She's never offered this before, never wanted the role.

"Thanks. I'll tell her."

She remembers his sister's name now: Mary. People called them Mary and Mattie, though they weren't a joke. They were something else: a sight people remembered because they didn't see it too often, a brother-and-sister pair sitting alone for the length of a lunch period, finding something to talk about the whole time.

He wanders into the living room, stops at a picture on the mantel of her graduation, where she stands between her parents, smiling cross-eyed at the tassel dangling from her mortarboard. "You want to know what I remember about you from high school?"

Her heart quickens as she imagines any number of embarrassing details he might recall: *You dated gay boys, you had an elaborate hairstyle.* ("Yes," she would have to admit, remembering the hours she spent wielding a curling iron in the bathroom, more often than not with Suzette perched on the toilet, saying: "Jesus, Cara, enough already. You're not curing cancer there.") She wanted so much back then, costumed herself so elaborately to get it.

"I remember you used to play the flute. Is that right?"

It's such an odd thing that she laughs. "Yes, that's right, I did." Her first two years in high school, and of course it was the flute, the instrument choice of all shy girls. She quit junior year when playing in the band required marching at the football games, where she would have had to wear an embarrassing uniform with a hair-crushing hat. "I didn't play for very long. I wasn't very good."

He shrugs. "I don't know why I remember. I must have seen you at a concert." Again, he lets his hands say something he isn't. "Older girl . . ."

She blushes and looks away, as it occurs to her: he's younger than she is, by two years at least. "How did you become a detective so young?"

He shrugs. "Small department. It's not so hard."

"Were you a regular police officer for a while?" She doesn't know the lexicon of this world.

"On street patrol? Sure."

She tries to imagine him wearing a uniform, writing out tickets, breaking up parties. "Some people love that, they're good at it, and they stay with it. I didn't."

"Why not?"

"I don't know. I like this part. Solving puzzles." A beeper on his belt goes off, cutting short the conversation. "Look, I've got to get back. Call if you need anything else."

She holds up a hand to wave good-bye as he disappears out the door, already dialing one-handed a phone he has produced and unfolded from his pocket.

After he leaves, Cara gets an idea. It's only nine o'clock, still early enough that she can call Morgan and ask if he would mind meeting her at the school playground in the morning.

"Sure. I mean, you know, I could do that."

"I want it to be just the three of us. If we go early, no one else will be there, right?"

"I guess. Okay."

After the bathroom, Adam didn't want to see her at recess. He didn't want to go with her into the woods. He's never heard this rule, but he knows it must be one. *No going into the woods; no leaving the playground.* It scares him to break rules, and he doesn't want to. Then she found him at the swings and buzzed her lips together. A machine sound, like a lawn mower, no teeth, just lips. He leaned closer to see if she had a machine in her mouth making that noise.

"Elephant," she said. Adam has never seen a real elephant, but this sounded the way the pictures looked. He smiled because he wanted her to do it again. She did once and then she told him it was time to go.

You go, he wanted to say. *Not me.* After recess was spelling, after spelling was movement room. He didn't want to miss movement room.

"Come on, Adam. You said. Remember?"

When they arrive, Morgan is already there, wearing the same clothes he had on Saturday, which makes her heart lift: Does he know how much this helps, that Adam often recognizes people not by their faces but by their clothing? She sits down beside him, leaves Adam to stand in the geometric shadow pattern of the climbing structure. "I wanted to see if being here might help Adam tell us what happened. Not in words maybe, but in his own way. Maybe we could just watch him, get some clues."

They look over at him. "Do you want to come over and say hi to Morgan?" she calls, though she doesn't expect this to work, because there's no urgency to her voice, no imperative behind it. Then he sur-prises her; he steps out of the shadow, walks over to the bench, and stands before them without rocking or humming, as if he's a perfectly fine boy; only with eyes that she recognizes: on the ground then way up to the sky. "Hi, Morgan."

She shakes her head, stunned. In three days, he's chosen to say the same two words twice: *Hi, Morgan*. There must be a plan to this. He is gathering his words, deciding what to say, how and when to say it, and Morgan is part of this for no reason that she understands, but in his pres-ence, the fog dissipates slightly—Adam can hear again, respond to sug-gestions. "Do you want to go over to the swings with Morgan?"

She watches. She's right: he's heard her, he's thinking about it.

"Uh, I have to say, swings make me a little bit sick to my stomach," Morgan says. "I have this problem where I sometimes throw up."

She doesn't take her eyes off of Adam. His expression changes as he looks over at the long chains and rubber *U*'s dangling above muddy ruts. Maybe this is a bad idea. Maybe this will push him to some edge, but she has to find out. She speaks softly: "Adam sat with Amelia on the swing set. That's the last thing they did before they went for their walk. Do you remember that, Adam?"

"Oh wow," Morgan says.

She can't look at Morgan, can't look away from Adam. "Why don't you go, Adam? Morgan will sit next to you. He doesn't have to swing. It'll be okay." She has to believe this is right, that any movement at all is better than paralysis. Adam steps toward the swing set. "Go with him," she whispers to Morgan. "Sit next to him and watch. I'm going to walk away, but tell him it's okay, I'll be right back. And then watch everything he does very carefully. I'll explain this later."

As Morgan walks away, she calls, "Nod if it seems like he hears anything."

Morgan turns around, nods experimentally, *Like this?*

Yes, she nods back, then slips around the back of the structure, the far wall of the school to the other side of the basketball court where a trash bin sits beside a muddy gully. Hidden behind the Dumpster, she watches the boys sit down on the swings. From this distance, she sees that Morgan's lips are moving, he is talking to Adam, though it's impossible to hear what he's saying so she waits for him to stop, then takes the chance: Just a decibel above a whisper, a hundred yards away, she says, "Say 'Hi, Morgan,' " and waits.

Adam's head is dipped into his jacket, obscured by his collar. She can't see his face or his lips, but a second later, Morgan nods.

She moves back farther. The muddy gully extends to the start of the woods that has been roped off with fluttering yellow police tape marked CAUTION. It seems strange that the police aren't here, but perhaps three days after the fact, it's no longer necessary to keep a crime-scene vigil, though even she knows—she thinks it, as she moves closer: *Criminals always return to their scene.* This should be terrifying, being so close, yet oddly it's the opposite—more like a relief at last, because she wants to know what Adam saw. She doesn't go under the tape; she has to stay focused on the matter at hand. She is farther from Adam now, maybe seventy-five yards, and she needs to try different sounds. She has planned this out, has a purse full of possibilities. First, a telephone she can press to call herself, which she does. Even from this distance, she can see Adam's response: he turns around in the swing, looks toward the woods so quickly that she has to jump back in the shadows to avoid being seen. She moves again, farther away. She has a Walkman with headphones, which she knows is a stretch; Adam's hearing is extraordinary, far beyond most people's, but it isn't bionic. In the past, he has been able to identify the music someone wearing a Walkman two seats in front of them on the bus is listening to—but at this distance, which is, essentially, a football field away? She turns it on, way up, holds the headphone in the air. Nothing. No nod from Morgan.

"Excuse me?"

She spins around, so startled she drops the Walkman on the ground. There's a policeman behind her, emerging from the trees, his uniform dotted with bits of leaves. She knows that he's about to tell her to leave, this isn't safe, isn't allowed. "Wait—" she says, holding up a finger. A tiny bit of song spills from the headphone hole in the Walkman lying on the ground. It distorts the music—opera—so that it sounds like she's listening to chipmunks singing. "Just watch." She holds up her hand to quiet him before he can speak because she needs perfect silence to demonstrate what she's just figured out: Morgan is nodding, Adam is turning, looking around. "He can hear it. He can hear a Walkman dropped in the woods."

If it had been a telephone, or voices, Adam would have heard it but wouldn't have cared. He would have stayed where he was, parked safely on those swings, but she knows this because she knows her son, knows music is a string that pulls him up, through rooms, out doors, away from her. She knows before she turns around exactly what she'll see: Adam is out of the swings, crossing the field, moving toward them.

"The guy had a Walkman," she tells the officer. "He had bare feet and a Walkman."

"Cara—"

She turns around to see: it's not just any policeman, it's someone she knows, a face she can't place right away and then she does. "Oh my God," she says, staring now. "Teddy?"

He nods, though it's instantly clear this isn't a reunion, or a happy co-incidence. He's a policeman and she's in trouble. "You shouldn't be here.

I've called the station. Detective Lincoln wants to meet you back at your house."

She nods, and retrieves the Walkman. She wants to say, *It's so strange, Teddy, I've just been thinking about you and Suzette.* She wants to grab his hand, squeeze it and say, *How is she?* but he won't look her in the eye. She stands there, her face frozen in expectation as he speaks into a walkie-talkie and tells someone at the other end that he has the subject in custody.

Adam remembers hearing something. A tiny trill, like a bird singing, a perfect song of notes that climbs up and down. She heard it, too, because they were walking now, getting closer and she could sing back. "This is what we do," she said. "He plays the flute and I sing it back."

He wants to hear more, wants to look inside her throat. It's beautiful, not scary, and he moves closer, following her, walking so close their shadows bump and touch and then disappear into the unbroken shadow of trees and forest. The songs call and answer each other. A bird sings, *Come, it's okay.* Another sings back, *I'm on my way.* There's no spelling to worry about, nothing bad can happen, this is the language he understands perfectly, these notes flying high through the trees and leaves, meeting midair, dancing together, invisibly.

"Come on," she says. "We're running out of time. He won't wait forever."

Sitting beside Matt Lincoln on the sofa, Cara explains herself. "Music is the one thing Adam cares about the most. If every other neural pathway's been blocked, music is the superhighway open to Adam's brain.

He has perfect pitch, a perfect memory for music. He can sing back any-thing he's heard once, any song, any language. I've been going over this and over this, and I keep thinking that for Adam to have fallen apart so completely, music must have had some part in it. Someone was singing, music was playing, something. Last night, for the first time in months, he asked to watch *The Magic Flute* and I kept thinking, *Why this one?* And then it occurred to me, it's so simple, really. There's a forest full of music. Papageno's playing his flute, the fairies are singing. That's what took him out there. There was music in the woods."

Lincoln nods, writes all of this down. He is all business now, as if he never stopped by last night, as if they never got into high school reminis-cences. He shakes his head: "It's interesting, I'll admit. But you shouldn't have gone there by yourself. Frankly, that was a dangerous and stupid thing to do."

"I *had* to. I had to see what he could hear. And it's amazing—he could *hear* a Walkman."

"Why are you so sure he heard music?"

"That's what draws him. That would have compelled him enough to break a rule about leaving the playground."

"Any music?"

"He has favorites. An opera would have been the biggest lure. Some-thing more contemporary would have been less likely. He doesn't really respond to rap or hip-hop."

Surely he sees the way this helps, that it rules out a world of teenage suspects.

"All right, Cara, I'm going to be honest with you," he says. "These ideas are good, but I've got a DA's office that's already written Adam off. That's how these guys think. They want a perfect witness who can testify in court, they want a case they can prosecute, neat and tidy. Now, my instincts are different. I think, if I've got the right guy, I'll build the case. I'll shred his alibis, I'll get a confession. I'll do whatever I have to. But in this instance, I have to say—I agree with them. I don't think anything Adam does or says is going to tell us much." He shifts in his seat, looks at the door Adam and Morgan have disappeared behind. "Watching Adam now, the way his eyes stay down on the ground, the way he shuts out what's around him, I have to say: I don't think he saw anything."

Cara shakes her head. "Of course he saw something. *Look* at him."

"There's no question he's traumatized, I don't doubt that. He knows everyone around him is upset. He knows something bad happened, but does he know the girl is dead? Have you *talked* to him about it? Explained dead?"

What can she say? *We're getting there? I will?* "No," she says.

"Look, it's not just Adam. A lot of kids are terrible witnesses. This happens all the time, a kid stands ten feet from a murder, and you want to know what they can usually tell you? The color of the guys' pants. They're too scared to look up. Faces are scary. Most of the time, a kid standing in the same room when a murder takes place can't tell you what weapon was used. They can't *see* that stuff. Their brains don't process it."

Cara guesses he's talking about three- or four-year-old witnesses— that the preschool brain is developmentally unable to fathom such a thing. And maybe he's right to put Adam in this group. It's sad yet also a relief, actually: Maybe the mazes and walls of his impenetrable brain have, in some way, spared him.

Except for sitting on the swings at the playground, Morgan hasn't been alone with Adam before and it's hard to judge what he should do after Cara asks him to stay with Adam in the family room while she talks to the policemen. "Want to play Boggle?" he asks, though Adam doesn't seem to be listening. He is staring out the window, his back to Morgan.

He can hear Cara talking to the policemen in the other room. If this doesn't work, he'll go listen at the door, try to hear what they're saying, he decides, and then Adam turns slightly, away from the window, and Morgan tries again. "Do you want to play Boggle? You don't have to."

Instead of answering, Adam crosses the room to the shelf, pulls down the Boggle box. He carries it to the table, opens it up. Morgan thinks, *It's interesting how Adam understands more than he lets on.* Adam takes out the Boggle cube, shakes it, and holds up the timer. It occurs to Morgan that maybe he could just ask, *Hey, Adam, who killed the girl?* He takes a seat, picks up his pencil. Now that he's thought of the words, it's hard not to say them. They're stuck in his mind.

Though it's a bad jumble of letters—only two vowels—Adam starts writing and for once in his life, Morgan doesn't care about winning, doesn't pick up his pencil or write anything at all. He stares at the sand timer and leans across the table. "Hey, Adam. About that girl . . ." he starts to say, and then he looks down and notices the words Adam is writing. They're impossible, way too long for words on a Boggle list, which should be only three or four letters each. Morgan can't read them all—Adam's handwriting is terrible—but he looks at the letters in the game, looks over at the list. It's ridiculous. He's got *elefant* written down and there isn't even an *E*.

"There's something else," Lincoln says. "This morning we got the autopsy back, and blood loss suggests she'd been dead longer than we originally thought, approximately an hour when we found her, which means the perpetrator didn't run away because he heard the police. He got interrupted at least thirty minutes before the police got there. The most likely scenario is that Adam stopped him."

Cara looks up, surprised. *"Adam?"*

"It might have simply been with his presence. He might have appeared, and the guy was startled enough by the prospect of an eyewitness to run away. That's a possibility. There's another, though." He hesitates. Cara looks over at Teddy, who has accompanied them home and now stands in the living room, his arms folded. After all his silence, it finally occurs to her: *Teddy's angry at me. It's been ten years, and he still thinks what happened is my fault.*

Lincoln keeps going: "The question we're asking ourselves is why, when a guy has been so thorough in his cleanup, which he has—we found two tire marks on the side of the road, but not a single footprint around them, meaning the guy must have prepped somehow, planned what he was doing, really quite meticulously—so why would a guy this thorough not have killed Adam as well?" Cara swallows and nods. *Is Teddy hearing all this? My son almost died and you're still mad at me?* "One idea we have is that he knew Adam and liked him well enough to spare him. Or simply knew his limitations as an eyewitness. If we go with that theory, it puts Adam at an increased risk right now, which is why we want to station an officer here at your house. For the time being, we'll ask that you not take Adam out without letting us know. And, obviously, that you not return to the crime scene."

"All right," she nods, and instantly worries: *Will Teddy be the first officer he stations?*

Lincoln looks down at his notebook, turns a page. "There's one more thing from the autopsy notes. We have very little evidence that Amelia put up a fight—no defensive wounds, nothing under her fingernails—which could suggest a couple of things. She knew the assailant, or she was attacked too quickly to fight back. It's rare to find so little forensic evidence on a victim, though it happens, it's possible. The thing is: some fibers were found on her clothes."

He stops talking, forcing her to look up. "And—?"

"And they're a match to Adam's sweater."

For a long time, she doesn't say anything.

"That might not mean much, but it does mean they didn't just walk out there together. At some point, they touched."

After he leaves, Cara is grateful to remember that Morgan is here and will need a ride home; she has to find car keys, her wallet. "I'm allowed, right?" she says, her first words to Teddy since Lincoln has left. "I'm allowed to drive this boy home, am I not?" *If he's angry at me,* she thinks, *I'll be angry back. It was ten years ago, and it wasn't all my fault.*

"Yes. You're allowed."

In the car, alone with Morgan and Adam, Cara talks quickly. "I *had* to go there, had to test the sound dynamics. See if something he heard might have made him cross the field, which is exactly what happened. They're going to thank me for this, I swear to God. I'm going to be right. What I don't understand is how Adam and Amelia got across without being seen. A huge empty expanse of green—how can two kids cross it without being noticed?"

"It isn't empty," Morgan says.

"Yes it is. They're not allowed to play soccer at recess."

"They don't play soccer. They play this weird game, Battle Zone, where you're not supposed to get seen. So you run across, and if you're seen someone points a finger at you and that means you're dead. People start dying a few minutes before recess is over. They lie down on the grass and teachers don't care. They just blow their whistles and tell people to come in."

"Kids are lying around on the field pretending to be dead?"

Morgan shrugs. "Not always. But yeah, sometimes. I don't know.

They used to play that game last year. Maybe they stopped. It's stupid. Stupid people play. Maybe Amelia and Adam ran into the woods to get away from that game."

"God, it reminds me of why I hated elementary school." Cara shakes her head. "The only thing I hated more was junior high."

He stares at her, eyes wide, as if this is a stunning revelation. *"Really?"*

"Everyone is so self-conscious. I always got caught up in things that didn't matter—who was my friend, who wasn't."

"I don't have any friends."

She smiles. "Oh, Morgan, I'm sure that's not true."

"It is. That's why I'm in this group for people who have no friends. It used to be I didn't care. Now I guess I do. A little bit."

She doesn't know what to say. "Well, Adam and I are your friends now. That's a start."

He nods, and seems to think for a moment. "Why would Adam and Amelia have walked out to the woods? Were *they* friends?"

In all innocence, he's posing the question she can hardly bear to consider herself. "I don't know. I don't know anything about her." Maybe she has made a mistake, not pursuing this more. Maybe she can't bear to hear what she fears: The girl *did* like Adam, pursued him somehow. She looks at Adam in her mirror, sees from his expression that he's listening to the music playing thinly over the radio, hearing none of this conversation, which means she might as well be honest, make it clear to Morgan. Every year, during the first week of school she takes pictures of his classmates and glues them to a poster board with MY FRIENDS written at the top. It's a way for Adam to learn names and faces, and she's also hoped, to understand an abstract word like *friends,* that they are meant to be children, approximately his age, though it's never really worked. When asked to choose a friend for an activity, his eyes always flick first and most hopefully at the teachers, even though time has taught him that Mrs. Wolf and Mrs. Ellis are not choices he's allowed to make, that friends are not the bosomed women he feels most comfortable around, but the unpredictable, frightening boys around his height who play games at recess that he doesn't understand. "I think that, for Adam, friendship has a different definition. He thinks of teachers as his friends or other adults. He's never had another child as a friend. Other kids are usually . . . confusing to him." It's hard for her to admit, but maybe her saying this will help Morgan see why he matters. "That he's even talked to you, played a game, gone and sat on the swings with you, all of that is very unusual for him."

Does he understand what she's trying to say?

"This detective says they touched, that she's got his clothing fibers on her, but he hates being touched. He'd do anything to avoid it, so I don't really understand how that could have happened." It's taken years of practice to learn the sort of touch his body can bear, and now she knows it well, deep pressure, bear hugs. What Adam hates above all is the incidental touching that happens daily between children: shoulders brushing, fingers tapping. If his sweater fibers are on her body, does that mean she terrified him in some inadvertent manner—did she brush his arm or pluck at his sweater long enough to unloose fibers?

"Because I could find out," Morgan says.

She looks up into the mirror. "What do you mean?"

"I know a few people from her classroom. I used to volunteer in there a little. I could go back. See what they say."

Back home, Cara is grateful for the smallest of favors: Teddy is outside, seated in his car, which means there's no need for a conversation that dances around what neither of them, apparently, wants to talk about. She steers Adam inside to the family room where she finds his Boggle list that makes no sense: *elefant, tres, berd, flut*. Adam's spelling is bad but not usually this bad. It means these are words he's heard or thought of but hasn't seen in print any time recently. Nor do they have much to do with the letters in the Boggle cube. She carries the list over and kneels down in front of him. "What is this, baby? Why did you write elephant?"

She doesn't expect an answer of course, but his vacant stare unnerves her. "Can you read this, sweetheart? What you wrote?" She holds the paper up because sometimes this works—he can read an answer he would otherwise not be able to give. This time, though, he doesn't.

His eyes move away and she lowers the paper.

That night, she makes a bowl of chicken soup that Adam will only eat if she lifts the spoon to his mouth. She dips the spoon carefully, no noises, nothing to startle him. His eyes are absent, his face empty of expression, though his lips open each time to receive the food.

Before dinner, she picked out the books they'd look at as they ate. This is one of their oldest traditions, what they do to get through the meals she insists they eat together as she always did with her parents. Usually, she lets him pick two and she picks two. His choices are always childhood favorites: Dr. Seuss books, *Farmer Duck*, books most nine-year-olds have long outgrown. Her selections usually have an agenda, books about bike riding or fractions, the things he needs motivation to learn. Tonight, though, she moves one of his old favorites—*Green Eggs and Ham*—in between them. It only takes a few pages to remember that she hates this book, and the way it goes on, foxes and boxes, goats and boats. Years ago she used to push it, back when the goal of her home-spun curriculum was "trying new foods." Now Adam loves the book but still eats approximately the same five foods every night for dinner: rice, peanut butter, chicken, ham, carrots.

Halfway through, she tries an experiment and skips a whole chunk of text. Usually, with an old favorite, his brain won't allow it. He'll back them up, fill in whatever should come next; pore over the page until the rhythm is correct again. This time, though, he says nothing. He doesn't notice. She skips some more, her heart beating, fearing she might cry if he doesn't stop her soon. She stops reading, closes the book, and they sit, for a length of time she can't measure. Then, out of nowhere, Adam opens his mouth and says in a voice not his own: "Watch yourself!"

She stares at him, stunned. "What was that, baby?"

He rocks in his chair, his hands on the table edge.

"Adam, sweetheart. Say that again."

"Watch yourself!" The voice is low, exactly like a grown man's. It's uncanny, the imitations he's capable of. There's almost an accent to it, but what would it be? Swedish? German? Adam gets up from the chair and circles the table, humming. He doesn't seem upset by the memory, though it's hard to say—agitation and excitement can look the same with him. "Did a man say that to you? In the woods?"

He shakes his head, looks around the room, and then at her, per-plexed, as if he has no idea what she's talking about.

Later, she straightens the kitchen, gathering her thoughts before she calls Lincoln to tell him—that if Adam didn't *see* anything, he *did* hear something, and his brain is like a tape recorder with a playback mode. He can remember anything he's ever heard, and now he has remembered something. His ears were still operating, in their extraordinary fashion, taking in everything, she thinks, and then she turns and sees something she hadn't noticed before, tucked behind the garbage can. There's a tuft of white fur. At first, she fears it's some small dead creature, then she bends down and takes a moment to realize exactly what it is: the rabbit's foot from his backpack, pinned to the ground by a steak knife driven through its center.

Alone at night, June waits for him to come, planning speeches she wants to say, but fears she never will. This murder has made her worry about everything—Teddy, his safety, all of her students. She worries that without warning, anyone might die suddenly, never knowing how she feels about them. With Teddy, she has held back for so long, she hardly knows how she'd express herself now. Such was Teddy's naïveté at the beginning of their relationship—when it was all nervous coffee dates—that she thought of him as a student of sorts, someone who needed and would follow her gentle instructions. ("It's okay to undress me," she once whispered in the dark. "Okay, sure," he said happily.) Now, every night, she fears getting a phone call telling her he is dead and this will be the tenderest thing she can remember saying to him.

When Teddy finally comes, it is later than usual, almost one o'clock; she opens the door and sees, on his face, something is different. "I met the boy," he says.

She knows, without being told, who he means. His hands are shoved in his back pockets, his equipment sags down on his hips. There's an urgency to what he wants to say but no words to say it. "He doesn't talk," he says.

"Yes he does. Not very much, but he does talk. He will again." She has spoken with Teddy about her work, and about these kids. He shouldn't be shocked, but he obviously is.

"But his mom is right there, talking to him the whole time, explaining things to him, like he understands everything. And then I look at the kid and I think maybe he does. I look at them together and I think maybe there's something I don't get."

She knows how hard it is for Teddy to accept complexity in others—that Cara, who once hurt Suzette, might also be worthy of sympathy or even admiration. "She's done a good job with him. Everyone says so." Now he must be going over it all, trying to understand. He has built his life around caring for a sister who's been hurt by a friend and something that happened in the past which June knows nothing about. She takes him in her arms, pulls him inside, and soon they are lying on her bed. She knows the pieces of his uniform by now, the clips and the buckles; even in the perfect darkness of her bedroom, she can free him from this armor he's adopted to take on the world, protect himself from pain he doesn't understand.

Though Suzette scored higher on the SATs than anyone else in their class, she announced early in their senior year that she had no intention of applying to college. Teachers tried to talk her into it; the guidance counselor even offered to fill out an application for her. "Just leave your options open," he said, but she refused. "If I want to be an artist, I don't need college, I need to make art," she told him.

True to her word, she got a job in the hospital administrative office where her mother had started working again, and kept up with her art, renting studio space in the basement of a church. For two years she and Cara both lived at home until finally Cara, desperate to escape the generous and overindulgent love of her parents, talked Suzette into renting an apartment with her in town. By this time, they moved in such different circles that it was sometimes hard to remember what they had in common besides the past. Cara took classes at the community college, worked at a restaurant, and went out at night after her shifts with crowds of nineteen- and twenty-year-olds who drank their meals. Suzette spent all her free time painting and going by herself to movies that Cara had never heard of. Cara couldn't understand Suzette's new taste for solitary pleasures. "Why don't you just ask me to go with you?" she'd say, and Suzette would smile. "I like going alone. I see things better that way."

After a while, it seemed to Cara that, living together, they saw each other less than they did in high school, which made her sad but seemed to be a choice Suzette was making. "I don't want to hang out with your new friends, Cara," Suzette would say. "I'm not all that interested in meeting more bartenders."

Cara couldn't say what Suzette was doing with most of her time except spending it alone, churning out canvases that no longer looked like anything except explosions of vivid and sometimes disturbing colors, and logging in her hours at the hospital doing clerical work in an office on the same floor as the psych unit. One evening, four months into their bifurcated apartment life, Suzette came home and announced: "You want to hear something weird—who I saw today?" There was a bit of pep in her voice, the old *you're never going to believe this*. "Kevin Barrows."

Cara felt her stomach tighten. "In the *hospital*?"

"Yeah, but not as a patient. Get this—his *mom* is the patient. I actually talked to him for a while. He said she had some substance abuse problems, only he pronounced it *sustenance* abuse. 'Too much sustenance?' I said. He was nice. He laughed."

She looked wistful, but even this wistful smile was the happiest Cara had seen her in months. "You should ask him out," Cara said, and saw a glimmer of consideration pass over Suzette's face. Once she'd started, the idea became a mission, an answer to the last eight months of Suzette's isolation. "Call him. If I know Kevin, he'll never be the one to call you. You'll have to make the first move."

Suzette stared down at her hands. "You're the one he loves."

Cara walked over, sat down next to her. "That's not true. After we visited him that time, I sent him a card and he never wrote me back."

Suzette nodded, as if to say, *Maybe you're right. I guess I could do this.* This wasn't like them at all, wasn't the pattern of their friendship: Cara getting the phone, looking up the number, offering to dial it for Suzette.

Suzette finally did call Kevin, but not until weeks after Cara's initial suggestion. By that time Cara was caught up in her own love-life drama, the first one she didn't share with Suzette. His name was Oliver; he taught her Writing for Business Majors class, and he was the opposite of every man she'd been drawn to in the past: hair unkempt, pens that leaked black-ink circles on his pockets and fingers. Some days he taught a whole class with his fly halfway down. Ostensibly, this was a business writing class—cover letters, résumés, project proposals—but on the first day he announced, "I don't want to be here any more than you do." None of this was interesting to him, none of this applicable to life success as he saw it. Instead, they spent class time discussing op-ed pieces in the local newspaper. She can still remember one debate over the licensing for a strip club on the outskirts of their town. "Is this not free speech?" Oliver asked. "Is stripping not a form of self-expression?"

She looked across the room at one of the few other women who came to class regularly but, like Cara, rarely spoke. *No,* they both said with their faces. "How many people here think there ought to be a strip club in this town? Raise your hands high. Don't be shy. Maybe you won't take your mother there, but you believe a town government shouldn't legislate what we choose to do with our entertainment money—or, more important, limit the opportunities women have to make some pretty good money."

Every hand went up except Cara's and the other woman's. Oliver turned to Cara for the first time and stared down at her. "Why not?"

Cara swallowed and said, "Because they hurt everyone. Crimes get committed. Money isn't always a good reason to do things."

For a long time, she stared at the floor until she realized the sound she heard was him, clapping slowly as he circled the room. "Excellent answer. Nice to see someone thinking for herself." After that, she began reading the paper more, trying to anticipate what he might bring up. She formed more opinions, outlined arguments she might present in class. She loved the unreadable way he had of presenting his arguments, how she never knew what he really thought. Over time, it was clear he liked this class, that even if most teaching was a burden, this combination of students wasn't. He Xeroxed extra articles, once passed out his own letter to the editor. Of course, there were students who complained and some who registered a protest with their absence. One day, out of a class of twenty-two, only six showed up. Oliver held out his hand toward the empty seats. "Ah. What to think, what to think? A flu going around perhaps? Rampant infection of the student body?" His eyes settled on Cara. "Or is it *moi*?"

That afternoon, they walked out of class together, fell in step talking, and discovered that, in the Byzantine maze of the college parking lot, their cars were parked beside each other. "Is this gray Toyota you?" he said, laughing with astonishment as if this coincidence represented something bigger. After that, they walked out to their cars regularly and began speaking more candidly: "I like this class, I really do," she said once. The next day, he admitted, "I noticed your pen wasn't working. I thought of giving you mine, but I worried it might look a little—I don't know—too friendly perhaps." She blushed, though this was a community college where friendships between teachers and students were not so unheard of. Many students were adults, making transitions. Most people left class and went to work, some came in uniform, or nurse's shoes. One woman was a school bus driver who walked out every day seven minutes early. "Nothing personal," she always said. To Oliver's admission of noticing her struggle with a dead pen, Cara said, "I wanted to write you a note. Ask if you'd like to go out to lunch sometime."

A week later, they went.

A week after that, she brought him back to the apartment. Some instinct told her to keep this private, to say nothing even to Suzette, who came home the same week full of energy after her first lunch with Kevin: "He's so *interesting*, Cara. You wouldn't believe it. He's had such an interesting life." Cara waited for the joke the old Suzette would have made, but none came: "He's got enough money from his accident settlement that he doesn't have to worry about jobs, so he works with underprivileged kids. There's one named Carlos, who he spends every afternoon with because the mom has to work and has no child care."

They were twenty years old. "He should be going to college," Cara said.

"He doesn't want to go to college. He's not interested in all that. He's interested in using what he's been through to help people." For the first time in memory, Suzette was drinking a beer and taking sips from a glass that left a smile of foam on her upper lip.

Cara stared down at her. "See? What did I tell you? Mr. Perfect."

After that, a space opened up between them. Cara stopped telling Suzette where she was going at night or inviting her along. Some nights she changed and left before Suzette got home and the next day neither one mentioned their previous evening. When she brought her professor home during the day, she cleaned up afterward so there would be no trace of the man she had never once mentioned to Suzette. When she asked about Kevin, she got shorter answers. "He's fine. Very sweet."

"But what's *happening*?" She stared at Suzette. This was all new, keeping secrets from each other.

Suzette shrugged. "It's nice. I like him. That's all."

"Come on, Suze, tell me what's going on." Cara was in the mood suddenly to push the matter. "Has he kissed you?"

"I'm not going to say. It's private."

"Oh please. I tell you everything."

"That's not true."

Cara studied her friend. Did she know what was happening?

As time went on, Suzette stopped mentioning Kevin completely, or only did so in odd, circumscribed ways. "Kevin's mom is fine," she said one day. "It doesn't make sense that she's even in the hospital, when she's more together than most mothers. She tries to be honest and open about things. She's very open with Kevin about her problems and with me, too."

"What are her problems?"

"Well, I mean, I probably shouldn't tell you. It's private to the family."

Was Suzette part of the family now? Later, she offered this: "Kevin's thinking about getting into teaching. He wants to go back to college and get his degree."

Cara stared at her. "How does he go back to college when he never went to begin with?"

"You know what I mean. He's registering next week at the community college. Actually, I might register with him. It could be nice. We could take a few classes together, share the cost of books."

How could this happen? How could Kevin and his needs have talked Suzette into something a dozen adults had not persuaded her to do? Cara tried to point out the obvious, that Suzette graduated third in their class and Kevin had barely graduated at all. "Why are you doing this when you could get in anywhere?"

"That's not true."

"It is true. Look at your grades. Look at your scores."

Suzette shook her head. "He can't go by himself. I promised his mother I'd do this. She's worried that if he tries to do this by himself, it'll be a disaster."

They started in January, with identical class schedules, though all their classes were at night, when Cara wasn't there. "It's *fine*," Suzette said. "It's all stuff I'm interested in, too. Once he gets the feel of it, he'll start taking classes by himself."

It wasn't fine, Cara came to understand gradually, though Suzette never spoke her complaints aloud. She simply said less and less as time went on. She told fewer stories of Kevin's kindness; eventually she began to admit she wasn't sure if Kevin would pass all his classes. "He has trouble organizing himself," she said once.

Cara tried to help, offer suggestions: "You can't do this for him," she said. "Maybe this isn't the right thing for Kevin. Maybe you should be thinking about yourself."

"Oh that's nice," Suzette said. "That's a really nice answer."

"Suzette. I'm just saying, it's hard for anyone to understand why you're doing all this for him." By this time, Cara had come to understand there wasn't any element of romance in this.

"We're friends," Suzette said. "He feels like the best friend I have right now. To me, that means something. Friendship means you help the other person. You stand by them. If it means making a sacrifice, okay."

Cara understood this was about more than just Kevin, that she had failed Suzette, had failed Kevin as well, in some way she would never understand, and now the two of them stood together, in alliance and apart from her. She had no better friends to show for herself, nothing to mitigate the loneliness of her own failure. She also understood there was something strange—in all these months, she'd never once seen Kevin, and never heard a message from him on the machine. She assumed it was intentional, that he was avoiding her, and then one night Cara came home to the sound of the shower and found Suzette sitting in her underpants and bra, motionless, on the sofa. "Suze?" she said, to no response. She went into the bathroom and turned off the water, which had grown ice cold. She came out, touched her friend with her wet hand. "Are you okay?"

Suzette didn't look up, didn't say anything.

Later that week, Cara ran into Suzette in their neighborhood drugstore, moving slowly, a fan of coupons clutched in her hand. Cara had gone there intending to buy a home pregnancy test and had thought, for a moment, Suzette was following her, suspicious and knowing, even in her current absent state, about the fears and hopes Cara had intentionally kept to herself. But after a minute of watching her, leaning on her cart like an old woman, Cara knew this was something else. "Suze!" she said, getting close enough to touch her shoulder gently.

Suzette stopped, turned around in slow motion. "What are you doing here?"

"Nothing. Just shopping. What about you?"

"I have to buy soap," Suzette said too loudly. "Everything's dirty."

Cara looked around, softened her voice to a whisper. "At home?"

"I need ant traps and soap. There's ants everywhere. In the bed, in the sink, everywhere."

"I don't remember seeing ants."

Suzette narrowed her gaze over Cara's shoulder then turned. "Never mind."

Cara left the store with Suzette and put off buying the pregnancy test when Suzette announced the next day that she was going home for a while. A weekend, maybe, or a week. That night she packed two enormous suitcases with what seemed to be everything she'd owned in the apartment. In the confusion of the days that followed, Cara found the number she'd once looked up for Kevin and dialed it. She apologized for calling him, but said she wanted to ask what was going on with Suzette, if he knew how long she intended to stay at home. He listened without speaking. "This . . . is . . . weird," he finally said. "I don't really remember her. I remember—well, you."

"Oh," Cara said, panicking. How was this possible—how had Suzette gone so crazy so quickly? "She told me she had run into you, but I must have gotten confused. Maybe it was a different Kevin. So I'm sorry. I'm kind of embarrassed."

"Don't be. I'm happy to hear from you."

The following day, Oliver began class by telling a story that surprised everyone: "So this weekend my wife and I were driving back from the beach, and what did we hear on the radio?" The boy next to Cara said, "What?" just as Cara thought, *Your what?* The tin-tasting nausea in the back of her mouth moved from her throat to her stomach and down to her feet. After class, Oliver walked out with another student and never lifted an eye in her direction. He had obviously arrived at some kind of decision, and this was his way to tell her of it.

She called Kevin again that night, asked if he'd like to have dinner sometime.

She still hadn't taken the test even though she had some signs of pregnancy—tender breasts, morning nausea that abated with a cracker—she drank at dinner because she had read in a book: *Don't worry too much about alcohol consumed before you knew you were pregnant.* If she was pregnant, there was a small window here, one night to decide the rest of her life, and she needed it. With a glass of wine, she felt happy for the first time in months. It had been almost two years since she had seen Kevin, and he looked surprisingly healthy, with a full beard and a flannel shirt that made him look rugged, in spite of the cane he still carried and hung on the back of his chair. Seeing him again, away from the eyes of others she must have been far too conscious of back then, she allowed herself the luxury of all thoughts, including this one: how handsome he was.

"So Cara, Cara, Cara. Tell me all about your life," he said after she sat down. "Are you a marine biologist yet?"

She smiled, shook her head. "Not yet. Why don't you start? Tell me about your life and then I'll tell you about mine."

The surprise—and it occurred to her, he always surprised her—was how honest he was. The kidney transplant had been terrible, and set him back for a long time. He couldn't leave the house, couldn't make it back to school. "I was going to go to graduation. That morning I was all dressed, my parents were in the car, and I couldn't move. Couldn't even stand up. My parents panicked and took me back to the hospital." He paused. "Wearing my suit, I remember that."

Only then did Cara register the most significant change—his speech was still halting, with strange articulation, but he had words now, at his disposal: "Now I get how depression takes over your body. At the time, I couldn't see it. In the middle of it, you can't see anything."

She leaned toward him, thinking of Suzette, of the possibility that if she asked, she might understand this hole in her life better: "What happens? What does it feel like?"

"Oh God," he laughed. "You don't have your senses. You can't taste anything or smell. Once, I put salt in my coffee and didn't notice. My mother tasted it later and told me."

"So what happened?"

He gave a smile so broad his whole face seemed to wear it. "Medication. Can't you tell? It's made me fat and happy."

Being with Kevin made her feel everything at once: lonely, abandoned, terrified of some decision she'd already made. Later, when it was her turn to talk, she tried to explain without specifying anything: "I don't think I want some big career. I know I'm supposed to, but I just don't. I want to have a different life." She thought of her parents, the quiet happiness of their lives, marred only by the miscarriages her mother had suffered before Cara—the miracle—arrived and stayed. "I think everyone wants to pretend we're adults now. I go to these parties and everyone's smoking and drinking, like at last we can, this is what we've all been waiting for, and it's *not*." This was the first time she'd thought about all this, how unhappy she'd been. For so long, she'd narrowed her thoughts into a tunnel of cheerful optimism for Suzette's sake: *This party might be great,* she'd say. *They have friends who are in a band*. What was she *thinking*? Suddenly she saw, in the perfect clarity of Suzette's absence, that all of it had been awful. Until now she hadn't let herself see the life Suzette was going crazy to reject.

"Ah, parties," Kevin said, grinning now, his whole face alive. "I went to one once. You want to hear what happened?" She smiled and nodded. "It was a football-player party. Or, more pathetically, an ex-football-player party. It was in Scott's basement. Dark, okay? With these huge overstuffed sofas, the only light in the place trained on the keg, and big drunk Scott—I think honestly intending to have a conversation with me—comes staggering over and sits down on top of me. For like thirty seconds, he sits there, saying, 'Wait? Kevin?' "

She laughed, knowing already something had shifted, a decision had been made. This made no sense, but it was true: he seemed like the first genuinely happy person she'd seen in years. She would bring Kevin back to the apartment she couldn't face spending the night alone in.

The next morning when she woke up, Kevin was gone. On the glass coffee table he had left a wax paper bag with a chocolate chip cookie inside, and a note underneath: "I bought this last night, and then I forgot to give it to you. K." The cookie was enormous and Cara ate the whole thing, thinking, for the first time, with unbridled glee, *Maybe I'm eating for two.* The night produced a tectonic shift in her worldview: Oliver mattered little, college even less. Suzette's breakdown wasn't a tragedy, but a road sign pointing Cara onto a path she must have seen when she stood in the bookstore thumbing through *What to Expect When You're Expecting.* Kevin wasn't the end of that path, he was a catalyst onto it, a way of seeing different versions of possibility: life could have no taste for a while, and then it could return.

Truthfully, what she saw in Kevin was hope for Suzette's return. Three weeks later, she went over to Suzette's old house, found her sitting in the kitchen wearing sweatpants and an old Mickey Mouse T-shirt. She was better already, Cara could tell. She smiled when Cara walked in, then rolled her eyes at Teddy's insistence on making tea for everyone. He was a tenth-grader now, taller than both of them, but he still had his quiet, boyish sweetness. "Look, Teddy, I'm fine," Suzette said as he set mugs down on the table. "Maybe Cara and I will just talk by ourselves if that's okay."

He hesitated, then walked out. Alone, they sat for a minute in silence.

"So I'm sorry for getting so crazy on you."

"You weren't crazy, Suzette."

Suzette held up a hand. "It's better to be honest," she said. "I'm trying to sort out what happened in my mind. I wanted to be ready to grow up and be independent. I kept thinking, 'Look at Cara, she's not afraid of things. She just does them.' You don't look at something and see a thousand ways it could go wrong. You just do it."

Cara thought about the secret she had come here to tell her. "Not always."

"No, it's a good thing. It's great. I'm trying to learn how to be more that way. Braver. Not so worried all the time about how things might not turn out right."

"You already seem better."

"I am. I'm getting there." She reached a hand across the table and took Cara's.

Cara hadn't planned any of this specifically, hadn't picked her words yet or how she would say this: "There's something I want to do, Suzette." She leaned across the table, whispered in case Teddy was somewhere, listening. "I've thought about it a lot. I'm sure it's the right thing. I know it. I feel it."

Suzette stared at her. "What?"

And she told her, said it out loud for the first time in her life. "I'm pregnant and I want to have a baby. I want you to help me. You'll be the one who knows what to do. You practically raised Teddy. And all those years babysitting. You'll be great."

Suzette looked at her. "Even after all this?"

Cara said the truest thing she could think of. "Of course. You're my best friend."

Suzette didn't return right away. For four months she lived at home, working part-time and attending an outpatient program she only described vaguely to Cara: "There's some group therapy and individual therapy. It's good. It helps." Cara understood Suzette's troubles were related, in some way, to her mother's breakdown after the divorce, which they bore witness to for years, but never talked about. But her mother was better now, working again, which Cara saw as an optimistic sign. Suzette was getting this out of her system; she'd be back again soon, stronger than before.

In all that time, Kevin floated like a secret, in and out of the picture.

The first time they saw each other after sleeping together, Kevin surprised Cara by delivering the very speech she herself had prepared. "I'd like us to be friends," he said, fiddling with a ceramic dish of sugar packets on the table where they were having lunch.

"Okay," Cara said, stunned.

"It's not you, believe me. I know myself a little bit better now. I know what I need to be careful of. Too much drama isn't good for me." He spoke quietly, but was sure of himself.

"Am I a lot of drama?"

"To me, I guess, yes. I don't know what your life is like. Does it feel like drama?"

He didn't even know the ways that it did, that he was right. "I suppose," she said.

He meant it about being friends, he told her. He didn't have very many, just a few from his old war-games days, some football players. "Most of them went away to school. With the ones who are around, I'm sort of the token geek, I guess. I've never been friends with a girl before."

Suddenly she saw what he was saying—real friendship, like she'd had so little of. "Okay," she said, meaning it.

And for a time, they tried it—they went out to the movies once and sat with a king's meal of concession food in their laps, as if reiterating the point with every handful of food: *See, we're just friends. Friends don't worry about greasy hands or Dots breath later.* Another time he brought her to a meeting of his Dungeons and Dragons club, a collection of oddballs she recognized from high school. She couldn't play, of course; the rules were ridiculously complicated, full of heated battles between two people shaking fistfuls of dice. These were the kinds of boys she didn't let herself contemplate much when she was in high school, her eyes trained so fiercely on popular girls, on boyfriend prospects.

By the time Suzette was ready to move back to the apartment, Cara's friendship with Kevin had lost all its momentum. She was too unpracticed, didn't know how to end an evening without awkwardness. Too many times, she sat in his car, engine idling, door handle half-pulled, and said, "So . . . what? Give me a call sometime?" Every evening felt like a buildup to the same sad wall. "I had fun tonight," she'd say, and mean it—they did have fun, laughing about elementary school teachers or the names some restaurants gave to hamburgers. She never told him she was pregnant or about her intention to keep the baby. Anytime she contemplated doing so, she thought of the first thing he'd said in launching their friendship: *Too much drama isn't good for me.* She also discovered the surprising ease of keeping the secret. For months, nothing changed but her breast size and the inner workings of her body's chemistry. It wasn't until she was five months along that she began leaving the button of her jeans undone beneath her sweater. If he noticed, he certainly made no remark about that or the beers she no longer drank.

They also spoke surprisingly little of Suzette. Cara hesitated to mention her, given the embarrassing way it factored into their reconnection. She never wanted him to ask, "Why did she lie?" She didn't want to contemplate such a question herself. Instead, when it came up, she tried to be frank in a way that mirrored his own honesty and allowed no speculative questions. "I think she's struggling with her own depression, but she's getting a lot better. She's much stronger, much clearer these days. She knew what was going on, got help right away."

He nodded through all this. "Good," he said, and looked away, apparently uncomfortable with a tale of problems so similar to his own.

He worked now, four days a week, at a record store in town. Once, on the eve of Suzette's planned return, she walked in and surprised him. The instant he saw her, she could see this wasn't a good idea. He was seated on a wooden stool, behind a cash register, wearing round wireframe glasses she'd never seen before. When he saw her, he took the glasses off. "What are you doing here?" he said, not smiling.

"I just thought I'd stop by. Maybe pick something out for Suzette. She's moving back in next week." She flipped through the contents of a rack as if this really had been her intention. Her back hurt these days and she'd begun to feel something like movement, a rippling flicker, like a fish swimming freely inside her. "I'm *allowed*, right? To come into your store?"

She meant this as a joke, a way to let him know how unfriendly the expression on his face was. "It's just"—he looked around though they were alone—"kind of a *girlfriend* thing to do."

She stared at him and a minute later walked out, her abdomen sloshing.

For weeks, she kept expecting him to call, kept planning explanations she'd offer to Suzette, who had never, in the four months since she moved out, mentioned his name. When the time came, she decided she would be honest: *He told me he never ran into you.* They would have the conversation, leave all this behind.

But he didn't call; he never called, and her calling him would only necessitate an explanation, at last, of the baby that was now making himself known, visible every night when she lay in bed and watched tiny bumps roll across the drum of her stomach. She and Suzette established a cautious balance with each other. Suzette talked about needing to have some boundaries from the start, and Cara understood from her tone that this meant more than rules about housekeeping duties. "We need to decide what we're going to expect. We're not going to just make plans and not tell each other."

Cara understood the mistakes she had made in the past, leaving Suzette alone too often. With her due date looming, her stomach growing, she felt a desperate certainty. "I'll be home, I promise. I won't do that old stuff."

Suzette nodded. "We need to share in apartment work."

"I know. I will."

"I can't be the only one who buys milk and coffee."

"That's right. You're right."

"And on weekends, I may need to go home. I can't promise I'll always be here, either."

"Okay. That's fine."

In between conversations like this one, there were also good times— going to birthing classes, buying baby supplies. Cara kept busy with preparations and gave herself no time to consider what had happened to Kevin or why their friendship had dissolved so swiftly in the wake of a single, inexplicable misstep on her part. She assumed that it was her fault, that visiting him at work violated some rule to the measured friendship they'd erected. She missed him but, truthfully, felt a certain sense of relief that not seeing him at all, by some choice on his part, left her with one less person to explain herself to. It had been hard enough with her parents, who greeted her announcement with perfect silence and then, from her mother, an uncharacteristic burst of tears. The tears came during what she'd anticipated as the hardest part of the conversation: the question of paternity. During the course of her prenatal visits, a sonogram had determined the fetus to be smaller, less developed than he should be, given the dates she'd provided. Cara heard this, unable to pull her eyes away from the frozen black-and-white picture on the monitor screen—he looked like a Martian, painted gray, with a broken string of pearls loosed from his neck. "That's the spine," the technician had said, slightly bored, as if it were obvious, and Cara felt a trembling sense of pride at the miracle of this accomplishment, a feeling she hadn't experienced in years. She'd done it! Something her mother had struggled with so, and only succeeded at once. "He's normal," the doctor said, "Just smaller than we'd expect, which means you might have been slightly off on your dates."

Only later did she contemplate this long enough to consider the possibility that when she slept with Kevin claiming protection she didn't have, she wasn't already pregnant. "I don't know who the father is," she told her parents. This was easier, she'd decided, than any other explanation she could offer: *He's married; he was a friend, now he's not.* She tried to make it clear, even through their tears, *It doesn't matter.*

Explaining any of this to Kevin, including the slim possibility he was involved, would only be a trial, one she was happy to avoid, mostly because she was happy about everything. As the pregnancy progressed, her happiness grew until she felt guilty by the size of it. Her parents came around, agreed to help her financially; Suzette was back, doing well. The world was lining up to allow this wonder to be truly hers. Soon, she'd have a baby.

The last night of their birthing class, she and Suzette went out to dinner to celebrate an end to meeting with people they had nothing but due dates in common with. They sat, giddy with excitement, toasting with their water glasses, and Cara looked up to see, across the restaurant, Kevin and his mother standing in the doorway.

He made slow progress toward them, his expression shifting as he took in her changes. She didn't warn Suzette who was approaching slowly behind her. Instead she let a silence fall, and when he got to their table, she understood—in Suzette's gasp of surprise, in the awkward way Kevin stepped back and looked away—that all those months ago, Suzette hadn't lied. Kevin had.

After that, came a terrible night of confession.

"I only slept with him once," Cara said. "After you moved out and he told me he'd never run into you at all. I didn't know what to think. You were gone and I needed a friend." She hesitated, wanting Suzette to understand—it hadn't been Oliver who broke her heart. "It felt like you were my family, and you left."

"That's ridiculous," Suzette snapped. "You have a family."

"There's a difference. You're my chosen family. And Kevin and I were just friends. Right away, we decided just to be friends. He was the one who insisted on that. He was the one who didn't want anything more to happen."

Suzette stood in their living room, shaking her head, looking around the room slowly as if she were trying to memorize its contents before she stepped out of it. "I can't do this, Cara," she said. "I don't want to do this."

Cara leaned over her enormous belly. Sometimes in Suzette's presence she tried to draw less attention to her pregnancy, to sit straighter, keep her hands off her abdomen. Now, with three weeks to go, it was impossible. "Do *what*?" She was growing defensive, already self-protective. She had a baby to think about, something more important than these dramas.

"I can't keep doing this. Living your life."

"Is that what it is?"

"My God, don't you *see* it? This baby will come and I won't be his mother. I'll be what I've always been—your friend. That's ridiculous. It's idiotic. Nobody should do that."

Cara sat back. They had talked about this, of course. Not enough, perhaps, but they had said it would be a new kind of family. "Someday, there'll be a sit-com of this and we'll have lived it," Cara had said, straining slightly, as she always did, to see things optimistically.

Suzette stared at her, long and hard, her eyes trembling with the weight of words she wasn't saying. "I'm not going to be your labor coach. It's too much for me. I can't do it."

"Fine," Cara said, thinking of Kevin's words: *Too much drama isn't good for me. To me, you're drama.*

"This isn't really friendship, Cara. Don't you see that?"

The next day, Cara came home to find cardboard boxes stacked up in the hallway. Seeing them, she actually felt a little relieved. She was nine months pregnant, on the brink of becoming a mother and a new person with a past she could divorce herself from. She didn't have the time to wonder why she had this effect on people, why her friendship was more than Suzette or Kevin could bear. She couldn't examine it, could only decide: *Never again.* Never again would she risk this mistake, believing that real love, sustained love, lived safest and longest, went deepest in friendship. Suzette had already moved out once and broken her heart. Kevin had abandoned her for the crime of stopping by work. Never again would she reach out to people who might recoil from an outstretched hand. And she hadn't.

After Suzette moved out, there was some attempt at rapprochement. Cara's mother stood in as her labor coach, but Suzette came to the hospital bearing a guilty bouquet of Mylar balloons. "He's beautiful," she said, pushing the balloons in the door. "I can't believe how beautiful he is."

To Cara's exhausted post-delivery eyes, Suzette seemed too cheerful, too obviously relieved to have spared herself from assisting in Adam's arrival to the world. She hugged Cara, who sat stiffly in bed and whispered, "Thanks."

"I want to come visit when you get him home."

"Okay," Cara said, too weak to argue.

Two days later, Adam came home, a wailing, howling infant, beset by eczema, chronic ear infections, a digestive tract that produced only vomit and viscous green diarrhea. Within a month it was clear she needed help, so she moved back in with her parents. Within six months she felt as if she had aged a decade—had become an exhausted, middle-aged twenty-one-year-old who pushed a stroller for miles to service a baby who needed constant movement to sleep and soothe his nerves. Suzette visited a handful of times, and invariably each visit ended in some eruption from Adam, wails that jolted Suzette out of her chair, out of the house, leaving in a flurry that felt more like an escape. Cara remembers all those visits as strained and awful, full of nervous small talk, everything real between them unspeakable.

Alone with her mother, Cara kept up a front of stoic cheer about her squalling baby. Every night they asked themselves the same questions as he cried in their arms—Is he tired? Is he hungry?—when he was none of those things. He was a boy at no peace inside his skin. If other babies quieted by being picked up, he would squirm from the hands that held him, arch away from Cara's breast, stiffen in her arms. In the terrible isolation of Adam's infancy, she felt certain the problem lay with her, and she wanted to understand what she hadn't had the courage to ask Suzette before: *What am I doing wrong? Why is my love such a terrible thing?*

Once—on Suzette's final visit, the last time she laid eyes on her only friend—in the quiet reprieve of a nap from Adam, Cara whispered the truth that she needed to tell someone: "There's something wrong with me, Suze. My baby doesn't want me. I'm not meant to be a mother." It was terrifying to speak this way, in a frantic, candid rush, but she had to, had to get it all out, dredge up the truth and lay it out for someone. "He tries to get away. Even when I hold him, he doesn't look at me. Sometimes he's fine and he'll only start crying when I pick him up. Last week,

I took him to the doctor's office and the only person who could calm him was the receptionist." Suzette stared at her. "I need to know," Cara said, frantic with exhaustion. "Just tell me, what's wrong with me? What am I doing that's so awful?"

Suzette never spoke, never answered the question.

"Wow," Lincoln whistles after Cara tells him what Adam said. For the story to have any impact at all, she has to explain echolalia and how it works: "There's immediate echolalia, where he repeats the last thing you've just said. Usually that's a way of processing or affirming what's been said. I ask, 'Adam, you want a cookie?' and he says 'Cookie?' which means yes. But there's also delayed, where it comes later, sort of a playback mode. Sometimes it's lines from movies, or things teachers have said. He tends to repeat warnings a lot, or rules. I think it's his way of remembering them." Of course maybe Lincoln knows this already.

"And you think this was something he heard in the woods?"

"Yes, I'm sure of it."

"It's not from any video, right? David, my nephew, does videos."

"These days the only thing he watches is opera. If he was echoing an opera, he would have sung it. The thing is—there was definitely an accent to it." She takes a moment to remember exactly how he said it. *Wach youseff.*

"Can he do it on command? Could we get a tape of it?"

"No, it's too unpredictable."

"But there was an accent, you'd say?"

"Yes. Definitely."

She also tells him about the rabbit's foot and the only thing it could mean: *Yes, Adam was looking, yes, he saw what happened and was telling them, in his own way, what weapon had been used.*

"We should pick up that rabbit's foot. If it belonged to Amelia, maybe we can trace where she bought it."

"Is there a toy store that sells these things?" Cara asks. It seems so macabre—a dead animal's fur-covered appendage.

"We'll see," Lincoln says. "No stone unturned."

Cara doesn't tell him the other part of the story, the thing that happened after she pried up the rabbit's foot and showed it to Adam. She expected him to break down, have an episode of some kind, and instead he seemed to snap out of whatever trance he'd been in. He looked at the rabbit's foot, then down at the book they'd been reading, and smiled to discover what it was. He took the spoon and began feeding himself. A minute later, he pointed to the book as if he couldn't think why she wasn't reading it.

The next morning in the kitchen, it's the same. He doesn't speak, but he's back with her in some way that he hasn't been for days. He's hungry, opening the refrigerator, bending down in search of something to eat. Eventually he reaches for some orange juice, pulls it out, gets himself a cup. "Adam?" she says, watching all this.

He looks up at her and smiles.

"Good morning," she says.

"Good morning," he says.

A half hour later comes another shock. Standing in the kitchen, she turns around to discover he's right behind her, fully dressed, with his backpack on. Just as she catches her breath from this surprise, there is an-other, fast on its heels.

"School," he says. The first word he's spoken, unechoed, in four days.

Morgan can't control the places his thoughts take him. Like recently he's been thinking this: Maybe if he gets to be good enough friends with Cara, she'll consider inviting him for a sleepover, something he's never done before because he doesn't have any friends. Maybe if she does that, he can pack enough clothes for two nights, and if it goes well, he'll just stay on. He'll tell her he can stay with Adam if she wants to run an er-rand, which he could, she's already said Adam likes him. Hard to be sure when someone doesn't talk, but he believes her.

Of course, it could also be a disaster. There would be food to think about—he'd have to bring his own, unless he told her which brand of macaroni and cheese to buy. Which hot dogs he can eat. A lot of people think hot dogs are all the same, because they don't realize they're not. There are very different colors, and some hot dogs have things that can only be described as skins. But if he made a list—what he'd need, what to remember—it might work out.

He might spend one night a week, then four. Something like that.

Then he wouldn't have to be here when his mother figures out what he's done. Wouldn't have to face what he imagines she'll say. "My son," she'll call him. "My *son* did this." He has thought about it a hundred times. Maybe she'll start by saying, "My son did *this*?"

It's only a matter of time before she finds out. He knows that much.

When he looks back, Morgan can see that he's been making certain mistakes all his life. In kindergarten, he once cried when the paper apples fell off the paper-apple name tree—cried for so long and so hard that his mother was called and appeared in the nurse's office to say, "For God's sake, Morgan, stop crying already," which he did because he was so surprised to see her, so grateful and relieved. *My mother!* he thought, understanding that with her here, it was over now, the paper-apple-tree nightmare.

After that, there were more mistakes, episodes he can't explain. In first grade Tianna Bradley hit him on the playground, and instead of hitting her back, he hit himself, over and over, until a small group of children gathered around him to laugh. "Why'd you do *that*?" his mother asked him when he told her about it, later, in tears. He couldn't explain himself, or why these things happened.

In second grade, he decided to stop crying so much. "That sounds good," his mother said when he told her. "If you see me crying, pinch me really hard," he told her, based on a *NOVA* show he'd seen the night before about mice being trained with electrical shocks. His mother thought about this, then nodded and shrugged. "If you say so." He stared at her, suddenly anxious. What if he was crying over something real, a lost jacket, for instance? Would she really pinch him then?

For two weeks he's been carrying this horrible weight around, picturing his mother's face, imagining her disappointment. He certainly didn't mean to start the fire. He'd meant only to ruin his shoes so his mother would be reasonable and buy him a new pair. If they were melted, he thought, she'd see he couldn't wear them. She wouldn't say things like "They cost three hundred dollars, Morgan. They're orthopedic, of course they're ugly. I'm sorry, but you have flat feet. You got them from your father, don't blame me."

They looked plastic.

In homeroom, a girl named Wendy with blond hair asked if they were.

"No." Because he couldn't think of anything else, he added, "They're orthopedic."

"Oh my God," she said and turned away.

This was the problem: they didn't burn. They didn't even melt. He sat there for an hour holding up match after match and nothing happened. The mistake—and he knows this now, no question in his mind—was wondering if something was wrong with his matches. They weren't really burning, he thought. They weren't really matches. That's when he tried them, as an experiment, on a bush. Did that mean it was an accident? He couldn't be sure. Would anyone believe that he'd tried to stop it, even peed on the bush, as he'd seen his father do once on a camping trip? "Nature's fire hydrant," he'd said, peeing forever, as his father could, a happy smile on his face.

Of course, for Morgan it didn't work because nothing worked for him the way it was supposed to. Could he explain that to people? That he was good at many things, or had been once—geography, spelling, science fair projects—but he had a small bladder?

"I have learned this," he wrote in his confession. "There are times in your life when only one thing matters. You have what it takes or you don't."

Adam wants to get back to school, to find the girl, warn her not to go into the woods again because he remembers what the woods has now: leaves on the ground, muddy dirt that squishes brown moons onto their shoes, a man with a yellow shirt, waiting. He needs to talk to her, not anyone else, because the rules are very clear. "Don't tell anyone," she said. "Whatever you do, don't tell."

He is surprised at first. His mother says yes.

"If you're sure about this," she says. She claps her hands together, turns around, and says to the refrigerator, "He says he wants to go back to school."

On the bus, though, he starts to worry. Things feel different. Glenn, the driver who usually calls him Chief, who should say "Howdy, Chief," instead puts out his hand and says, "Good to see you, Chief." Adam walks by the hand he can't touch into the seat behind Glenn that looks the same but feels different because there isn't enough noise, there's the thrum of the engine but no voices on top of it, no screaming children.

When he gets off, Phil is there, putting a hand on his shoulder, which he shouldn't do. "Good to have you back, buddy," Phil says, but he can't answer because there's a crowd of shoes around him. He has to concentrate on these if he wants to find the girl's brown sandals. Most days she wears yellow socks, but sometimes she wears other colors, too. Pink. Or orange. If he sees them, he will go closer, tell her what he needs to: *Don't keep walking*.

There are rules to school that get him from one place to another safely without looking up. He walks along walls, knows from the floor pattern and the sound of pipes where the water fountain is, so he can circle around, can touch each letter on the silver bar: P-U-S-H.

He can't look for the girl now, with so many people and voices all around him.

He hears his name, feels people touch his shoulder, his backpack, but he doesn't look up. He needs the classroom, the schedule of the day posted on the wall, math, language arts, social studies. He needs everything to move around him as it always does, until 11:15, when the clock hands click onto the tilted *L* where they need to be for everyone to stand, move into lines that say, at last, it's recess.

All morning Cara keeps moving around the house, too nervous to sit. To busy herself, she's tried calling Carol, the school occupational therapist, to ask if she worked with Amelia at all. Mostly she's curious to find out if the girl was clumsy, if maybe she fell down on their walk and grabbed Adam's sweater on the way. Carol said she knew Amelia a bit, and had done some initial testing the first week of school, but hadn't been able to come up with much. "She was a puzzle. There was quite a bit she couldn't do, which made me worry that I'd started the testing at too high a level, which can frustrate the kids, make them shut down and skew the results. But she seemed unfazed by the whole thing. At the end she asked me if I had any pets and we talked about animals for a while."

Two hours earlier, Cara had put Adam on the bus because she wanted to reward him for a nearly perfect morning. She checked with Bill, the officer stationed in the car out front that morning, who radioed the station where they'd said fine, they'd send extra security. Now she worries about everything that might happen: other children pointing at Adam, whispering around him, extra security officers who will feel, to him, like terrifying strangers, pressing down. Why didn't she think of this? Adam will go to school expecting what he cherishes most—everything the same—and it won't be so. There will be new rules, more people, differences he'll feel but not understand. She needs to go there, sit as inconspicuously as possible in the back of the room and watch signs of the composure he kept all morning to break, for anxiety to replace it, and then fear, then a fit.

On her way out the door, the telephone rings. She lets the answering machine click on, hears Matt Lincoln's voice behind her: "Okay, Cara, it looks like we've got something at last. I've told everyone about the rabbit's foot, and they think maybe he can help us. We need Adam to come down again after school today. We've got another psychologist in, a Dr. Katzenbaum, who says she knows him. We're going to try and get Adam to ID the guy."

"You don't have to finish it now, buddy," Phil says, pointing to a work-sheet of number problems. "We have a little bit of catching up to do, but not that much."

Adam thinks, *If I don't have to, I won't.* I'll choose *"No, thank you."*

He could say *No, thank you,* out loud with his voice, but it doesn't seem like he has to even do that. The worksheet disappears.

"You want to just hit the library? Check out the music books, maybe?"

The clock is in a *V*, 11:07—if they go to the library, he won't be here for lineup. He will miss recess, which sometimes happens. It disappears without him.

He doesn't answer. Doesn't move.

Phil stands up. "How 'bout it, big guy. Library time?"

No, he shakes his head. Points to the clock.

"I know what time it is. We're not going out to recess today. We're doing something else. We're going to the library, or the resource room. Your choice."

No. He has to go to recess. He has to find her.

Phil sits back down, leans into his ear too close. "Look, it's not my decision; they're telling me you can't go outside for recess, okay? Ms. Tesler, the principal, says so. You don't want me to get in trouble with Ms. Tesler, do you?"

Adam hears himself say his first word of the day: "Recess."

"Nice job. Nice to hear you talk again."

He says it again. "Recess."

"Just not today. Maybe tomorrow or the next day."

He feels the noises rising up inside of him, a humming that builds to torn sounds and broken glass. He needs to find the girl. Tell her about the rabbit's foot. "You take this," she said. "Don't show anybody. Don't tell anyone you have it." She held it out in her hand, and for a long time, he didn't take it because he didn't know what it was. He thought maybe it was a dead mouse like the one his mother found once in the basement and brought up on a shovel to show him. "Look, Adam," she said and he did, and for a long time he couldn't tell what it was because its feet were in the wrong place and it had no ears. Then his mother pointed out the parts: "There's his tummy. See his little teeth," and he felt dizzy because the mouse was upside down. It must have made him sick to be carried like that and then his mother said, "Don't touch. He's dead," and Adam understood *dead* meant "asleep upside down." *Dead* also meant "forever" and "Don't touch," which is why he didn't touch the rabbit's foot for a long time.

"Here," the girl said. "You have to take it. Just take it and hide it and don't show anyone. If you show anyone, they'll know I gave it to you."

Now his mother has found it and knows.

He has to go outside for recess, has to find her and tell her, *My mother knows.*

"Just take it easy, Adam. No screaming, okay?"

He feels Phil's hands on him, pressing his shoulders and he folds himself down, ears between his knees. He knows the sounds filling the room are coming from him because when his face is between his knees the sound circles back inside of him, up his legs through his stomach and back out his ears.

"We're getting someone, okay, buddy. Just calm down."

He hears chairs pushing around him.

"Can you stand up? If you can't stand up, that's okay. Someone's coming."

He wants to break something. Breaking a glass breaks this circle of noise going in and out. He can't breathe, but he must be breathing because the sound is still there. He can't feel his arms or his legs, can't feel where they are, if he even has them anymore. His eyes are shut but he sees things anyway, red and pink. The red is moving, like a circle or water, getting bigger and he knows if this doesn't stop soon, there will be no pink left.

"His mom is in the building. She's on her way."

"Did you hear that, buddy? Your mom is here. She's going to take you home, okay? And we'll try again tomorrow. Does that sound all right?"

He hears her voice, his mother is here.

"Baby, we're going home. I'm taking you home," his mother says.

When she pulls him into her lap, he can feel his pants are wet, which she doesn't notice for a while and then she does. "Oh, sweetheart," she says. "This is my fault. I shouldn't have let you come. You were just so determined, weren't you?"

He wants her to explain to everyone what he needs to say but can't. He needs to find the girl and stop her. His mother knows, she must, because she found the rabbit's foot.

Then, instead of explaining, she stands up, carries him out of the classroom, the wrong way down the hall. He tries to get her to stop with his body, to turn around and carry him the right way, out the back door to the playground. He screams again, louder this time. In the open tunnel of the hallway, the noise travels without walls to stop it. He hammers his head on her shoulder. Scream, pound, scream, pound, so the noise and the feeling become the same thing and he feels his mother start to run. There are people running around her; someone shouts, "Should I call 911?"

Someone says, "No, no, no."

He realizes it's him, saying *No,* screaming into the empty space above her shoulder that jiggles as the world dissolves into nothing, faces that wobble and disappear, until he's outside the building, then inside the car and then, when he breathes, he listens and hears: there's music again. His opera.

Hansel and Gretel. He stops screaming because he knows this one, remembers it all from a few notes of music. He needs to listen carefully to every piece of it, hear the whole story again, because all he remembers is a boy and a girl go into the woods and never come out.

"Okay, so I'll tell you what happened," Chris says to the group. "But then I'd just like to please drop the subject. I'm a little bit tired now of everybody mentioning it all the time. I don't see why people can't just let it go."

Chris has a new habit, Morgan has noticed: leaning over in his chair so he can step on his own hands.

"You were in a garbage can, Chris," Sean says.

"Right, right. I know that already. I was in a garbage can. Big deal."

"You crawled in yourself."

"I was looking for cans. In science class we get ten points extra credit for bringing in recycling. That's it. End of story. I was not in there eating my lunch, as everyone likes to say I was. Let's just get that straight."

"But, Chris," says Marianne, "do you understand now that your science teacher never meant for you to go through the trash?"

"Yes, yes."

"That going through the trash is probably not a healthy or safe thing to do?"

"I'm hardly going to do it again now, am I? After the whole school has gotten their jollies out laughing at me. I may look retarded, but I'm not, okay?"

"I think maybe you're exaggerating, Chris. The whole school wasn't laughing at you."

Unfortunately he isn't exaggerating. The whole school has been talking about it all day, most of the kids laughing. Morgan doesn't want to think about this, though. He doesn't want to think about anything except his after-school plan to go over to the elementary school and find out whatever he can about Amelia. Even Marianne coming up to him, asking if she might speak with him after group today, hasn't distracted him from thinking about his mission.

When Chris is finished, Marianne asks how people are feeling about Amelia and the investigation. This is their first meeting since the murder, and she looks around the room. For a long time, no one speaks. "It's like the only thing anyone wants to talk about," Sean finally says.

"Well, that's pretty natural, Sean."

"But what are we supposed to *say*?"

"When something bad like this happens, sometimes people say 'I'm sorry.' "

"I didn't do it."

"Right, we know. But even if you didn't do it, you can feel sad that it happened. Saying 'I'm sorry' can mean 'I wish it hadn't happened.' "

Sean shrugs. "I didn't know her."

"No, that's right. A lot of people didn't know her. Does the idea that it happened so close to this school scare people?"

Chris huffs forward in his chair. "It doesn't scare me, but that's because I have so many other things weighing on my mind right now."

"Like what, Chris?"

"Just things. In four weeks it'll be Thanksgiving vacation, and three weeks after that will be Christmas, which means I'll get vacation, then I'll have to come back to this dump hole and feel like killing myself all over again. There's state testing in December, which I'll probably fail, and geometry, which I'll for sure fail. There's PE, where they give you like one foot of room to change your clothes and if you bump into anyone they yell at you and call you a fag."

"Chris."

"Yeah?"

"We're talking about Amelia Best. Remember the importance of staying on topic."

Lately Morgan has been wondering if Chris is getting worse. There's something he does with his mouth and cheeks, a kind of scrunching that's meant to reposition his glasses, but never works. His glasses stay balanced on the tip of his nose, and his face looks like he's undergoing electroshock therapy.

After group is over, Morgan stays in his seat. When everyone has left, Marianne picks up her tote bag and carries it over to the chair beside Morgan. "It's actually Chris I wanted to talk about," she says. "I'm a little bit worried about him, and so is his mother."

Morgan nods and tries to picture Chris with a mother, but he can't. He's always had a hard time picturing anyone else's life.

"He's alone quite a bit after school, and his mother worries that that might be a problem. I'm wondering if you would consider bringing him with you on one of your visits to Adam's house? When I originally spoke with Adam's mother, she welcomed the idea of having more kids. She requested it, actually."

Morgan doesn't want to do this, but he doesn't see how he can say no. If he wants to get a sleepover invitation, he'll need to keep surprising Cara with everything he's capable of—getting information on Amelia, producing friends to come with him. He pictures Cara's face, her smile when she opens the door. "Sure," he says. "Yeah, okay."

In PE that afternoon, Chris doesn't dress for volleyball. He tells the teacher he has an ankle that's bothering him and is maybe sprained, and he limps from lineup to the bleachers, where he sits down, bends over, and sticks his fingers inside his shoes. After teams are drawn up, Morgan volunteers to be out first and joins Chris at the bleachers. From experience, he knows it's possible he'll be forgotten for twenty minutes or more, longer if his team has any players on it serious about winning. "So, Chris, what's wrong with your ankle?"

Chris sits up and shrugs. "Nothing. I'm faking. I had to."

On certain matters, Chris is braver than Morgan, who dresses every day for an hour of getting hit by balls, without believing he has any other options. "Are you okay?" Morgan asks softly, because he doesn't look like he is. His lips scrunch up, his eyes dart around the room.

"No, I'm terrible. Some people's lives are okay, mine isn't. I'm thinking about never coming to school again as long as I live."

"Wow." Morgan nods. "Really?"

In front of them, a girl calls out zero-zero service and swats her ball into the net.

"Here's the thing," Chris says. "I *had* to go through the garbage. I was looking for something. Everyone wants to talk about this murder, but no one wants to *do* anything about it."

"What do you mean?" Morgan whispers, low, as an example for Chris to follow: *People like us, we whisper in places like gymnasiums. We don't talk loud, don't let ourselves be overheard.*

"Just never mind."

"Do you know something, Chris?"

"Yes, okay. Are you satisfied? I know something, but I'm not going to tell you because if I do, they'll kill me—and if you know, they'll kill you, too."

Morgan knows this probably isn't true. In group Chris likes to talk this way, about everyone who wants to kill him and who should be in trouble but isn't. Morgan watches his team rotate without him. One boy looks up and notices Morgan, who half stands in response, until the boy raises his hand to say, *No that's fine. You stay there.* He turns to Chris and wonders if he should ask now about coming to Adam's with him. Maybe if Chris comes with him, he'll find out whatever Chris thinks he knows

about the murder. "So, Chris, Marianne said you might like to do something after school sometime."

"What do you mean?"

"I've started my volunteer project, where I go to this guy Adam's
house and visit with him. She thought you might like to try that
sometime."

"Are you *kidding*? You want me to go over to *that* kid's house?"

Morgan isn't sure what to say. "Yeah."

"Do you *know* who he *is*?"

Morgan wants to explain this right, convince Chris to come with him
today, after he's gone to the elementary school. "Yeah, Adam saw the
murder, but that's what makes it interesting. There's police involved and
clues, and he's got this mother who goes to the crime scene, even though
that's against the law." Morgan stops because Chris looks as if he's
maybe having an asthma attack. "Are you okay?"

Chris looks around the gym and leans closer to Morgan. "Trust me,
okay? You don't want to know this stuff."

For the rest of the period, Morgan tries to imagine if it's possible that
Chris really knows something. Just before the bell, Chris squints over his
glasses as if he's just thought of something new. "Come to think of it,
though, maybe I should go to Adam's house. What difference does it
make if I'm never coming back to school again, right?"

Morgan has no idea what he's talking about. He wants to ask, but
then two boys walk by, say "Faggots" loud enough for everyone to hear,
and that's that.

"He had an episode this morning, but he seems to be better now," Cara
tells Lincoln over the phone. Oddly this is true: Adam does seem better.
After the terrifying fit he threw in the school hallway, he was fine in the

car and by the time he got home, he'd recovered enough to ask calmly for a ham sandwich. Her hands were still shaking, her breath ragged from the ordeal, though she should remember this is how it could be with Adam—a terrifying eruption could arise as inexplicably as it passed minutes later, with no evidence beyond the shattered nerves and broken plates it left in its wake. But never before had it been quite like this: Never had it drawn such a crowd of worried faces, never had someone offered to call 911.

"Of course," she said. "But, sweetheart, can we talk first, about what happened at school?"

"Don't want to talk."

This is her old Adam. With enough words to say that he hates words. "I know, baby, but we have to. That was very scary what happened at school. You getting so upset like that. It scares people and worries them. I got scared and worried. People think you might be hurt. They don't know why you're screaming that way. Can you say why you were screaming?"

He doesn't answer. *Don't tell anyone what we're doing,* she said. *It's a secret.* His mother knows, though. She must. He doesn't need to tell her. He tries this: "Did Phil say library or resource room?"

"Is that what Phil said?"

"Library or resource room." He rocks, happy with those words.

"Was that a bad choice? That sounds pretty good to me."

"Library." Now he's stuck on these words, and can't find any others. "Resource room, recess." Because they're all *R*s he can get them out. It's okay to say recess with other *R*s.

"You don't have to go outside for recess. I told Ms. Tesler maybe you shouldn't."

"Rain," he says. "Red." Coming out of his mouth, the words surprise him. "Wrinkle. Right. Wrong. Rhinoceros."

She laughs, claps her hands together. "Lot's of *R*s, Adam! What does it mean?"

Nothing. He can't say. He closes his mouth. He doesn't know where the *R*s came from.

"Can you tell me what they mean?"

No, he can't. He doesn't know.

"Well, anyway. We have something we have to do after lunch." His mother stands, moves around the kitchen. It's hard for him to watch and hear at the same time. He hears this part: "Dr. Katzenbaum will be at the police station." Then she says something about a tape recorder, but he can't hear what, can't listen anymore because there's a knife in her hand going straight down into the mustard.

Because of bus scheduling, the elementary school gets out forty-five minutes after the middle school, which means there's time for Morgan to go back, find Leon, ask him his questions. It won't be easy, he fears, and it isn't. Outside the front door to the elementary school, five adults wearing neon orange name tags, stand guard as part of the new Parents on Alert program he's heard about on TV. He walks up to a tall man. "I have to go inside. I need to speak with someone in the SPED room," he says, because lying hasn't occurred to him.

The man looks him over and nods. "Fine. Hurry, though. School's almost out."

Walking down the hall of his old school makes Morgan think about the past and wish he'd appreciated all this while he had it—bathrooms everywhere, thigh-high water fountains. Outside the SPED room, the door opens and Ms. Daly, his old friend, steps out. "Oh, Morgan, good. I have to check on the vans, there's been some problem. Do you mind coming in for a sec? There's only ten minutes left. You can keep an eye on things while they're finishing some worksheets."

"Sure," he says, nodding.

Inside, it's obvious why he's been entrusted with this job: there are only two students, one of whom is Leon, who would sooner wet his pants than leave his seat without teacher permission. He doesn't recognize the other one, a small black kid wearing a green-and-white shirt with *Patriots* written on it.

"Morgan!" Leon says. "Do you want to play checkers?"

Morgan smiles. "Okay, sure," he says and crosses the room to the shelf of battered game boxes, pulls down checkers. He knows he doesn't have much time, that Ms. Daly will be back any minute. "So, Leon, you must have known this Amelia girl, right?" He divides up the checkers, half of which are pieces of red and black paper, cut into circles.

Leon's mouth rounds to an *O*. "Oh yeah. She's dead. They killed her."

"Who killed her?"

"I don't know."

"But you knew her, right?"

"Yeah, sure."

"What was she like?"

"Girly. That's what Jimmy called her. Girly-girly." Leon looks like he wants to laugh, and then he does. "Jimmy knows all about her."

From across the room, the boy who must be Jimmy turns around and looks at them. "Shit, Leon, I don't know anything. All I know is that I saw her go out to those woods a bunch of times. No one wants to say that, but it's true. The police and the teachers, they're all like, we don't know how she got out there and I'm saying, I know, okay? She walked. Once I followed her, so I know where she went."

"What happened when you followed her? Was anyone else in the woods?"

"Nah."

"So she was just out there, by herself?"

"Yeah."

"What was she doing?"

"Shit. I don't know. Just being herself. Singing, I guess. That's what she did."

"She sang?"

Leon nods his large head up and down. "A lot."

"There was one thing that freaked me out, though." Jimmy leans way over, his voice low. "It was like there was something singing with her. At first, I thought it was birds, and then it was like uh-uh, that's not a bird, that's a flute."

"There was someone in the woods playing a flute?"

"That's what I thought. Then it stopped. It freaked me out a little bit and I left."

Leon seems eager to get in on this conversation. "You want to know what else she did?"

"Sure."

"She drew. She wasn't supposed to. The teacher said no drawing, but I watched her." He points to a chair in front of his.

To Morgan this seems like a less interesting revelation than the one about the flute playing in the woods, but Jimmy has turned back around, is bent over his work again. He looks at the desk Leon points to. He wants to go over, see if anything is drawn on it. "Where are her pictures?" Morgan asks, just as the door opens and Ms. Daly appears.

"Your van is going to be ten minutes late, Leon. I'm sorry about this. About the last thing we need at this point is confusion and disorganization, but there you have it. You can stay with me until it comes. Thank you, Morgan, for stepping in. You can go now—do whatever it was you were doing." Does she remember that he no longer goes to this school? That technically, he isn't supposed to be there? Apparently not.

"Sorry, Leon, but I gotta go." Morgan holds up a flat hand because high fives are big in the SPED crowd and it's a way to avoid a hug from Leon. "See you later."

Leon hooks two fingers onto his bottom teeth and leans into Morgan's ear. "Her pictures are in Candy Land," he says, wrapping Morgan up in the hug he was trying to avoid.

Later, Morgan waits in the bathroom and watches until he sees Ms. Daly walk Leon to his van, and then he slips into the room. Candy Land is on the top shelf, meaning he needs to get a chair to pull it out, but once he does, he knows he's got them. He doesn't stop to look. *Jackpot*, he thinks, sliding the stack of papers covered in line drawings into his backpack.

They went to Dr. Katzenbaum twice around the time Adam turned four. Mostly their sessions were demonstrations of play, the doctor down on the floor, crouched with Adam in front of a marble run. It had been inspiring to watch—how Adam darted peripheral looks at her, how he tried once to look down her blouse, to touch her bracelet, signs of sincere interest on his part. Once, she got him to help her water plants. "First it's my turn, then whose turn is it?"

Those were the days of stubbornly reversed pronouns. "Your turn," Adam whispered.

She picked up his hand, laid it to his chest. "My turn." She kept going. "Dr. Katzenbaum's turn, now who?"

"Your turn."

She picked it up again, touched it to his chest. "M-m-m . . ."

"My turn."

They worked on the chest-tapping prompt for months before he got it. Cara remembers saying to someone, "If he could just get pronouns, I'd be happy forever." Of course, it hasn't worked that way; with every accomplishment, a new goal appears, something else to work on.

They get to the station and in the hallway find Lincoln, who explains what they're going to do. "We want to meet first with Dr. Katzenbaum in the interview room. Then if he's doing all right, we'll take him downstairs to look at a lineup. You can watch him, tell us when you think he's had enough, and we'll stop. Does that sound okay?"

Behind him, there's an even larger crowd of onlookers than there was the first time. Cara recognizes some of the faces, wearing the same skeptical expressions. As he claps his hands and glances at the others, it occurs to her: *He's taken a risk here. He's talked to them about autism and told them it's worth giving Adam a second chance.*

"Yes, thank you," Cara says. "That'll be fine."

Dr. Katzenbaum wears the same oversize red-frame glasses she wore four years ago. With short hair and a beakish nose, she looks like Sally Jesse Raphael's more serious sister. "We're going to play a game, Adam. You need to look at me and listen to what I'm saying," she says. She knows these kids, knows how to speak to them. She's already brushed away pointless puppets and distracting crayons, and in four seconds she gets further than the first time Adam was in this room. He turns his head, lifts his eyes to her mouth. "Listen, Adam. I'm going to say one word." Her finger moves, becomes a number 1 in the air. "And you're going to say the first word you think of. Not a sentence, not two words, just one."

The power of this woman's voice is such that sitting in the observation room, a mirrored window away, Cara leans forward in her chair, holds her breath. "SNOW," she says and Adam—is it possible?—leans toward her.

"MAN," he says.

"Very good," Dr. Katzenbaum says, as if she isn't surprised.

"HALLOWEEN."

Adam hums, thinking for a long time.

"Come on, baby, Halloween," Cara says aloud, though he obviously can't hear her.

"PUMPKIN," he finally says, and Cara exhales.

"She's good," Cara says to Lincoln.

"He's better, too," Lincoln says. "That's nice to see."

As the words get harder, Cara's surprise grows. First one word, then another; one word, then another. She feels breathless, giddy with the peek into the contents of Adam's brain.

"LEMON," Dr. Katzenbaum says.

"SOUR," he answers.

Where did that come from? Cara expected him to say yellow. Where did he learn the word *sour*? Lincoln won't understand the thrill of this, or how remarkable it is to hear logical connections, not rote repetition, or drilled answers. Why hasn't anyone taught her this game before? It's as if all these years of insisting on sentences might have slowed Adam down, been a mistake.

"PLUMBER," Dr. Katzenbaum says.

In the old days, Cara designed Adam's curriculum into units: holidays, seasons, workers in the community. She used photograph flash cards of workers to drill a standard answer. "What's a plumber, Adam?" she'd say, and to get his reward, he'd have to give an exact answer: "A plumber fixes pipes."

Now Adam answers, "SINK."

It takes Cara's breath away. He hasn't gone for the obvious choice: *pipes*. He has carved a different pathway in his brain, has put a word to what he saw in the picture and then—this is the thrilling part—has *memorized his own thought*.

She turns to Lincoln. "This is extraordinary," she says.

He nods, speaks into a microphone in his hand. "Good, Dorothy. Why don't you start?"

Cara looks at him. *Start what?*

Dorothy nods. "GIRL," she says.

Adam shakes his head. "BOY."

"GIRL IN THE PINK DRESS."

Oh God, no, Cara thinks, then watches Adam carefully. "WOODS," he says.

"Very good, Adam. You can say 'stop' anytime. MAN IN THE WOODS."

Adam rocks and hums. Cara holds her breath. "YELLOW."

"Good, Adam. Yellow what?"

"Yellow . . ."

"Yellow pants?"

Cara can see Adam's agitation mounting. Others might not see his fingers curling around the lip of the chair, but she can.

"Yellow shirt?"

"Yellow shirt," he says and his eyes travel to the mirror they are watching him through.

"Yellow shirt, very good. You've done a good job, Adam. Do you want to take a break?"

He stands up without answering and moves over to the mirror. Usually Adam hates mirrors; once, he broke one that a speech therapist was using, but now Cara watches, her breath held in anticipation of catastrophe, some revisitation of his morning outburst. *He's going to throw him-*

self against it, shatter the glass, she thinks, but this is nearly the exact opposite, a quieting of his whole body, one finger outstretched with the silent concentration it would take to catch dust. His hand opens and he presses one palm, then the other, to the mirror, hard so the flesh lines look like a starfish's underbelly inching along the glass tank wall. She would stop this now, but his face is serene, intrigued by this strange rectangle, this mirror that isn't really a mirror. She leans in; if he can see through this thing, her face is right here, so close he could touch it. Maybe he smells her, or hears her heart beat. She almost whispers, *Adam,* and then his mouth opens. "Hair," he says.

"Jesus Christ," Lincoln says behind her and stands up. "Go," he points to a uniformed officer in the room with them. "Right now. Tell Lou."

Cara turns around. "What?"

He doesn't answer, speaks into the microphone. "That's enough for now, Dorothy. We're going to take him downstairs."

"What is it?" There is movement all around them, except for Adam, who stays glued to this mirror, suspended in the utterance of this one word.

Lincoln turns to her. "The guy we've got downstairs is bald."

With Amelia's drawings tucked safely in his backpack, Morgan gets home from school to find his mother standing in the kitchen, holding his notebook. He's been waiting for this, knew it was coming. He never tried to hide the notebook; in fact, he's done the opposite: some nights it sat on the dining room table, beside the papers his mother spent the meal reading. He's wanted her to find it, and get this over with, just not now, not today, when he has made arrangements to take Chris over to Cara's, when he has a backpack full of pictures to show her.

"What are we going to do?" she says.

He takes a stab. "Nothing?"

"No, Morgan. That is exactly what we're *not* going to do. I'll tell you what we're going to do—we're going to go to the police."

"But I'm supposed to meet someone. A friend."

For a second, this stops her. "Who?"

"You don't know him."

He sees the surprise on her face. *First a fire, now this? Out of nowhere, a friend?* "Well, sorry. We're going to the police. We're telling them what happened."

In the car, she is surprisingly quiet. She doesn't ask the questions he readied answers for by writing them down. She doesn't scream or cry, as he assumed she would. *When it all comes out,* he thought, *it will be over. This bubble we're living in will break like glass.* She speaks for the first time when they pull into the police station parking lot. "Five years I've worked on saving that wetland. Five years of my life up in smoke." Her voice is steady and flat. She turns away from him and opens her car door.

"Mom," he says, but she is gone, marching toward the double glass doors, gripping her purse, circling around a broken beer bottle in the parking lot.

Inside, Morgan hears her ask a police secretary if they might speak to an officer in charge, please. "About what, ma'am?"

"It's private," his mother says, too loudly. "But important. My son has information about a crime." Saying this, she attracts the attention of two uniformed police officers standing by the front desk. Morgan hopes they'll think this is related to Amelia's death and let him speak to someone working on that. By comparison, his own crime will seem minor. Then his mother folds her arms over her chest. "It seems he's set a fire."

This is what happens, Morgan plans to say. *People go crazy. It can happen to anyone at any time.* Look how it happened to him. His mother didn't see, didn't understand how bad it was. She didn't think he needed a group. "You're fine, Morgan, my God. A lot of people don't have friends. *I* never had any friends," she said.

The secretary tells them to wait, have a seat please, that someone will be with them in a moment. His mother sits beside him, her open purse piled in her lap. "You want gum or something?" she says, digging through her bag. He shakes his head. This isn't anything like what he imagined. His mother seems to be her ordinary self—eyes darting, impatient with bureaucracy. "Nice to keep us waiting," she says, folding some gum into her mouth.

When he first told her about joining the group, she seemed angrier than she is now. To him it had come as such a relief: *There's a group at school, Mom. Where they explain everything you're doing wrong. They tell you exactly what your problem is and then you fix it. You make friends because you're not doing all the wrong things anymore. They tell you what's wrong with your clothes, what kind of shoes you should be wearing.* She hated the idea, everything about it. "It's all a lot of brainwashing," she said. "It's going to be a group that says you need hundred-dollar sneakers. I can't stand that. Some people are different. Some people do odd things. In my day, that wasn't a crime."

She doesn't see how much depends on having friends, how without them, you've got lunch hours, passing periods, bus rides, before and after school, great chunks of the day to spend trying to be invisible.

When they are finally assigned a police officer to speak with, there is some debate about whether his mother should go in with him.

"I'd prefer to speak with him alone," the officer, who is a woman, says.

"I'd like to hear what my son has to say."

Morgan stares at the ground, fearing this will lead to the explosion he's anticipated. His mother doesn't mind making public scenes—it's even possible she prefers them.

"Why don't we let him decide?"

Morgan studies his shoes—the flesh-colored orthopedic ones, the same shoes he wears all the time now, to punish himself. He can't look at her face. "Alone, please," he says, his voice tiny.

His mother folds her arms over her chest. "Fine," she says.

"If you'll just wait here, we'll call you in after we're through."

He tells the woman the whole story, that he went out there intending to burn his shoes, not the land, not fourteen acres of salamander habitat and home to a nesting beaver pair. "They're wetlands. You don't think of wetlands burning," he points out, though of course at the end of a dry summer, they will, he's learned.

"This is very serious," she says. He wants to point out that it could have been worse, he could have killed a girl and he didn't. "I can tell you right now the best-case scenario and the worst-case scenario." The best case is a probation period with a mandatory weekly attendance at a fire-starters group where he will learn about fires and the damage they cause. He will be given assignments about fire safety, personal fire prevention, community service related to fires. He wants to explain that this isn't necessary, that he has no interest in fires, no intention to start any more.

The other possibility is detention time. She studies her own notes, as if it might be up to her right now to decide. "Can you tell me a little bit more about what you were thinking? Why you went into the woods with these matches?"

He does the best he can: he tells her that he wanted his life to change, wanted his mother to see that he had problems, that his shoes were a problem.

"Shoes?" she says.

He points to his feet. "They're orthopedic." She looks down and nods, makes a note.

He doesn't say the other part, that there was more to it than his shoes. He doesn't tell her there was a plan behind the whole thing, because the plan didn't work so what would be the point in mentioning it at all?

Cara lets Dr. Katzenbaum take Adam downstairs while she walks with Lincoln, who explains: "We were going with some of the things you've given us. This guy walked into Nancy's Diner on Route 19, wearing flip-flops, two hours after the murder took place. His hands had dirt on them—no blood, but dirt—and his demeanor was agitated. Here's the thing, though: He was carrying a tin whistle in his pocket and he played it, went around from table to table, asking other customers if they wanted to buy one, saying it was good for bird calls."

"Oh my God," Cara says.

"Does a little flute in the woods sound like something that might have drawn Adam?"

"Yes. Absolutely."

"We figured. The man has no alibi. He admits he was out walking in woods that day, but doesn't remember which woods. We wanted to see if we could get Adam to come up with any link before we took him down. I'd say this was a pretty good one. Better than I'd even hoped for. Apparently he used to be some kind of musician, but there's a history of relatives pressing him into treatment and him refusing. Last time he was on the Bayfield Psych Unit was three months ago. He has no prior arrests, no history of violence, though there's one incident of aggressive behavior reported against a nurse at Bayfield. We're getting more specifics as fast as we can. My hunch right now is that we've got him. I gotta say, Adam saying *hair* right now . . ." He shakes his head, lets his mouth turn upward. It's the first time since that night at her house when they talked about high school that she's seen him look relaxed, even happy. He's even told her to call him Matt. "You were right. You said barefoot and music." He laughs. "You ought to think about getting into this line of work."

The elevator stops. The doors open on Adam standing beside Dr. Katzenbaum wearing a smile, as if to say *Mom! You're here, too! Isn't this wild!* This is how life with Adam has been: frozen in the past for days, and now he's here again, every hour surprising her: first a morning outburst and now this—composure, compliance. "Hi, buddy! Fancy seeing you here."

"Police!" he whispers, grinning.

"I know. Isn't it funny? There's police everywhere. I think because it's a police station."

Adam laughs, and everyone laughs with him at the impossible wonder: *A police station!* They all smile, shake their heads, and open the door to what feels, at last, like the beginning of the end.

Dr. Katzenbaum takes charge of Adam for the lineup, which Cara is grateful for because when the men walk in, it takes her a minute to recall how, but she remembers one of them. Finally it hits her: he was a musician giving children's concerts back in the days when she drove anywhere for an outing that would hold Adam's attention. Cara moves away. She understands that she must stand back, not let Adam see which one she recognizes. There are six men in all, four of them bald, or nearly so, which Matt has explained is necessary—Adam can't just pick out one dominant feature; he's got to get the right person.

"Look at me, Adam," Dr. Katzenbaum says, his face to hers. She knows the commands exactly as Cara would give them: simple, direct, with as few words as possible. "Now, point to . . . *man in the woods*."

He's meant to do something, but he doesn't know what. The buzzing gets louder like it always does if no one is telling him what's going to happen but something is meant to.

"Just look around, Adam. See if anyone looks familiar."

There were pants, brown pants with lines down them that ran shadows to his feet, which were dirty with leaves between his toes. All these pants are tan called khaki or blue called jeans, and all of these men are wearing shoes, so there's nothing for him to do or say except that every time he turns around someone tells him to keep looking.

"He's here," the girl said. "He just wants to talk to you."

The man shook his head. "He just wants to meet you, that's all."

He remembers all this, but doesn't know what it means. There was more than one man. There were other feet, other voices. He remembers voices: *Shit. What the fuck?* Words his mother says don't ever say, so he doesn't, though he doesn't know why. Once, his mother called them unpleasant, which is the same thing she sometimes calls certain smells he can't smell so he also doesn't understand. He starts to rock, but it's better here, he's okay. He's not at school, where he has to worry about the girl. He knows she's not here, not at a police station, he doesn't have to worry about her here, so it's okay. He remembers they were in trouble, remembers someone saying, "Shit, we're gonna get in trouble." But he was buried by then, in a hole of bushes.

Cara thinks of something: "Adam has a hard time with faces, but he might recognize feet. Can you have them take off their shoes?"

Matt squints his eyes and considers this idea. Finally, he nods and a voice announces over a loudspeaker to the men in line, "Please remove your socks and shoes."

The man Cara remembers complies without bending down. He steps out of shoes that are too big and unpeels his socks with toes as dexterous as fingers. They all watch, momentarily mesmerized by this mini freak-show demonstration. When the socks finally come off, Adam backs away from the window, shaking his head.

Dr. Katzenbaum kneels down beside him. "Use your words, Adam." They wait forever.

Something grumbles inside him, words rising, being pulled like a magnet up. Now, they're here, inside of him. He opens his mouth. "WHAT THE FUCK ARE YOU DOING!"

Morgan will get a court date, the officer explains. He'll tell his story to a judge who will decide on his punishment, taking into account his clean record, his actions since the crime, his willingness to come forward and volunteer the information. "Some of these things will work in your favor," she says. "But you have to bear in mind this was the worst fire our conservation land has suffered in ten years. It decimated an ecosystem, countless animals suffered. You will need to be mindful of that in every choice you make for the rest of your life. You've seen how easily life can be taken away, how actions have tremendous consequences."

He nods; he has. Knowing they are coming to an end because she's moving toward the door, he takes a chance. "Can I ask how you're doing on the Amelia Best case?"

She stops beside her desk. "I can't talk about that, Morgan. But why do you ask?"

"I know someone who might know something."

She narrows her eyes, weighs this possibility. "Hmm. I can tell you, because it's going to be on the news soon. We've got a suspect in custody."

"Who is it?"

"I can't tell you."

"Is it a kid?"

"I can tell you that much. No. Why?"

He thinks about Chris. "I believe a kid did it. A kid who's making threats on other kids who might know."

"Why do you think that?"

"I can't tell you."

She smiles. "All right. I'll tell them what you've said, but just so you know, kids can do terrible things, but it's not very likely that one did this. You shouldn't worry about this, Morgan. You should worry about yourself."

Out in the hallway again, the station has swelled with people and it feels suddenly like a hubbub of activity. This must be related to Amelia, he thinks, remembering the officer's words: *We've got a suspect in custody.* He looks around the room to see if there's anyone he recognizes in the crowd and then he does: Cara across the room, standing between two policemen. She sees him at the same time he sees her. "Morgan!" she calls, smiling and raising one hand up. "Did you hear? They've got the guy."

Morgan looks back to where his mother was sitting but isn't anymore. Her purse is gone, her jacket, too. "That's great," he says, and then he sees Adam, too, standing beside an older woman wearing glasses. He doesn't want his mother to walk up and see him talking to Cara. "I should go," he says.

"Okay, well. I'm happy, we're all happy. We'd love to see you soon, Morgan. And bring this friend of yours. Marianne called and told me all about him."

For the first time since they got to the police station, he remembers that he was supposed to pick up Chris to go over to Adam's this afternoon. He never called, never told Chris he wouldn't make it, but how could he? "Okay," Morgan says, wishing it was possible to come right out and tell Cara what's on his mind: *I was wondering if I could come live with you for a while. Not forever, of course. Just until this fire business blows over with my mother.*

Instead of walking away, Cara steps closer, puts her hand on Morgan's shoulder. "Even if this investigation is over, Morgan—if Adam goes back to school—we'd still love to see you." Before he spots it coming, or braces himself for it, she wraps him up in a hug. "Your friendship has meant a lot to both of us."

The whole ride home, Morgan's mother is silent. He can't stop thinking of Cara's hug, and her hair that smelled like coconut shampoo. The way she asked him to keep coming over, makes him feel like he *can* go there for a sleepover, like she might say yes, even if he tells her he needs certain foods and can't sleep with any kind of fan on in the room or doors open even a crack. He looks over at his mother, who has said nothing since they got in the car. He's pretty sure she's thinking up punishments, trying to decide exactly the right one. Grounding him won't work because he never goes anywhere; forbidding TV isn't good because he hardly watches it. He knows why his mother is having trouble with this: he doesn't do much, except visit Adam.

Realizing this fills him with dread, though. What if she takes this away? What if he can't show Cara the pictures that Amelia drew, and sit beside her as she goes through them? What if he can't watch her face when she gets to the last three pictures in the stack?

They get home and walk inside without a word. He tries to read her body language as she slides off her shoes and rubs her eyes with the heels of her hands. Though it's six-thirty, fifteen minutes after their usual dinnertime, she makes no move to start cooking. It scares him not knowing what will happen next, what she'll finally say when she says it. As she moves around the kitchen and punches Play on the answering machine, he imagines his mother did see Cara hug him and is about to tell him he must never—will never—see that woman again, or her son, whatever his problem is. When his mother gets going, she can be horribly mean; sometimes he can't believe the names she's called people who walk by their card table. He is so busy imagining what she might say, he almost doesn't hear what is being said: Marianne's voice on the answering machine, asking him to please call her at home, that there's a problem with Chris. That he seems to be missing.

An hour after they get home, Cara's happiness begins to dampen. The whole time at the police station she'd felt euphoric—Adam had communicated! Had solved the crime after all! In his own fashion, he'd been as useful as a typical nine-year-old. While he never pointed to one suspect, echoing when he did, at exactly the moment the man Cara recognized took off his socks, communicated enough. He'd said what he had to—*hair* and the words this man had given him—they all heard it, no one doubted what it was or thought for a second that those might have been Adam's own words. She watched a smile pass from one officer to another, watched as it turned into nods, then laughter, a single hand clap, then action. They didn't even need what she had to offer, whispered to Matt as he issued instructions to officers around him. "We know that guy. We've seen him before."

Matt stopped. "How?"

"He's a children's musician. He calls himself Busker Bob. We went to his concerts when Adam was younger." She remembers him surprisingly well: the trademark pair of patchwork pants that he always wore, quilted from beautiful pieces of velvet and satin, dotted with small mirror chips and buttons and safety pin chains he'd link charms onto. The pants must have weighed four or five pounds and made a tinkly sound when he moved. Ironically, one of the things Cara remembers most about him was his unusual gentleness. With a wide, plate face and a big smile, he must have been the quietest children's performer they ever saw, leaning over his guitar, as if every song was a secret he could only tell the kids, who knelt, breathless, in the front row. It had a funny effect—kids inched forward, one knee at a time until he had a horseshoe of sticky faces breathing into his guitar. "Oh, don't touch," he'd whisper, holding up a single finger. "Don't touch."

In those days, surrounded by other three- or four-year-olds, Adam could often pass as fine—even better than fine, sometimes. He was a boy who sat motionless, enrapt for the duration of any musical offering, and she often got compliments on his looks and his perfect concentration. Other mothers would say, *Is that one yours? I'm impressed.* With his little adult face, the way he cocked his head and wrinkled his eyebrows at people's laughter, the exact expression an adult would use to say *That's not funny*, Adam often impressed people, especially in an environment like a concert where he was at his best. But there was something else she remembers: Busker Bob could tell.

After his shows, Busker Bob always opened a duffel bag filled with maracas and bottle-cap shakers and let children play as he moved around the room in some fashion of a parade. Sometimes it worked, sometimes, with too many toddlers in need of naps, it didn't—but Adam was always there, trotting behind, as close as possible without physically touching. One time, parading Bob made an unexpected turn and the laws of physics worked against Adam, crashing him into the object of his obsession. Afterward, Bob watched Adam go through one of his standard touched-by-a-stranger responses: he turned in three circles, said

I'm sorry, I'm sorry, under his hand. Bob looked down at him and up at her. "He's a little different, isn't he?" She's never forgotten that moment or the horrible way it cemented something about Adam's future—that even in places where they came to get away, they didn't, really.

"How many concerts of his did you see?" Matt asked her.

"Five maybe, but that's a guess. Maybe less."

"But that would qualify you as a regular, wouldn't it?"

"I don't know. He had a once-a-month gig Saturday mornings at the community center. Some days, he got thirty or forty people there."

"Is it possible he registered Adam's autism?"

"Yes, actually. I think he might have."

"What did he say?"

" 'He's a little different, isn't he?' "

"I beg your pardon?"

"That's what he said to me. There were maybe thirty kids there, and he picked out mine and that's what he said to me. My only son. Four years old."

Matt noted all of this, scribbling furiously, nodding as she spoke. Cara smiled in spite of herself. This story was good, she could see, more than they'd even hoped for. This man knew Adam's limitations, let him live because of them. Around them, people moved by, patted her on the shoulder, offered congratulations. "Great thinking about the shoes," a man she'd never seen before said.

Before they'd left the station, she looked for Matt again across the room, crowded with people. When she caught his eye, she mouthed *Thank you, Matt,* and he smiled in a way that caught her breath. For the first time, she thought: *My God, he's a person. An unmarried person who isn't afraid of Adam or his autism.* She felt a little silly, unsure what to do, so she made her hand into a phone. *I'll call you,* she mouthed and a second later, he did the same, looked as silly as she had. *I'll talk to you,* he said into his pinky finger.

Back home, Cara feels her relief dissipate into a growing shadow of doubt. They all heard the way Adam said his echoed words: in the accent she heard before and could describe, but couldn't place. They heard each man say his name, a tiny snippet of a voice sample, five words for each of them—"My name is . . ."—and in that sliver, Robert Phillips, Busker Bob, was the quietest, the one who seemed closest to tears or emotion, which they all must have noticed (impossible not to), but did they also hear what she did, right away? There was no accent.

She worries this over in her mind for hours. Maybe she didn't make the rules of echolalia clear enough. They don't understand that Adam has no ability to fabricate or embroider, to apply an accent or borrow one. His brain is a tape recorder with an invisible Play button. This accent is part of it, and the man they've got doesn't have one.

Later, she thinks of something else: Adam knows the word *bald*. They drilled it as a joke when they were teaching him the adjectives *long* and *short* with pictures of hair cut out from magazines. They added two pictures of bald heads because Adam loved them, thought they were so funny. They would flip through the cards and Adam would say, "Long, long, short, long, short, short, *bald!,* long, short." So why would he say *hair* to describe its absence? There's only one answer: he wouldn't.

That night, Cara thinks of an experiment to try. In the old days, Cara used to buy every CD being peddled by any performer they went to because it was a way to teach past tense, to retell their stories. *(Remember his pants? Remember that guitar?)* Did she buy Busker Bob's? She fears his comment about Adam might have made her mad enough not to. Then she digs through the shoe boxes in the bottom of their stereo closet and is astonished to find a cheaply reproduced CD cover with Busker

Bob's photograph on the front, a red, hand-colored background. "Adam?" she says. "I want you to listen to something."

She turns it over, unsure if Adam will put this together, or react at all. She holds up the picture for him. "Do you recognize this guy? We saw him in a concert a long time ago and now we just saw him again at the police station." She tries to keep any weight out of her voice, to sound only passingly curious, *Do you remember this coincidence?* She puts on the CD, and Adam does what he's done his whole life when music plays: he crouches beside the speaker, presses his ear to it. His head nods in time and, after two choruses of "If I Had a Rooster," she asks, "Do you remember this guy at all? It was a long time ago. Maybe you don't."

He can't possibly. The last time they saw him was five years ago, half his lifetime. Then she looks down and he's staring at her, his face furrowed in thought. "Pants?" he says.

She moves quickly, finds a newspaper with Amelia's picture in it. He remembers this guy, he's calm, he's here, responding, she can't lose the opportunity. She turns off the music and asks him to come sit next to her on the sofa for a minute. "This is Amelia, Adam. The girl you went into the woods with. She was your friend. You talked to her on the playground sometimes, she sang songs. And then you went out to the woods and she got hurt. Very badly hurt. Do you remember that?"

He doesn't look up. When someone steps out from behind the tree, he sees toes, a bare foot, and looks away.

"She got hurt in the woods and they're trying to figure out who did it. Sometimes this happens, baby. Sometimes people do terrible things. They don't know what they're doing, they don't mean to, really, they have a bad brain that's telling them to hurt somebody."

He sees shadows and hears her voice. He didn't know her name, didn't know she had one.

"Do you remember seeing Busker Bob, Adam? Was he there in the woods? You need to answer this question, Adam. You can nod yes or no."

He remembers this, knows the answer. He nods yes. Yes, he nods. He was there. Yes.

"Okay," she breathes out. "He was there. Good job, baby. And did he hurt her? Did he have a knife?"

His face twitches in surprise, almost a readably normal expression: *A knife?* And it occurs to her, *My God, no one's made this distinction, asked him this question specifically: Was he the one who hurt her?* In weighing their questions carefully, paring them down for simplicity, they've entirely forgotten this possibility: he might have been there and not done it; there might have been someone else.

Later, after Adam has drifted off to sleep, Cara calls Matt and tells him about the conversation. She has waited three hours because she wants these doubts to have no merit. She wants him to say, *We've got a confession. It's over. Don't worry anymore.* "I'm wondering if more than one person might have been in the woods. I know you've said you don't think that's possible."

All the buoyancy she heard in his voice earlier in the day is gone. "Unfortunately, we can't arrest the guy. Something's happened."

She doesn't speak because suddenly fear knots her stomach, as if she knows what he's going to say before he does: "Another kid is missing."

June never watches the morning news shows, never turns on the TV for company, fearing that if she does, she might begin to resemble Suzette, who spends her days in the flickering presence of ubiquitous TV news. Usually, Suzette watches without the sound, but she never turns it off, even when Teddy asks her to. "I like to see what's happening," she says, as if this is her compromise with the world she can't live in. She will keep it on, in the corner, thirteen inches wide, even as she goes about her day, working on her paintings and at her computer, in the dancing light of stories playing silently on the screen. June turns it on this morning because her nerves are frayed and she can't stop thinking about Teddy, who came over last night after his shift spent parked in front of Cara and Adam's house. He is changed by what's happened, more unsettled, more talkative; maybe they both are. Instead of falling into bed and sleep, they sat on June's sofa side by side, holding hands. She watched his face, listened to him circle around the things he couldn't tell her, until he decided what he could. "I keep thinking about Adam and what Suzette used to say about him." She knows he hasn't been home in three nights, that he comes to her cottage now for showers and food, perhaps to avoid facing his sister, though he doesn't say this directly. "She hasn't seen him since he was a baby, but I remember she used to talk about him a lot. She used to say he scared her, that even though he was just a baby, he seemed to understand what was going on around him."

June only knows a small piece of this story—that Cara and Suzette were once roommates who planned to raise the baby together, and at the last minute Suzette backed out.

"At first, she thought it was her, that he knew what she'd done and cried more whenever she came to the house. She thought he was freakishly gifted or something. Then, on her last visit, she realized, no, there was something wrong with him—very wrong—and she couldn't go back. She couldn't see him anymore. She was scared that it was somehow her fault."

"What would that have to do with what's happened?"

"I keep thinking there's something compelling about this kid that the investigation is missing. They're focusing everything around the girl— where she's been, who she's talked to. But I look at how the body was found, in a little clearing, ten feet in front of the bush Adam was hiding in, and I'm thinking, isn't it possible—isn't there a chance the guy was after *him*? That Adam was his target and the girl was just *there*?"

After that, June lay in bed for hours and imagined someone targeting Adam, someone still out there. This morning, when she woke up, Teddy was long gone. She remembers him getting up in the middle of the night, talking on the phone in the kitchen and then coming back, fully dressed, to lean over her and say, "Something's happened. I'll call you later."

Now she knows what it is: a child's picture flashes on the television, a blond-haired boy, wearing glasses, who looks like he's twelve or thirteen years old. "A town already on high alert following the murder of ten-year-old Amelia Best now faces the possible abduction of another child. Late yesterday afternoon Chris Kolchak, a thirteen-year-old boy who attends Kennedy Middle School a hundred yards away from where Amelia Best was found slain in the woods, disappeared from his home. Chris was last seen in front of his house, apparently waiting for a friend to pick him up. Nobody saw him leave, no witnesses saw any unusual activity or unfamiliar cars in the area. Anyone with any information is asked to call this number . . ." A minute later, his mother is on the screen, crying mascara down her face, staring directly into the camera: "If anyone knows anything, has any information about my baby, I'm begging you please, call the police. He's a sick boy and he needs his medicines."

June holds on to the edge of the sink to steady herself. She'll need to get to school as fast as possible; there will be more meetings, more outsiders telling them what to do. "In the slim chance of a repeat incident . . ." a counselor once told them, and June can't even remember what followed because she hadn't let herself hear it, couldn't entertain the notion when the bulk of her job had become paranoia control.

At school, the morning meeting is impromptu, with as many people here as are able to be. Marianne Foster, a guidance counselor at the middle school, leads the meeting, which includes enough faces June doesn't recognize to presume this is a joint meeting for the two schools. June walks in on Marianne midpoint: "Chris has a degree of obsessive-compulsive behavior, and a diagnosed anxiety disorder. Following Amelia's murder, he was exhibiting elevated signs of stress. He felt very persecuted, obsessed by bullies. It's possible—we're praying—he has run away to escape some imagined or legitimate danger. We're asking people to tell the kids that we have no evidence Chris has been hurt. We are working on the assumption that he's alive somewhere, hiding from what he perceives to be dangers, and we need any information kids might have about where he went. Chris can be quite a talker, as anyone who knows him can attest, and it's our belief that wherever Chris has gone, he probably told someone."

June admires Marianne's fiery conviction, this energetic certainty that good counseling efforts will find Chris and return him unharmed. But Marianne hasn't yet had one of her own students die, hasn't learned that it can happen in a matter of minutes, that her ardent belief it's not possible will not make it so.

Morgan wonders if this is all his fault. Obviously, to a certain extent, it is. If he'd picked Chris up as he was meant to, Chris wouldn't have been standing outside, wouldn't have gotten kidnapped. Last night, after they listened to Marianne's message, Morgan's mother asked him to please just tell her what was going on. He told her the truth, that he didn't know. She kept going: "I just want to understand this, all right? All of the sudden I have no idea who you are—you're setting fires, you're hugging some strange woman at the police station. Who *was* that, Morgan? What's going *on* here?"

He has told her nothing of his two visits with Adam because if he is going to disappear, he needs to have a few secrets of his own. Sunday morning, before meeting Cara at the playground, he had told his mother he was going to the library. His heart beat as he said it, the first lie he'd ever told her, not counting, of course, the day of the fire when he sat for three hours in the same chair waiting for her return and then said, "No, nothing," when she asked him, "Is anything wrong?" Now he wonders if Chris was thinking along the same lines, if he was arranging his own escape.

"She isn't anybody, Mom. I don't know what you're talking about."

"That woman at the police station wasn't anybody?"

"No, I've never seen her before."

"I don't understand you, Morgan. You're not a very good liar. You obviously know her somehow, right?"

In his mind, he is already packing his suitcase, making a list of necessities. He will need a few things from the pantry his mother stands in front of.

"Do you know what she's talking about on this message? Do you know this Chris guy?"

"I was supposed to meet him after school today."

"Oh my God, and now he's missing?"

He will need macaroni and cheese, bottles of Yoo-Hoo, Life cereal for the morning.

"Morgan, that's *terrible*."

It is. He knows it is. But what can he do? He's guilty of too many things to be guilty of this, too. He thinks about water, tries to remember if Cara has a filter or if she drinks tap, which he can't do. Drinking tap water, to him, tastes like drinking a pipe. "Do we have bottled water?" he asks and she stares at him.

"Morgan."

"What?"

"This boy might be *dead*."

"Oh I don't think so," he says, spying two bottles of water on the shelf above her shoulder.

It's seven o'clock in the morning when Cara opens her door, expecting one of the bleary-eyed policemen stationed outside awkwardly asking to use her bathroom, and instead she finds Morgan, standing on her porch with a suitcase beside him. "I have something to show you," he says.

He offers no explanation for the large suitcase he rolls in the kitchen. Instead, he opens his backpack, pulls out a file folder of papers. "Here they are," he says.

"What's this?" She has hardly slept at all. Instead, she lay awake all night, going over the horrible roller coaster of her day. Last night, she made the mistake of watching the news until she couldn't bear it anymore—a boy only four years older than Adam? What does it *mean*?

Morgan hands her a stack of pictures. "Amelia drew these. I found them at school. No one's seen them yet. Mostly they're of animals and buildings. But there's a few of people."

She flips through and sees that some of the drawings are remarkable— far more sophisticated than most ten-year-olds could do, though even as she thinks this, it also occurs to her: what does she know of how most ten-year-olds draw? She knows only Adam, who draws people as balloon-headed stick figures and animals that look like lopsided forks. Amelia's drawings of horses are something else entirely: rich in detail, manes, bri-dles, whiskers, and even though it hardly seems possible, the suggestion of personality. She's good at drawing eyes, which must be what distin-guishes them—makes one horse look playful, another more reflective. Her furniture includes a desk and a chair with erased lines that show she was using these objects to work on perspective. Cara studies the desk drawing, which doesn't work exactly—a pencil cup teeters on the edge of the desk as if it's trying to throw itself over—but still: a ten-year-old recognizing there are rules to drawing and trying to teach herself?

Upstairs, she hears Adam awake, moving around. She moves to the stairs and calls out, "Adam, sweetheart? Guess what? We've got a surprise! Morgan's here."

Morgan follows her, keeping himself inches from the hand that holds the drawings he wants her to keep looking at. She wants to get breakfast on, get the morning started. She has decided what's important is getting Adam back to school, into his routine. She doesn't want to let his meltdown yesterday stop them, but apparently Morgan isn't going to let her put his pile of paper treasure down. "Keep going," he says, poking his finger at them. "It gets better."

She worries: What would "better" be in Morgan's mind? She hears Adam on the steps and suddenly fears that he will come down in his pajamas and have Morgan see, right away, that he still wears a Pull-Up to sleep, that if he didn't, she'd be washing sheets every morning. She shouldn't care about these things, but she does, feels the embarrassment Adam never would. "Morgan, look. Adam can feel a little shy in the mornings. Would you mind sitting in the family room for a minute?"

"Just keep looking." He can't let go of this, can't read her hints.

"Fine." She keeps flipping through the drawings: a tree, some flowers, a dog sleeping on a rug. Toward the bottom, she finds the first sketches of people—about ten of them—which aren't as detailed or alive as the earlier ones of animals: these are all flat, almond-eyed faces, staring angrily off the page. Except for the hair, it's hard to tell the men from the women, the young from the old. She gets to the bottom and hands them back. "They're great, Morgan. Good job. Maybe we should show them . . . " She hesitates. "I don't know, to Amelia's mother maybe?"

"Don't you get it?"

"Get what?"

"Look again."

"Morgan. It's early. We've got school today." She eyes his suitcase again. What's he *doing* here this early? She looks at the pictures again just as Adam appears in the doorway, scratching his head, pajama bottoms wrinkled around the damp bulge of his Pull-Up.

"See? *See?*" Morgan grins wildly now, so excited she fears he might stab a hole in the paper with his finger. "They're of Adam. Three of them. All of Adam." She goes back and looks. The last three are all of a young boy with—it's true—similarities to Adam's features: his wide brown eyes and (this startles her a bit: why didn't she notice it the first time through?) his unusually long eyelashes. The nose might be off—too short, too flat—but the mouth is right, the shape of his lips, the tiny curve in the corners. The more she looks, the more she can't get over that she missed it the first time: It *is* Adam, his hair, curlier on one side than it is on the other, his ears that stick out a bit behind his hair, one of the few physical flaws on a face that is otherwise so perfect.

"My God, Morgan, you're right. That's amazing," she says, though now she wants to put the pictures down, save them to look at when she can bear to contemplate the possibility they suggest: a girl so interested in Adam that she studied his face, memorized its details.

"But did you see the other one?" Morgan says when she tries to lay them on the table.

"Not right now, Morgan. It's hard for me to look at them, okay? Do you get what I'm saying?"

"Just this last one, I swear," he says and reaches into the stack to pull one out that she saw originally and flipped past, thinking only *generic woman,* and her heart freezes: it's a turtleneck she knows, earrings she recognizes. It's unmistakable, though she passed right by it before: it's a drawing of her.

She turns away from Morgan, steers Adam back upstairs, to the toilet, to the sink, into clothes. When they come back down, Morgan is at their kitchen table, eating a bowl of cereal from a box of Life she doesn't own. His suitcase is open, revealing its contents, which is mostly food. "Okay, Morgan, you need to tell us what you're doing here."

Dressed and awake, Adam suddenly seems tickled by the novelty of Morgan at their table. Beside her, he rocks back and forth. "What are you doing!" He giggles and turns a little circle.

"My mom has to go out of town for a night. I'm fine staying by myself, but I thought I'd drop these off and see if you, you know, needed anything or wanted maybe for me to sleep over tonight."

She laughs in surprise at the offer. They've never had a sleepover, of course; it's possible Adam doesn't even know what this means. But maybe this is a good idea; maybe it will get them through the day, take their minds off of Chris and everything else that's going on.

"What do you think, Adam? Do you want Morgan to sleep at our house tonight?"

"Sleep at our house," he says, tightening his circles, turning so quickly she finally puts a hand on his shoulder to slow him down.

In every class, people are talking about Chris, but Morgan doesn't want to think about Chris. He wants to think about sleeping over with Cara and Adam, about his mother coming home to find the house empty, her own suitcase gone. He imagines her not noticing at first. She will make some phone calls, start her evening reading and then it will dawn on her bit by bit, the missing food, his toothbrush gone, his clothes and books. And then she will see the only thing he's left behind—his orthopedic shoes—and she will know that this is it, that he's going to live with Cara, for two days at least, which is as long as he estimates his food supply will last.

In social studies, Morgan gets a pink office summons slip, which is usually reserved for people in trouble, but in the office Marianne tells him, "You're not in any trouble. This is about Chris, obviously," and Morgan is relieved. Apparently she hasn't heard about the fire yet, doesn't realize that actually, yes, he *is* in trouble. "We're talking to as many of his friends as we can today, but you're the person we wanted to start with."

A police officer leans on the desk beside her, with a notebook in one hand and a pencil in the other. Morgan nods and tries to think what he might say.

"You and Chris were meant to go over to Adam's house yesterday afternoon, right?"

"Yes."

"And what happened? Why didn't you?"

"My mother made me do something else. It wasn't my choice."

"What did she make you do?"

He hasn't planned what to say, hasn't decided ahead of time to lie, but then it comes so easily he can hardly believe it. "She made me go to visit my grandmother." Lies are confusing, though. They mean anything could happen—Marianne could know his grandmother, could know that she died six years ago.

"Okay." She nods. "And did you call Chris to cancel your plans?"

Morgan shakes his head. "No."

"Do you understand, Morgan, that when you make plans with people you have to be responsible to them, let them know if you can't make it?"

He feels the room start to spin. She's saying that Chris missing is his fault, too. Everything is his fault. There'll be no getting away from it, no escaping to Cara's house, home of the one face who always looks happy to see him.

"It's okay, Morgan. You made a mistake, but it's not your fault that Chris disappeared."

It's too late. Morgan has started to cry, hard enough for the police officer to hand him a box of Kleenex. "Why don't you tell us what you two talked about yesterday?"

Morgan blows his nose: "His problems, I guess. That people liked to pick on him. Amelia's murder."

"What about Amelia's murder?"

Here it seems okay to tell the truth: "That he knew something about it."

Marianne looks at the officer and back at him. "What did he know?"

"He said he couldn't tell me because then somebody would kill him."

"That's what he said?"

Only now does Morgan realize what he's saying, what he's known but hasn't let himself register all this time. "I guess maybe Chris knows who did it."

"Did he tell you, 'I know who killed Amelia Best'?"

"No. But I think about the bullies and the people Chris was always talking about putting on a list, and I have to wonder."

"Wonder what?"

"If one of them did it."

"Now, Morgan, there's no question that Chris was distressed about bullying. People picked on him, and that made him very upset."

"Yes."

"But do you see how there's a difference between Chris saying 'I know people who *should* get in trouble for being mean' and 'I know the person who killed Amelia Best'?"

"Yes. I see there's a difference."

"Is it possible he was saying 'I know people who are so mean they could have killed her'?"

Morgan shakes his head. It's obvious to him now, so obvious he can't think why he didn't see it sooner. "I think he knows whoever went into the woods. It's one of the guys who likes to bully him."

There are three that he knows of, for sure. Maybe more. He needs to make a list, start writing names down.

All morning, Cara moves restlessly around the pile of drawings she doesn't want to contemplate. The picture of her sits on top, accurate enough for Morgan to identify, though he couldn't even know what Amelia's got right—the clothes, the jewelry. What did he see to recognize this blank-faced woman with unsmiling, empty eyes, as her? Is it possible this is what she looks like now—that she wears her loneliness when she doesn't even realize it, as a permanent expression on her unguarded face?

For three days Cara has thought about making this call. The number is easy enough to find in the phone book; she dials it quickly before doubt can set in. "Mrs. Best? It's Cara Miller, Adam's mother. I wanted to call and tell you how sorry I am. If there's anything I can do . . ." She has had no practice for this. She's friends with no mothers of other children because she's never known what to say to any of them.

"Please," the woman says. Her voice is soft, reassuring. "Call me Olivia. I've wanted to talk to you, too."

"I have some drawings that Amelia did at school. A friend found them and brought them to me." She moves around the kitchen, picks up a dirty knife, then puts it back down. "They're very good. I thought maybe you might want them."

In the background, Cara hears a little girl's voice.

"No, not that one, Katie," the woman says.

My God, Cara remembers, this is why she can sound reasonably normal: she has other children. She isn't so horribly, unassailably alone, as Cara would have been if it had happened to her. "Maybe this isn't a good time. I just wanted to let you know we're thinking of you." She hesitates. There's more, of course, but how can she ask the question most pressing in her mind right now. *Did Amelia talk about Adam at all?* She looks down at the pictures, the drawing of Adam, touches the tiny line of his ear. *Is it possible they were friends?*

The woman must be moving around. She hears a baby cry, and the TV come on. "Look—would you like to come over? We're new in town, and I don't really have any friends yet. Our days have been so full of police. It would be nice to talk to another mother."

Cara can hardly think what to say. "I could bring these drawings."

"Yes, please do. I'd like to see them."

Cara didn't go to the funeral because there was only a small, private one; she only knows this family from the news snippets she's watched after Adam's gone to bed. The father works as a supermarket manager, the mother wears glasses and never, that Cara saw, cried on camera. They don't blame the school, they've said several times, but they are interested in seeing a fence erected, something to keep kids out of the woods. Cara wonders if she could ever be so pragmatic herself. Her child is dead and she's talking about fences? Who is this woman angry at, if not the school?

They live in a condominium sandwiched between identical units with no numbers over the door. "We're the one with the red Dodge minivan parked in front," she said, though she could just as easily have said, *We're the ones who look like a plastic toy factory exploded on our front lawn.*

Olivia answers the door wearing a pink jogging suit and holding the baby. "You'll have to excuse the mess," she says. In her free hand is a half-eaten apple, in the other, beneath the baby's bottom, is a wadded-up paper towel. She introduces her children, baby Benjamin and three-year-old Katie, sitting inches from the TV and pointing a stubby finger at the screen. "It's on the lamp, Steve! Look on the lamp!" Cara can hardly believe such a sentence coming out of such a tiny person, but she always feels this way around typically developing kids—to her, they all seem wildly precocious.

"I'm sorry about this, but the only thing I can offer you is an apple. My husband brought home a crate of apples from the store and I've got apples, apples, apples coming out my ears."

"An apple sounds great," Cara says, realizing she's hungry, that in the surprise of Morgan's visit, she forgot to eat breakfast. "Here are the drawings," Cara says, laying the pile on the kitchen table. She has taken the one of herself out and left it at home on the kitchen table, along with one of Adam, which she wants to show him when the time is right. "She was very talented."

For a minute Olivia says nothing. She puts the baby on the floor, turns to the pile, and touches the top one. Cara watches him crawl straight for the apple box, pick one out, and roll it toward his mother's feet. When she looks up, she sees tears in Olivia's eyes. "I'm sorry," Cara whispers. "Maybe I shouldn't have brought them."

She shakes her head. "No, it's all right. You say your friend found these at school?"

"Yes."

"Do you know where?"

"I guess in one of the games."

She nods. "She must have been hiding them. I told her she wasn't allowed to draw at school anymore. That's all she did at her old school. They never demanded anything of her, never held her to any expectations at all. She couldn't *read* because they let her do this all day long." She points to the drawings and steps back, accidentally kicking an apple by her foot.

Cara knows that Amelia was in the special ed room, but no one has ever told her why, or what Amelia's diagnosis was. "She had trouble reading?" Cara says, then adds quickly, "Adam had a lot of trouble, too. Especially in the beginning."

"She was years behind. We had to get her out of the old school; they weren't doing anything for her. It was terrible." It's amazing to see: Olivia *is* angry, but not at *this* school. "They told me she'd never learn to read, that I wasn't doing her any favors by pushing her to do things she couldn't." Across the room, the baby has begun a game of freeing every apple from the confines of the crate. Around him, a dozen apples rock gently. "You want to know who taught her to read? I did. This summer. Ten years old and she finally learned to read."

"What was the trouble exactly?"

"She had about four different diagnoses. We used to say her medical record looked like an alphabet soup. Finally they settled on PDD-NOS."

Cara stares at her, stunned. She knows this shorthand: PDD-NOS, pervasive developmental disorder—not otherwise specified.

"It's a way of saying she was on the autistic spectrum, but they don't really know exactly what's going on."

"She was on the spectrum?"

"Oh sure." Olivia nods. "More so when she was younger. She drew all the time, played with her stuffed animals, hated going anywhere, hated leaving the house. We had these window blinds and she would open and close them, open and close them all day long."

How is this *possible*? "Why didn't anyone tell me this?"

"No one at the school knew. I kept her records back. Her father and I never agreed on this. He didn't see the progress she was making, but I did. I was with her all day, I heard her talk about wanting friends. At night, she would lie in bed and talk about wanting playdates and then, when I tried to set them up, everyone said no." The tears still hover in her eyes as she busies herself picking up apples. "With one girl I broke down and begged her mother. I said, 'My Amelia needs help with this. She needs to practice playing with other children her own age. Would Katie consider just coming over once and baking some cookies with Amelia?' "

"What did she say?"

"That she felt bad, but she didn't think she could force her daughter to do it." She wipes her eyes and shakes her head. "I was going to give them her records, I just wanted to wait a little bit—see if she did better without the label."

Cara almost can't bear to ask. "Did she?"

"I think so. She liked this school. She was learning some things. I could see that."

Cara can't get over it: Amelia was once autistic and now recovered enough that no one along the way—June, Phil, no one—had recognized this possibility? What had Phil said? *She might have had some special needs?* She wants to say it's not possible, and then she wants to ask, *How did you do it? What worked?* "She must have been doing so well," Cara says softly. "What therapies did you use?"

"We tried a lot of things. I think changing her diet made a difference."

Cara nods. When Adam was first diagnosed, the Internet was full of research saying that autism could be an extreme manifestation of a food allergy. Every mother she met online yanked dairy and wheat out of their houses, and the testimonials flew back and forth, everything punctuated with exclamation points. "He's speaking in sentences now!" "I can vacuum the house without hysterics!" "He plays with something other than the bath plug!" After starting him on the diet, Cara saw changes with Adam, too—saw the fog start to lift. In three months, he gained nine months of language. He started putting words together, using short sentences, talking with something like emotion in his voice. Now the years have crept by and she's lost touch with all those mothers, stopped logging on for company every night, though she's always wondered: did the others keep going, or did it work the way it had with Adam, in bits and pieces that sometimes made it seem as if nothing good had happened at all? He has sentences now, and language, but all of it is a far cry from normal. She knows the diet works because when they slip off of it, he slips, too, and spends a day spinning circles in the corner, but she's always wondered: if this was the problem and it's been corrected, why isn't he normal?

She looks at Olivia. "The diet did it?"

"I don't know. Sometimes I thought so, but she still had stomach issues. She wasn't always continent, exactly."

Cara nods. "Adam has accidents, too."

"It used to be she didn't care. Then recently she started being very embarrassed." She hesitates. "And secretive. Some days she came home without any underpants on, and I would ask her what happened and she wouldn't tell me." She isn't crying anymore, but her voice betrays the effort not to. "I've wondered if maybe she went out to the woods to bury them. I don't think it was her first time there." Her head bends under the weight of this admission. "Once she brought home a bag of underpants that were covered in dirt, two pairs, and I didn't know what to think. I said, 'Amelia, what is this?' "

Cara thinks about the rabbit's foot, found and never explained, these conversations without answers. She knows what it means to have a child who remains, in every fundamental way, a mystery. "What did she say?"

"Nothing." She shakes her head and bends down to collect the apples. "I'm sorry she took your son out there, too. I'm sorry he got involved."

Cara reaches over and touches Olivia's arm. "You mustn't think it was her fault."

"No, I know. I just wanted you to know that I'm sorry. She liked Adam so much."

Cara stops. It's the first time she's ever heard someone say this. "What did she say about him?"

"Oh, funny things. That he hummed a lot. His hands—what did she say about his hands?—they danced when he was happy. That's how I guessed he was probably autistic, too. These last few weeks she didn't want to go to school, and then she'd remember: 'Recess Adam?' And I'd say, 'You have to go to school to see Recess Adam, right?' "

My God—it sounded like a conversation from her own house.

"She wanted to invite him over, and then she changed her mind. She knew where he lived, and I think she was scared of what he'd think of this apartment."

Adam? Was she serious?

"I told her he probably wouldn't care, but she was nervous. She actually said, 'He'll think we're poor,' and I said, 'Honey, we *are*.' "

Driving over here, Cara had tried to imagine what she would say, what she would want to hear if the situation were reversed. She could only guess this: she'd want to hear people tell her any minuscule anecdote they remembered about him. She'd want to gather proof that for all of his deficits, Adam mattered to others, had an effect, a place on this earth. She reaches across the table to touch this woman's hand. "I know that Adam was changed by Amelia. He's different now, since his friendship with her."

This seems to be the right thing. Olivia looks up, a damp smile on her face. "How?"

"Well . . ." Cara tries to think: what is a good example? "Adam isn't as verbal as she was. Especially in describing anything abstract like his own emotions. But I can see him thinking about her sometimes. He went to school the other day, and got very upset, had more of a meltdown than I've seen in years, and I have to assume it's because he misses her. It was right before recess when they usually saw each other—" She stops speaking. For the first time, it occurs to her: *Did he think he would see Amelia at recess yesterday? Is it possible he doesn't realize she's dead?* "He can't tell me what happened in the woods or why they went out there, but I can tell he's thinking about it. He keeps wanting to watch this opera, *The Magic Flute*, where everyone's in the woods and magical things are happening and I keep"—she hesitates, choosing her words carefully— "hoping that's what it was like. That they were on an adventure, sharing it with each other."

Olivia nods, crying quietly, a hand over her face. "I just wish—"

"What?"

Her eyes are red, filled with tears. "I wish I'd been more patient with her. I have the two little ones, and sometimes Amelia was more work than both of them, going on and on, repeating and repeating, hanging on my arm. Sometimes I would say, 'Amelia you have to go to your room, I can't stand it anymore.' "

Cara has had these moments, too. Adam stuck in a groove. A few months ago they had a blowup when he wouldn't stop saying "An old man in Texas," a phrase he'd heard on the radio, over and over. "What does it even *mean*?" she screamed, and left the room, slamming the door so he would understand: he couldn't just do this, annoy people to death. Afterward, she went into his room, where he'd buried himself in his bed. She lay down beside him and whispered, "I'm sorry," which gave him new words to lock on to. "I'm sorry, I'm sorry, I'm sorry," he said over and over. They were terrible, those fights.

"I've done the same thing," she says softly. "I know how you feel."

Now that he's put the pieces together, Morgan walks back to algebra and thinks about the one time he saw Chris actually being bullied. It was early in the morning, before school started, and at first he didn't realize it was Chris. He recognized three ninth-graders from their black leather jackets circling around a kid who held a purple backpack in front of his face, and then he recognized the familiar, high-pitched voice. "God, you guys. Why don't you just leave me *alone*?" They were poking at him with sticks, jabbing his knees and then his shoes.

Now Morgan realizes there are things he might have done to help. He could have yelled; he could have found a teacher or Marianne. At the time, though, none of these possibilities occurred to him. When he recognized Chris's voice, he turned his eyes away, down to the floor. He walked away and tried to forget the whole thing, the way he does when he isn't sure, but suspects, people are being mean to him. He didn't really know the boys, who hardly come to school and study so little they carry no backpacks, but there are other bullies, a list he could start with the oversize woodshop boys who are fourteen and already shaving: Randall Im, Chris Wyant, Brad Stonewall. He could also include the small-but-mean boys: Harrison Rogers, Wilson Burnstein, who once, in fifth grade, called Morgan a homo for going into a bathroom stall to pee. For a month afterward, Morgan drank nothing at breakfast and never peed at school. A comment like this can be much worse than name-calling, Morgan has learned. Someone whispers, "Freak," when you're walking down the hall and it's possible to believe that he might be thinking of a book or singing a song. Someone looks you in the eye and calls you retarded, though, and it's harder to ignore.

If it's one of these guys and Chris knows, one thought occurs to him: Maybe other people know, too. Surely it's possible, but how can he ask without anyone finding out? He looks over his list and gets an idea.

During lunch, he visits every bathroom in the school and leaves the same Magic Marker message: DO YOU KNOW WHO KILLED AMELIA BEST? IF SO, PLEASE WRITE YES BELOW. On the last three bathrooms, he added,

Please NO Jokers or Fakes. This is Serious. You will Not Have to be Personally Identified. We Respect Anonymity.

Of the four stalls he writes this in, he spells *anonymity* different each time.

As Cara drives home from Olivia's house, her mind fills up with all the questions she didn't get to ask of this woman who feels like the first new friend she's made in years. Does she know what Adam and Amelia talked about? What they said in their private moments on the swings at recess? Cara assumes that Amelia, with more language at her disposal, did far more talking, but is it possible that Adam told her some version of the terrible bike story? Did he say *Bike ruined, no bike anymore*? Is it possible he said, in some way that Amelia understood, *My mother drives me crazy, she cares about the stupidest things*?

He must have said something, or pointed her out, at least; otherwise, how would the girl have known who she was? Why would she have drawn a picture of Cara wearing an expression that looks mostly like fierce and angry determination? All she's ever wanted for Adam was what this girl got: a chance at recovery, to make connections, friends of his own. Cara knew the path to such a goal could look serpentine, but there was a logic to her efforts. Forcing him to learn how to ride a bike, to play Uno, to watch television shows that didn't interest him was part of that plan. She'd watched other boys his age ride bikes together, play cards on the bus. She saw how little they talked during such activities and she thought, *My God, he could do this.* But she'd never explained it to him that way, never told him the real goal behind pushing him into activities he instinctively resisted. It stuns her to realize she never had a conversation where she explained: *It's good to make friends. Here's one way to do it.* She always assumed he wouldn't understand.

And yet, surely what he had with this girl qualifies as friendship. Though it might have looked quaint to others, like little more than singing side by side on the swing set, in their world it was private and monumental. In all the emotions washing through Cara, one of them must be happiness. Adam has made his own friend once, he'll do it again; he's taken a step into his own life, away from her. It's what she's wanted and prayed for all this time. But now that he has, she wonders: If Adam is getting better, even incrementally, where does that leave her?

At home, she walks in as the telephone rings and picks it up gratefully, because any voice at all would be preferable to the lonely thoughts ricocheting around her brain. "Cara? Is that you?" she hears and looks out the kitchen window, thinking it must be Teddy, calling from his car parked in front of her house. They've had a handful of strained exchanges as he periodically makes use of her bathroom. "How's your family?" she tried once, to which he said only, "I don't have one. I'm not married." Maybe he's calling now to make amends for such an absurd response and finally talk about what they have in common.

"Teddy?" she says, squinting out the window.

"No," the man says, and she sees that Teddy is in the car, but he isn't on the phone. He's sipping coffee, staring ahead.

"Who is this?" She looks down at the phone, this voice she recognizes but can't place.

"It's me. Kevin."

"Oh my God."

This call is so strange, coming on the heels of her visit with Olivia. Any other time her defenses would be up. With her tone of voice, she would say, *No, Kevin, it doesn't work this way. You can't drop in and out of people's lives; you can't be both charming and deceitful.* But being with Olivia has been so unsettling, and has reminded her of the past, when she had people her own age to talk about her life with. The whole drive home she's been thinking about Kevin and Suzette, her last real friends, and here he is now, as if summoned by her thoughts, calling again.

"Hi, Kevin," she says quietly. She certainly isn't going to let all her guard down, laugh with delight, say, *Long time, no see, Kevin*. But she also can't deny this: it's nice to hear his voice.

"I just wanted to see how you were doing. I heard what happened to Adam, and I wanted to say I'm sorry. I'm just so sorry. You must be having a terrible time."

"How did you hear?" Maybe she should get used to this by now. Theoretically, Adam's name has been kept out of the papers, carefully withheld, but the reality is, everyone knows.

"Suzette told me. I—she heard from her brother, I guess."

Jesus, she thinks. *I should hang up now.* All of these years, he's still in touch with *Suzette*? Still friends with her after nonchalantly denying he ever ran into her?

"I've tried to keep up with her. She's not doing that great, and I don't want her to think I've abandoned her."

You didn't mind abandoning me, Cara wants to scream, but instead, because this is something she hasn't heard before, she asks softly, "What's wrong with Suzette?"

"She gets these panic attacks, and it's left her scared to leave her apartment. She doesn't go out at all anymore, as far as I know. I try to get there once or twice a month at least. I don't always make it, but I try."

It's sad to hear this, but not a shock. She had always had an agoraphobic's aversion to leaving their apartment. ("Why go out for beer when there's two in the fridge?" used to be one of her favorite responses to Cara's invitations.) To Cara, what's interesting is the way he says this, making it perfectly clear that there's no romance, making sure she knows: *I do the decent thing, I stop by.* Maybe she's being too hard on him, to still wonder about that lie he told so many years ago. It was a complicated time; everyone acted badly, in one way or another. "Oh, Kevin," she breathes. "I wish—"

"What?"

"I wish I hadn't asked so much of Suzette. I asked for too much from her and made it impossible to stay friends at all." She wants to understand all of this better, understand how they came to be at such an impasse.

"You're not the reason she has panic attacks, Cara. She's had this problem for a long time. Medication hasn't helped, neither has therapy. She just lives with it, works at home. Her brother lives with her, so that helps. Panic attacks limit what you can do. She tends to avoid whatever sets them off, which is probably why she's avoided you."

It's never occurred to Cara that Adam's meltdowns might have been worse for Suzette than they were for her. At the time, Cara was so caught up in her own frantic efforts to stop his wailing that she didn't think about anything else, but surely it's possible they left Suzette feeling breathless, too, paralyzed by her own inability to help. They were like best friends who'd gone to war together and were forever driven apart by the terrible sights they'd jointly witnessed. Maybe that isn't a fair comparison, but it feels right somehow—they haven't wanted to see each other because they can't bear what they've seen each other go through.

"I don't know, Cara. I've wanted to call you for so long. I've thought about it and thought about it. Finally I decided just to do it."

She doesn't like the image of Kevin sitting at home for the last ten years, debating the pluses and minuses of making a phone call—it makes him seem sad, with too little to do with his time—but there's also this: all her other well-wishers and phone callers have dribbled away. He's here now, being what seems at least reasonably genuine.

He keeps going: "Sometimes, when I'm driving to work—or my mother's driving me—I remember these strange things from high school. Does that ever happen to you?"

"Sure, Kevin. Of course."

"I remember something you said in class about *The Scarlet Letter*. How maybe Hester liked having the *A* on her chest, because it freed her from having to live the same life as everyone else. Do you remember that?"

"No."

"You said it sounds nice to have no obligations to anyone except her child."

Did she really say such a prescient thing? Anticipate her own future spent with a scarlet *A* for autism printed over everything? "That's weird. I don't remember that."

"Maybe I remember too much."

"It's okay," she says because the truth is, she doesn't mind hearing this—doesn't mind having him remind her who she was before Adam came along to make her someone else.

"I remember the way you watched me in fifth grade, turning around in your seat."

She blushes, grateful that he isn't here to see. "You're right, I did."

"Of course, what was I doing?" He laughs. "Staring at your little outfits. I think maybe we were watching each other all those years we never talked."

It's funny, she thinks: they've never before mentioned the time between fifth grade and twelfth.

"I was waiting, getting myself ready for some big move, and then I kept getting so sick. But the other day it occurred to me: that's what worked, didn't it? Almost dying. That always got your attention. That's why I didn't go to graduation."

"What do you mean?"

"If I went, you might not have talked to me, but if I didn't go, I knew you'd notice."

She remembers sitting on stage that day, five rows behind the empty seat left symbolically open. "That's Kevin's chair," Mrs. Murphy, the orchestrator of the day's pageant, said. Other missing students had their places filled in, so the picture from the bleachers was a solid continuance of black robes with a single, folding-chair hole. Cara spent the length of graduation watching the chair, expecting Kevin to appear at any moment, in a wheelchair, or behind a walker, inching his broken body into it.

"I did." She knows it's dangerous, going too far back, admitting too much. "I noticed."

"I remember the letter I sent you."

She doesn't say anything, but wonders where this conversation is heading.

"And what you sent back."

Should she remind him that she was a nervous teenager, afraid of everything he represented—real love, commitment, everything that would entail? Should she tell him she composed different answers, one he probably would have liked better? There's danger in anything she says, so she stays quiet.

"So why don't you tell me about your life?" he says to rescue them from silence.

"Maybe you already know this, but Adam has developmental delays. And that's been my whole life, pretty much. Just focusing on him, helping him get better."

"Is he? Better?"

What can she say? What would Kevin's mother say about Kevin? Suddenly she doesn't want to dance around the word, she wants to be honest. "He's still autistic," she says. "He always will be, I imagine, but he's better than he was. He reaches out more, tries to connect. He had a kind of friendship with this girl, apparently. They played on the playground, and sang songs. I wouldn't have believed it, but everyone keeps telling me it's true. She chose him or they chose each other—I don't know. So, yes, I think maybe he's better."

"Good," he finally says. "And what about you? Are you better?"

How can she answer this? Once, she wanted love to come into her life and take it over and then, with Adam's arrival, it did. At the time, it had felt as if the long wait was part of it, the way this child mirrored the men that came before, the reticence she had always been drawn to. All her life, she picked men who eluded her and then was given a child who did, too. "What do you mean?"

"Are you happy? Are you married?"

Married? Surely he knows this much. "No, Kevin. I'm not married."

"Because maybe we could have lunch someday. Or dinner. Any meal would be okay."

She laughs. Her heart softens, begins to see a new possibility. Surely she doesn't need to tell him it's too late for romance, too much has happened, but it occurs to her that perhaps this is a chance to learn what she has spent nine years trying unsuccessfully to teach Adam—the delicate and fragile intricacies of real friendship. It has been so hard without any of her own to hold up as examples. Perhaps this is what they need more than playdates for Adam or social skills groups, or Friendshipmakers.com, a Web site devoted to teaching conversation and play to children that Cara leaped on when she first heard about it, ran home and subscribed to, only to discover list after list of dubiously helpful advice, like one of their top-ten suggested conversation starters: "Do you have a favorite doughnut?" Maybe what they need are less of those things and more examples for Adam to observe of friendship around them, of people talking to each other, asking questions and listening to the answers. Maybe—after all this time—this is what she and Kevin can ask of each other and offer back in return. "Sure, Kevin. I'd like that."

After she hangs up, she decides that's not all she wants. There's something else. She runs outside. Holding her sweater closed against the cold, she taps on the window of Teddy's police car and bends down as it lowers. "I want to see Suzette," she says. "I need to talk to her."

For a long time, Teddy stares at her, as if he's absorbing what she's asking in pieces. "Right now?"

"Yes, right now. School's not out for two hours. I want to go now."

For the rest of the day, Morgan visits the bathrooms as often as he possibly can. For three hours, his graffiti goes without response, then at the end of the day, he climbs the stairs to pee in the privacy of an empty third-floor bathroom and finds, written in pencil below his Magic Marker message: *Yeah, I know.* The writing is tiny, but thrilling, so pale it's as if the person wrote it halfheartedly, a handwritten whisper.

He needs to act fast. In five minutes this bathroom will have people moving in and out of it. He has thought of several contingency plans for this possibility: *Write me a note and push it through locker number 2536* might become an invitation to the derelicts who push lit matches into lockers. His best hope is a message that will be missed by the thugs and read by the person that matters. *Meet me in Rogers Park after school,* he writes in pale pencil, and then, to ensure privacy, he blackens out what came before. After that, he moves down hallways, studies the faces of strangers for the shadowy, haunted look of knowledge. Someone at this school knows something, he thinks, counting off the minutes until he will, too.

· · ·

Maybe this will be a mistake, but Cara doesn't want to doubt herself now or question what she's doing. Kevin's call has shot her full of adrenaline, and she's on a mission to make some amends, offer apologies and explanations and get some of her own. For years, she's thought of her past as a shadowy series of misunderstandings best left unexamined. Whenever anyone has asked about Suzette, she's said the same thing, "Something happened but I don't really know what," as her only explanation. "We don't talk anymore." Now they *will* talk and she'll understand better what happened all those years ago to drive them so far from each other's lives.

The apartment that Teddy and Suzette share in Chester is a twenty-minute drive away, which is a risk. If Adam has another episode and the school calls, it will take some time to get back to him, but so be it, she decides. She needs to do this. As they drive, Teddy fills in the details, tells her a bit more than she got from Kevin. *Suzette has kept up with her painting, she works from home as a graphic designer for Web pages. And no, she never leaves the apartment, hasn't for more than a year.*

Cara shakes her head. "A year? Really?"

"It's more common than you think. Especially these days, when people can work at home, and order groceries online. She doesn't really need me to live with her, but I don't want to move out yet. Even though she says I can, I don't want to leave her alone."

Cara hears all this and tries to take it in. "I didn't know, Teddy."

"No. Of course you didn't." Without having directly addressed the issue, he seems to have let go of his anger, which is a relief.

"When we were kids"—her voice wavers—"she was so sure of herself in ways that I wasn't. She didn't care what other people thought. She felt so strongly about certain things." She tries to remember exactly what she means, and can only think of the last subject Suzette felt strongly about: Kevin. *Friendship means you help the other person. You stand by them.* Why didn't she remember this and realize Suzette couldn't possibly have lied about her friendship with Kevin? How had Cara managed, at such a crucial juncture, to see so little?

"Having Adam was the first time I was absolutely sure of what I was doing. It's the only time in my life like that. And I remember thinking, *I just want to do this one thing, be like Suzette and sure of myself on this.* I don't think I ever could have done it if I wasn't friends with her first." She's never thought about this before, but saying it now, she realizes it's true.

Chester is a fading, sad town, once dominated by a now-defunct aluminum factory. The playgrounds have signs declaring DRUGS WILL NOT BE TOLERATED HERE, NO LOITERING, NO TRESPASSING AFTER HOURS, NO GLASS CONTAINERS, precautions against crime they grew up oblivious to. The apartment is behind a post office, with a long ramp sloping downward to the front door so that, going inside, Cara feels like she is entering a basement. Inside the front hallway, Cara hunches over when her head almost whacks a copper pipe. It's not a basement, though, it is an apartment, with narrow windows along the top of three walls and—for a second Cara's breath catches—Suzette's art on all the walls. She recognizes one piece, done after they graduated from high school. It's a self-portrait, though Suzette never called it that because it's a headless study of her naked body after a bath, reflected in a full-length mirror as she bends over to dry her leg with a towel. Cara had always loved this one, mostly because the body was so accurately rendered, so instantly recognizable: the mole on Suzette's ankle, her knobby kneecaps, her pointy, cornucopia-curved breasts.

Teddy calls out, "Suze! I'm home. I brought a surprise."

There's a silence, and then a voice from the bedroom that Cara recognizes perfectly. "What does that mean?"

Before Cara can say anything, the bedroom door opens for a second and closes again. Though Cara didn't see her, didn't turn around fast enough, Suzette obviously saw Cara.

"What the hell are you doing, Teddy?" she calls.

Cara steps toward the closed door. "Don't be mad at him, Suze. I made him bring me. He wanted to call first, and I wouldn't let him because I didn't want you to say no. I just want to talk to you. I want to figure out what happened between us."

As she talks, she sees the knob on the door turn. "What happened between us?" she calls without opening the door. "Maybe we should just start with hi first."

Cara smiles. "Hi."

The door opens. "Hi."

She looks beautiful. Her old hair, thin and wavy, a battle of cowlicks she used to fight and lose, is entirely gone, and a crew cut stands up haphazardly, away from her head, so short in spots her scalp is visible. It's a terrible haircut, but it doesn't matter; she still looks good. Without much hair, her face jumps out, her eyes look huge and beautifully blue. "Wow. Look at you, Suze. You look great. You really do."

"That's not true, but it's nice of you to say."

"No, it is true. I like your hair that way. Short like that." She wonders why this is the first thing she can think to say when they were never friends who focused on looks. They never dyed each other's hair, never did each other's nails.

Suzette runs a flat hand over the bristly rug of hair. "This is kind of sudden."

"I know, I'm sorry." She recognizes this new Suzette better in parts—she knows her hands, her shoulders, better than this whole creature she's become. "Teddy, would it be all right if Suzette and I talked for a few minutes by ourselves? Would that be okay with you, Suzette?"

"I guess," she says, softly.

"All right," Teddy says. "I'll go for a walk and be back."

Suzette tells her she needs a minute to save what she's working on and change her clothes. She's wearing a T-shirt that's so old Cara is almost sure she recognizes it and gray sweatpants with a red stain on the knee. When she comes back out, she's wearing jeans and a black turtleneck. She goes into the kitchen and pours herself a glass of water.

Cara starts with what she's planned to say: "I know this was all a long time ago, but I wanted to say I'm sorry, Suze, for everything that happened. I wanted the baby to be an answer for both of us. And it wasn't, of course. It was an answer for me, and I shouldn't have asked you to give up so much to help me with a baby you never planned or asked for."

"I shouldn't have said yes, and then changed my mind."

Cara shakes her head. "It's strange to remember it this way, but I honestly think one reason I let myself get pregnant is that I thought you would like it. I thought it would bring us back together again and give you a baby to take care of the way you'd taken care of Teddy."

Suzette smiles and shakes her head. "Nice thought. Apparently not the right one."

"I've been trying to understand why you got so angry with me, though—why we couldn't see each other at all."

"You didn't even know, did you?"

"Know what?"

Suzette turns to the one window in the kitchen that looks out over the childless playground. A pair of birds perch on the motionless swing set. "Kevin had this plan. He wanted to win you over and dump you, but he wanted it to be big, like you were supposed to really fall in love with him and then he could hurt you the way you had hurt him back in high school. I was supposed to talk about how great he was and act like I was in love with him and that would open the door. Pique your interest."

Cara has come here wanting to talk about Kevin, and the surprise is that Suzette brings him up first. "Why did you want to help him do something like that?" Cara asks.

"I was so confused, and you were so . . ." Suzette goes to the sink, turns on the water, and lets it run. "Sure of yourself."

"That's not true."

"That's what I saw. It was such an awful time for me, and you were so oblivious."

"I knew you weren't happy."

"But you were supposed to be devastated. Your life was supposed to be ruined, and you didn't even see that. You were just happy to be having a baby."

"I *was* happy."

"So you see—it didn't work. First Kevin left, then I left, and you didn't care."

"Yes I did. I cared." It's been nine years and Cara still thinks of stories to tell her. In her mind, Suzette is still there. Surely she can see this, can sense it. Or maybe not. Maybe too many years have passed now and they are both too altered by the lives they've ended up with. For a while, they stand there, each of them weighing her own regret. "I don't know if he told you he was going to do this, but Kevin called me and asked if we could see each other sometime."

Suzette nods. "I figured he would. Sooner or later."

"I want to see him, but I don't want it to be like last time. I don't want to sneak around."

"Do you want to date him?"

"I don't think so. But I want to see him, see if it's possible for us to be friends. Do you think it is?"

"He's not the same person you remember. He's in a wheelchair now, did he tell you that?"

She tries not to let the surprise of this register on her face. "No."

"He'll probably be mad at me for telling you. He wants you to think of him as nondisabled, mostly independent. Using the wheelchair is related to the kidney stuff. I think he can still stand occasionally, but not much. Not often that I've seen. We've stayed friends because look—" She gestures around. "Accessible apartment. An old man lived here before Teddy and me. Kevin can visit me and actually go to the bathroom by himself. The thing is, sometimes he's fine, and sometimes he's not. Sometimes he has dark periods and I don't hear from him. He disappears and I don't know what happens to him."

Cara nods, and looks around the room at some of the paintings she's never seen before. They're different from her old work—more accessible, more realistic. One is of a beach, with water in the background. Though it has no person in it, it feels like a portrait nevertheless. A towel in the foreground is arranged with objects—a pack of cigarettes, sunglasses, the shadow of a dog. The more Cara looks at it, the more she thinks the dog—or more accurately, its shadow—is the real subject of the painting, the source of the tension. Where has the owner gone, leaving the dog behind like a possession? Then it occurs to her to wonder: How has Suzette painted the rocks, even the lichen, and the perfect light of a searing hot day from this hole in the ground?

"I paint from memory," Suzette explains, before Cara has a chance to even ask. She points to the beach scene. "That's Truro, where we went as kids."

Finally Cara is old enough to look at these paintings and offer a reaction. "They're much more realistic." And they certainly are—the cigarettes have a brand name and matches tucked inside, the shadow has fur, clumped distinctly enough to know the dog is wet. Cara doesn't say what she's thinking: it's as if to see the world this clearly, Suzette has had to distance herself from it. "I love these," Cara finally says. "I really do. If I had any money, I'd buy one from you."

They smile and each offer a halfhearted laugh.

Cara means it, and Suzette obviously appreciates the sentiment, but she feels like it has left them without anything more to say. She hears Teddy's footsteps coming back up the hall and remembers something. "I brought some pictures I want to show you, get your opinion on . . ." She goes to her purse and pulls out the folder with a few of Amelia's drawings, the two she had kept and a few others that Olivia had given back to her, saying, "You keep some of these. I want other people to remember Amelia, too." Cara wants to get to know this girl, understand her better, and maybe Suzette, with an artist's eye, can help. She hands them over, and Suzette looks through a few. "My God, did Adam do these?"

"No. Amelia. The girl who—"

Suzette nods, and keeps looking. "Wow, how old was she?"

"Ten."

Suzette shakes her head. "Remarkable." She begins studying each one slowly, as Cara watches, waiting for Suzette to get to the one of her. Maybe this is why she's brought them—to see if Suzette will recognize the sad portrait faster than Cara did. Behind her, the door opens and Teddy steps in. "We should get going, Cara. School will be letting out soon."

"In a minute," Cara says. She wants Suzette to go faster, get to the ones on the bottom. She doesn't even care about the one of her anymore, she wants her to see the portraits of Adam. *There he is,* she'll say quietly. *There's our baby.*

When she gets to the one of Cara, it's clear right away that she does recognize it. She stops, looks up at Cara and back down at the picture. She stays on it for so long that Cara begins to worry it was a mistake to bring these; this picture reveals too much about her life. She can tell

Suzette that she's fine, that she and Adam are doing well, moving along with their lives, but Suzette has only to look at this and see for herself that it's only half true. For a long time, they stand there, with Teddy now looking on, and then Suzette surprises her: she says nothing, but she reaches out and takes Cara's hand. Maybe this picture has done it, has told her as much as she needs to know to even the balance between them—Suzette's had her struggles, and so has Cara.

Cara wants to say something, but the moment passes. Suzette moves on to the next picture and the next, until she stops again on one of an old woman with curly hair and exaggerated lines on her face. "Oh my God," Suzette whispers, and Cara leans closer to see what has struck her about this one. It's not anyone Cara recognizes. She looks angry and unsettled, as if this is the only emotion the girl knew how to draw. "These are just very good," Suzette says, shaking her head. And that's all.

Driving home with Teddy, Cara studies his profile from the passenger seat. She thinks about the little boy she remembers him being—how he lived for Suzette's attention, how some afternoons Cara would come over and find them curled on the sofa reading Dr. Seuss books. It's never occurred to Cara before how watching Suzette mother another from the age of twelve might have shaped her. All their lives, Suzette seemed older than their peers, wiser and more mature, because she cared nothing about her own social standing: she had this at home, a boy who depended on her completely. At the time, Cara complained about all that it took away—they hardly went shopping, they rarely went out—but somewhere she must have registered everything it gave to Suzette: The strength to care little about smaller matters, the confidence to make her own decisions. Of course, it was also a complicated blessing. Suzette probably didn't go away to college because she didn't want to leave Teddy. Moving out to live with Cara, she fell apart away from him. Now he is caring for her in a life that must look to other people like a limited

and sad one, but is it? Or is it something else entirely—closer to the life
Cara has had: attending to the needs of another, so delicate and so great
there are times Cara thinks no one who hasn't done this can know how it
feels, how sacrifice rewards itself, how large and consuming this kind of
love can be. Sometimes she thinks: *This is more than most parents are lucky
enough to have.*

She stares at Teddy's face, inscrutable and distant, and wishes it was
possible to ask.

At the park, Morgan expects to find someone he recognizes: maybe a fellow group member or another school wallflower who's been lurking in
the same shadowy corners as he has for the last three months. Someone
who's listened in on the conversations of people who don't even see that
he's there. He isn't afraid until he walks up the street and sees, in the distance, a girl he recognizes: Fiona, the black-haired, braceleted girl he had
once talked to outside of Marianne's office. Surely, this is a coincidence
or a mistake, he thinks, until she walks up to him and says, "I thought it
might be you."

How is this possible?

"I use that bathroom sometimes," she says, matter-of-factly. "No one
ever goes in. No one cares. I can't deal with the girls' bathrooms. You
should go in one, you'll know what I mean."

Morgan doesn't want to think about girls' bathrooms or talk about
them, either. "What do you know about Amelia?"

"It's not Amelia I know about, it's Chris. He's on my bus." She stares
at him, twisting a piece of her hair, as if now that she's here, she's not
sure she wants to say anything.

Morgan nods. "And?"

"The day after the murder Chris sat in front of me and started saying all this stuff about how he hopes people realize how bad it can get, that people can die from bullying."

"Like bullies killed her?"

"That's what I thought, but then yesterday on the bus, he told me it was all over, he wasn't going to go to school anymore, that he was going to go to the police and turn himself in."

"For what?"

"He said he was the reason Amelia was dead, and he couldn't live with the guilt anymore."

Wow, Morgan thinks. This is extremely interesting and he's an extremely good detective to have gotten to the bottom of this. "So Chris killed her?"

"He said no, but that he was responsible." Her voice begins to waver a bit, and Morgan steps back. He has seen her cry once; he certainly doesn't want to see it again.

"You don't have to cry," he says more abruptly than he means to, and suddenly it's too late, the tears are there again, rolling down her cheeks.

"He was trying to tell me something more. He was trying to talk to me and I cut him off because I didn't want people on the bus to think we were friends. I told him I had to do my homework. Now maybe he's dead and it's my fault because I was so mean to him."

Morgan wonders: if he died, how many people would cry when they remembered how badly they'd treated him? For now, he offers this: "You can hope maybe he's not dead. If he isn't, I think you should tell him you're sorry and offer to sit next to him on the bus. For like a week. That would be good."

Fiona looks up at him and wipes at the tears with the back of her hand. "Maybe you're right."

Afterward, Morgan walks away and marvels at what he has learned: Chris is involved in some way, or at least feels responsible for Amelia's death, and also this—sometimes people feel bad afterward for being mean.

At home, Cara thinks about Kevin and everything Suzette told her—that he loved her and also wanted to hurt her. There has been so much she hasn't seen, ways she has hurt people that she only recognizes now as she guards Adam against such pain. How can she blame Kevin? She went to great lengths to befriend him, to make tapes for him, then dropped the friendship once it gathered the weight of expectation. She thinks about him being in a wheelchair, and the oddity that he didn't tell her himself, that he's kept certain secrets for reasons she doesn't understand.

Of course, it occurs to her: so has she.

If an impartial outsider looked at their lives, weighed the sins of omission, it's likely that Cara would be found at far graver fault. As she waits for Adam's school bus, she can't shake the uneasiness her visit with Suzette has left her with. It's such a sad picture to look back on, how each of them had approached adulthood and independence but then retreated into her own isolation. Without seeing each other for nine years, they have defined the outlines of each other's lives—as if having tried to connect and failed once, they both decided they would no longer try.

Cara wonders what would have happened to her friendship with Suzette if Kevin had never entered the picture. Surely for a time, Suzette had fallen in love with Kevin, with all his potential, and had seen what her presence in his life could help him achieve. She broke every tenet of her self-determined path: she attended college with him, made his success her goal, and—what happened? Did he tell her, *No, it's Cara I want,* or did she sense it gradually, with conversations that returned to winning some battle Cara never knew was taking place? Maybe—Cara hopes—she wasn't the central issue. She thinks of Suzette's words: *Sometimes he has dark periods . . . He disappears.* She's thought so little about the end of her friendship with Kevin and his disappearance; now that she does, it occurs to her that she'd seen glimmers of it coming. The week before she stopped by his work and saw him for the last time, they'd gone out to dinner and Kevin had gotten infuriated at a waiter who couldn't understand what he was trying to order. After trying twice, the waiter turned to Cara and asked distractedly, "What's he saying?"

"I'm sitting right here!" Kevin screamed. "And I'm saying *grilled chicken sandwich.*"

Though Cara understood, when Kevin got angry, his words got tangled in his mouth, grew more incomprehensible. It sounded like he was saying *girl chicka satchel.* Cara translated quietly, and the waiter disappeared, but that single outburst left Kevin breathless, choking down his water. "I'm sorry," he must have said three times as the red drained out of his face, and they searched for some topic to recover their evening with. Eventually they found one and all was fine until the waiter brought their food and laid each place before them saying, "Here you go, ma'am," and then, very pointedly to Kevin, "I'm sorry, sir."

Kevin huffed at the apology and instead of accepting, said gruffly, "Just watch yourself."

She remembers this moment, etched in her mind because even then she had had the thought: *He really holds on to grudges; he doesn't forgive easily.* Now, watching Adam get off the bus, it feels as if her heart is turning over in her chest. *Just watch yourself,* he said.

And then it's as if she's swimming through water, hearing and not hearing voices above her, knowing they are there, shouting something, the aural version of a smudge, a blur, words erased, and then she emerges out of water to perfect clarity—it's her mother, laughing, her father beside her, a grill in the distance, meat popping on it, all of it fine, except that it's not. Suddenly her heart freezes at the thought:

she knows who Adam is echoing. It's not an accent; it's a speech impediment, muscles lost, control gone, one side overcompensating another, a face at war with itself. It's Kevin's voice. He's been echoing Kevin.

In his mind, Morgan makes a list of things he needs to tell Cara about: (1) About the fire. (2) About Fiona. (3) About Chris, who may be responsible for Amelia's murder, but also might not.

"Oh, Morgan, I'm so glad you're here," Cara says when he gets there.

Something is obviously going on. There is an old lady and a policeman in the kitchen, and Cara is pulling on a jacket. "I have to go out for a little while, but Wendy is going to stay here." She points to the old woman, who holds up her hand. "I promise I won't be gone long. You guys can—" She stops for a second. "What can you do? Play games, I guess. Whatever you want. Adam's in the family room, there's food in the refrigerator. Are you hungry?"

He shakes his head, and her eyes settle on the suitcase still standing in the corner of the kitchen. "You brought your own food, right? You can eat that if you need to."

She is obviously nervous—three sets of eyes watching her—which makes Morgan feel surprisingly relaxed. What he needs to tell her can wait; in a minute, she'll be gone and he'll be alone with Adam in the family room, asking anything he wants. Maybe they'll play Boggle, or maybe he'll just ask if Adam has seen any boys with glasses in the woods carrying knives lately.

Cara has called over Wendy, the retired nurse and old family friend who lives next door and has, in a pinch, babysat for Adam in the past, though

Cara rarely calls on her, in part because she rarely needs a babysitter, but also because seeing Wendy—her mother's age and her mother's old friend—is always a little sad for both of them. Usually they can't make it through an evening without Wendy saying at some point, her eyes shining with tears, "She'd be so proud of you, Cara. Everything you've done. How Adam's doing. She'd be very proud." Cara loves hearing this, but can't bear the flood of emotion it precipitates in her chest: the terrible throat tightening, the fear that she, too, will break down and cry. Now, struggling to keep control of herself and everything she must do, she is all business and instructions with Wendy: dinner here, games in the family room, Morgan may eat whatever he wants.

She has asked Teddy to drive her over to Kevin's and stay in the car outside his house because there is no way of knowing what to expect. She has told Teddy (and herself) that it's possible he wasn't in the woods at all, that Adam is echoing his voice and his words because he saw him in some other situation. But by the time she knocks on his door, her fear has been swallowed by a rising tide of anger that leaves her voice shaking and thin when he opens the door and rolls back in surprise to see her standing there.

"I'm sorry I didn't call first, Kevin, but I have to ask if you've seen Adam or been with him anytime lately." There's no sense in exchanging pleasantries or saying hello when this is what she's come to ask him. She doesn't even want to look at him, doesn't want to take in what's different, what's the same. Instead, she stares at the wheelchair he sits in and the faded running shoes he's wearing.

"I was there," he finally says. "In the woods. Did he tell you?"

She wants to back out and run straight to Teddy's car, tell him to call Matt right away.

"Let me tell you what happened, Cara. Let me tell you the whole story before you do anything. I didn't kill that girl, if that's what you're

thinking. I didn't do anything, but for four days I've been trying to figure out what I should do, and finally I thought, *I'll tell Cara everything
and let her decide*. That's why I wanted to get together. I need you to
know exactly what happened."

Hearing this, she lets herself look up from the wheelchair, at his
face; she has gone so long without seeing him, she's forgotten the very
details she has lived with all these years—that his dark hair curls in
the same way around his ears, which also stick out just a fraction. His
eyelashes are the same as Adam's, the shape of his fingernails. She isn't
sure what to think of it—if he really looks beautiful, or if she just loves
the pieces of his face that she looks at every day. "Okay," she says.
"Tell me."

"I just wanted to meet him. That's all. I'd seen him once before,
about three years ago, at the library. He wandered away from you and
came right up to me. I saw what he looked like and I thought, *This is it,
she's going to come over and we're going to talk about this*. And then he
walked away. He knew you were looking for him, and I watched him
smile and hide between two stacks. You kept saying, 'Adam, this isn't
funny,' and then you'd laugh, and I wanted to say something, but it was
nice just watching you play the game."

She actually remembers the time he's talking about. She'd worked for
so long at teaching Adam hide-and-seek, had labored through so many
failed attempts, when she closed her eyes, counted, then opened them to
find him standing beside her, confused. On her hiding turns, she had to
be blatant—hide only her head under a pillow or stick two feet out from
under the table—or Adam would forget the game entirely and wander
over to his window. She remembers the library because it was the first
time she really couldn't find him. It's hard to wrap her mind around this:
that Kevin's been floating around, seeing them, knowing bits and pieces,
but not the whole story.

"I knew there was something wrong with him—that he didn't talk or something—but seeing you guys laughing, I thought, *They must be okay. They look okay.* It made me want to get to know him. That's all."

She doesn't want to think about this, that in denying Kevin his paternity she made some huge, irrevocable mistake. "Tell me what happened in the woods."

"I used to go out there and watch him. I could see him from the woods and I just liked watching the things he did. He always walked this yellow line first, back and forth, and then he'd go to the tires and sit inside. And I saw there was one girl this year who sought him out—Amelia. She'd find him in the tires and sit down next to him. One day that girl came out to the woods, like she knew I was there, waiting for someone to help. So I talked to her, got to know her a little bit, and she said she'd bring him out. We set the whole thing up, and they came, and for a while I just couldn't believe it: he's so beautiful, Cara. I'd only ever seen him close up that one time. I just—I didn't know what to say to him. I wanted to say, 'I think I'm your father,' but I was scared. I didn't know if he'd understand that. I kept thinking I should have had a present with me. Something to break the ice. That's what absent fathers do, they show up again with presents. I hadn't gotten ready like I should have. I kept trying to talk to him, and I couldn't get very far—"

Cara can picture this all too easily. In any situation where conversation is expected of him, Adam will wander away, avoid it if he possibly can.

"Then I looked up and saw that Amelia had found a knife on the ground. She held it up and I told her to give it to me, but she wouldn't. She saw that it was making me nervous, and I know it's terrible to say this, but the truth is, she was a weird little girl. She seemed like she was trying to play games or something. Then this guy walked up, wearing no shoes—pretty agitated. He kept saying 'What are you doing here?' I said, 'Nothing, we'll leave, it's fine,' and then he saw the knife and he said,

'What's that?' He was obviously very upset or disturbed, or something, so I said, " 'Give it back to the man.' "

Cara shakes her head. "That's what you *said*?"

"I keep going over it in my mind. I don't know what I was thinking. I wanted to deflect the tension; I thought the knife would be safer in his hands than a kid's. Obviously, I regretted it the minute I said it. Right away, I saw this was dangerous, so I tried to get to Adam first, make sure he stayed away. When I turned around, Amelia had given the guy the knife, and I knew, the way he was holding it, it wasn't his. He was turning it over in his hands, and she was standing a few inches away from him, and when I got closer, I could hear she was talking to him, asking him why his clothes were so dirty, why he had no shoes on."

"Oh God." Cara can hardly bear to hear this.

"I tried to get her to stop, Cara. I tried to get over to her, but when I finally did, it was too late. It just happened so fast."

"Why didn't you go to the police right away?"

His hands hang limp in his lap. Even in the gray, dim light of the entryway, she can see that he is crying. "I couldn't, Cara. What would they have said? I was trespassing on school grounds, soliciting juveniles. In my mind, I've kept thinking: *I finally meet Adam, and talk to him and if I go to the police, the next time I see him I'll be sitting in jail.* But now I've decided I have to do whatever's best for Adam. You tell me what to do. You decide."

She doesn't hesitate: "Go to the police, Kevin. I'll come with you. There's a detective there I like. He'll understand. I promise."

All day at school, June overheard every possible rumor about Chris—that he was dead, that he'd been kidnapped, that he'd run away and was living in a garbage can now. She listened carefully, as Marianne had told them to do, and in a whole day of conversation, there was only one thing she heard that had a ring of truth to it. It came late in the morning as she was trying to segue the group into reading time. "I know that kid. I've seem him out there before," Jimmy said.

June stopped, her hands full of workbooks she was handing out. "Where?"

"In the woods."

"You saw Chris Kolchak in the woods?"

"Yeah. It was weird. It was like he was talking to himself. Or crying or something."

"Was anyone with him?"

Jimmy thought about this, folded his lips up, and shook his head. "Nah, I don't think so."

"When?" she asked, even as she told herself, *Don't dwell on this, don't scare the other kids*.

"I don't know. Maybe a week ago."

She knew it was possible—that the kids played farther out on the field than they were technically supposed to. Something about the way Jimmy said it, and the way no one else in the room picked up on it except her, made her think it must be true. He wasn't trying to shock anyone, because he hadn't realized, apparently, that this might be important.

When she got home this afternoon, she'd put in a call to Teddy, and now she's waiting by her phone for him to call her back. She feels like this has been her last four evenings—waiting by the phone, worrying about him, saying very little when he finally comes over. It's as if love has reduced her to long wordless nights spent picturing the day he will be borne away from her, injured or killed, or simply taken in by a woman more suited than she is to being with a cop. June knows all the reasons she's not a good candidate: she worries excessively, she doesn't own an iron or any black shoe polish. There are women who are good at caring for these details—she met them last August, at the station picnic, where every other woman except her carried a baby in her arms. They were nice and interesting—some were cops, too, or had been for a while, all of them as committed to the job as they were to their men. "It's a little like marrying into the army," one of them had said, staring at June hard, to make sure she understood.

June doesn't know if this is what keeps them from discussing their future and moving in together, or if it's just Teddy and the duty he feels to take care of his sister. "She practically raised me," he's told her, to explain. "When I was six, my mother fell apart and Suzette did everything for me—cooked dinners, played games, read me books. I'm not crazy today pretty much because of her," he would say, cheerfully, perhaps not even recognizing the irony: *But do you see? She is.*

In any conversation about Suzette, he always insists this is a phase, something she will pass through and get out of in time. Only once, that June knows of, did Suzette try getting treatment for her agoraphobia. It involved behavioral retraining, and leaving the house in gradual increments. You don't go out and try to make it through the grocery store the first day. You drive halfway to the store, then turn around and come home. You don't set up failure, you reward yourself in small stages, first for walking ten feet from home, then twenty, then half a block. You train your nerves to exercise willpower, build up the muscles of calming thoughts. At the time, Teddy worked with her every day after he got off from his shifts. They'd go out late—eleven o'clock at night—and take a twenty-foot walk down the street. "Wouldn't she be less scared during the day?" June would ask.

"No. The night is good for her. She sees less. Too much light is one of the problems."

Back then, June had felt hopeful; one night they made it to the grocery store and bought strawberries as a reward. Then Suzette announced that she was no longer interested in going to this doctor or trying these trips. "My life is fine," she said. "I like it the way it is."

When Teddy finally calls, he tells June he won't be coming over tonight, that he needs to go home and be with his sister. She should expect this, she knows; he hasn't been home in days; Suzette needs him, too, and June has had more than her usual share of his time. She decides to skip telling him what Jimmy said today and concentrate on something far harder for her to say. "Teddy? There's something I want to tell you."

"Yes?"

She doesn't know where he is calling from, if he's alone in his car or at the station surrounded by people he can't talk in front of. For a week now, she's been perched on the edge of speaking her most guarded thoughts aloud to him. She has been in love before, certainly, has had her heart broken, more than once, but it's never felt quite this precarious, as if the drop will be greater, the fall worse somehow. "Ever since this business with Amelia, I keep thinking how important it is to tell people when you have a chance, what they mean, how important . . ." June, with her degrees, all the words in the world, stammers over the only ones she can find to say. "I care about you, Teddy. So much. I don't want you to get hurt."

Is this what she means?

Among all her fears about getting more involved with Teddy—that she'll lose interest in him, that he'll lose interest with her—there is also this: cops get hurt and they die. *It's like marrying into the army.*

"What are you talking about, June? Are you breaking up with me?"

"No!"

How has she tried to communicate one thing and accomplished the opposite? "Look—I've got to go . . . " he says and a second later, he's gone.

After Cara has spent the ride over in Teddy's car reassuring Kevin that Matt Lincoln will be sympathetic, he is nothing but officious and terse when they get to the station. In less than a minute, he's separated them into different interview rooms and now he sits across from Cara in narrow-eyed disbelief of the story she's told him.

"*When* was the last time you saw Kevin Barrows?"

"About four months before Adam was born."

"And you've never seen him since?"

"No."

"Any contact in any fashion? Phone calls? Letters? Anyone in your family have any contact with him?"

"Not that I was aware of."

"But presumably he's developed an interest in Adam because . . ."

"He believes he's Adam's father."

"Is that true?"

She takes a deep breath. "It's possible. I don't know for sure."

He shakes his head in a way that Cara has a hard time reading: Maybe Cara should have told him this sooner; maybe it's old-fashioned disapproval on his part, that after all these years, it's still possible to judge her for the unpardonable crime of once sleeping with two men in the same month. "You know, I have to believe that my decade-old sex life isn't the issue, here. The issue is that you have a witness—a perfectly cogent, verbal witness—saying that Busker Bob—Robert Phillips—is the guy. Whatever it is, Kevin has his own reason for not coming forward sooner, but four days late is better than never, right?"

Matt's obviously not going to back down. "It's not quite that easy, Cara. Number one, Phillips passed a polygraph test. Admittedly, these aren't one hundred percent reliable, but in this case, I feel like it's fairly significant. Number two, we've picked up his footprints about forty yards away from the crime scene, but there's nothing around them—no partials, nothing. Even if the guy took off his thongs and tiptoed up to the scene, crawled, got there on his *knees,* there should be *something,* and there's not. As far as we can tell, what he's told us is true: He never got closer than forty yards away. He says he heard a little girl singing when he played his flute, that's it."

"He's also been diagnosed with a mental illness, am I wrong?"

Matt holds up a flat hand. "I'll grant you. But we've also got Barrows telling us a story that has some problems to say the least. If the girl picked up the knife and handed it to Phillips, where is the knife now? Phillips had nowhere to hide something like that. We would have found it by now—it would have turned up in the woods, buried in a bush, or under some leaves."

"What does that have to do with Kevin's story?"

"The reason we can't find the knife is that it went home with someone."

She stares at him. "You think Kevin took the knife home with him? That's absurd." Even as she says this, she understands what he's getting at: Kevin's story doesn't hold up completely. He has painted a picture of himself in the woods, tongue-tied and awkward, saying too little or all the wrong things, so why would Adam have echoed words of anger? It's a question, certainly, but in her mind, not a major one, because she believes that if he's lied about the details of this story, its essence is true. His guilt is tied up to his own bad judgment: his being there at all, his contacting Adam without her permission. These aren't small matters, and she will certainly have to think a long time about whether Kevin can see Adam in the future, but this also isn't a matter for the police to make judgments on, and she feels hugely annoyed that an hour earlier, she was making great claims to Matt's sensitivity. If she could, she'd lean forward and tell him off: tell him that maybe he doesn't understand the nature of long and embroiled friendships, that people can affect each other without seeing one another. That they can undermine and hurt each other even if they also, in a fashion, love each other, too. And that these relationships, fraught as they are, produce actions that don't always follow logical paths.

The longer she sits here, the more certain she is that she's right. Whatever the holes in Kevin's story are, whatever he's too embarrassed to say, he was there out of love, acting in the driving force of its name. And what she can't get over—what kills her, really—is that it wasn't love for her that sent him sneaking around, on a mission of subterfuge. It was love for Adam.

"Kevin didn't kill her. I know him. He couldn't have. I'm sure of it."

He holds up a finger, as if to say, *Wait, one more thing.* "I'm assuming there's something Barrows probably hasn't told you." Cara stares at him and waits. "He probably hasn't told you that he's spent some time in jail."

Chris doesn't know how long he's been here. He knows he fell asleep and woke up. He knows it was dark for a while and then light again. He's eaten through all the food he brought, a backpack stuffed with fruit. He can't help himself, every time he gets nervous, hears a noise, imagines what might happen here, he returns to his backpack and eats some more. He's needed to go to the bathroom for about six hours now, but he doesn't want to try until he's finished with what he has to do. He's got his designs, his notebook propped open under a rock. For a while he thought this would be too hard for him, his arms weren't strong enough; he'd only brought what he could fit in his backpack, so he doesn't have a real shovel, only a garden trowel of his mother's.

He planned for this to take two hours.

That he's been here at least twenty-four is further proof that nothing works out for him the way it's supposed to.

But now it's okay. Now he's getting somewhere, crouched on the soles of his feet, hugging his knees as he stabs at the rocky ground. It's a beautiful hole, deep enough that it's an effort for him to get out, long enough that he can lie flat without touching any sides. These are the dimensions he needs. It must look like a coffin, he's decided, because that's what it will be.

Morgan didn't expect it would be this easy. With Cara gone, and a nervous old lady in her place, he can ask Adam anything he wants. He could even suggest going up to Adam's room, which he does. Wendy doesn't follow them. She isn't like Cara, who hardly lets Adam out of her sight. So far, he's asked Adam about a few of the names—Randall Im, Wilson Burnstein—and Adam has said nothing, just stared at him blankly. "How about a guy with glasses?" Morgan asks, and Adam blinks. Forget it, he decides.

He'll try something else.

Alone in Adam's room, he pokes around for a bit—Adam kneels on his bed, picks up a small blue blanket, and drapes it around his shoulders.

"So Adam," he says. "About this girl, Amelia?"

He hears footsteps on the stairs. He'll have to act fast, then he thinks of something else. He kicks the door shut and the footsteps stop.

Cara has to leave Kevin at the police station, she has no choice. She doesn't believe what Matt is suggesting, that Kevin might be guilty, but she can't stay any longer to argue her point. It's nearly six o'clock and

Adam will need her; he'll want dinner soon, and his usual routine, especially after this unprecedented length of time with another child.

She isn't allowed to see Kevin or say good-bye, so she asks a station secretary to call his mother, tell her where he is and what's going on. On the drive home with an officer she's never met before, she wonders for the first time: Where *is* Kevin's mother? She remembers Suzette, in the flush of discussing her friendship with Kevin, talking as frequently about his mother as she did about him. *I don't think she has so many problems. At least she talks about them. At least she's honest.* In all these years, Cara has thought very little about those months before she first became pregnant, when Suzette came alive again with stories to tell, about Kevin and his mother. She realizes now that she never believed his mother was the patient. That whole time, all those stories, she assumed Kevin was the patient, volunteering with children who were in the hospital. She assumed this because it fit the picture of Kevin, forever in her head, lying in bed, whispering: "My body is finally falling apart." Kevin was the weak link, his mother the steely rod anchoring him to life, pulling him back, time and again. How could the woman Cara remembers, with her lipstick and curlers, her gaze fixed so steadily on the face of her fragile son, have allowed herself a breakdown?

She never knew the answer to this. Her brief adult friendship with Kevin had presumed that Suzette had met neither one of them at the hospital, that everyone was fine, except of course Suzette. When she understood that the truth was far more complicated, steeped in countless lies that weren't Suzette's at all, she was a month away from giving birth, which made it possible to say to herself: *I won't think about this now, I'll think about it later.*

And then she saw a different way out. Kevin might be Adam's father, but he also might not be. She could decide for herself not to decide.

Make true what she had said to her parents: *It doesn't matter who the father is. It's not important.* She kept it up steadfastly through prenatal visits, through hospital admissions, through birth certificate application forms. *Father: Unknown,* she wrote each time. Toward the end, people began to question her more; in the hospital she got assigned a social worker who told her, five hours after she'd delivered Adam, that there were men who sued former girlfriends for access to the children they'd never been told they had.

"No, no," Cara said, staring down at the baby in her arms, already serious, brow already furrowed in doubt about this business of leaving the womb. "That won't be the case here."

"Look," the woman finally said. "Any way you want to cut your cake, you can. I'm not going to tell you how to live your life when I don't know you from Eve. But every book you read, every study says, a kid who knows his father is a more grounded, healthier kid. You hear what I'm saying? I'm not talking the guy has to be a zoo dad or what have you. I'm saying knowing is better than not knowing. A name on that birth certificate is whole lot better than no name."

Even in the face of this large, persuasive woman's obvious logic, she didn't cave in. She simply said, "It'll be okay. In this case, he'll be okay. I promise."

In all this time, she's never doubted this decision, or the certainty she made it with. Three years later, she sat through neurologist appointments, with their battery of genetic questions, and didn't doubt herself. She understood that a named father wouldn't change what was happening; that Adam's brain, his stalled development, had nothing to do with missing a father.

She arrives home to find Morgan and Adam perfectly content, sitting at the dining room table playing Sorry. She watches for a while, knowing the logistics of this game are too complicated for Adam, though he seems happy enough to let Morgan move his piece while he rolls the dice and says "Sorr-eee," each time.

"Is everyone here okay?" she asks Wendy, who is sitting on the sofa.

"I think we're fine. Everyone wanted hot dogs for dinner, so that's what they ate."

She turns back to the boys. Adam is kneeling on his chair, leaning forward over folded arms so his nose can hover a few inches above something that has caught his interest on the board.

"Seven," he says, studying the dice, his chin furrowed in concentration.

Morgan looks closer. "Eight actually. Five plus three is eight."

Cara smiles. Rain Man, he's not.

"Oh yeah. Eight, eight, eight, gate."

"You want to move, or you want me to move for you?"

"Move for you, move for you," he giggles, and now it's clear what's caught Adam's interest, what he's loving about this game: the knocking sound Morgan makes moving the piece forward. Click, click, click, click, click. Adam is helpless with laughter. Cara laughs, too, catches Wendy's eye. She smiles and nods. "They're fine, really."

Later, Morgan agrees to watch an opera with Adam, but five minutes into it, he wanders out of the family room and finds Cara cleaning up in the kitchen. She turns and smiles. "A little bored with opera?"

"Yeah." He shakes his head. "It's like all in a different language or something."

"It *is* a different language. It's German."

"Oh. I don't know German."

"Neither does Adam."

"So why does he like it?"

She shrugs. Though she's tried, she doesn't really understand it herself. She has sat with him through countless opera videos and they all remain a mystery to her—people flinging their arms, chins quivering under heavy wigs. When he watches, she usually sits beside him, trying to piece together a plot he never cares about anyway. "These two either love each other, or else she's his mother, I can't tell which," she'll say to Adam, who will beg, with his eyes, for her to stop talking.

"So there's something I wanted to talk to you about," Morgan says.

"Okay." She dries her hands, and turns around to face him.

Morgan speaks quickly, staring at the ground. "The first thing is, I started a fire on my mother's land. Well, not her land, but the land she's been trying to save. Now it's all gone, the beavers and salamanders, everything is dead."

Cara widens her eyes. She remembers the fire, three weeks ago maybe. The papers were full of it—pictures of firefighters bent over beside the ash-covered ground and blackened tree skeletons. Arson was suspected, but couldn't be proved. "On purpose?"

"Not exactly. But it wasn't exactly an accident, either."

What does this *mean*? What sort of boy has she let into their lives?

"I never meant for it to happen the way it did. I'm going to make up for it."

"How?"

"I'm going to solve this murder. I'm going to figure out who did it and then no one will be mad at me anymore."

"That's why you've been coming here? To solve the murder?"

He nods. "Yeah. I mean. Yeah."

"You thought Adam might tell you what he hasn't told the police or me?"

"He might. You never know."

Cara is surprised by how quickly and completely anger sweeps through. She has spent all day responding reasonably to shocking revelations and now, at last, this one has pushed her over the edge. "Adam *likes* you, Morgan."

He doesn't seem to hear. "If I solve the murder, then no one will think about the fire anymore. They'll just think I'm great. My mom won't be mad. Neither will Marianne, or the police officer, or the judge. There's a judge, I guess, who decides my punishment."

"Adam has never had a friend before. For whatever reason, he likes you, Morgan. He's happy when you're here, he says your name, he wants to spend time with you. That's all very different for Adam. If you don't feel like you can be a real friend to him, I don't think you should stay here tonight. I think you should leave." As she says these words, her breath goes shallow. Why is she forcing the issue when she could just as easily swallow her pride, tell herself it doesn't matter, what matters is getting through this, Adam waking up tomorrow with a smile on his face, believing he's had his first sleepover? She knows mothers who all but bribe kids to come for playdates, so why is she suddenly insisting on sincerity?

"You want me to leave?"

She takes a deep breath. "No, I don't. It's been a long day. I'm feeling defensive."

"Because maybe I should. I'm starting to think my mom might be worried."

She stares at him. "Wait a minute. Your mother doesn't know where you are?"

She calls Wendy back over, explains what is going on: that there's been a change of plans: she's running Morgan home. In the car, he surprises her. For a while they drive in silence and then, out of nowhere, he asks: "So who's Adam's dad? Some guy, right?"

"Right," she says carefully. "Adam doesn't see him."

"Yeah, my dad blows me off, too, sometimes."

"He didn't blow us off, Morgan. When I found out I was pregnant, I knew I wanted a baby, so I decided to have him by myself."

"See, I don't get that. Why would people want this thing that ruins your life?"

She knows she shouldn't be angry at Morgan, but she can't help herself. "It doesn't ruin your life, Morgan," she says curtly. "I don't know where you'd get that idea."

"I don't know. I think maybe it ruined my mother's life."

As she pulls the car into the driveway, the screen door opens, and a silhouetted figure leans out of the house. "Please say that's you, Morgan."

He opens the car door. "It's me, Mom."

Cara watches him walk up to the porch, watches the two figures stand there for a full minute without touching. Cara can't hear what they say but stays in the driveway as long as she can—until one figure steps aside, lets the other walk in first and then follow.

Frankly, Morgan is surprised. He knew his mother would be angry, that she'd probably lose the cool she's kept since finding out about the fire, but unless he's mistaken, it looks like she's been crying, too. "I can't bear this, Morgan. I came home today and you weren't here and I thought you were dead."

They are seated side by side on the sofa, and she's leaning forward, her head in her hands. He can't tell what she's doing, so he leans forward to peek in between her fingers. "Are you crying, Mom?" he whispers.

"Jesus, Morgan."

"I'm just asking."

"I know I'm not a perfect mother. I know that. I know you wish your life was different and you think you need these touchy-feely groups I can't stand. You don't need to burn down any more wetlands to tell me not to push my opinions on you anymore. I see it. I've learned my lesson. I just keep thinking, *My God, is he going to die to prove his point?* Are you going to get yourself killed and then I'll finally see—yes, you're your own person. Oh God, Morgan." She never talks this way. Ever. She raises her voice about water pollution levels and air quality, not him. Now he can see: she *is* crying. He's never seen this before, never in all his life has he seen his mother cry. "I keep thinking, *What would I do if you died?*"

"Are you serious?" he says. Obviously she must be, but he's not entirely sure.

She nods, takes a deep breath. "Oh, Morgan." She's done now. Whatever mood swept over her is gone. Her hands are down, splayed over her knees like a benched basketball player. She shakes her head. "I'm all right."

"Okay," he says. "Are you *sure*?"

Though the tears scared him, he wants to go back, touch something that might produce them again. He has spent his life crying too much, too often, tears shed in the offices of guidance counselors and principals who could only ever think of one thing to do: call his mother on the phone. "Because it's not like I want to die or anything."

"What *do* you want?"

"New shoes, I guess. Friends, maybe."

"Is that really so important?"

"I guess so, yeah."

"I don't have any friends."

"I know, Mom."

"I have you. That's it."

"I know."

"I'm not saying that should be enough for you. I'm just saying that's what I have. You're what I have. You're my whole life." One tear leaks down her cheek, travels to the corner of her mouth, and stops. "That's it."

"I know, Mom," he says, though he wonders if he ever realized it before now.

All night, June has been watching the local news that is covering the search for Chris nonstop. Volunteers have come out of the woodwork, dozens of them, to search the five-mile radius surrounding Chris's apartment, an effort that is slowed down, slightly, by two bodies of water—a duck pond beside his condo complex, and Lister Lake, a mile away, where divers have been working all day and now, into the night. Chris's mother has reappeared beside the lake to weep once again on camera. "My Chris *hates* water—he's terrified of it. He won't go near it."

June wants Teddy to call back so she can tell him what's more important than her feelings at this point: that Chris was seen once in the woods, talking to himself, possibly crying. It means he's gone there before, that it's a place he seeks some kind of escape to. It's also not in the radius they're searching.

"If he hates water, that means he hasn't gone near it," she says, realizing too late that she's talking out loud, to a television set. She feels like she's losing her mind. She needs to get hold of Teddy again, tell him this tip about Chris. Maybe it's nothing, or maybe it will be the break that they need. Finally she breaks down and calls his apartment and, to her surprise, gets Suzette, who says she hasn't heard from him since the afternoon.

"He said he was going home to talk to you."

"Is that what he said?" Suzette's voice sounds shaky, as if she, too, has been waiting for a call all day.

"Yes. He definitely said he was going home." He'd been working a straight twenty-four-hour shift, after which they're required to go home—go someplace—and get some sleep. So where is he?

Suddenly it's clear, though, that this isn't what's worrying Suzette. "June, can I get your help? There's a person I need to talk to and I can't get there by myself."

"You want me to take you somewhere?" She can hardly believe it.

"Yes. I do."

All this time, June can only remember being alone with Suzette the one time when she told her she was glad she wasn't a waitress and twenty-two. "Are you sure?"

"I'm thinking about this boy, Chris. It's someone who might know something; she might know what happened to him."

"I'll be right over."

When she hangs up, she looks at the TV and knows suddenly where Teddy must be. Even though he's off duty, officially encouraged to get some sleep, he is with the search teams looking for Chris. He's combing the ponds, the abandoned fields, looking for anything—a sock, a shoe, an earpiece from some eyeglasses—because now she is beginning to understand what this job means. No police officer will go to sleep, or go home, or do anything else, with a child in his town still missing.

It's dark when June arrives. She knows Teddy won't appreciate her getting involved; he believes Suzette's condition is something other people can't understand, that only he knows his sister and how fragile she is. As June drives up to their apartment, though, Suzette stands out front looking fine. "Thank you for doing this, June. I couldn't ask anyone else. I was going to phone a taxi and then you called." June remembers Teddy describing their late-night walks—how her body froze up two blocks from home and she couldn't walk anymore. Now she was going to call a taxi, venture out on her own? "What's this about?" she says, watching Suzette carefully.

"An old friend of mine came by today and brought some pictures that

Amelia had drawn. I recognized one. I think it means something. I need to find out."

"*My* Amelia?"

Suzette blinks, seems to have no idea what June is saying.

"Amelia was my student."

Suzette shakes her head. "Really? You *knew* her?"

Has Teddy told her nothing? "Yes."

"Then maybe you would have an answer to this—how did she know Evelyn Barrows?"

As she drives home from Morgan's, it occurs to Cara that she could swing by Kevin's to see if he's back from the station yet. When she does, the house is dark, but a car is in the driveway that she doesn't remember seeing before. This must be his mother's car; if she's at home, he must be, too, she thinks, ringing the doorbell. Standing on the porch, she remembers the last time she saw Kevin's mother, in his hospital room where he almost died. She remembers her face, lips folded in apprehension, her silence, and the way she refused to fill in the awkward gaps of conversation, to make the visit easier or see it as something relatively simple: two girls coming to cheer Kevin up. To her, it obviously wasn't; there was far more to fear than Cara could even recognize at the time. Now she does. She thinks about the argument she's just had with Morgan, this instinct to protect Adam at any cost. What would she do now if Amelia, with her blond hair and blue eyes, showed up on their doorstep asking for Adam?

When the door finally opens, Cara hardly recognizes the person in front of her. She remembers a woman who came to school wearing curlers and lipstick, as if her face was divided, one half readying for an evening out, the other half all set. She was never beautiful, but there had always been something striking—or maybe just noticeable—about her. She was the first woman Cara ever saw smoking an ultrathin cigarette; from far away it looked like she was dragging on a knitting needle. Now it looks like she has been doing little else for the last fifteen years. Her skin is mottled, leathery, and wrinkled, her eyes shadowed in dark circles as if she hasn't slept in days, though she is wearing a nightgown. "Mrs. Barrows?"

"What are you doing here?"

She didn't know if Kevin's mother would remember her. Now it's obvious: yes, she does. "Can I come in?"

Mrs. Barrows seems to need a moment to think this over. "I suppose," she finally says, and then, before Cara can begin any of the vague speeches she's planned to deliver—*I had to take him to the police; in the long run this will be better, you'll see*—the woman whispers, "Will you excuse me for a minute," and disappears. Cara stands in the entryway, and, unsure what else to do, closes the door behind her. Her first time here, she had stayed outside, too focused on Kevin and what he was saying to go in and look around, but now that she does, she can hardly believe how dingy the place is. In the corner there's a Hefty bag of garbage that has been sitting there long enough to have leaked a coagulated puddle onto the floor. A cardboard box in the far corner seems to be the repository of mail, but it's not the week's worth that Cara lets pile up on her table—this is an avalanche, six months or more of unopened envelopes and grocery store circulars.

She steps inside farther, her senses alive. How did she not notice the musty smell her first time here? She peeks into the kitchen, which looks like a flashback frozen from a time of bad decorating ideas: the floor is carpeted, the counter covered in linoleum tiles held in place by a row of ancient appliances: a toaster, a blender, a rusting silver bread box. Nailed to one wall is a wood-stained box holding a miniature decoupage scene of a kitchen. Cara tries to imagine Kevin's mother in better days, constructing this box, which looks eerily like a small coffin. After a few minutes, she wonders if it's possible to leave without saying anything more, slip back outside, shutting the door soundlessly behind her.

Just as she decides she will let herself do this—it's been too long a day, this house is too sad for her to think about the lives of its inhabitants—she hears a sound in the foyer. A key turning in the lock on the front door.

She spins around to see Mrs. Barrows in the kitchen doorway. Cara had assumed she was getting dressed, putting on her face, attending to the hair that Cara remembers always being styled or in the process, but now she stands before her unchanged, except that over her nightgown she wears a bathrobe. "Have they arrested Kevin yet?"

Cara's breath goes shallow. "No. They're not going to. He hasn't done anything wrong."

She hears this and nods carefully. "That's right. He hasn't. That's what's important. Why don't you come into the living room? There's something I want to show you."

Cara follows her into the living room, which is in slightly better shape than the other rooms she's seen, but not by much. The furniture is still intact, if twenty years old, but the far wall of the room has been used for miscellaneous storage—a pair of skis lies on the floor, an old guitar leans against the wall, a pile of dresses still on their hangers lies across a cardboard box that seems, from the glimpse inside that Cara gets, to be filled with more mail.

"Come sit, I want to show you something." She walks over to the bookshelf and pulls out a stack of photo albums. "I've got some pictures here. You'll like them. The top three are Glenn, my older boy, the bottom three are Kevin."

Cara stares at her, then turns back to the front door. *Is she serious?* "I wish I could, Mrs. Barrows, but I can't stay too long. I have a little boy waiting for me at home. I just wanted to check in and see if you'd heard from Kevin."

The woman sits down on the sofa, opens the top photo album. "Oh, don't go. Look at my pictures for a minute." She opens the book and pats the sofa beside her. "Please."

Cara walks over and sits down beside her.

"This is Kevin's book. It starts after the accident." She opens it to a montage of gory hospital photos: Kevin, eleven years old and lying in bed, his face and head covered in bandages stained in quilted patches of pale yellow and orange disinfectant. One picture, a close-up, is all pillow and bandages, the only recognizable feature, Kevin's lips, cracked with dried blood. Silently, his mother touches each picture and then turns the page. "This is after the bandages came off."

Cara forces herself to look, though the second page is, if anything, grislier than the first. Kevin's head is shaved, a line of black staples runs a train track across his scalp. His face is misshapen, both sunken and swollen, colored in shades of yellow and burgundy. "Why are you showing me these?"

Mrs. Barrows lifts her eyebrows in surprise. "I don't think they're so awful, do you? Look at where he was and look at him now. He's beautiful, isn't he? You think he's beautiful, don't you?"

It's terrifying to sit here, to see what a lifetime of caretaking can do. Mrs. Barrows looks like a shadow of the woman Cara remembers—erased of all color, even her hair is a strange silver-flesh-gray, a mane of curls that's no color at all. Sitting beside her, so close, Cara notices something strange: her hair has shifted—the part in her tangled curls sits a little closer to one ear. *My God,* she thinks, *she's wearing a wig.*

The woman nods and turns another page to photos that chronicle

Kevin's therapy: Kevin standing between two parallel bars, two aides on either side; Kevin on a floor mat wearing matching green sweatpants and sweatshirt, one leg lifted to touch the flat, hovering hand of a therapist. More pages, more pictures, many now with Kevin's mother in the background. Though Kevin sometimes does, she never looks at the camera, never takes her eyes off of whatever Kevin is doing, even if it is only sitting and smiling. For Cara, the pictures are unsettlingly familiar. She has books like this at home because she, too, has chronicled the minutiae of Adam's life. His first five years are pasted laboriously into a dozen different scrapbooks they used to bring to speech therapy because photographs were so crucial in teaching Adam the components of his own life: *Here's your bedroom, your kitchen, your grandparents.* She still remembers this: the first time he said *Mom,* he was pointing to a picture.

As the woman turns the pages, touching each image—Kevin drinking from a cup held by a nurse, Kevin asleep in a wheelchair—Cara recognizes more details: the same fine-motor pegboard she used with Adam; the animal lacing cards she used to make him sew. In one picture, Kevin even looks the same age as Adam now, looks exactly like him, staring into a mirror on a speech therapist's table, making his mouth an *O.*

"I wanted to remember all of this," Mrs. Barrows says, as they near the end. "As hard as it was, I knew I'd look back on it as the best thing I'd ever done. And it is." She nods with great certainty. "I did as much as I could. I stopped at nothing. Of course now Kevin is so angry with me he doesn't remember any of this."

Cara gets up; she can't sit any longer beside this woman, can't look at these pictures for another minute. "Why is he angry with you?"

"He thinks I do too much for him. But I have to. He doesn't realize. He wants to feel independent. He says, 'Mom, I need to take care of myself.' Meanwhile, when's the last time he's been inside a grocery store? Ask him that."

Cara moves around to the back of the sofa. She doesn't know what to say or where to stand. "A long time, I bet."

"Years. That's all I'll say. Years. All I've done is tried to ensure that he has the best life possible."

"You've done a good job," Cara says, because she wants to get out of here, get home to Adam, and she feels like she will need to earn this sad woman's permission before she'll be allowed to leave this house. "You've been a good mother . . ." she says and then looks down to see, beneath the window, leaning against the wall, several flattened sheets of muddy cardboard, crisscrossed by tire prints. "What are these?" she asks, pointing to them.

"Oh those," Mrs. Barrows looks and waves a hand. "We have to use those or Kevin's chair will get stuck in the mud."

"Where?"

"Outdoors. Sometimes he takes these walks in the woods."

Cara looks over at her; in the light of the lamp beside her, her hair looks horribly artificial, no better than a doll's. Does she realize what she's saying? She thinks of Matt's words—*You collect two hundred cigarette butts, five of them with lipstick, what does that tell you? Someone wearing lipstick has been there, smoking.* Cara comes back around the sofa and stands in front of the woman. "Were you with him, Mrs. Barrows? Did you help Kevin get out to the woods?"

"He wanted to see the boy. He tried to go by himself, and finally I said, 'Kevin, let me help you.' You'll soon figure this out—there's not much a mother can do after a while, but I can help him get where he needs to be."

Cara thinks of more things Matt has said: *The guy must have prepped somehow, planned what he was doing, really quite meticulously.* This cardboard could explain why there were so few footprints. "So you were there when it happened?"

"Kevin has done nothing wrong. *Nothing*. He's had a very hard life and he's asked very little of other people." She stares at Cara so there can be no mistake. "He's asked very little of you, and you've taken a lot. He's angry with me, but I only did what I had to. What any mother would do."

Why wouldn't Kevin have included this part? As long as he was admitting as much as he did, why wouldn't he also have said, *My mother was there. I needed her help?* She thinks of Suzette's words: *He wants you to think of him as nondisabled, mostly independent.* How sad that he would admit to so many things, but not that he still needs his mother.

"I've tried to protect him. All his life I've said, 'Choose your friends carefully.' You care about the wrong people, you'll only get hurt." She shakes her head and stands up. "You might have thought a little bit more about the impact of your actions on other people once in a while. I understand that I'm not supposed to blame you, but I'm sorry, I do."

Cara feels the air go out of her body. Mrs. Barrows's wig is so askew now it's hard to notice anything else, and Cara thinks of Adam, the one word he's found to describe his time in the woods—*hair*—and slowly, it dawns on her: What if Kevin's mother wasn't just a witness? What if she isn't just a sad figure, broken and crazed by a lifetime of tending to a boy who's never really recovered? What if she's the one who killed Amelia?

Cara starts to back out of the room. "I've done a lot of things wrong," Cara says.

"You certainly have."

"I took Kevin for granted. I was too focused on my child."

"That's right."

"I tried to build a circle around us. I wanted our life to be private. Just ours."

Mrs. Barrows shakes her head. "It doesn't work that way."

Cara's heart speeds up. Her palms turn cold and clammy. She needs to get herself out of here. "I need to go home," Cara says, working to keep her voice steady, to betray as little emotion as possible. She moves sideways, away from the window, afraid to turn her back to the woman which perhaps is a mistake. It confirms what they both know. Now there's no need for the shred of pretense. "I'll kill you if you leave," she says.

How? She wonders. Is the knife in her bathrobe? Is this tiny woman going to come lunging at her? For a second, this ludicrous image energizes Cara. She's not a little girl taken by surprise; she can fight this woman off and save herself, if only she can find a way out of this house.

"You can't go now. I have a knife."

Cara doesn't move. "If you kill me, Mrs. Barrows, how will that help Kevin?"

"I should have done it a long time ago."

"No," Cara says. The woman does indeed have a knife she's pulled out of her pocket. It is narrow, as thin as a steak knife, but much longer, and serrated. Cara remembers hearing one of the main things gleaned from Amelia's wound: the knife was serrated. "I know what you're thinking, and it's not the answer."

"You don't know what I'm thinking."

"I do. For the last five days, I've been lying awake every night, thinking about this girl who came into my son's life." Cara keeps her voice level, her words steady. "I was horrified that she'd been murdered, of course, but in some way I was glad she was gone, because it meant she couldn't make some choice down the line that would devastate Adam. Couldn't befriend him for a year and then decide, next year, to make fun of him on the playground." Cara can see that this is working. The woman's eyes are turned away, but Cara can see in her posture, her hands, that she is listening. "But now I'm starting to think maybe I was wrong. Maybe this girl wasn't a distraction, maybe she was a measure of success I couldn't see. Maybe Adam's friendship helped her in some way, and he understood that." She slows down now, to choose her words carefully. "I know that Kevin's friendship helped me. Even if we couldn't sustain it. Even if he made that choice—" She pauses to ensure the words are clear: *He made the choice*. "I know that he loved me. I know his heart is good, that his intentions are loving. And he knows that mine are the same. And I think it's possible to feel sustained by certain kinds of love even when you don't see that person. Knowing that Kevin is here, with us, watching over us, thinking about us, has sustained me. Don't ruin what's left of Kevin's future. He still has a chance. Don't ruin it, Mrs. Barrows."

Behind her, Cara hears a car pull into the driveway.

"He's not entirely innocent, you know."

There are footsteps on the gravel walk, coming up to the house. She hears a female voice, not Kevin as she expected. Cara looks up. "What do you mean?"

Cara takes a step into the entryway. In the corner of her eye, she can see the kitchen, a red painted door on the far wall. There's a clear path to the door, no chairs or table blocking the way. The question is whether it's locked, and how hard it will be to find her way from the dark, fenced-in backyard to her car. She will need to make a run for it, trusting that this woman's reflexes are slow, her experience with a knife marginal.

"Ask him yourself. Ask him why it's taken him nine years to get in touch with you. Ask him if he knows anything about your poor parents."

Cara flies then, jerking around so fast her shoulder hits the doorway with a smack that momentarily sends her reeling off course, then surging toward the back door. Behind her, there's movement, a scrambling, objects falling to the floor.

Miraculously, when she gets to it, Cara finds the door open and a second later, she's outside, enveloped by darkness and cold night air. She jumps off the porch and crouches into the cover of bushes beside the house to wait.

Behind her she hears someone ring the front door bell, open the door, and then call out, in a familiar voice: "Evelyn, it's me."

From her spot in the bushes, Cara creeps closer to the window. She doesn't understand, doesn't know how it's possible. She stands up to see what she can through the window: the back of Kevin's mother, standing in the doorway and, behind her, Suzette walking in, opening her arms, and saying, "I'm so sorry, sweetheart. Just tell me what happened."

June doesn't know if this is right or not, but Suzette has insisted that she drop her off. "I'll be fine. I promise you," she said, though she didn't look fine anymore. Her eyes darted from house to house, window to window; her hand shook slightly as she reached for the door. "I have to do this by myself. I'm asking you, please. Come back in an hour." In her voice, June heard a core of steel, a determination to do whatever she had to without assistance. She thought, *Maybe this will be a breakthrough, like she never had taking her two-block walks with Teddy.*

"Okay," she said. "I'll be back." Maybe this is a mistake or maybe it's what Suzette needs most: to be trusted, given a chance.

With an hour to kill, the only place June can think to go is the parking lot behind the school that overlooks the woods. She won't go hunting, won't do anything dangerous, but maybe she'll see if there's any sign of Chris. When she gets there, it's amazing: there are no other cars, no sign of life, but there in the woods, a light is flashing. It's a dim orange glow, a weak flashlight on the last of its batteries.

Before getting out of the car, June makes one last call to Teddy's cell phone and, miraculously, he answers. She's so relieved to hear his voice again, so happy he's alive and apparently fine, that she almost tells him she loves him right on the spot.

But of course that would be silly. What's important now is finding Chris, tracking down this light in the woods. She tells him where she is, what she's seen. "He's been out there before apparently, during school hours."

"All right. I'm coming over. Stay right where you are. Don't go in by yourself, okay?"

"Okay."

"Promise me."

In the distance, the light turns off, as if whoever's holding it has seen her car, or somehow heard this phone call. She gets out of the car and moves soundlessly across the field where she knows the older children sometimes play a complicated game of tag that, until Amelia's murder, supervising adults had allowed in a tacit agreement to choose some battles over others. No one, that she's heard, has ever mentioned this fact to the police, but she wonders if it isn't an important facet of what happened: that children had been allowed to extend their own boundaries.

At the edge of the wood, she steps in the direction she believes the light was coming from.

She hears a sound that no animal could make—a stick hitting dirt, with labored breathing behind it. As she moves into the grove of trees, a branch catches her shirt and she cries out in startled terror. Beneath a moonless sky, it's impossible to see anything but the branches directly in front of her face, so she moves by feel, inching forward, her hands in front of her, trying to make as little sound as possible. If the killer is out here, he won't have an easy time finding her, she tells herself, and creeps forward in the direction the sound was coming from. But what will she do if she does find danger? She has no protection, nothing on her that resembles a weapon. If someone lunged at her right now, she hardly knows what she would do except execute the vaguest plan of self-defense—a knee to the crotch, fingers to the eyeballs.

Except for the leaves beneath her feet, the only sound in the woods now seems to be coming from her own body—her heart pounding, blood rushing in her ears. Then she sees it again, a flash of yellow light. Out of the silence, she hears something high-pitched and, after a moment, realizes what it must be: a child crying.

She moves faster, ignoring the branches that snag at her clothes. Something tears her sleeve and she yanks it free, and only feels, a few seconds later, that it's scratched her, too. She touches her arm and feels a trickle of blood.

She finds him, finally, by nearly falling on top of him. In the fading glow of his dying flashlight, she can see the outline of the boy—the hunch of his shoulders, his shoes, the edge of his glasses—curled at the bottom of an oval-shaped hole, five feet long and several feet wide. He is so bent on his work digging this hole, he doesn't look up and see her standing over him. She levels her voice to a whisper and tries to calm her thundering heart: "Are you okay?"

It's amazing, really: he keeps stabbing at the dirt, doesn't even lift his head to see who she is, to realize he's being rescued right now.

"I'm digging a hole," he says.

From what she can tell, it's an extraordinary hole, a feat of persistence. "Why?"

"I can't tell you."

In the distance she sees the lights of Teddy's car pull into the parking lot. "Everyone's been looking for you, Chris. They're all worried about you. They think maybe you've been hurt or kidnapped."

"No, I had to do this."

There's a trick she has from her years of teaching, an intuitive strategy that sometimes works wonders and sometimes backfires: *Join them. Bend down. Look at the same thing they're looking at.* "Do you mind if I get in? See how deep it is?"

"Right now, eleven inches."

"Wow," she sits down, lets her feet dangle in. They can touch the bottom, but barely. "So you've been at this for a while?"

"All night. I didn't want to sleep, but I might have, for a little while." He is squatting on his feet, hugging his knees.

"Gosh. Quite a project."

"If I didn't have to I wouldn't, believe me. It's not like I enjoy this kind of thing."

"Okay." She nods, and because this feels like an opening, she takes a risk: "Why did you have to do it?" She tries to make this sound casual, conversational, as if her next question might be what kind of music he likes.

"Because it was *my knife,* all right? The whole thing was *my fault.*"

"Oh," she nods. "You brought a knife to school?"

"I *had* to. I had no choice."

Behind her, she hears Teddy approaching. He's got a flashlight, a radio squawking. In a minute this will all be over, out of her hands. He'll have called for backup, alerted the throngs of searchers, and she'll be a hero for finding this boy, but she knows he will clam up the minute this begins. "Wait!" she calls loud enough for Chris to snap his head up, look at her for the first time, so she can see his face, covered in dirt except where his glasses are, making him look like a caught animal at the bottom of some terrifying shoe box.

"Why did you have to bring a knife to school?" she asks.

And he tells her the whole story, staring up, tears leaking muddy trails down his cheeks, so sad that she fears that even when Teddy slips up beside her, takes her hand in his, she will cry herself for the pain these children have endured, for the ways they have found to carry on.

. . .

Cara tries, but can't hear what they're talking about. Kevin's mother is angry, working herself into a rage, screaming at Suzette, who stays amazingly calm. She can only hear snippets of what they say: "I tried to call you—" "Where is he now?" "You don't have any choice, Evelyn."

She creeps around the side of the house until she finds a place from which she can hear better. "You need to go, Evelyn. Now. It will only get worse for him."

Mrs. Barrows is silent, seated in a chair, her head bent. Whatever she was yelling about is over. "We can call now, or we can wait for my brother's girlfriend to come back."

How extraordinary to watch Suzette move carefully around this woman. She touches her shoulder briefly, then moves away, picks up the knife that has dropped to the ground. Cara thinks of the old Suzette she remembers so well, carrying food to her mother, tapping lightly with a fingertip on her door. She's been good at this her whole life.

Suzette goes to the phone and picks it up. "I'm going to call and in a minute, they'll be here, and everything will be okay." She moves into the other room to make the call, and Cara watches Mrs. Barrows sit by herself, her head in her hands, as she breathes slowly, in and out.

When the patrol car comes, the driver turns off the lights halfway up the street. She can hear the radio when both doors open and two officers step out. She is paralyzed by the spectacle, unable to leave, as she watches Mrs. Barrows, still wearing her bathrobe, hands cuffed behind her, walk out to the car. It's an oddly slow drama, and also quiet; no words are spoken that she can hear, no sounds at all but the crackle of their radio. It's only a full minute after they've pulled out that she realizes Suzette didn't go with them, that she must still be inside, making no sound. She creeps around to the front door and peeks. There she is on the floor, the phone still in her hand: in the wake of the stress she didn't show a few minutes earlier, Suzette has fainted.

Once Chris starts talking, he apparently can't stop. He keeps going and going, telling June everything as they walk to the ambulance and ride to the hospital, where they are greeted by news cameras, doctors, police, and his parents. By the time he's settled into a room, he has told her the whole story, in large and small detail, and when she is finally alone with Teddy again, she tells him what he said: "Apparently he's been persecuted every morning at school for the last year and a half. It started innocuously enough, with bus-stop teasing, but built up from there. Eventually this group of boys—there were three of them, primarily— stole his glasses and broke them. From there, it escalated: two weeks ago, somebody urinated in his backpack, and last week he found a brown bag of *crap* in his locker."

"Jesus," Teddy says, shaking his head.

"He went to the authorities, tried to get these kids put on report, but it didn't do any good. They'd already been put on detention. The guidance counselor was involved. Apparently he was being told to try solving the problem himself. He was meant to take steps to avoid these guys, stay out of their way, not do anything to provoke them, as if this might all be *his* fault."

In the ambulance, Chris told her what precipitated the knife. "They said that somebody had offered to pay twenty-five dollars to break my arm and thirty dollars to break my leg."

"Who would have—" she started to ask, then stopped. The detail is so odd, she fears it must be true.

"I don't know. They wouldn't say who offered it. Apparently someone who hates me and has a lot of money to throw away."

She nodded her head to tell him, *Keep going*.

"So I knew they would do it. They'd already taken these scissors and cut bald patches in my hair. And another time, they poured gasoline on my shoes." He held out a fist, uncurled a finger for every infraction he'd endured. When he got to five, he curled it up again. "I had to bring a knife. I had to do something. I was trying to fight back."

June nodded, heard herself say, "It sounds like a good idea."

When June finally left Chris in his room, alone with his mother and father, she walked out beside Teddy and got into his police car. She had already been photographed and filmed, told she would be on the evening news. When asked to give a statement meant to reflect the euphoria of the moment—*He's fine! He's been found! He's with his parents now!*—she looked into the blinding white light of the camera and said, "I hope the children who are responsible for this know who they are and will come into their own justice very soon."

Now June sits alone beside Teddy, who has remained at her side, nearly silent through all of this. He offers what must feel, to him, like the best thing to say, "I had some trouble with bullies when I was younger. People made fun of me because I was odd and shy and my mother sometimes walked outside wearing her nightgown."

He has said so little about this part of his life before now that June isn't sure what to say. "What did you do?"

"My sister helped. Or at least she tried to. I still spent most of my childhood afraid of bullies. I remember in junior high, they used to make me eat the lit embers of cigarettes."

June stares at him. She can't help it; she's crying again. "Oh my God, that's terrible."

"It was. But you know what? I've never smoked a single cigarette. I could thank them for that." He shakes his head. "Kids survive. You'd be amazed what they go through and survive. He'll be okay."

She wants to tell him now how she feels, wants to tell him maybe they should do something more than just survive. "Earlier tonight, Teddy, I wanted to say something—"

"What?"

"That I love you, and I don't know why it's so hard for me to say it."

He takes her hand, pulls it into his lap, and spreads it over his knee. "Because it's hard. But I love you, too."

But there's more. For the first time in her life, she doesn't want to hold back. She wants to make a scene, make demands, say something absurd like, *You need to choose me, not your sister.* She wants him to feel what she feels—torn open by this. "I want us to have more." Her voice is tiny; it sounds as if a stranger is speaking. "I want us to live together."

And then it's as if a silence has engulfed them; words have left the car and only their hands can speak for them; he picks hers up, sandwiches it carefully between his, pressing her fingers, curling his palm into hers. "Yes," he finally whispers. "That sounds like a good idea."

As soon as she gets home, Cara tries to put together the pieces of everything that's happened, make sense of it in her mind. In the eerie silence after Mrs. Barrows was led away, Cara crawled inside the house and roused Suzette, who sat up and blinked as she looked around, trying to remember where she was. She was better soon enough, or at least able to move into the kitchen, where Cara got her a glass of water and pointed out the decoupage box on the wall. "Didn't we used to do things like that?" she said, and Suzette rolled her eyes, as if to say *Speak for yourself.* Cara desperately wanted to understand everything—*How was Suzette friends with Kevin's mother? How did she know to arrive just then?*—but she also wanted to find the common ground of their old friendship, remember the ways they used to log in the hours of their life together.

Eventually Suzette explained: Kevin had always tried to work; he was happier being busy, getting out of the house. But in the last few years it hadn't been easy and he'd been fired from a few jobs. When his settlement money ran out, he had to take a job he didn't much like in an office supply store a half-hour drive away. It was in Chester, near Suzette's apartment, and after dropping him off, his mother would stop in and visit Suzette. Sometimes she would stay a few hours, talking as Suzette worked. "For some reason, it didn't drive me crazy. I don't know why. I was fond of her, I guess. I always have been. I suppose because I always thought she was a good mother to Kevin. I always *admired* her—I really did."

Cara shook her head in disbelief. "Did she talk about going with Kevin to the woods?"

"No, never." She thought about it for a moment. "The thing is, she talked about you a lot. She was always a little obsessed with you. Even more than Kevin was, I think. It was her idea, years ago, that I should lie and tell you she was in the hospital, not Kevin. She wanted you to think that Kevin might have a few physical problems, but mostly he was fine."

"Why did it matter what I thought?"

"I don't know. She always wanted you to believe that Kevin had made a lot of progress."

In truth, Cara understood this impulse: she did the same thing with people who saw Adam infrequently—especially doctors who ran their assessment tests every other year. She would drill him for weeks ahead of time, try to guess the questions that might be asked, all so she could hear a lab-coated stranger say, "He's getting better." There were so few ways to measure success, one simply did this, chose arbitrary judges. She thought of Mrs. Barrows pulling out the scrapbook, insisting that Cara look and be reminded that it was a long, hard road. She knew already, knew the road well.

In the end, the conversation ran out of steam. Cara couldn't bring herself to say, *Tell me, really, what your life is like,* embarrassed at the thought of the limited answers she would get, and Suzette never asked anything about Adam, even the most basic questions like what grade he was in now, or what he liked to do. They filled the time as they never had when they were little girls, with talk of other people: Kevin, his mother, classmates they'd both long ago lost touch with. When the time came to leave because Teddy and June showed up at the door, they both seemed grateful for the reprieve from the conversation they were having such a hard time sustaining.

Now, she wishes she'd tried a little harder. Maybe she should have mentioned Matt Lincoln, seen if Suzette remembered him sitting with his sister in the cafeteria, which she probably would. She would remember odd details—that he wore a Def Leppard T-shirt or had clear braces, but she'd also remember what was important. "He was a nice kid," she'd say. "I remember that."

That night, after Cara has finally gotten Adam to sleep, she moves around the house, straightening up and trying to put Evelyn Barrows out of her mind, when the doorbell rings. She moves toward it tentatively; it's close to midnight, too late for visitors; it can't be an officer needing the bathroom, because for the first time in days, no police car is parked in front of their house. She snaps on the porch light and sees, first, the silver bars of a wheelchair.

"I need to talk to you, Cara," Kevin calls through the door.

"It's late, Kevin. You shouldn't be here."

"I don't know why my mother is doing this. She didn't kill the girl."

Her heart begins to race. If it wasn't his mother, that only leaves one person. "I can't let you in, Kevin. I'm sorry."

"She wasn't even there."

"Yes, she was. She told me she was."

"She was there the times before, when I talked to Amelia. But when I finally went to meet Adam, I didn't tell my mother I was going. I didn't want her to be part of it. I wanted this for myself. I wanted to look like a real father and I didn't think I could with her around."

Cara hears the emotion in his voice; she knows he must be telling the truth now, just as she knew, vaguely, that he wasn't before. She opens the door and steps outside. "I'll talk to you on the porch. I don't want you to come inside. Adam's asleep. I don't want him to wake up." In truth, for all his acute hearing, Adam wouldn't wake up; once he's asleep nothing wakes him up except the mysterious rhythms of his own brain.

"I got Scott to bring me. He laid out the cardboard, and then I told him I wanted to be alone and he went back and waited in the van at the edge of the woods."

"Why did your mother let everyone think she killed Amelia?"

"I don't know. She must be thinking I did it. That she has to protect me."

"Did you?"

"*No.* Cara, listen to me. Here's the truth I couldn't tell you before. I left. I set the whole thing up, and then I panicked. After all this time, I finally saw Adam—he showed up with the girl and he was wearing these funny little shoes, those slip-on sneakers, and I thought, Jesus, all these years you've been buying him shoes. You take him to the shoe store and he probably doesn't like it and you talk him through it, promise him something if he'll try on this pair. I just thought, if I had this kid I wouldn't know how to buy him shoes. I wouldn't know how to talk to him, how to get him through something."

"You learn it, Kevin. It's not that hard." It's late and she's tired; she's running low on patience.

"When I saw him standing there, I knew the whole thing was a mistake. He was humming and rocking back and forth, and I could tell he was nervous. The girl started talking to him; I couldn't hear what she said, but I could tell it helped. She was trying to get him to come over to me and then he looked up at me and made this perfect eye contact. Like he recognized me and he understood. I swear that's what it felt like."

She knows this feeling, the magic of Adam's eye contact when it comes; she also knows how it can be unsettling, and make her forget whatever she'd been trying to say.

"And I panicked. I looked at him and thought—*My God, he's got a life, here*. He's got you, he's got school, he's got this friend. If I come along, I'll just screw it up somehow and I thought it would be better if I left. So I did."

"You didn't talk to him at all?"

"No. I rolled myself back up to the car and told Scott to get the cardboard. He did—it took him about a minute and we left."

"You didn't say *anything*?" How could Adam have echoed him if he didn't talk?

"I might have yelled something to Scott, I don't remember."

" 'Watch yourself'?"

"Yeah, I guess. I didn't want him to talk to them or say anything."

"So maybe you said, 'What the fuck are you doing?' "

He looks down in his lap. "Maybe."

"Why did you tell me that whole story before about the homeless guy?"

"I knew the police had him. I assumed he did it, and I didn't want to tell you the real story."

"But that man couldn't have. He never got close enough."

"I don't know, Cara. Someone else must have been there, then."

"But *who*?"

"I don't *know*."

"How long were you there?"

"Five minutes. Maybe less."

Which meant there was plenty of time, forty-five minutes, maybe; anyone could have come along. "You left two scared kids alone in the woods and you just drove away?" She says this, though she's no longer thinking about his irresponsibility or his terrible judgment. She's only thinking, *My God, we're back at the beginning.* Someone is out there still who killed Amelia and will, if it's possible, want to kill Adam.

"It's not Evelyn Barrows," Matt Lincoln tells Cara needlessly, when she calls him after Kevin has left. "The knife isn't even close to a match. She's a crazy lady telling a crazy story. It's sad, but it happens. I'm sorry you got caught in the middle."

"And Kevin?" she asks tentatively.

"Not him, either."

"How do you know?"

"A few reasons. The wound, primarily. Had to have been delivered by someone standing, someone probably between five-six and five-eight. We tried to get Barrows to admit he could stand up, which he never did, but the real clincher came when he tried to sign his statements. The guy has phenomenally weak hands; he can hardly hold a pen." She thinks about the cartons of yogurt she used to open for him. *My God,* she thinks, *he's right.*

"Did he tell you the whole story?"

"That he left them alone there? Yeah, basically. It's like this guy did all the sinister stuff—the planning and prepping—and then left them alone long enough for someone else to come along and do the dirty work."

"Does it seem strange, that all these people were out in the woods that morning?"

"No, actually. There's two footpaths, one from the road and another, less obvious, from the middle school. On any given day, we're guessing seven to ten people on average might come through there. Kids come down from the middle school. They're not supposed, but they do. You probably heard we found the missing boy, and that's where he was. In the woods."

She hasn't heard. In the last five hours, she hasn't turned on the news. "And . . . ?"

"And he's fine. I'm going over to talk to him right now. So far, he's not saying anything about why he was there. But we're figuring, odds are, it's got to be related."

After she hangs up, she turns on the news to a reporter standing in front of the local hospital where Chris has been brought. She describes his condition as fair, dehydrated but stable, after a twenty-four-hour absence in which he eluded a townwide search to find him. "The school and these woods are nine miles from his home. Local authorities are currently investigating how he made it so far from his house without being seen, and how he could have remained so close to school personnel the whole day and still escaped detection. So far, we have little information to go on, except that he was determined to stay hidden and he did."

That night she lies in bed, picturing the path Matt Lincoln described, leading from the middle school into the woods. Maybe she has all along been scared of the wrong things—of menacing strangers and the faces from her unresolved past—when the greatest danger is really the inevitable future: Adam growing up and going on to middle school, where the world will move at a less forgiving pace and those who can't keep up will suffer the consequences. She thinks about Morgan and the fire he started, his strange determination to solve a murder that has, for almost a week, stumped everyone else. Suddenly, she remembers an arrangement, made with the middle school guidance counselor for Morgan to bring a boy named Chris over. Is it possible Morgan knows this boy? She keeps coming back to his confidence that he could solve this case, and she wonders: *Why would he be so certain of that unless he knows something the rest of them don't?*

When Morgan wakes up, he can hardly believe his eyes: Cara is standing in his room, staring down at him. At first, he thinks he must be dreaming, and then he looks around the room, sees that it's almost nine o'clock. His mother must have decided he doesn't have to go to school today. He feels like finding his notebook, writing it down: *Surprise Number Seven From My Mother: School isn't necessary after you've spent an evening afraid your son is dead.* Come to think of it, there's also this—*Surprise Number Eight: She let Cara in.*

"I'm sorry to wake you up, Morgan, but I have to ask, how well do you know Chris?"

He sits up in bed. "We have PE together. And that group I told you about. Sometimes we eat lunch together, but that was only twice. I don't know if we'll ever eat lunch together again."

"Do you think it's possible he could have killed Amelia? I keep wondering how he stayed in those woods all night, not scared of the killer, unless maybe he was the one who did it?"

Morgan can't believe she's asking him this. It's amazing, really. All last night after they learned where Chris had been found, he'd wanted to talk about it with someone, but his mother refused. She wanted to pull out scrapbooks and talk about the good old days before all their problems started. ("Remember this?" she kept saying. "Remember when we went to Gettysburg? That was fun.") Now Cara is here, asking him the questions he's been asking himself. "I considered that, actually, but I don't think so. I have a different theory." He reaches under his bed for his notebook and realizes this is the first time someone who isn't a relative has been in his bedroom, seen his stack of notebooks. "My theory is that Chris knows who did it, but feels like if he says anything, they'll kill him because—well, they probably will."

"Someone in your school?"

"I have a list here, actually. Of everyone I ever saw or heard about bullying Chris."

He has a lot of lists, unfortunately, and it takes him a while to find the right one. As he flips through pages, she looks at the headings of some of the others: *Possible Suspects: School Employees*. She reads one name and raises her eyebrows. "Mrs. Tesler, the *principal?*"

"I have my reasons. The important thing is to rule out no one."

Finally, he finds it. *People Who Bullied Chris*. It's fourteen names long.

"Wow," Cara says. "That's a lot of names."

"Some of them are people who made fun of him behind his back. They're just mean, not cruel." To Morgan, this is an important distinction. Mean people use words, cruel people use other things.

"Did you ever *see* anyone bully him?"

Morgan nods. Suddenly he's afraid Cara will ask him, specifically, what he saw.

"Physically try to hurt him?"

He nods again. He hasn't told anyone what he saw because he's been trying so hard, for so long, to forget it—the sticks jabbing at Chris, how one went into his knee and another stabbed him in the waist so hard he buckled over and his glasses fell to the floor. How one of the boys, wearing black motorcycle boots, stepped on the glasses. Morgan has tried very hard to put these details out of his mind.

"I saw something once. Where these kids were doing stuff with sticks," he whispers. He shakes his head; he doesn't want to say any more. "The day it happened, I set the fire."

In his mind, it made sense: a crime had been committed and someone should be punished. His mother believes certain things are simple. If people are mean to you, you tell a teacher. She doesn't understand about repercussions. That telling on people means they torture you more. They sit behind you on the bus and melt the straps of your backpack with a lighter, or else they pull hairs out of your head one by one. Sometimes they trip you in the bus aisle or make you give them your arm so they can write in ballpoint pen *I'm a Fag* on the pale underside where the skin is thin and it really hurts. He's told no one these things because he wants to pretend they happened to someone else, which seemed possible when he saw what they did to Chris, how his nose was bleeding by the time he crawled over to his glasses and tried to put them back on, how the blood and the snot made lines across his face, and then he saw that Chris had wet his pants which made him remember doing the same thing during the arm-writing episode, which made it seem possible—he can't explain exactly—that none of it was real.

It's confusing, though, because the harder he tries to forget, the more he can't remember what's happened to him and what's happened to Chris. He can't tell Cara all this because, really in the end, there aren't the words to explain how complicated middle school is.

"Can I take this list?" she asks softly. "Maybe this will help Chris. He needs some help, and this could be a start."

Morgan nods, but he doesn't look up, because if he looks up he might cry. He doesn't want to tear the list out of the notebook, so he finds a piece of paper and copies it over.

"Why don't you put a star by the names of the ones who seemed like the biggest problem," she says and he can do this. As long as he doesn't have to say anything, he can write down the names, and star what he knows.

Overall, Chris is pretty happy with himself. True, he said too much to the teacher, but he only told her one story and it wasn't the whole one or the real one, which means, for now, he's safe. It was hard to stay quiet with her because she had a nice face, and was crying when he looked up from his hole, which made him wish she was one of his middle school teachers so he could make friends with her and maybe eat lunch in her classroom and play checkers afterward, the way he did with Mrs. Montgomery in fifth grade, before his life got complicated by everyone hating him so much.

In the hospital, he figures out that not talking to the police is surprisingly easy: he pretends there is glue on his mouth and if he says anything, his lips will tear off.

"Can you tell us what you were planning to do with the hole?" the detective asks him. "Because it's a gorgeous hole. A lot of work."

Yes it was, he doesn't say.

"Kind of like you wanted to bury something, maybe?"

Yes.

"Or somebody?"

Maybe. Chris has seen how easy it is to do. How it takes no time. How you just have to be careful afterward and clean up better, not leave a body lying there for anyone to find.

"What was your plan, Chris? You must have had a plan."

No plan.

"You were out there by yourself, all night long. You must have known people would be worried and looking for you, right?"

Well sure. My mother, of course. He knew she would cry and worry about his asthma inhaler, which he forgot to pack. But he also thought: *If everyone is worried, then the one who matters will come looking.* This was the only way.

"I have a feeling this has something to do with Amelia Best. Can you nod, maybe? Just tell me, yes or no, does this have to do with the little girl? Did you know her? Or see her, maybe?"

Chris has seen how easily it can happen. How you don't have to be particularly strong. You only have to be angry and take people by surprise.

"The girl who died, Chris. Amelia. Did you ever see her at all?"

He can't see her now, but he can hear her voice. It's like it's inside his head, telling him what to do. *There's a man,* she said, *I need to find him.*

"Do you know who killed her? Did you see it?"

Chris thinks it's interesting how no one believes he did it. *Someone like me, it's not possible. Because they don't understand it* is *possible.* If someone is pushed far enough, he'll do what he has to. The detective keeps talking, which makes Chris do an old trick: he stares so hard at the man's lips moving that he can't hear a single word he says.

After the detective leaves, his mother cries on his bed for a while and his father does his nervous blinking at the TV, which is tuned to news because Chris isn't going to unglue his lips, even long enough to say, "Remote, please." His parents seem to think the news is fine to watch, though his mother is on it, holding a plastic ziplock bag with his asthma inhaler in it. On TV, she says she's the happiest mother in the world to have her boy back, safe and sound, though looking at her now, crying on his bed, Chris has to wonder. He shakes his head. The only thing that matters is what they say at the end: "At this point, the boy has refused to answer all questions from authorities about the period of time he spent missing."

If I'm watching this, Chris thinks, *he is, too. He'll think I'm amazing, doing all this for him, because he'll have no clue.*

"Here's the list," Cara says. "I know it seems silly, fourteen names of middle schoolers, but I swear Matt, I think this might be something. It's clear that Morgan was fixated on the murder, and maybe Chris was, too. Morgan came into our life because he wanted Adam to help him solve it, but I'm honestly thinking he might already know more than he's letting on."

"Like what?"

"That he's witnessed certain things. That he's seen a capacity for this kind of violence. He's got lists and lists of suspects—these ludicrous lists, the principal, half the teachers at the elementary school, the nursing staff—but buried in there are some names he obviously wants us to have, but can't bring himself to say out loud."

"Interesting." Matt Lincoln studies the list, frowning, one finger raised to his lips. "We've talked to some of these guys already. Randall Wu, Harrison Rogers, this Welton character. None of them terribly pleasant guys, I can tell you. You know, it's funny—we had all three of them in for the arson investigation a few weeks ago, and we go to talk to them about the murder and they're all full of attitude: 'Anything happens in this town and you want to pin it on us.' It's like, boys, take a look in the mirror, at the boots and the chains, and take a wild guess why you're being questioned."

Cara stares at him. "They didn't start that fire."

"No, I know."

"Why did you question them?"

"We thought we had an eyewitness. Someone claimed to have seen them there."

"Who?"

"It was a telephone tip, but they had the clothing right. And it was corroborated by a second witness."

"And both those tips were telephoned in?"

"I believe so, yes."

"Is it possible they were from kids?"

"Kids can make tips. They sometimes do."

"But would you have a recording of them?"

"We'd have a record. Not a recording. Why?"

"Because I keep thinking the fire is connected to all this. Morgan saw some bullying and wanted to stop it somehow, or express his outrage, I don't know. But he set the fire the same day he saw some particularly gruesome incident. It makes sense that afterward he'd call in a fake tip, try to get those kids in trouble for something, even if it wasn't what they actually did."

"Hmm."

"And maybe Chris called in, too. And maybe they found out who was ratting on them."

"But what does that have to do with Amelia's murder?"

"Think about it," she says, though the truth is, she doesn't know. If they were angry at Morgan and Chris, why would they kill a girl from the elementary school, a girl they couldn't have known because she only moved to town six weeks ago?

"Jesus Christ," Matt says, slamming his pen down on top of his list. "I just thought of something." He's out of his chair, bent over to dig through a stack of file folders behind him.

"What?"

He finds a file, starts flipping through pages, flipping some more, shaking his head. "Idiot," he mumbles to himself. "I'm an idiot."

"*What?*"

He finds his piece of paper and pulls it out, lays it next to Morgan's list with the three starred names. "This one," he says, pointing to the second starred name. "Right there. Harrison Rogers. They call him Hare."

Morgan's mother thinks he should visit Chris, that if he wants friends so much, he should learn how to be one. He wants to tell his mother Chris is part of the whole problem. *If I'm not careful, I'll become exactly like Chris and I won't even understand how it happened.*

He doesn't say this out loud, but his mother must hear what he is thinking.

"Don't do that, Morgan. Don't do to Chris what other people have done to you. You want some friends, this is how you start. You call him up. You say, 'May I come over?' "

When Morgan calls to ask about visiting Chris, he talks to Chris's mother, who sounds happy enough to have him come over. "Sure," she says. "He's talking again, thank God, just not about the woods. You ask about that, he'll do a little zipper thing with his mouth. Just keep him on other subjects, and he'll be all right."

Which sounded fine to Morgan, but now that he's here, it's hard to think of anything else to talk about. Chris is lying in bed, even though, technically—or according to the TV reports anyway—there's nothing wrong with him. Morgan wants to ask him everything that he's not supposed to from what he's heard so far: *Did the knife really belong to you? What were you going to do with it?* He knows what it feels like to stand alone in the woods and feel capable of doing anything at all, even breaking the law. What he really wants to ask is: *Did you want to kill someone? Do you still?*

Morgan thinks if he could get up the guts to ask Chris that, maybe he could tell him how he'd tried to get Harrison put in jail weeks ago. The problem with telling Chris is that it was a stupid idea, and it didn't work. It would also involve telling Chris he saw him get beat up and wet his pants, which is a topic Morgan doesn't feel like getting into right now.

He's afraid it might make him start crying or admit some of his own troubles along the same lines, his own day spent in wet pants, a sweatshirt tied around his waist, red lines down his arm where words had been.

Chris doesn't seem particularly happy to see Morgan, but he also doesn't seem *un*happy to have a visitor. He sits up in bed, looks around the room. "You want to see my origami collection?" he finally offers.

Morgan can see it, on the shelf, rows and rows of folded figurines, some so small they look like wadded-up gum wrappers picked up off the street. *Not really,* he wants to say. Instead he points. "You did all these?"

"That's right. On the far left is a giraffe, then a hippopotamus, an egret, a platypus, and a swan, of course. I design my own, which is really hard to do."

And sort of pointless, Morgan thinks, when none of them look like the animals he's named.

"I could teach you if you want. My mother says most people aren't interested in origami."

"I'm probably like that," Morgan says. "Not so interested."

"Yeah. That's okay. What are you interested in?"

"I don't know." He almost says some of the old things: Civil War, trains, U.S. presidents, his quarter collection. Instead, he opts for this. "Mysteries, I guess."

Chris surprises him. "Like what happened in the woods for instance?"

"That's one."

It didn't work. None of it worked.

Chris was going to kill him and now he can't, and finally he's realized: *Why bother not talking now, when it makes no difference what I don't say?*

For a day, Chris has been thinking about ways he might kill himself.

It seems like the next logical step. He's thinking about doing it the hardest way possible—drowning himself, which isn't easy when touching water makes him hyperventilate. He wants to do it the hard way so that, at the last minute, he doesn't think about any good things in life and change his mind.

He's not even sure if he should bother trying, though, when nothing works out for him. Not planning a murder, not trying to foil Harrison's revenge. Now that he looks back, though, he has to admit it worked for a while. He still thinks of those ten minutes before they walked into the woods as some of the happiest minutes he's had in his life.

For two weeks, Harrison had been talking about breaking Chris's arm for calling the police, and trying to pin the fire on him. He told him people were going to pay him to do it, people who were sick of his ratting-out ways. Chris didn't deny doing it—it was certainly possible that Harrison *had* set it, the way he'd been carrying lighters for years, flicking them at the bus stop, setting everything on fire: blades of grass, farts, the white thread fringe on girls' miniskirts. Once Chris watched him burn a live cricket. As it turned out, though, Chris was wrong. Harrison couldn't have set the fire because he was at school, doing detention when it started.

"I know it was you, and you're going to die, you little piece of freakshit," he said the day after Chris called the police. Harrison, more than the others, liked to drag things out, spend days talking about what he was going to do, which bones he would break, how he would break them. "First I'm gonna do your arm. It's easier than you think." The night before it was meant to happen, Chris stayed up late, making a plan. He knew he needed a weapon and an element of surprise. He decided this: he would agree to a face-off, and then he would control it. If he'd known anyone with a gun he would have used that, but as it was, he settled on what he had: his mother's kitchen knife, wrapped in a sock, stored in the bottom of his backpack. He knew he couldn't bring it into school, that if anyone found it he'd get suspended, so he left it in the woods still wrapped in the sock. Knowing it was there was like having a test you knew ahead of time you were going to cheat on, and get away with. It made him feel lucky; made him say "Fine" when Harrison said they should just get this over with and skip third period.

"Okay," Chris said. "But we should go to the woods so no one tries to stop us."

Harrison stared at him. "Seriously?"

"Sure. Why not?" Before this, he'd never done anything except beg for these boys to leave him alone.

"You want me to break your arm?"

"Maybe you can, maybe you can't. I know a little judo."

His eyes narrowed. "How much judo?"

"A little."

Chris saw then how easy this was; that strength came simply from not looking afraid. Walking out to the woods, he talked the whole time, told Harrison about his hospital stays. "If you break my arm, I figure I might get a night, tops, but that'll be good. They get some stations at the hospital I don't get at home. They also have Nintendo. You'd be surprised what they have."

Harrison stopped walking. "Are you a fucking freak or what?"

Chris shrugged. "I suppose so. You're not the first person to ask me that. There's one guy on the bus—Neil I think his name is—who asked me that once and I said, 'Yes, is that a problem?' See here's the funny part. Well not funny, ha ha. But I've occasionally wondered if you *like* being mean or if you feel like you *have* to be so that no one thinks you're a freak, too. But in a way, it's too late, if you don't mind my saying so, because the way you dress and your friends—well, a lot of people think you're a little freaky, too, Hare. Do you mind if I call you Hare?"

"Yes."

He was enjoying himself so much he couldn't stop. It felt like the best time he'd ever had. "Hare! Hare! Hare!" he called, because in a minute, he'd reach down, pull out his knife, and be the last one laughing.

"Just shut up, freak show. Shut the fuck up."

He didn't, of course. He kept talking and talking until they got in the woods and then he stopped talking, because he knew, right away, something had happened. They weren't alone. When he went for his knife, the sock was there, but the knife was gone, which meant none of this would work, that he would get his arm broken, and would also get in trouble for the knife.

Now he understands how much he did wrong, all the countless mistakes he made. If he hadn't brought the knife, hadn't stashed it in the woods, hadn't egged Harrison on because it felt so good—if he'd done a dozen things differently, the girl might still be alive and not in his head where she sits, all the time now, wearing her pink dress and telling him what to do.

Cara stays at the station long enough to see Harrison Rogers when he's brought in. He's a red-headed kid, covered in freckles, dressed in a black T-shirt, black jeans, and black shoes, trailed by a mother who's screaming about police harassment of a minor. "It's the third time they've questioned him. Three times I'm talking about. Anybody does anything in this town, my son gets interrupted with living his life to talk to police. I'm telling you, I want to talk to whoever's in charge around here."

She is so loud that even her son seems embarrassed to stand near her. Matt steps forward, holding out his hand. "At this point, I'm in charge. Detective Sergeant Matt Lincoln, ma'am. We appreciate you coming down."

"You the guy we talked to last time? About the fire?"

"I am. Yes."

" 'Cause he didn't start no fire."

"That's correct, ma'am. We don't need to ask any questions about that."

While the mother huffs from side to side, her arms folded across the expanse of her large chest, her son seems to shrink at her side. He leans against the wall, picks at a thumbnail, shoulders hunched, one foot resting against the shin of his other leg.

"It's persecution is what it is, and you better believe tomorrow I'm calling a lawyer."

Matt lowers his voice to a whisper. "We told you, Ms. Rogers, that you *should* have a lawyer present. We told you what he's here for." Saying this, he makes it sadly clear: this woman is terrified and putting on a show. She's heard one story and has told herself another—that this is nothing, more harassment because her boy wears too much black to school.

She waves a hand around. "No, no. Let's just get this over with and get home."

"No, Ms. Rogers, I can't recommend that. We have a lawyer here who can represent Harrison for the time being and also answer any questions you have."

To Cara it's obvious: Matt doesn't want to take a single step without this, no matter what the woman says. "I have to say, it'll be much better for Harrison if someone is there, protecting his interests."

She rolls her eyes. "Look, whatever. I don't care."

Cara watches the boy, and wonders if he hears this. His expression is dead, as if he long ago stopped listening to most of the things his mother says. The look creates a strange disconnect—his face seems much older, as hard as a streetwise twenty-year-old who's seen too many things to register much, but his body is surprisingly small, with boyishly thin, broomstick arms and tiny feet. Registering this, she notices something else: he's wearing slip-on sneakers, like the kind she buys for Adam, who still can't manage shoe tying on his own. They're black, a color she would never buy for Adam, but when she looks a little closer, she sees: they're the same brand, with—she can tell by the way he's standing—the exact same sole.

Here it is, she thinks. *Here's why it looked like only two sets footprints.*

She tries to signal Matt, who has moved away from Harrison's mother to deal with logistics—securing a room, locating the lawyer. Cara slips up behind him and whispers, as he reads a note in his hand. "He's wearing the same shoes that Adam has."

Matt nods over her shoulder, holds up two fingers to a secretary in the corner. "Room two?" he calls and then turns to Cara. "I noticed that," he whispers.

And a minute later, they're gone.

There are parts Chris doesn't remember at all. He remembers the girl showed up, said she needed to find a man in a wheelchair, that she was trying to help him and he had left. Harrison saw it first, that she was holding the knife.

"Give it," Harrison said. "Give it here." He held out his hand, and then Chris wondered if there was something wrong with her, because she didn't do what Harrison said, didn't hand over the knife. Instead, she stared up at the trees, smiling like she didn't hear Harrison at all.

He remembers this: she started singing, which made Harrison scream, "Give me the motherfucking knife or I'll hurt you," which didn't make sense because he was mad at Chris, not at her, but then he thought about earlier, how having a knife made him strong and not having it paralyzed him. And then it was like Harrison forgot all about Chris, forgot he was even there, because he was just mad at the girl, who wasn't doing what she was told and wasn't scared the way she should be. She was singing in his face, asking him questions that made no sense about people who weren't there, dancing around, holding the knife up. One minute, she was worried about the man in the wheelchair, the next she was leaning into Harrison's face, asking what he called those things on his skin. "Are they still freckles when there's so many like that?"

Chris knew that if she wasn't holding the knife, Harrison would've hurt her. He would've pushed her down to the ground and made her eat a piece of paper or perpetrated one of his other favorite tortures, but that long shiny knife meant she could do what Chris had just discovered. She could say anything at all. "Freckles are like dirt, only they don't come off," she said, touching his face and then—he still doesn't understand this—she looked down at her hand, saw the knife in it, and dropped it.

Chris had no chance, he was too far away. Harrison grabbed the knife.

The girl floated away and Harrison's voice changed to soft, like he'd gotten a new idea. "Hey, come here for a second. I want to show you something," he called to the girl as he reached for his pants. Chris thought, *Oh God, he's going to pee on her the way he peed on my shoes.*

He unzipped his fly and pulled his thing out. "Come here!" he said, waving at her with the knife. Chris looked away, started thinking of other things, like the English class he was missing, and how in math if they finished their work, they were allowed to read the comics the teacher kept on his desk, how there was one Chris loved with a villain named Viscous Liquid.

"Come here, girlie. I won't hurt you, I promise. I just want to show you something."

Chris tried to think about Viscous Liquid and his father, Venomous Hate, who set up the laboratory where he grew his only son, a villain who could go from human to liquid and back again in seven seconds.

"I know the guy you're looking for. I've seen him. Come here, I'll tell you where he is."

Chris wanted to say *No, don't believe him. Don't go,* but he couldn't speak, couldn't open his mouth or say anything, because if he said anything Harrison would remember he was here and break his arm and maybe do worse with the knife. He thought about Viscous Liquid, who stuffed himself into people's mouths to drown them, and then disappeared without a trace. Chris tried to picture his own mouth filling up, stuffed with needles and dirt from the forest floor, rocks and blood, and maybe his own sock. It didn't matter what Chris said or didn't say because Harrison went over to her, grabbed her around the shoulders, and whispered into the back of her head, "What did I just say? Do you see how I have the knife now? How I could hurt you if I wanted to?" He started pulling her. "I don't want to hurt you, though. I want you to come over here. I want to be friends and you can see what I have. What it does. It's like a surprise."

She walked with him because she had no choice, and Chris hoped that maybe she was young enough that she wouldn't know what was happening to her or remember it, anyway. And then he saw her feet dig in the mud, like maybe she could stop what was happening with her toes. "No," she said and that's when he knew she wasn't too young, she was something else—crazy maybe, because she started calling really loudly into the trees, "I'VE BROUGHT HIM! I HAVE HIM! DON'T BE SCARED. I'LL HELP YOU TALK TO HIM!" And saying all that, being so weird, making no sense, she somehow got away. Harrison had her for a minute, moving her where he wanted her to go, and then she flew away, no problem, like nothing, and he was standing there, alone, with his thing hanging out of his pants.

Chris doesn't remember exactly what happened next. Harrison's face went red like his hair and he exploded. Chris thought maybe it's possible that real people can morph into other forms or energy forces. That they can get so angry they transform the landscape like volcano lava or a snowstorm. One minute everything is one color, and the next, it's another color entirely, which is how it felt, when he had her and lost her and then lunged at her again, and Chris thought there was a scream, but no sound came, only Harrison's mouth stretched open like a scream and everything went quiet, with only breathing and the sound of bodies colliding, and Chris squeezed his eyes shut the second he saw the knife disappear into her dress, inside a ring of blood, because he was scared that if he kept looking, he'd see organs slide out.

"Jesus fucking Christ. Look what you made me do," he heard Harrison say. "You gotta fucking help me, this is your fucking fault." And he knew that it was his fault, that he'd started it all by trying to speak up. That if he'd stayed silent and said nothing, they would have been fine. Chris didn't need Harrison's threats, or his talk when they walked back about killing him if he said anything. He already knew what he would do. He'd decided as he watched Harrison pull out the knife—his hands shaking—and wipe it off with the sock to stuff it in his jacket pocket. He knew when he closed his eyes and heard for the first time, what the girl had been listening to instead of Harrison—that somewhere else in the woods, a tiny flute was playing as if none of this had happened. Which is what he decided he would tell himself until he found a way to kill Harrison.

Morgan is pretty sure he's stayed long enough. They've talked mostly about hobbies and all of Chris's seem a little strange, to be honest. For a while he was into hot-air balloons, then tractors; now he's mostly interested in antique outboard boat engines, which seems strange to Morgan given Chris's feelings about water. It makes Morgan nervous to have so much in common with Chris, or at least this: old passions that don't work anymore. He thinks, *If Chris ever comes over, I'll have to hide most of my stuff.* Then he thinks of another possibility: Chris sitting in his room, looking over his notebooks, nodding and wheezing, pointing a bony finger at one of his gravestone rubbings and saying, "Wow. Where'd you get that?" Maybe his old life would look different with someone to show it to. Someone who understood.

"I should probably go," Morgan says, and looks at the clock to see he's only been here twenty-five minutes, that it just feels like two hours. "I'll come back, if you want. I don't mind."

Chris looks out the window. "Do you want to know why I went to the woods? The second time, when I ran away?"

Morgan sits back down. So far as he knows, Chris has told no one why or how he did this yet. "Sure."

"I knew Harrison would come out there eventually, looking for me. I was going to kill him and bury him so no one would find the body and no one would care because the world would be a better place without him. He'd just be a missing person."

Morgan can't believe he's saying this. For a second it feels like Chris is telling him everything, and Morgan fears maybe his brain will explode with all this information. He takes a deep breath and remembers this: Harrison's name was on the list he'd given Cara, and he'd put a star by it. "Wow. I have to say, I wouldn't mind if that guy died."

"Now I keep thinking—" Chris starts to say more, and then stops.

"What?"

"There's a reason I can't do it. It's like that girl is inside of me."

Morgan looks at the door and back at the clock. One minute has passed since the last time he looked. "*Inside* you?"

"It's like she keeps talking about this man and how she's trying to help him, but he ran away. I keep hearing her voice saying this stuff."

Morgan tries this: "Sometimes when I keep thinking about something I just tell myself: *Stop.*"

"It was like she was in the middle of something and we stopped her. She kept saying, 'He's hurt and I need to help him.' "

Chris must be trying to imitate her voice, but he sounds like he's doing a Snow White impersonation. Morgan wonders if he's having a nervous breakdown or if this is what going insane looks like.

"I keep thinking, what was it she was trying to do? Like maybe I could help. It was something about this man."

And Adam, Morgan thinks. *Don't forget Adam.*

"Anyway." Chris turns from the window, looks at Morgan, and seems to remember who he's talking to. "You should probably go. If you want, next time, I'll show you the rest of my origami. There's a frog that's pretty good, and a few more giraffes."

It's twenty-four hours before Cara gets the whole story from Matt, who calls her at home. "This kid is a real case. It took an hour and a half, but we got a confession. For a kid, that's a long time. Usually they break down right away, but this one, he let his mother do all the talking, and then finally, in the middle of her going off on some tangent, he just exploded like a volcano. Started calling her a freak case who had no fucking clue what she was saying, that she should try shutting up for once in her life. Nice kid. He's a real gem."

This should be a relief, Cara thinks. *It's over,* she tries to tell herself, but all she can think of is the boy standing in the hallway wearing shoes that reminded her of Adam, with a mother she can't help feeling for; a mother whose life, as she's known it, has just ended.

"Did he say *why*?"

"I don't know if there is a why. He says it wasn't his fault, of course. It never is. His story is that he and Chris went out to the woods to fight and the girl was there already, holding a knife. She wouldn't leave them alone; she kept getting in Harrison's face, asking him if he had seen a man in a wheelchair. I presume she must have been looking for Barrows."

Cara thinks of something, and can hardly believe what this story suggests. "Wait a second. Adam wasn't with her?"

"Doesn't sound like it. Harrison says he never saw another kid, though obviously Adam must have heard them shouting."

"But he didn't see her get killed?" This comes as such a genuine relief and surprise that she wants to dwell on it.

"We don't think so, but there's a lot we don't know yet, a lot of questions we still have."

"Like what?"

"Like, according to Harrison, she wouldn't back away, wouldn't leave them alone. She kept asking the same questions over and over, and eventually she started singing in his face. But why would a young girl do that to an older kid who obviously looks threatening? Why wouldn't she have backed away?"

Cara knows the answer, but doesn't know if she's supposed to say it. Obviously, Olivia has chosen, even in death, to spare Amelia the taint of labels. "Because she was autistic," Cara says. "It was mild, but she would have had some residual tendencies. Singing in someone's face to dispel tension is a very autistic thing to do." Cara can picture the whole scene, all too easily. In the days after her parents' accident, Adam coped with her grief, the mysterious disappearance of his grandparents, the stress of everything, by singing "The Wheels on the Bus" over and over, so incessantly that she finally had to threaten to take away all opera videos unless he stopped.

Matt whistles in surprise and then lets it go. "You know what I keep thinking?"

"What?"

"Adam gave us the name two days ago. He told us who did it. It's incredible, really."

Adam nods because nodding means you're listening and he is.

"She's dead," his mother tells him. "Someone got so mad he accidentally killed her, but I don't think he meant to, because she was a very nice girl. She was your friend and she shouldn't have died, but she did and I'm sorry baby. I'm so, so sorry, but that's what happened."

Now he knows. Dead means forever and don't touch, and she's up in heaven where Grandma and Grandpa live, which is maybe in the clouds and maybe not. Once, his mother told him heaven is with God, and once Mrs. Ellis, his kindergarten teacher, said she didn't know where God lived, maybe in the clouds, maybe in plants and trees. It quiets him to know that she's dead but maybe living inside of trees, inside the woods she always wanted to go to.

Dead means he won't see her again because he's never seen his Grandma and Grandpa again.

Dead means people cry, though he knows he won't.

Dead means throw it away, like flowers or batteries.

Dead means asleep but you don't wake up.

He can hear her in his mind. Remember her singing. He never got to see the inside of her throat, but he can imagine it if he wants to: a long row of strings and tiny felted hammers, or a little bird with a beak that opens and closes inside of her mouth.

He doesn't have to worry about her anymore. Doesn't have to go back to school and look for her shoes. It's a relief to know this.

Sad, maybe. And a relief.

At night, Cara has an old dream she used to have years ago—that Adam comes to her bedroom one morning, speaking in full sentences, original thoughts, woven into paragraphs. At first, she is surprised and then, the longer he speaks, she is less so. They aren't the thoughts of a typical nine-year-old, but they sound exactly like Adam, the way he must think: "I heard something interesting. A *clackety-clackety*." In these dreams, her impulse is always the same; if handed an Adam who could freely talk, she would start asking questions, which come so easily, it's as if she's been expecting this at any time and is ready: *Why do you laugh at fireworks? Cry when the water goes down the drain? Why do you hate certain doors at school? Why do you love Mr. Rogers still?* In the dream, there are answers for every question; simple, if-she-thought-about-it obvious answers. *Fireworks are dancing star rockets, funny. Water down the drain dies. Doors should open out, not in. And Mr. Rogers? His shoes.* When she wakes, she wonders why she didn't ask him to tell her more about what happened when he was with Amelia. *What exactly did you see in the woods? How bad was it?* She believes she knows her son, knows the answers already if they could come, but this part still eludes her.

She has seen Busker Bob's testimony and, from it, she knows that Adam *did* wander away from Amelia, doing what he naturally would have done, following the music, to find his way to Busker Bob. She knows it must have been Adam by the way he described him, standing across a clearing, listening to his flute, tracking the music with his hand. In the statement, Robert Phillips was kind enough to add this: "When I stopped playing, the boy sang back the last seven notes I played—quite lovely, perfect pitch."

It also says Adam didn't stay with Busker Bob for more than about seven minutes, though.

To cheer Adam up, Cara checks out one of his old favorite videos from the library: *I Love Dirt Movers and Construction Machines*. It's been years since she's let him watch this one, targeted to toddlers, mindless and full of slow-motion payloaders shifting mounds of dirt, but five minutes into it, he's grinning. She's happy, too, because earlier today Morgan called to ask if he could stop by to bring a few things back that he borrowed from Adam.

When the doorbell rings a half hour early, Cara jumps up, and cries, "He's here! It's Morgan, Adam," from the other room, before she opens the door to discover it's not Morgan.

It's Kevin, again. She steps back, and takes a breath.

"I wanted to talk to you a little bit. I thought if I called first, you might say no."

He's probably right, but now that he's here, she doesn't have much choice. "It's okay, Kevin. You can come in."

He rolls himself to the living room, to the shelf where Adam's baby pictures sit beside one of her parents at their thirtieth wedding anniversary, looking surprisingly young: her mother in a flowered dress, her father in a suit she later had to give to the funeral director to bury him in. For a long time, Cara doesn't say anything. Finally, Kevin breaks the silence.

"You probably heard I spent some time in jail."

She nods, though he doesn't look at her.

"It was a first offense. My mother hired a good lawyer, so I could have gotten out of it, but I didn't even try, because the night I was arrested something bad happened."

She thinks about what his mother had said: *Ask him if he knows anything about your poor parents.* She doesn't want to ask, though; she doesn't want to hear what he's about to tell her.

"I was with them the night they died, Cara. It was terrible. I'd been out with Scott, who was dealing coke back then, and we were driving around town celebrating, and we saw your parents coming out of a movie and the first thing I thought was, *Great, I can ask them how you're doing.* I forgot . . . that they wouldn't know who I was. That I only knew them because I knew everything about your life. When I walked up, they looked confused, so Scott said, 'He knows Cara,' and right away, your mom said, 'How?' and I felt bad. I was high and I'd walked up to some old people and started some conversation like I was out of my mind. I started to leave, and your dad grabbed my shoulder and said, 'No, we'd like to hear how you know her.' Your mom was crying. Scott was so nervous he said, 'Oh fuck,' and started to laugh."

Cara can hardly bear to listen.

"I said, 'I'm sorry. We were friends a while ago, no big deal.' And your father said, 'It is a big deal. There's a child involved.' See, here's the whole thing, Cara—I knew you had a child, but I had *no idea* it could be mine."

She stares at him. "What did you do?"

"They walked out to the parking lot. We got in our car and I told Scott to follow them."

"*You* were in the car behind them?"

"We weren't that close. We didn't *do* anything. I swear to God, it wasn't our fault. I just wanted to know if Adam was my kid."

"You were *with* them when they died?"

He nods. "I felt terrible, Cara. It was awful."

How can he say these words—how terrible he feels, how awful it was—when he will never understand her loss that day, that one afternoon she had a family and the next day she did not?

After the accident she was desperate to get the name of the people in that car, because her loss so consumed her she thought knowing everything would alleviate it somehow. Though her mother, in the passenger seat, died instantly, she knew her father stayed alive for nearly an hour and she had always wanted to find out whether he said anything in those final moments. Now it doesn't matter; she doesn't want to hear. Her parents died in a terrible moment of confusion, their disorientation a measure of their great and often unspoken love for her. It's too much.

"You need to leave, Kevin," she says simply.

"The police searched the car, busted us for possession—but I swear the accident wasn't our fault."

He has said this so many times tonight, she fears he must believe it—that nothing is his fault, though he has been involved in the deaths of three people. "Get out. Right now, get out."

Behind her the doorbell rings, startling her for a moment. She opens the door to find Morgan standing on the porch, a brown paper grocery bag in his hand. "I can't really come in. My mother's in the car. I just wanted to return some things I took." He hands her the paper bag and she opens it to see, on top, the sweater Adam was wearing the day Amelia was murdered.

"Okay," she says, trying to steady her voice. "Thank you."

"I'd also like to say I'm sorry, and if you're ever looking for a volunteer again, you can call me. I promise if you invite me back, I won't steal anything next time. I like Adam. I like spending time with him." He doesn't look her in the eye when he says this, but it doesn't matter. She believes him. His words are delivered with such sincerity that, for a moment, she forgets about her anger at Kevin.

To her surprise, Adam suddenly materializes beside her, which means he must have heard Morgan's voice and left his video to see him. She smiles down. "Morgan says he'd like to come over again, Adam. What do you think?"

Adam rocks and smiles. "Hi, Morgan! Sorree!!"

"Yeah. We could play that game again. I don't mind."

"Sorreee. I don't mind Sorreee!"

"It's not my *favorite* game in the world, but it's all right."

Adam turns a circle and stops, pointing his nose in Morgan's direction. Though his eyes drift sideways, she knows he is offering his best approximation of eye contact. She expects him to echo and in a sense he does: "What's your favorite game in the world?" he asks.

For a moment, it doesn't hit her right away. It's a question, a *WH* question, that he's asking voluntarily of another child. She hasn't prompted him, hasn't thought ahead of time of what he should say. She's never seen this before; in truth, she never thought it was possible.

"I don't know. Clue is all right, but I don't think we should play that."

Cara's impulse to steer this conversation and cue Adam's responses is so strong, it's nearly impossible to stop. But she does. She takes a deep breath and waits.

"All right. No Clue, then."

She exhales. *My God, they've done it. They've made a decision, a plan to not play something.* In the awkwardness that follows, Morgan peeks over her shoulder, sees Kevin sitting in the living room behind her. He looks at Kevin, then back at her. "Uh, Cara—could I speak to you in private for a minute? Like alone?" He points to the porch, and she follows him outside because Adam seems fine, humming obliviously.

"What is it, Morgan?"

"I just have to ask: Do you know that guy? The one in the wheel-chair?"

"Yes."

"Okay, because this is a little weird. This is what I wanted to ask you about. I've been talking to Chris, and he told me that in the woods, Amelia was looking for a man in a wheelchair. Supposedly she kept say-ing, 'There's a man in a wheelchair and he needs my help.' "

Cara stares at him. "That's what she *said*?"

"Over and over. 'He's scared and he needs help.' "

She looks inside through the glass pane of the door at Kevin. He has pushed himself into the kitchen and now sits across the room from Adam, who notices, for the first time, this delightful surprise: a wheel-chair in his kitchen! Amazingly, he looks fine, as if he doesn't remember seeing Kevin before, he's only curious about this contraption and all its gizmos, interested enough to not mind stepping closer to the person it contains.

He's scared and he needs help. "Those were her last words?"

"I guess." She can't hear what's happening inside, but through the glass she can see: Kevin is talking about his wheelchair, pointing out the different parts, and Adam is listening, hovering inches from the joystick that has captured his attention. She could have told Kevin that talking to Adam wouldn't be as hard as he feared, that he's sitting in a wheelchair, which alone would hold Adam's interest for the better part of a week. Watching them is sweet, but it also makes her nervous.

"So anyway, what I might do is tell Chris that I think I've found the guy. He might want to come over, talk to him, find out what sort of help he needs."

"I think I know," she says.

Morgan looks up, surprised. "You *do?*"

This is part of something larger, part of letting Adam grow into his own life where pieces of it exist separate from her. Kevin has made bad choices in the past that have caused irreparable damage, but there's also this: so has she. And it's possible he could be good for Adam. She wants to try: for Adam's sake, and Kevin's, maybe her own; at this point, she can't even say for sure.

A week later, Cara sits in a local roadside hamburger stand that has been around so long she remembers riding bikes here with Suzette to split a paper boat full of fries. Now she watches Kevin, parked with a quarter resting on each of his knees, marveling at Adam, who is still playing the same game of pinball after ten minutes. "You'll see," she said earlier, changing only one dollar. "Adam's weirdly good at pinball." She can't remember when they made this discovery—maybe two years ago—but it's been a godsend on rainy days when she can take him to an arcade, steer him to the pinball machines no one else cares about and, for two dollars, can keep him occupied for most of an afternoon. She studies Kevin's face, the shocked look of awe and delight. "He's *unbelievable,* Cara."

She laughs. "I told you."

"It's like people should see this kid. I'm signing him up for competitions."

"Sure, Kevin. What competitions are you talking about, exactly?"

"Don't they have pinball tournaments anymore?"

"Maybe in Russia."

"I'm going to look into it."

She laughs, even though it feels a little forced.

She wishes it was easier to talk to Kevin. This is their first outing, but he has called twice to set it up, and both times his voice on the telephone has filled her with some combination of panic and dread. She fears saying the wrong thing, leading him on, or not saying enough and losing him completely. It's a delicate balance, like tiptoeing through a minefield of dangerous possibilities.

Earlier in the week, she invited Matt Lincoln to lunch, telling him she had some questions and a favor to ask him, presumably so he wouldn't get the wrong idea, and then she proceeded to change her outfit three times the morning before she met him. When he arrived, she almost laughed out loud, to see that he'd made a similar effort: his shirt was clean, freshly pressed, his face shaved, his hair damp, which could only mean he'd gone home from work and showered for lunch. After that, talking to him wasn't nearly as hard as she feared it would be. She remembered her old self, the jokes she used to make standing at parties, drinking beers and wearing halter tops. With him, she could even make some of the old ones—about teachers in high school, the old football coach. Eventually they got onto more serious topics. Matt told her more about his nephew, and she told him the one thing she thought was most important in the beginning. "Every parent wishes they'd started therapies—whichever ones—sooner. Try everything. The more, the better. He'll change a lot, you'll see." He nodded at this. "Who knows? He might turn out fine. But whatever happens, life gets much easier, much better than you think it will be." She also wishes someone had told her this—that adjusted expectations aren't a tragedy.

Technically, she asked him to lunch because she wanted him to return the bag of belongings that Morgan brought over, all things that apparently Adam had but that must've, at one point belonged to Amelia: a book with her name written inside, another with a horse on the cover she'd copied in one of her drawings. There was also a pencil, some rocks, and—Cara's heart almost stopped—two unmatched girl's socks. How did Morgan find these things, and know they were Amelia's, unless Adam understood what he was asking and told him somehow? She wanted to call Morgan and have him explain exactly what was said, what Adam did, and then she thought, *No, let this be private. Let them have their own friendship and their own exchanges.*

In the last week she has realized that having so many answers has only opened up more questions, harder ones to answer. How did Amelia convince Adam to go with her? Did she say "Your father is waiting? He wants to meet you?" Could he understand such a promise? She thinks about her impulse to probe, to find out everything she can about Amelia, who will, in the end—whatever she finds out—be just a girl, a ten-year-old with a mysterious mix of strengths and deficits, calculation and innocence. She could accumulate details, a thousand scraps of information, and still never know what was said in the bathroom, what was sung on the swings. Maybe in the end what she's after doesn't have much to do with Amelia at all. Maybe what she wants is Amelia's perspective—what she saw in Adam, what drew her to him, because the real mystery of Cara's life has always been the same one: Adam.

Matt said he'd be happy to take Amelia's belongings to Olivia, which left just her questions. Really there was only one: "Do you remember where the sweater fibers were found on Amelia's body?"

"On her collar, I think. Around her shoulders and neck."

She nodded again and thanked him. "That's what I thought."

Outside the restaurant, he walked her to her car and stood with the paper bag filling his arms. In the sunlight, she saw traces of the boy she remembered: in his small crooked smile, the way his teeth overlapped. He was the first man she'd felt comfortable with in so long, and it made her want to reach across the space between them and say something to make her thoughts perfectly clear: *If you'd ever like to go out at night, I can get a babysitter.* She almost said it and then held back, even though she suspected it was hovering in his mind, too, behind the rest of their talk.

There's time, she tells herself now, sitting in the diner. What's important, for the moment, is getting this right with Kevin and Adam. Over hamburgers that Adam eats bunless with his fingers, fiddling with the wheelchair joystick, Kevin tells them about his life and she gets the idea it hasn't been so different from hers, living at home, surrounded by the past. When Suzette's name comes up, he tells her, "Her brother is moving in with his girlfriend, did you hear that?"

She pictures Teddy and June, on the doorstep to retrieve Suzette that night at Kevin's house. It was such a startling surprise—like seeing two characters from different movies turn up together. Then after a minute, she could see easily: yes, they were a couple, the way they worked together, the way they talked to Suzette in similar ways, matter-of-fact and reassuring ("Mrs. Barrows will be okay . . . I'm going to drive you home . . . June is going to follow us there . . .") She watched them and thought: *This is how people weather crises and survive. They focus on details, on rides and food. They move, by instinct, through pain, and stick together.*

If she wants Adam to know his father, she needs to be fair and perfectly clear. She waits until he has floated away, back to the pinball machine. "There's something I have to say about getting together again," Cara says. "There have to be some rules. I don't think it's a good idea for you to be alone with him. At least until we've really gotten to know you again."

To her surprise, Kevin smiles and nods. "Fair enough," he says.

"But I've thought about this a lot and I think it could be good for Adam to have you in his life. It would widen his world and eventually, I hope he can learn ways that he could help *you*. I know that would be good for him—to not always be the one being taken care of. To feel like he is strong and capable sometimes. I don't think he gets a lot of chances to feel that way."

Though Kevin doesn't answer, he nods, looking down at his wheelchair. He seems to understand what she's trying to say.

When they get outside, she remembers the one question she's wanted to ask him because she'd once asked Matt and he couldn't answer. "Do you happen to remember, when you saw Adam in the woods, early on—was he wearing his sweater or holding it?"

"Holding it, I think. I remember thinking it was cold, that maybe he should put it on."

They stand in the parking lot, beside Kevin's van with its mechanized wheelchair lift, and Adam bounces in happy anticipation of seeing the ramp lower, the same thrill he gets from his forklift videos. "Thank you for everything, Kevin," she says.

As the ramp lowers slowly, Adam squeals and claps for this small mechanical wonder of a show. "Thank you for everything, thank you for everything," he echoes, his face inches from the levered mechanical box that makes the ramp work. Kevin rolls next to Adam, points to one of the levers, shows him what he needs. "When I say go," he says and rolls himself onto the ramp. He nods and Adam does it, throws the switch that raises Kevin up to his car and tilts him inside. Even Cara has to admit: as machines go, it's a pretty good one.

"Thank you, my small Pinball Wizard," Kevin says once he's inside, leaning over his lap toward Adam, who giggles and doesn't look up.

In the car ride home, alone with her thoughts, she goes over it all in her mind. Kevin didn't ask why she wanted to know about the sweater, for which she is grateful. Maybe, when he knows Adam better, she'll explain what she believes it means, as she breaks down the time line of events in the woods, how it must have all transpired from Adam's point of view. For a period there were a few people, talking in ways that Adam didn't understand, and then for a while there was music, beautiful and ethereal, that took him away. She knows that Adam must have stayed as far away as possible, for most of the time, but eventually he must have done something else, too. After everyone was gone, he must have emerged from the bushes and gone to his friend, comforted her in the only way he could think of, by putting a sweater around her neck that would approximate his blanket, by tucking it in, holding it just so. She will never know what, if any, words passed between them, but she knows he did something most children his age could never manage. Maybe he sang a color song, or a hummable snippet from one of his operas. Maybe it was less romantic: "The Wheels on the Bus" crooned frantically in her ear as life slipped away. But she knows this much, is sure of it, even as it stuns her to imagine: he stayed with her the whole time, unafraid.

ACKNOWLEDGMENTS

We are currently in the throes of an autism epidemic that is being fought in Washington, D.C., in laboratories, and in a million homes around the world. While parents, given the choice, might not have volunteered to join this battle, scores of unsung heroes have, and I thank every teacher, paraprofessional, therapist, school nurse, cafeteria worker, and principal's secretary who has taken the time to befriend my son, and in so doing, has widened his world and helped him to believe there is a place for him in it.

I also want to thank the many people who helped with various aspects of research for this book: Cathy Baechle, Doug Bolton, Jay Federman, Laura Lefebvre, Brent Nielsen, Steve Paterniti, and Derek Shea. And to dearest of readers: Mike Floquet, Bill Lychack, Bay Anapol, Beth Haas, Bill and Katie McGovern, Simon Curtis, and Elizabeth McGovern. I especially thank my brother, Monty McGovern, for reading a rewrite at the last minute and offering suggestions that made such a great deal of sense I took the extraordinary step of using all of them. Huge, huge thanks to Molly Stern, Mary Mount, Clare Ferraro, and everyone at Viking for their intelligent criticism and their enthusiastic and generous support of this book. And last, but not least, it has to be said that my life and times as a struggling writer changed a great deal for the better the day, four years ago, that Eric Simonoff called and kindly offered to represent me.

Finally, a portion of all proceeds from this book will go to support Whole Children in Hadley, Massachusetts, a resource center for families raising children with special needs, and I want to thank my intrepid cohorts there: Sue Higgins, Lisa Kirwan, Noreen Cmar-Mascis, Bob James, Sam McClellan, and especially Carrie McGee, whose bright and benevolent spirit has taught all of us a great deal about loving our children patiently and well, for who they are and for everything they *can* do.

A PENGUIN READERS GUIDE TO

EYE
CONTACT

Cammie McGovern

AN INTRODUCTION TO
Eye Contact

When Cara is called in to her nine-year-old son Adam's school one afternoon, she tries not to expect the worst. Because Adam is autistic, Cara—a single mother—has spent many hours with his teachers, principals, and guidance counselors discussing her son's development, and it isn't unusual for Adam to throw a tantrum at school that would necessitate her presence.

But today is different. Adam is missing, and he hasn't been found in any of his usual hiding places. He broke a rule (which he never does) and disappeared during recess, presumably having left school grounds. When the police find him later that afternoon, Cara is stunned to find out that Adam—who has no friends at school to speak of—was in the woods behind the school with a fellow student. Her name was Amelia Best, and she was found dead, stabbed in the chest.

The community is thrown into crisis, with parents fearing for their children's safety and teachers at the local schools doing their best to help their young students cope with this tragedy. Cara is convinced that Adam can help the police solve this murder, but he has retreated back inside himself after the incident, despite recent signs of improvement. Though Detective Matt Lincoln is skeptical about Adam's ability to aid the investigation—child witnesses are difficult enough, but what can he do with one who won't even speak?—Cara refuses to give up on her son, who has become her entire life since the death of her parents in a car accident. She tries in vain to get him to participate in his usual communication games and finds it difficult just to get him to look at her. Willing to take a risk in order to bring Adam around, she agrees with a local schoolteacher that an older boy's companionship might help and invites Morgan over to visit.

Morgan, an eighth grader at the local middle school, has some troubles of his own: while he isn't autistic or developmentally disabled, he attends classes with a special group at his own school, which he refers to as "the group for kids who have no friends." He faces constant tormenting from bullies at recess, and though he likes the teacher of his special group, Morgan doesn't share a bond with any of his classmates. It is clear from the start that he is harboring a terrible secret of his own. When Morgan meets Adam, Cara is shocked when Adam speaks his first voluntary phrases since the murder. As the two boys begin spending more time together, Adam offers his own clues to Cara that are difficult to decipher but might be important to locating the killer. But Morgan's secret, as well as some old friends from Cara's past, threatens to obscure the path to the truth behind Amelia's death.

As Cara and Detective Lincoln draw closer to the resolution of this awful crime, Cara is forced to come to terms with the consequences of decisions she has made—including the choice she made as a young woman not to include Adam's father in his life—and realizes she is not alone in her pain and isolation. In order to get to the murderer and bring Adam back to her, Cara must find it in her heart to forgive and be forgiven. Cammie McGovern's *Eye Contact* is a heartrending portrait of a mother's relationship with her son and a psychological thriller that keeps the reader guessing up to its final pages.

A Conversation with
Cammie McGovern

1. Like Cara, you are also the mother of an autistic child. To what extent did your own experiences inform your writing? What, if any, misgivings and difficulties did you encounter in approaching such a personal subject through fiction?

About four years ago, I started writing a nonfiction account of our experience in the early years just before and after our son's diagnosis of autism. It's a time when you feel frantic to be doing as much as possible because everyone tells you the early years are the most important, but no one can say with any certainty what that help should look like or which therapies will work best for your child. I used to devour every account I could find of parents in a similar situation, looking for clues, for children who resembled my son, and for what strategies worked best. Eventually, as we emerged from that time, I thought it might be a service to other parents to write about our own story and the discoveries we'd made, often by trial and error and muddling through a lot of mistakes. The more I wrote, though, the more I realized how hard it is to write a memoir well and sustain a narrative that doesn't have a clear ending in place. I'd already published one novel and many short stories. I'd spent the last fifteen years as a fiction writer, and I knew how to create a story and keep it moving along with suspense and surprises better than I knew how to report the countless ways that those years were hard and lonely for our family. Now, I'm glad I put aside the nonfiction version. I think there are quite a few wonderful memoirs of parents who've tackled this struggle in interesting ways (two favorites are Beth Kephardt's *The Slant of Sun* and Pat Stacey's *The Boy Who Loved Windows*). By returning to my comfort zone of fiction, I suppose I'm hoping to accomplish something with a different audience: that people looking for a good mystery might read this and also learn a bit about autistic spectrum disorders. As the numbers of children being diagnosed with autism continue to rise, it seems important to tell as many stories as possible that show what I've seen and know—what's hard for these kids and also how brave they can be, facing down their fears, overcoming extraordinary obstacles, and reaching out to other people.

2. One gets the impression by the end of the book that this has really been Cara's story, but Eye Contact *is told from the point of view of multiple characters, including Adam, Morgan, and June. What made you decide to write* Eye Contact *from a number of different perspectives? Did you ever consider writing it from Cara's perspective only?*

I initially wrote most of the story from Cara's point of view, when I first envisioned the book as a story centered around a terrifying scenario that most parents of autistic kids would relate to: What if, after years of laborious therapy with some success gaining language, play skills, etc., your child witnessed some traumatic event and lost everything in a single day? My first draft was much less about who did the crime and more about the history of Adam's therapy, where he'd been and how far he'd come. My husband read that draft and thought it seemed too much like a memoir with a story laid over it. He encouraged me to let the story take over and not be afraid to make it a murder mystery, with different people acting as detectives, pooling their knowledge. At the same time, I had begun sitting in on a few different social skills groups with middle-school-aged boys, and I so fell in love with some of them and the way they talked about their struggles that I wanted to introduce a character who would act as a kind of apprentice detective with Cara but who would ultimately also help her understand Adam a little bit better.

3. Eye Contact is an insightful look at the relationship between a mother and her son, and a portrait of a community, but it is also a riveting murder mystery. What aspect of the book came to you first? Did you set out to write a mystery or a literary novel? How did you strike a balance between the two?

I've always liked writing plot-driven stories, but was a little intimidated about saying I wanted to write a murder mystery. My background is an MFA at the University of Michigan and a Stegner Fellowship at Stanford and not too many people there are teaching or celebrating the joys of genre fiction. Not that anyone was putting it down; it just wasn't what we were reading or talking about or there to do. Now I feel like we're seeing more and more "literary" writers using a crime or a murder at the center of their stories simply because it puts every character on a precipice, raises the stakes, and launches a story that can still do all the same things a "literary" novel does, but can also be a page-turner as well.

4. It isn't clear who Amelia's murderer is until very late in the novel. Did you know who the killer was before you started writing? How did you decide who it would be and why did you choose that person?

I didn't know how the book would end for a long time and even changed the ending (and the killer) a few times after the book had sold. It's a tricky business because the ending has to both surprise the reader and have a feeling of inevitability to it. I switched it around so many times I think I lost track of what effect I was trying to achieve. I finally settled on one and at the last minute before it went to the printer in the UK (where the book was being released first), my brother, who's a big mystery fan, read it and said he liked the first version better for the three reasons he proceeded to list like the true mathematician that he is. I remember my heart sinking when I read his e-mail because I instantly knew he was right and I had something like twenty-four hours to change everything back.

5. There are a number of troubling incidents in the book that feature the cruel and heartless ways that children sometimes treat one another, but there are also instances where children feel strongly compelled to help one another and are kinder than their adult counterparts. What have you experienced, as a mother, that led you to write about these issues in Eye Contact?

When you're the parent of a child with autism, you are so prepared for cruelty and on guard about bullying that in fact what's surprised me much more is how many examples I've seen of surprising kindness and generosity on the part of kids my son goes to school with. I do think it's something that begins when kids are very young and blossoms with the children of parents who make the extra effort to teach their children about kindness and generosity toward all children, even those who are different or challenged, the sort who invite everyone in that class to a birthday party or have an odd kid over for a playdate. With these parents, children tend to learn an invaluable lesson about the rewards and pleasures of helping other kids, of not being frightened of differences and even about how to reach across them.

6. The accepted statistic for the current prevalence of autism is 1 in 166 children might be affected by some form of the disorder. At the moment, there is no cure. What do you think should be done on a larger scale in the United States to address the issue of autism? Are you actively involved in research on autism? Did writing this book change your perspective on the disorder in any way?

Though no one can say with any certainty what has caused the exponential increase of autism in the last twenty years, most doctors and professionals agree that it has to be partly owing to an increase in a whole variety of environmental toxins on genetically vulnerable, very young immune and nervous systems. I don't see how thimerosal being 50 percent mercury and used as a preservative in virtually all the vaccines during the years of the autism spike isn't at least one factor in the increase, but I also think there are probably many factors. I believe that 100 percent thimerosal-free vaccines are imperative now (a stand the CDC seemed to agree with when it recommended removing and reducing all mercury exposure), though currently only four states have mandated this and the federal government is mysteriously recommending the flu vaccine (the only vaccine that still contains thimerosal) to all pregnant women and children under three years old, exactly the group that should not be getting such large doses of mercury.

7. *What writers have influenced you, both on this book and others? Outside of questions of influence, who are some of your favorite authors?*

In the last few years, I have been reading a wide range of mystery writers, especially ones who invert the formula a little, like Ruth Rendall (and her Barbara Vine books), Minette Walters, Dennis Lehane, Denise Mina, Laura Lippman, Harlan Coben. I love all Jess Walters's books, but especially his second, *Land of the Blind*, and John Searles's *Strange but True*. I seem to be most drawn to books that put ordinary characters in the role of detective, where the clues to the mystery lie, at least in part, in their own past and in confronting certain demons they have let lie too long.

8. *It seems like Cara's life is even more difficult than those of other parents of disabled children, because she is unmarried and both her parents are dead. Although she seems to get along well with Adam's teachers and with the police who are investigating the murder, it is pretty clear she has no emotional support structure around her. Why did you decide to make her so isolated? How important do you think it is for a parent in her situation to have another adult to depend on—whether it is a spouse, a family member, or a close friend?*

I originally had Cara being a divorced mother but the further I got into the story, the more I wanted to raise the stakes for her by isolating her as much as possible. It does seem a bit cruel to put your main character in the center of a murder investigation and then not give her any parents, siblings, old friends, or neighbors who are particularly helpful or supportive of her. But here's the thing—even when you're happily married, as I am, with a wonderful and supportive extended family on both sides as we have, those early years parenting a child with autism can feel this isolated, or at least they did for me. It's not an experience you can share easily with your family or old friends because no one else is going through it. What Cara doesn't have that I found early on is a support group of other parents of children with special needs facing similar issues. For me, this made an enormous difference and was the beginning of putting my own child's challenges into perspective and discovering that yes, there really are blessings to be found along the way in this journey.

9. There are repeated mentions of how beautiful Amelia was for a girl her age, and when this terrible thing occurs to her, the question of sexual assault is immediately raised. However, it is not portrayed in a sensationalistic way—the young girl's sexuality is only pondered at length by sympathetic characters like June and Cara. Did you make any conscious decisions about how to deal with such a sensitive topic in this book? Was the lack of graphic violence and descriptions intentional?

These were the hardest scenes for me to write perhaps for obvious reasons: It's unsettling to contemplate violence and cruelty, especially being committed against children. For a long time, I put off writing them and put off determining exactly what had happened in the woods because I didn't want to think about those specifics. Finally, though, to have a book where you create a real sense of menace, you need to have a genuinely dark source for that. I tried to create a villain whose evil might be scarier because it reflects something familiar and recognizable in our society.

10. Do you think you will write more mysteries or "literary suspense" books in the future? What are you working on now?

One of the things I loved most about writing *Eye Contact* was creating a central character who, because of his disability, is as much of a mystery as the perpetrator of the crime is. Currently in America, 20 percent of our population identifies itself as disabled, an enormous group of people that has been underrepresented in books, movies, and TV. The fact that we see so few people with disabilities in the media adds to the mystery surrounding them, I'm sure, but sometimes the disability itself creates barriers—language is difficult, communication is broken down, physical logistics are hard. My next book, also a mystery, has a woman with cerebral palsy as a main character. She is the unlikely center of a love triangle and the victim of a crime committed in its wake. As everyone tries to figure out exactly what happened, they all begin to realize how little they actually knew about her.

QUESTIONS FOR DISCUSSION

1. Cara is not the only parent in the book who struggles with raising a child with special needs. Morgan's mother, Kevin's mother, and Amelia's mother are all in similar situations. What are the differences between the ways that they treat their children? Do you think that some of the mothers fail where others have succeeded? What do you agree and disagree with in each of their situations?

2. When Adam begins talking to the police and offering them clues, they have a difficult time understanding what he is getting at. For instance, one word he blurts out without prompting is "hair," which confuses Detective Lincoln because, as he says, "the guy

we've got downstairs is bald" (p. 157). However, this particular word becomes very significant later on in the investigation. How different would the search for Amelia's murderer have been if Adam had been an average nine-year-old? What kind of obstacles would have been avoided? What new difficulties would the police have faced?

3. On page 25, when she is being interviewed by the police, Amelia's teacher June is forced to admit that though she had planned on pairing Amelia with a partner from another classroom to help her development, she hadn't had the chance to do so. In the aftermath of a tragedy, people surrounding the victims often have feelings of regret, wishing they had done something differently that might have prevented what happened. Have you ever been through a situation like this one? How did you cope with your feelings of guilt and regret? How does June cope with hers? Are there other characters who feel similarly about Amelia's murder?

4. Cara and Suzette's friendship is a continuing subplot throughout *Eye Contact*, and there are moments when it seems like they are the best of friends and other times when they are very distant from each other. Many of their misunderstandings revolve around Kevin and the feelings each of them has for him. What reasons do you think that each of them has for caring about Kevin? Do you think their friendship might have lasted if they had confronted Kevin when they were younger?

5. Why do you think Suzette became agoraphobic? When Cara and Suzette were children, Suzette seemed to be the one who was more confident of herself and what she wanted out of life. What could have happened to her that caused her to become a recluse?

6. What does the title *Eye Contact* mean to you? It is mentioned a couple of times in the book in reference to Adam—one of the most

important things one can do to get an autistic child's attention is to gain eye contact—but it also serves as a larger metaphor for many of the characters and their relationships in the novel. How do you think the term applies to Teddy and June, for instance? Or Kevin and his mother?

7. When Morgan's mother takes him to the police after he's admitted to starting the fire, she says to him at one point, "You're fine, Morgan, my God. A lot of people don't have friends. *I* never had any friends" (p. 159). Many of the other characters in *Eye Contact* are similarly isolated from their peers. What does this say about the way that both children and adults in their neighborhood communicate with one another? What do you think about Morgan's mother's comment—is it "fine" not to have any friends?

8. When Morgan embarks on his own search for Amelia's killer, he forms an unexpected alliance with Fiona, another misfit student at the middle school. She tells Morgan, "the day after the murder Chris sat in front of me and started saying all this stuff about how he hopes people realize how bad it can get, that people can die from bullying" (p. 209). To what extent do you think Chris was right about this? Discuss some of the terrible things children do to one another in *Eye Contact* and whether you've observed this kind of behavior in young children you know. What are some of the ways this kind of cruelty can be prevented?

9. One of the results of Adam's autism is his appreciation for classical music and his love of opera. He has perfect pitch and impeccable hearing ability. Why do you think that a child who has such a difficult time with language and communication loves music so much? What are his musical talents compensating for? How might they be able to enrich his future life?

10. Amelia's mother fought to have her daughter placed in a special education classroom while Cara has been fighting since Adam was young to have him integrated into a normal classroom, with the help of an aide. How do you think their respective learning environments affected Adam and Amelia? In what ways might it have had an impact on the burgeoning friendship between the two children before Amelia died?

11. When Cara is thinking back over her relationship with Kevin, she admits to herself that "he's kept certain secrets for reasons she can't understand . . . [but] so has she. If an impartial outsider looked at their lives, weighed the sins of omission, it's likely that Cara would be found at far graver fault" (p. 210). What does the author mean by this? Do you agree with this statement? What are the sins of omission that Cara has committed, against Kevin, against her parents, against Suzette, against herself?

12. Although Adam is not a first-person narrator in *Eye Contact*, there are numerous sections that are written from his point of view. What did you learn about autistic children and how they see the world after reading this book? What preconceptions you have about childhood and communication are challenged by Adam's story?

13. Morgan is convinced that if he finds out who killed Amelia, he will be forgiven for the crime he committed. Many of the characters in *Eye Contact* are in search of a similar kind of redemption. Do you think any of them are capable of achieving it? In light of this theme of redemption, how do you feel about where the different characters end up at the book's conclusion?

For more information about or to order other Penguin Readers Guides, please e-mail the Penguin Marketing Department at reading@us.penguingroup.com or write to us at:

Penguin Books Marketing Dept.
Readers Guides
375 Hudson Street
New York, NY 10014-3657

Please allow 4–6 weeks for delivery.
To access Penguin Readers Guides online, visit the Penguin Group (USA) Web site at www.penguin.com.

FOR THE BEST IN PAPERBACKS, LOOK FOR THE

In every corner of the world, on every subject under the sun, Penguin represents quality and variety—the very best in publishing today.

For complete information about books available from Penguin—including Penguin Classics and Puffins—and how to order them, write to us at the appropriate address below. Please note that for copyright reasons the selection of books varies from country to country.

In the United States: Please write to *Penguin Group (USA), P.O. Box 12289 Dept. B, Newark, New Jersey 07101-5289* or call *1-800-788-6262.*

In the United Kingdom: Please write to *Dept. EP, Penguin Books Ltd, Bath Road, Harmondsworth, West Drayton, Middlesex UB7 0DA.*

In Canada: Please write to *Penguin Books Canada Ltd, 90 Eglinton Avenue East, Suite 700, Toronto, Ontario M4P 2Y3.*

In Australia: Please write to *Penguin Books Australia Ltd, P.O. Box 257, Ringwood, Victoria 3134.*

In New Zealand: Please write to *Penguin Books (NZ) Ltd, Private Bag 102902, North Shore Mail Centre, Auckland 10.*

In India: Please write to *Penguin Books India Pvt Ltd, 11 Panchsheel Shopping Centre, Panchsheel Park, New Delhi 110 017.*

In the Netherlands: Please write to *Penguin Books Netherlands bv, Postbus 3507, NL-1001 AH Amsterdam.*

In Germany: Please write to *Penguin Books Deutschland GmbH, Metzlerstrasse 26, 60594 Frankfurt am Main.*

In Spain: Please write to *Penguin Books S. A., Bravo Murillo 19, 1° B, 28015 Madrid.*

In Italy: Please write to *Penguin Italia s.r.l., Via Benedetto Croce 2, 20094 Corsico, Milano.*

In France: Please write to *Penguin France, Le Carré Wilson, 62 rue Benjamin Baillaud, 31500 Toulouse.*

In Japan: Please write to *Penguin Books Japan Ltd, Kaneko Building, 2-3-25 Koraku, Bunkyo-Ku, Tokyo 112.*

In South Africa: Please write to *Penguin Books South Africa (Pty) Ltd, Private Bag X14, Parkview, 2122 Johannesburg.*